Books by P.J. Parrish

DARK OF THE MOON

DEAD OF WINTER

Published by Pinnacle Books

ALONE IN THE WOODS

Louis scanned the snow. Now he could see prints, sloppy and distorted. The prints led off toward the pines

He picked up a stick and stepped forward. Something snapped in the distance. What was it? A branch? An animal?

Louis looked back toward the cruiser. A chill prickled his spine and his hand jerked to his radio.

A loud crack fractured the silence and, at the same time, something hit him from behind, slamming him to the ground. He couldn't breathe. Frantically, he tried to raise his face from the snow and immediately felt a sharp pain somewhere near his spine. He coughed, fighting for breath, trying to wipe away the snow.

God . . . he was hit.

DEAD OF WINTER

P.J. Parrish

PINNACLE BOOKS
Kensington Publishing Corp.

PINNACLE BOOKS are published by

Kensington Publishing Corp.
850 Third Avenue
New York, NY 10022

ISBN 0-7394-1492-5

Printed in the United States of America

TO MY SISTER,
WHO MAKES IMPOSSIBLE DREAMS COME TRUE

"Whoever fights monsters should see to it that in the process he does not become a monster. And when you look long into an abyss, the abyss also looks into you."
—Friedrich Nietzche
Beyond Good and Evil

One

It was just a dull thud, a sound that drifted down to him as he lay in the deepest fathoms of his sleep. He struggled up to the surface and opened his eyes with a start. Darkness, and then, emerging from the shadows, a bulky form and a glint of light. He let out a breath. Just the oak bureau, and his badge lying on top.

The sound had probably come from his dream, and the thought made him relax back into the pillows. But his ears remained alert for foreign sounds amid all the familiar groans and squeaks of the house.

He glanced over at Stephanie, snoring softly by his side. She always kidded him about his excellent hearing. "Tommy, baby, you can hear the snow falling," she said, laughing. Hell, sometimes he thought so, too. He pulled the quilt up over his wife's shoulder and swung his legs over the side of the bed.

He rose, shivering in the cold air, and went to the window. He pulled back the drape. Sure enough, it was snowing. Already covered the yard, leaving pillows of meringue on the kids' swing set. He gazed at the softly falling snow. First big snowfall of the season. It was beautiful.

His eyes narrowed. There was a truck parked across the street, a few houses down, in front of the McCabe house. The headlights were off, but he could see the trail of smoke coming from the exhaust pipe. He squinted, trying to remember if he'd seen it before. It looked to be brown, although it was so dirty he couldn't really tell. He felt his body tense slightly, that involuntary response to an unknown situation.

It was probably nothing. Maybe someone visiting the Mc-Cabes. But except for the Christmas lights around the front door, the McCabe house was dark. He squinted to see who was in the car and thought he picked out two forms. Shoot, it was probably that crazy teenager Lisa, necking with some boy just to make her old man mad.

He glanced back at the clock on the bureau. Three-ten. Late for a Sunday night, even for Lisa.

He shivered again, and he knew it wasn't from the cold. It was his body sending out its old signals, that familiar release of adrenaline.

Stephanie gave out a soft moan and he looked back at her. It occurred to him, as he watched her, that he should have told her what was going on. He had never held back things from her before and he shouldn't have now. But she was so happy in this place and he hadn't wanted to give her a reason to worry. This isn't like Flint, he had told her not long after they had arrived. They don't hurt cops in a place like this.

He hadn't really wanted to leave his old job, especially to work in this speck of a town in the Michigan woods. But the bullet he had taken in the shoulder by that crack-crazed kid had been the last straw. We're safe here, baby, he told her, we're safe here.

He moved silently to the closet. He ran his hand along the top shelf until it found the cold metal of his service weapon, a .357 Colt Python. He checked the cylinder and, with a glance back at Stephanie, tiptoed out of the bedroom.

The gun was cold; he could feel it against his thigh through the thin cotton of his pajamas as he crept down the hall. Outside the kids' room, he paused. The baby had colic and it occurred to him that it might have been just the child's restless thump that he had heard. He strained his ears in the darkness. Nothing.

Downstairs in the foyer, the white tile floor shimmered with

a kaleidoscope of color, created by the Christmas lights outside, refracted through the leaded-glass panel of the front door.
He stopped. No sound. Had the truck left? He looked out the
small window in the door, but couldn't see the truck.

He let out a breath of relief and turned away from the door.

A soft tap. Someone knocking. He drew back the curtain
and looked out at the face in the shadows outside.

A sharp, snapping sound.

His heart slammed up against his sternum, then froze.

It was a sound he had heard before. Too many times before.

The pump of a shotgun.

Dear God Almighty . . .

Glass exploded over, around and into him. He was hurled
back against the staircase. His fingers groped for the spindles
but he could not move. He couldn't feel his legs. He couldn't
feel anything. Except, except . . . except a horrible pumping.
His blood pumping out the black hole in his chest.

Oh Jesus, help me. Stephanie . . .

Then he felt nothing.

The colored lights danced over the white tile, turning the
shards of glass into gaudy jewels. Snowflakes swirled in
through the gaping hole in the glass window of the door, dying
as they hit the warm blood. A Christmas wreath lay across his
legs, its sound-activated battery pack sending out a tinny ren-
dition of "Silent Night."

A scream came from upstairs.

The man holding the shotgun looked up the staircase and
then reached into his jacket and withdrew a blue-backed playing card. With a flick of his wrist, he tossed it through the
hole in the glass. It spun to the floor, settling on the white tile
near the body.

"Merry fucking Christmas, Officer Pryce," he said.

Two

It was a lousy day for a drive. Smog-stained sleet left dirty streaks on the windshield. Slick patches of ice sent the tires spinning for grip. It seemed to take forever for the gray Detroit skyline to disappear in the rearview mirror.

The bad weather followed him as he drove up I-75, past the sooty factories in Flint and the sodden cornfields outside Saginaw. Somewhere north of a town called Standish, the temperature dropped and the sleet turned to snow. Now it was coming down hard, flakes so big he could make out their lacy patterns on the windshield before the wipers slapped them away.

Louis Kincaid followed a snowplow into a town called Rose City and pulled into a gas station. As he waited for the old man to fill the tank, he unfolded the wrinkled map. It couldn't be far now, maybe twenty-five miles.

"That's eleven fifty," the old man said, holding out a mittened hand. "Check your oil?"

Louis nodded. "Yeah, guess you better. Got a small leak."

The man eyed the scarred, white, '65 Mustang. "That ain't your only problem," he said. "That back right tire's bald."

Louis nodded grimly and the man trudged to the front and popped the hood. As he watched the man pull the dipstick, he thought of Phillip Lawrence's warning that morning. Take my truck, Louis, that Mustang will never make it. It looked like his foster father was right again, which bothered him. And it bothered him that it bothered him.

"It took a quart. You're gonna need another soon though."

"Thanks." He handed the old man some bills. "How far to Loon Lake?"

"Oh, 'bout thirty miles." His snow-encrusted brows knitted together. "You going up there for some ice fishing?"

"Nope. For a job."

The man nodded and handed back the change. "Well, good luck to you. Pretty place, Loon Lake."

"So I've heard."

As he pulled back onto the highway, Louis shook his head and smiled. It was obvious the old man had been trying his damnedest to figure out what business a young black man in a beat-up convertible had in Loon Lake. Phillip had warned him it would be like that. *I just don't think you'll like it there, Louis. It's a resort town, where rich white men from Chicago build hunting lodges so they have a place to get away.*

Louis reached down and turned the heater up to its highest setting. It answered with a cough and a sudden blast of cold air. He banged a fist on the dash, then switched the dead heater off.

A place to get away. That didn't sound so bad. It wasn't like he had such a great life back in Detroit. A roach-filled efficiency. And no job.

He shook his head, thinking back over the events of the last couple of months. Stupid. Had he really expected to walk into the station and get his old job back after being gone for a year? It had been official, his leave of absence, but by the time he got back to Ann Arbor, there were cutbacks on the force. *Last one in, first one out. Jesus, tough luck, Louis, you're a good cop, but you know how these budget things are, but if you need a recommendation . . .*

The next day, the letter had come. He could still see the envelope sticking out of his mail slot, with the damn royal-blue seal that had made his heart stop.

Dear Mr. Kincaid: Thank you again for your interest in the Detroit Police Department. We have given your application careful consideration and are impressed with your credentials. However, due to cutbacks in the City of Detroit budget, we will not be adding any additional officers to our force this year. Your application will remain active . . .

He saw the classified ad in the *Free Press* the same day. It was slipped in between the computer programmers and fast-food managers.

Police Officer. Loon Lake, Mich. Must be MLEOTC. $22,000. Physical/drug test required. Application deadline Dec. 18. 5 P.M.

Come back home, Louis, Phillip Lawrence had said. Just until you get your feet back on the ground. We're worried about you. Loon Lake isn't the answer.

The snow was starting to let up some. Louis glanced at his watch. It was four-thirty.

He straightened against the cold vinyl seat, his teeth chattering. A green reflector sign caught the headlights: WELCOME TO LOON LAKE, GATEWAY TO THE WINTER WONDERLAND.

The pines parted, opening onto a two-lane residential street, cast in the soft glow of old-style street lamps. Neat frame houses lined the street, with swings on the porches, smoke curling from the chimneys, and snowmen standing guard in the yards. In the dusk, ruddy-faced men shoveled their driveways. Louis drove past a redbrick school. Kids were sliding down a hill on cafeteria trays, chased by a barking golden retriever.

Louis continued down Main Street. There were garlands of lights festooned across the street and big plastic candy canes fastened to each streetlight. The store windows were filled with signs announcing Christmas sales. Women stood in knots on the snowy sidewalks, holding babies and packages.

"Christ," Louis muttered. "It's Bedford-fucking-Falls."

The thought made his mind trip back suddenly to childhood. It was a long-buried memory, and the suddenness of it was so acute, so unexpected, that it was like a sting in his chest.

It was 1967. He had been only weeks past his eighth birthday and had come to the fifth in a string of foster homes, arriving in the middle of a blizzard a few days before Christmas. There had been four other kids, all foster children and all white.

He had spent the day off by himself, eyeing the Christmas tree and presents, knowing there would be nothing under there for him. Later, he picked at his dinner and moped while the other kids played stupid games only they seemed to know and talked of things Louis knew nothing about.

A man had come in, a very tall man. Louis knew he was the man who owned the big house, another strange face, another foster father. The man told them all to sit in a circle. He handed each of them two Christmas cookies and a glass of milk and then turned on the television. Stale cookies and some stupid old black-and-white movie about some stupid white guy who worked in a bank.

Louis had stood up. The tall man asked him, gently but firmly, to sit down. He refused and the man repeated his request. No one was watching the movie. They were all watching him and the man. When the man told him a third time to sit down, Louis kicked the green paper plate, sending the cookies skidding across the floor.

"Testing me, Louis?" the man asked quietly.

"I don't wanna be here."

"Where do you want to be?"

"Home."

"This is your home now."

"I don't like it here. I hate it. I hate it."

The man came over to Louis, slipped an arm around his shoulders and guided him over to a sofa. Louis sat stiffly on the edge, staring at the TV screen. Finally, the man pulled Louis's rigid body into the crook of his arm and neither said another word for ninety minutes. When the movie was over, Louis stood up, walked to the broken cookies and picked up the crumbs.

He didn't understand the movie and sure didn't believe in angels. But after that, very slowly, he did come to believe in the tall man. He came to love Phillip Lawrence.

What was the name of that damn movie? Shit, it was all over TV every Christmas. *It's a Wonderful Life*. That was it.

A sign for the police station lay ahead. The station was nearly obscured by pines and evergreens. Louis swung into the small lot and cut the engine. The building was made of logs, like a ranger station. A smoking chimney reached into the gray sky and two bare maples formed a spindly tunnel over the sidewalk.

Louis got out of the car, stretching his stiff body. He was struck by the smell of the air—pine and smoke. He bent and checked his tie in the side-view mirror. He had spent almost eight hours on the road. His trousers were wrinkled and he felt dirty. What a way to appear for a job interview.

Louis stepped into the station, the heat from a ceiling vent raining down on him. The interior was paneled in a coffee-colored wood, and a brick fireplace in the back crackled with a healthy fire. A polished pine counter and a long, gleaming railing separated the work area from where he stood, set off by a small gate. On his left was a door marked CHIEF OF POLICE.

Louis walked to the counter, glancing down hungrily at a large tray of Christmas cookies. An officer sat at the rear desk, his blond head bent over a report. Louis cleared his throat.

"Excuse me . . ."

The young man looked up and smiled. He stacked his papers neatly, positioning them exactly parallel to the edge of the desk, and rose, coming toward the counter.

"Hello. What can I help you with?" The smile was genuine. He had pearly, straight teeth and closely cut hair. His skin was flawless and pink, and combined with the powder-blue police shirt, he looked like a baby shower gift. His silver nameplate said DALE MCGUIRE.

"I saw the ad in the paper," Louis said.

The officer's eyes moved over Louis's dark blue suit and he reached under the counter and produced an application and several other papers. He slid the stack across the counter. Louis moved the tray of cookies and turned the papers so he could read them.

"You have to do the app here. Chief wants to make sure you can read and write," the young officer said.

Louis nodded, reaching for his pen. "Have you had many applicants?"

"A few, but you're the last. Chief says deadline is five, he means five."

Louis glanced back at the empty chairs, debating whether to take a seat. His eye was drawn to a photograph on the wall. The photograph had a small black ribbon across the top left-hand corner. The handsome black officer in the photo was named Thomas Pryce. The plate beneath the photo said: IN MEMORIUM, JUNE 12, 1952–DECEMBER 1, 1984. Two weeks ago.

Louis turned back to see Dale McGuire staring at him.

"Is there something wrong?" Louis asked.

Dale smiled. "No, nothing. Would you like a cookie?"

Louis smiled and nodded. Dale pulled off the Saran wrap and Louis took a red Christmas tree. He munched on it as he filled out the application.

"L-17 to Central. We're back in service."

The sound of the officer's voice on the radio drew Louis's attention to the dispatch desk in the corner. The dispatcher was a walrus of a woman with a jet-black bouffant and fifties-style cat's-eye glasses. With a sigh, she lowered her paperback and keyed her microphone.

"Ten-4, seventeen. I have a message for you. Your wife requests you stop and pick up eggnog on the way home."

A voice came back, slightly chagrined. "Ten-4, Central."

"That's Edna," Dale offered.

Edna gave a wave from behind her Danielle Steel novel without looking up at Louis.

More calls trickled in, and Louis listened as he filled out the application. A lost dog. An officer stating he was checking on an elderly woman who lived alone. Another requesting jumper cables for a stranded motorist. It was unreal. All his adult life, he had set his sights on Detroit and the challenge of working for a big city department with plenty of action. But here he was. What the hell did this town even need cops for?

He glanced at Dale McGuire, who was rearranging tinsel over the computer. Still, there was something about this place. Something in the air, something . . . sweet and clean, more than just pine and gingerbread. He had felt it the moment he drove into town. He remembered something Frances Lawrence, his foster mother, once said, something about people having places on earth where their souls felt comfortable. Places where, as soon as you set foot in them, you felt at home. He had never felt that special pull to any one place.

"You know," Dale said, interrupting his thoughts, "the chief hasn't found anyone he likes yet. When you get done with that, he'll want to see you."

See him? Now?

"He's anxious to fill the job. Doesn't like working short-handed," Dale added.

Louis glanced at the chief's closed door. He saw his cold, ugly apartment back in Detroit and felt the sting of lonely and boring nights.

God, he wanted this job. He wanted it bad.

"The chief will see you now."

Louis looked at his watch. He had been waiting for two hours. He had read every flyer and wanted poster on the bulletin board and thumbed through the four copies of old *Na-*

tional Geographics three times. He stood up, smoothing his jacket. Dale led him to the chief's door and knocked. They waited until a commanding voice summoned them in.

There was no one in the office. Louis was wondering where the chief was when he heard the flush of a toilet from behind a closed door to his right. Taking a deep breath to relax, he looked around.

He stood on a blood red carpet, vacuum tracks still visible around the perimeter. The walls were covered with framed photographs, certificates, plaques and newspaper clippings. On the credenza below them sat a handsome chess set. Louis's eyes were drawn to two swords mounted over the credenza. One was gleaming steel, with gold cording. The other was old, foreign looking. Louis stared at it. Good God, was it a samurai sword?

The sound of running water came from the bathroom. The man was taking his time. Louis went to the credenza and picked up one of the chess pieces. It was a pewter pawn, in the shape of a soldier.

"Do you play?"

Louis turned. The man was about six feet, trim but broad-shouldered in his starched baby-blue shirt. His short hair was silver blond and his ruddy, clean-shaven face was that of a man only thirty-eight, maybe forty at the most.

"Some," Louis said with a smile. "But I'm no good at it."

"Maybe because you think of it only as a game," the man said. "It's more than that. It's science, poetry, mystery. Just when you think you are solving its secrets, it thwarts you."

"I never learned the strategy, I guess," Louis said.

The chief came forward to take the pawn from Louis's hand. "Anyone can learn strategy. Courage is what really counts, courage to use original moves that surprise your opponent."

Louis nodded as if in understanding.

"Like a Marshall swindle, or a Lucena position," the chief went on. He saw the blank look on Louis's face and smiled. "Or a gambit. You know what a gambit is, don't you?"

Louis shook his head.

"The gambit is when you sacrifice one of your pieces to throw an opponent off," the chief said. "There are many different kinds: the Swiss gambit, the classic bishop sacrifice, the Evans gambit. These moves are what elevates the game to artistry."

Louis nodded in acknowledgement, half expecting the man to ask him to play as part of the interview.

The chief turned, picking up Louis's application from the desk. Louis found himself staring at the man's face. It was chiseled, with a jutting jawline, broad forehead and strong brows shielding eyes the color of pale sapphires. Louis thought of a photograph in the *National Geographic* he had seen outside, a photograph of the mysterious ancient stone statues on Easter Island with their massive, powerful heads. His eyes went to the desk, looking for a nameplate. There was none.

"So, why'd you leave your last job?" the chief asked, looking up.

"It was personal. It just didn't work out."

"I called down there, you know, to your little town in Mississippi."

Great, Louis thought. "Who did you talk to?"

"A man named Junior Resnick."

Louis kept his face impassive. What a reference.

The chief gave an odd smile. "The man's obviously an idiot, but he likes you. Says that you've got no sense of humor, but you're a smart guy."

Louis stifled a smile. "I'm surprised. We had our differences."

The chief gazed at Louis, as if taking his physical measure. "Investigator," he said, tossing the application on the desk. "Impressive title for someone who hasn't seen his thirtieth birthday."

"That's all it was, a title."

"Well, when we give titles here, it means something. That's why we have so few." He held up the pawn and smiled. "But even a pawn can win a promotion, maybe become a knight or bishop, right?"

Louis nodded. The chief went back to the chess set and carefully set the pawn back down on its square.

"Tell me," he said, turning, "did you get the respect you deserve down there or was it as hard as I would suspect?"

Well, that was a unique way to ask if being a black cop in the South was a problem. "Respect didn't come automatically with the uniform down there," Louis said.

"It does here," the chief said. He went back to his desk and pulled a pack of Camels out of a drawer. He lit one and took a quick drag as he hefted a hip on the desk. Louis noticed how sharply creased his pants were. You could cut bread on them.

" 'Il n'existe que trois êtres respectables: le prêtre, le guerrier, le poete. Savoir, tuer et créer.' "

Louis stared at the chief.

"Do you speak French?"

Louis shook his head.

"It's Baudelaire. 'There exists only three beings worthy of respect: the priest, the soldier, the poet. To know, to kill, to create.' He smiled. "We're neither priests nor poets. That leaves soldiers."

He blew out a stream of smoke. His eyes seemed to change suddenly, turning cooler as he considered Louis.

"I can train a man to do almost anything," he said. "I can train him to shoot. I can train him to do the damn paperwork. I can even train him to kill. But there is one thing I cannot teach him. Do you know what that might be?"

Louis hesitated, trying to figure out the best answer. "A sense of honor?"

"Is that what you think I want to hear or is that what you really think?"

"Well, I don't think you can teach honor," Louis said.

"The one thing I cannot teach a man is loyalty."

This was getting weird. What was next, Buddhist proverbs? Haiku?

"But as long as you feel honor is so important, perhaps you can define it for me," the chief said.

"I'd say that honor is acting with integrity."

The chief shook his head. "That's a clean conscience." He pointed the cigarette at Louis. "Honor is an exalted existence, earned by sacrifice and courage. It's what makes you brave when you're scared shitless, and it's what makes that badge shine when you look in the mirror."

The chief paused to grind out his cigarette in a butt-filled ashtray. "So, does your badge shine?"

"Sir?" Louis had been looking at the photograph on the wall of the Army buddies, looking for the chief in the foursome.

"Does your badge *shine?*"

Louis wanted to say he didn't have a badge, but knew that was not what the chief wanted to hear. "Yes, sir."

The chief drifted behind him. Louis resisted the urge to turn around. He squinted at a framed newspaper clipping on the wall to see if he could read the name. This was nuts. He didn't know who he was talking to. He was beginning to wonder *what* he was talking to.

"Can you do a hundred push-ups?" the voice behind him asked.

"Yes," Louis said, hoping he would not be asked to prove it.

"Can you pass a drug test?"

"Yes, sir."

"What'd you qualify as?"

"On the range? Expert."

"You ever killed anyone?"

Louis looked back at him over his shoulder. "No, sir."

The chief came back to stand before Louis. "Could you?" he asked.

Louis detected a challenge in the tone. "Yes," he said. "But I hope I never have to."

The chief smiled.

He was blowing this. He could feel it.

"You ever had to fire your weapon at a human being?" the chief asked.

"No, sir." He hoped he wasn't going to be asked if he had ever been shot at. He didn't want to go into what had happened in Mississippi.

"You ever been reprimanded?" the chief asked.

"Once."

"What for?"

Shit. Keep it simple. "Insubordination."

"Define insubordination."

Louis wet his lips. "I did something—"

"I don't care what you did. Define the word."

"Technically, it's a refusal to carry out a direct order by a superior."

Again, the chief shook his head, a small smile on his lips. "It's not that simple."

What was *simple to this guy?* Louis thought.

"When an officer chooses a course not aligned with that of his commander, then that is a mutiny of sorts. And that is never acceptable." He looked at Louis. "Do you understand?"

Louis nodded.

The chief turned abruptly, going back behind his desk. He grabbed the pack of Camels and pulled another one out. "These are the rules and listen good," he said. "First, never tell me smoking is bad for my health. I know that. You get a suspension the first time and I'll fire your ass the second time. Second, never enter this office without knocking. I'll suspend you the first time and fire you the second."

He was hired. Shit, that was all?

"Sir, will there be an oral board?"

"I *am* the oral board."

"Testing?"

"You passed it once, didn't you?"

"Yes, sir."

"Third, you will always wear full uniform. That includes your gun. I catch you out of uniform, I'll suspend you. You'll be issued all your leather. You own a .357?"

"No, sir. Thirty-eight."

"In this department, everyone carries the same weapon."

Louis suppressed a sigh. He couldn't afford a new gun.

"We'll give you one at twenty-five dollars a week," the chief said. "You damn well better last long enough to pay it off. And don't lose it. It'll cost you five hundred dollars to replace it."

Plus, I'll be suspended, Louis thought.

"Plus, you'll be suspended." The chief paused, his eyes seeming to warm a bit. "Loon Lake is a good, clean place, Kincaid," he said briskly. "And this is a good, clean department. We may be small in size, but not in spirit. These men are top-notch officers, all good, honest cops. Every damn one of them, and we are a tight unit." He pointed to a small plaque on the wall. "We have a motto here: *Gens una sumus.*"

Louis waited, but no translation seemed forthcoming. "Latin, sir?"

"Yes. 'We are one family.' "

Louis nodded again.

"Never forget it. Your fellow officers are your brothers."

Louis nodded. The chief walked to the door and opened it. "Firearms testing is the first Thursday of every month. You fail, you go on suspension. Any questions?"

"None I can't ask the other officers."

"Let's go, then. I'll turn you over to McGuire."

Louis followed the chief to the outer office. Dale jumped up and came hurrying over.

"We share desks here," the chief said. "This is yours for day shift. It's Ollie's at night. That's Ollie over there, sucking down the caffeine. Wickshaw, say hello to our new man, Kincaid."

A tall, skinny man at the coffeepot nodded. Louis nodded back.

"McGuire will get you started on your paperwork," the chief said. "You need a day to go home and get your things?"

Louis looked at the clock on the wall. It was after 8:00 P.M. He would have to stay the night. "Yes, sir," he said.

"Fine. You can start Monday morning." The chief stared at Louis for a moment, then thrust out his hand. "Welcome to the force. I hope you'll be happy here." He smiled. It was a frosty effort, but not completely unforced.

Louis shook his hand. "Thank you, sir."

The chief walked back through the gate and into his office, closing the door. Louis looked at the desktop, feeling a mix of elation and apprehension. He couldn't believe it. Just like that, he was hired. A new job. A new start.

He looked at the closed door. The chief was kind of an odd bird, what with the French and the quotes. He was also a bit too spit-and-polish, but he seemed to lean in the right direction and maybe that was all that mattered. He surveyed the room, the fireplace, the tinsel-draped computer, and the photograph of Thomas Pryce. He felt a twinge of guilt that another cop had to die to make his chance here possible. But it felt right. This town, this job, at this time in his life. It felt right.

"Welcome to Loon Lake, Louis."

Louis shook Dale's outstretched hand. "Thanks. You know, no one told me his name."

"Gibralter."

"Like the rock?" Louis asked.

Dale smiled. "Yup. Brian Gibralter. But don't ever call him Brian. Or God forbid, Rocky. Nothing will get you suspended quicker. Trust me, I know."

Louis rubbed his face, suddenly tired. "I can't believe this. No test, no oral board."

"That's the way he does things."

"But fifteen minutes? What can he tell about me after fifteen minutes?" Louis asked. "Did he do that with the other applicants?"

Dale shook his head. "He only saw three others. He kept telling me none of them *looked* right."

"What?" Louis asked.

Dale's eyes drifted up to the photograph of the dead officer. Louis followed his gaze.

"He hired me because I'm black?" Louis asked, incredulous. "What, to fill some quota or something?"

"Hell, no," Dale said quickly. "Chief doesn't care about that stuff. I mean, you must've just said something in there he liked." He nodded toward the photograph of Thomas Pryce. "Like him."

Louis shook his head. "I don't follow."

"Thomas Pryce was . . . a good cop," Dale said. He shrugged his shoulders, looking for words. "Somebody you could respect, you know what I mean? I think maybe the chief saw something of him in you, that's all."

Louis looked up at the photograph of Pryce. "How old was he?" he asked.

"Thirty-two," Dale said. "You're the same height and build, you know. What size shirt you wear?"

"Sixteen, thirty-four."

Dale smiled slightly. "See? He won't have to buy new uniforms."

Louis stared back at Dale, not sure if he was kidding.

Dale picked up the Saran-wrapped tray. "Want another cookie?"

Three

"Raise your right hand."

Louis lifted his hand and took a deep breath.

"Do you, Louis Washington Kincaid, on this twentieth day of December, nineteen hundred and eighty-four, solemnly swear to uphold and enforce the laws of the United States of America and the great state of Michigan to the best of your ability?"

Louis looked down at the silver shield in Gibralter's hand.

"With professionalism, integrity and honor?" Gibralter added.

"I do," Louis said.

Gibralter slapped the badge in Louis's palm.

"Welcome to Loon Lake, badge number 127."

Louis heard soft applause and turned. Five officers stood in a half-circle, all dressed in light blue shirts, dark blue trousers, navy ties and billed Garrison caps. Louis pinned the badge on his shirt.

"McGuire, is Kincaid ready to go?" Gibralter asked.

Dale hustled over. "You sign that gun agreement, Louis?"

Louis nodded, watching the chief as he ambled away to talk to another man. "I signed everything. I didn't see a union card."

"You won't," Dale said quietly. "And we don't use that word in civilized conversation in this office, Louis."

Shit, a union-free department. That was scary.

"Read your manual, Kincaid," Gibralter said, turning back. "Ignorance is not an acceptable excuse here."

"Yes, sir."

"Your call number is 11. Loon-11," Dale added.

Louis would have laughed except for the utter seriousness on Dale's face.

"Chief, who you want to put him with?" Dale asked.

Louis looked at the officers. Christ. He was getting a training officer.

"Harrison!" Gibralter called out.

A man stepped out of the knot and sauntered over. He was about the same age as Louis. His thick hair was variegated with black, browns and auburn, like rich mahogany. He had expressive brown eyes that softened his slightly pitted face. There was a long, thin scar down his neck that disappeared into his blue collar. He looked up at Louis, shaking his head.

"Jeez, Chief, another six-footer. When you going to give me someone I can look in the eye?"

Gibralter, on his way back to his office, hollered back over his shoulder, "Buy some goddamn elevator shoes, for crissake."

Harrison grinned and thrust out his hand. "Jesse Harrison. Welcome to Loon Lake, Kincaid."

Louis shook his hand. "Thanks."

"You ready?" Jesse slipped his jacket over his arms and reached back for the car keys on the desk. On the ring was a dirty orange rabbit's foot. He saw Louis looking at it.

"Don't you say a word about my rabbit's foot," he said. "It brings me luck."

"In this town, why do you even feel you need it?" Louis asked as he followed Jesse Harrison out the door.

"Kincaid, I've been unlucky all my life. I was born on September 13, my badge number is 113 and when I joined this department, Gibralter gave me a call number 13. If you were me, what would you use?"

"My gun," Louis said dryly.

Jesse opened the glass door with his rear end. "I like a man with a sense of humor, Kincaid. We should get along fine."

The moment he got inside the police cruiser, Louis flipped the heater up to high.

"Living down South thin your blood?" Jesse asked as he pulled out of the station parking lot.

"Car wouldn't start. Had to walk in." He wondered how Harrison had found out so quickly about his stint in Mississippi.

"Where you staying, at the Loon Lake Lodge?"

"No, I rented a cabin on the lake."

"North or south side?"

Louis thought for a moment. "South. Just outside town."

Jesse swung the car down Main Street. "Good. You don't want to be staying up north with the Eggers."

"What?"

"That's what I call the rich tourists. You know, East Egg. You never read *The Great Gatsby?*"

"Saw the movie."

"Bad movie, great book." Jesse's grin had a touch of superiority to it. "I read a lot. Anything I can get my hands on. Lots of biographies, history books. I like psychology stuff best. The chief says I'm an autodidact. That means self-taught."

"Yeah, I know."

Jesse glanced over at him. "You went to University of Michigan, right?"

Again, Louis wondered how Harrison had found out so much about him so fast. "Yup," he answered.

"That's great," Jesse said softly, nodding his head.

They drove on, Jesse offering a lay of the land. The town of Loon Lake was clustered on the southeast end of the lake. Jesse explained that it was not hard to get the feel for the town's layout: the small commercial heart was bordered by the residential houses, perfect little square lots with chain-link fences that split the area into a grid. The city park, with its new baseball diamond, sat on a tract of pine-choked land just north of the residential area.

As Jesse drove up Highway 44, which circled the lake, the homes grew sparser, giving way to bait shacks, trailers and towering pine trees. Up on the north end, Highway 44 was intersected with dozens of narrow roads. They were the driveways of the tourists' properties, Louis realized. Most were gated or chained, with signs that hinted at the humor and hopes of the people who dwelled within—BLISSFUL ACRES, TWIN PINES, THISTLE DEW, THE LOONY BIN. Louis strained to get a glimpse of the houses beyond the thick trees, but could see nothing. Jesse told him that the locals didn't really mix much with the tourists.

"They look down their noses at us some," Jesse said. "You know, like we're a bunch of yahoos."

Louis smiled slightly.

"But we just smile and take their money," Jesse went on. "We're a big tourist destination here. Hell, if it weren't for the Eggers, Loon Lake would be just like all the other crappy little dots on the map up here."

Louis was looking out the window.

"You see that fire station back there?" Jesse asked.

"That new place?"

Jesse nodded, somewhat proudly. "Egg money built that place last year. Best in four counties. Bought the lights on the baseball diamond, too."

It took forty minutes to drive around the lake. As they came back to town from the north end, Jesse pulled out a bag of peanuts. Louis politely refused his offer to share. Jesse expertly popped open the shells and ate with one hand, his left hand steady on the wheel.

"Well," Jesse said, "I suppose I should fill you in on how things are at our house."

Louis hid his smile. Jesse had obviously seen too many cop shows.

"Gibralter's a great chief," Jesse said. "Runs a clean department and a clean town. What he says goes."

"I already got that impression. What's with the quotes?"

Jesse looked over. "What did you get, Baudelaire or Churchill?"

"Baudelaire."

"Chief's a smart man. Stanford grad, majored in Asian studies."

"Why'd he become a cop?"

Jesse shrugged. "He told me it was to piss off his old man, but I don't believe it. He was a captain in Chicago before this."

"What the hell is he doing here?"

"You're here, aren't you?" Jesse grinned as he popped a peanut into his mouth. "U. of M. . . . Isn't that supposed to be the Stanford of the East?"

"Harvard of the Midwest."

"Maybe that's why he hired you. A meeting of the minds."

Louis squinted out at the snowy landscape. "So, who's our shift supervisor?"

"We don't have shift supervisors here."

"Watch commander?"

"Don't need one. Chief's always there late, sometimes till ten or eleven. Anything comes up after that, we call him at home."

Louis shook his head. "A little thin at the top, I'd say."

"Chief likes it that way. Lean and mean. Alpha units all the way. Gibralter said if we think we need a partner, he'll buy us a dog. After the chief thinks you're broken in, you'll be on your own."

"What about that thin guy I saw last night? He was wearing a sergeant stripe."

"Ollie Wickshaw. Yeah, he's a sergeant, but he pulls a shift with the rest of us. He's okay, a little strange. Into that occult shit. Supervision isn't his strong suit. If it were up to him,

he'd rather be with his damn homing pigeons than human beings."

Jesse swung the cruiser off Main Street and into a residential
area.

"Anybody else have rank?" Louis asked.

Jesse shook his head. "There's only nine guys total on the
force, including you now. And we're all on the street, equal in
the eyes of the chief."

"And God," Louis added.

"One and the same, my friend."

They drove on in silence for several blocks. Louis gazed
out at the neat bungalows with their snowy yards. The sky
was a brilliant blue and cloudless. He sank back into the seat,
lulled by the heat.

What an odd departmental structure, he thought. A dictator-
ship, union-free to boot. But Gibralter seemed to be well liked
by his men. Hell, maybe having one man at the top was better
than the twenty layers of gold-plated bullshit most departments
had.

The photograph on the wall of Thomas Pryce floated into
his mind, and he wondered how the man had died. Had he
been killed in the line of duty? But what could get a cop killed
in a place like this? Walking into a bad domestic? That could
happen anywhere.

"Thomas Pryce," Louis said slowly. "How'd he die?"

Jesse didn't look over at him. "He was shot."

"On duty?"

Jesse's jaw moved. "No. In his own house. Someone walked
up and just blew him away with a shotgun."

"Jesus," Louis said quietly. He wanted to know more, but
he sensed Jesse didn't want to talk about it. Pryce's death had
only been a few weeks ago, and he knew how long it took for
a wound to scar over in a small department when a cop was
killed. He had been to only one cop funeral, right after he
started his first job in Ann Arbor. He hadn't known the man,
but he had felt the current of pain and anger that ran like some

subterranean river below the smooth daily workings of the department.

"You get the guy who did it?" Louis asked finally.

"No," Jesse said.

"So the case is still open?"

"Technically."

"Who's running it?"

"Nobody right now," Jesse said. "We don't have an investigator. That was Pryce's job."

"He was the investigator?"

Jesse didn't look at him. "Yeah, Pryce was the investigator. Not that we ever have much to investigate around here."

Louis thought he detected an edge in Jesse's voice. They rode slowly down the freshly plowed street for several minutes.

"So who worked the case?" Louis asked, unwilling to let it lie.

"Chief gave all of us bits and pieces."

"You got any suspects?"

"No."

"Any theories?"

"Chief hasn't really asked us for our theories. We sit around and speculate sometimes. The other guys think it's probably a prior bust, some perp Pryce put away."

"But?" Louis prodded.

"Pryce didn't have any big cases. Just little shit. Nothing worth getting shot for."

The dispatcher broke in with a vandalism call. Jesse keyed the mike and answered that they were on their way.

"Christ, I get tired of this Mickey Mouse shit," he said, swinging the cruiser into a driveway to turn around.

They drove several blocks, stopping in front of a two-story colonial. An old woman was out front, shivering in a pink sweater. As Louis and Jesse got out, she pointed to a life-size plastic reindeer lying in the snowy yard.

"Look at what they did! Just look!" she jabbered.

Louis looked down at the deer. Someone had knocked the head off and spray painted the words "Fuck You" on it.

"What are you going to do about it?" the woman demanded, her voice shaking as she clutched her sweater around her.

Louis frowned slightly. "Well, ma'am . . ."

"I demand you do something!"

Louis started to take out a notebook, anything to shut the woman up.

Suddenly, Jesse dropped to his knees and laid an ear to the reindeer's torso. Then he began pumping with both hands on the deer's chest. After a few seconds, he stopped, sighed heavily and dropped his head.

"I'm sorry, Mrs. Jaspers, he's gone," he said softly.

She glared at Jesse. "Officer Harrison, that is not funny."

Louis turned away to hide a smile.

Jesse stood up slowly, brushing the snow from his pants. "Kincaid, do you have a rape kit in the car?"

Mrs. Jaspers set her flabby jaw and wagged a finger. "I'm going to report you, young man. For all the good it does."

"Just having a little fun, Mrs. Jaspers," Jesse said, pulling out his notebook.

"That reindeer has been in my family for years."

"Well, maybe the life insurance can help with the burial expenses."

Mrs. Jaspers crossed her arms and began to describe the hoodlums. Jesse pulled the cap of his pen off with his teeth and started to write. Louis glanced up and down the street. Kids usually liked to see the results of their pranks and he suspected maybe the culprits were lurking nearby. But his gaze was drawn to the white house at the corner.

It was a pretty house, two stories, with green shutters and trimmed evergreens. Even the snow seemed to lie differently on it, a neat layer across the eaves and lawn. It was the kind of house you'd expect to find in *Happy Days*. Only this one had yellow crime tape strung around it.

"Jess, you need me here?"

"No," Jesse said, scribbling to keep up with the woman's talking. He spun around. "Where you going?"

Louis crossed the street and stopped at a black mailbox. Across the side it read: THOMAS & STEPHANIE PRYCE. He heard Jesse come up behind him.

"What are you doing?" Jesse asked.

"I'd like to go in," Louis said.

"What for?"

"I just would like to see the scene."

Jesse looked up at the house, then shrugged. "Go ahead. We've already looked a hundred times."

Louis trudged up the snowy sidewalk and stepped onto the porch. The green wood door was intact, but a piece of plywood had been nailed over the hole where the glass window once was. There were black smudges on edges of the door and the porch railings where they had been dusted.

Jesse came up the walk.

"What happened exactly?" Louis asked.

"Pryce came downstairs. He was standing behind the door when he was blasted through the window. It was a twelve gauge shotgun. Hit him in the chest. We found Pryce's gun lying on the floor.

"He pulled his gun?"

"Never fired it."

"What time?"

"About three-fifteen A.M."

"You get anything?"

"One boot print. And the guy next door heard the shot. Another neighbor thought he saw somebody in the backyard."

"Not much to go on," Louis murmured, his gaze roaming over the door.

Jesse let out a sigh. "There was one other thing."

Louis turned.

"We found a card next to the body."

"A Christmas card?"

"No. A card, like you play poker with. It had this weird drawing on the back."

"Of what?"

"A skull and bones, you know, like a pirate flag or something on a poison bottle."

"What number?"

"Huh?"

"The card . . . a number or a face card?"

"It was an ace."

"Of what?"

Jesse shifted uneasily. "Spades."

Louis watched him for a second, then turned away. "Think it was symbolic of anything?"

"I don't know," Jesse said. "Maybe it meant something, maybe it didn't."

"You sure Pryce wasn't working on something when he was killed?"

Jesse bristled slightly. "We went through the stuff in his desk, but there was nothing but a routine burglary of a tourist cabin. Other than that, I've got no clue what Pryce was doing."

Louis turned to look at him. "He didn't talk to you about what he worked on?"

Jesse picked at an evergreen. "No. He wasn't big on casual conversation. He never really talked to anybody about much."

"How long was he with the department?"

"About three years."

"Three years on a force with only nine men, and he didn't talk to the rest of you?" Louis said.

Jesse was looking up at him, but Louis couldn't see his eyes behind the sunglasses. "Yeah, that's right," he said. "Pryce wasn't your basic party animal."

"What does that mean?"

"It means he kept to himself. That's all it means."

Louis stared at Jesse. "What about you? Did you like him?"

Jesse shrugged.

"What about the chief?" Louis asked. "Did Pryce get along with him okay?"

"You'll have to ask the chief that."

Louis turned away, looking around the porch again. "Where'd you get the print?"

Jesse came up the steps. "Right here, where the overhang kept the snow off. We lost anything out there in the yard 'cause it was snowing like a motherfucker that night."

"You try to trace it?"

"Yeah, I did. It was from some company called Warden's. Cheap work boot, thousands of them sold around the state."

Louis reached for the doorknob, but Jesse caught his arm. "It's locked. Hold on." Jesse disappeared around the house. Minutes later, Louis heard sounds inside the house and the door opened. "Went in through a basement window," Jesse said.

The white-tile foyer was wallpapered in faded pink roses with green leaves. Louis glanced over at the staircase. The bottom four stairs, carpeted in pale pink, were splattered with dried, brown blood. There was a brown stain the size of a dinner plate on the bottom stair.

Louis looked left into the living room. It was empty of furniture, but little things, small plastic toys, dustbunnies and books, were scattered across the floor.

"They left in a hurry," Louis said softly.

Jesse came up behind him. "Mrs. Pryce took the kids and went back to Flint the next day. A week later, she came back for the body."

Louis went back to the foyer and started up the stairs, Jesse trailing after. Louis paused at the door of a blue bedroom. There was a wallpaper border of ducks and some toys on the floor.

"How many children did they have?" Louis asked.

"Two. One was just a baby."

Louis went down the hall to the master bedroom. The walls were painted a mint green. There were depressions in the thick carpet where the king-size bed had been. On the floor were bits of papers, some beads from a broken necklace and several magazines.

Louis went slowly to the center of the room. He thought he could still smell the scent of aftershave, hear the kids giggling. He closed his eyes and imagined the sound as the blast ripped through the door below. He saw Stephanie Pryce bolting upright in her bed. He turned and saw Jesse looking at him oddly.

"You take this kind of personal, don't you, Kincaid?"

"What do you mean?"

"I was watching you. It was like you could see it in your head."

"Sometimes it helps to try and get a feel for things," he said. He saw something in the closet and went to it. Hanging there were two Loon Lake uniforms, still in their plastic dry-cleaning wrappers.

"Damn, she just left them hanging here," he said quietly.

Jesse came up behind him. "I should take them, I guess," he said. "Chief asked me to two weeks ago."

Louis moved to let Jesse gather up the uniforms, turning to survey the empty room again. He saw a curled photograph on the floor and reached down for it. It was of a small child, light-skinned with a tumble of black curls.

"Is this one of his kids?" Louis asked.

Jesse peered over Louis's shoulder.

"Yeah."

Louis stared at the picture. "Is Mrs. Pryce white?"

"Yeah."

"Did you guys consider that a possible motive?"

"Sure. The wife had an ex-husband that we thought was weird, but the chief didn't agree."

"How long were the Pryces married?"

"Seven years."

"Long time for an ex to stew about something," Louis said, slipping the photograph into his jacket pocket. He walked to the window and looked out at the street. There was a little girl making snow angels on her lawn across the street.

"What was Pryce like?" Louis asked.

Jesse hefted the uniforms up. "I told you. He kinda kept to himself, so none of us really got to know him. He always seemed, I don't know, uncomfortable with us. He was . . . intense, off in his own world, a classic Type A personality."

Louis didn't answer, his eyes still on the little girl.

"Personally, I always thought maybe he considered himself an outsider because he was black," Jesse said.

Louis turned and stared at Jesse. "Was he?"

"Shit no, not from our side." Jesse stared back at Louis, determined not to let his discomfort show. "I just always thought he just needed to lighten up."

"Lighten up?"

"Christ, Kincaid. You know what I mean. You know, a guy might make a joke or something, about color or something, but they don't mean anything by it. But Pryce never saw it from that point of view. He just couldn't, you know . . ."

"Lighten up," Louis said tersely.

Jesse let out a sigh. "Shit, Kincaid. No way am I gonna get this right."

"Okay. Here's a home-run pitch for you. What kind of cop was he?"

Jesse thought for a moment. "Civil, even to the dirtbags," he said. "He was the kind of cop that polished his badge, buckles and probably his balls with Brasso."

Louis smiled slightly. Jesse's mouth curved up gratefully.

"Let's get the fuck out of here," Jesse said. "Chief'll ream me a new asshole if he finds out."

Louis followed Jesse downstairs and back out onto the porch. Louis held the uniforms as Jesse pulled the door closed to lock it.

"You think the chief would let me see Pryce's old case files?" Louis asked.

"What for?"

"See if there's any old grudges someone wanted to settle."

Jesse slipped his sunglasses back on and stared at Louis. "We tried, Kincaid. We talked to local criminals, retired criminals, local mental cases, Pryce's relatives. Hell, we even visited the Rambos up at Lake Orion."

"Rambos?"

"You know, those weird Vietnam vets who live in the woods? Chief thought maybe they just decided to start popping cops. I'm telling you, we talked our asses off. And we didn't find squat." Jesse started down off the porch.

"Jesse."

Jesse stopped and turned.

"I wasn't implying you didn't try."

"Sounded like it."

Louis hoisted the uniforms. "Sorry."

Jesse turned and walked back across the street to the cruiser. Louis followed. He laid the uniforms across the backseat and got in. They drove in silence, heading back to Main Street.

Louis pulled the photograph of the Pryce boy from his pocket.

Jesse noticed him staring at it. "I keep thinking of his kids," Jesse said quietly. "I keep thinking of those kids and hoping they didn't come down those stairs."

"Yeah," Louis said.

They were silent again. The radio crackled as a call came for another unit to assist an old man who had fallen on some ice.

"You know," Jesse said. "More cops are killed during December than any other month."

Louis didn't respond. They turned back onto Main, starting into the business district.

"Hey," Jesse said suddenly, "I almost forgot to show you the most important place in Loon Lake."

Jesse did a U-turn and pulled up to the curb.

"Ground zero," Jesse said with a grin. "Dotty's Blue Star

Cafe. The state's biggest deposit of natural gas." Jesse grabbed the mike. "Florence, this is L-13. We're 10-7 for a few."

Louis slipped the photograph of Thomas Pryce's little boy back in his pocket. His mind was working back, replaying his job interview with Gibralter, wondering if Gibralter intended to appoint someone to take Pryce's investigator job. If he himself had been interviewing for it, he wished Gibralter had told him. Maybe Gibralter had been doing just that and he just hadn't picked up the clues. He had worked for only two other men before. His first chief in Ann Arbor was as easy to read as a telephone book. But his experience with the sheriff in Black Pool had taught him that impressions and, worse, assumptions about character, could be dead wrong. This man Gibralter . . . What in the world was he? Soldier? Scholar? Dictator?

Louis shook his head. Whatever Brian Gibralter was, it was clear that beneath that starchy exterior buzzed a Byzantine brain.

A meeting of the minds. Shit, maybe that *was* why he had been hired.

Four

Louis lingered on the porch until the moon scuttled behind a cloud, then he went back inside the cabin. He stood for a moment, gazing at his suitcase sitting on the bed, then went to the kitchen. Grabbing a Heineken from the refrigerator, he popped it open and took a long drink as he surveyed his new home.

The place was a little shabby, but not bad for two hundred a month. The moment the real estate agent had unlocked the door, Louis had liked the place. The furniture was utilitarian, standard-issue rental stuff. But the wood floors, rough-hewn walls and log-beamed ceiling had a certain rustic charm. It was the fireplace that had cinched it, though, a huge stone thing dusty with soot and cobwebs. The agent was barely out the door with the signed lease before Louis was out back gathering wood.

It took four tries, but now a fire was blazing, softening the dark corners and dissipating the mildew smell with the sweet scent of burning wood. Louis looked down at the rug in front of the fireplace. It was a bear rug, dusty brown and pocked with moth holes. He had found it rolled up in the closet. It smelled like dirty sweat socks, but he doused it with some foot powder from his ditty bag and it had settled down. The taxidermist had given the bear a maniacal grin, and as Louis stared down into the animal's glassy eyes, he found himself smiling.

Damn, he liked this place.

He took a swig of the beer. Setting down the bottle, he went outside to get some more firewood.

It was quiet—no wind, no animal sounds. He stopped, staring out at the frozen lake. The strong pine scent pricked his nostrils, reminding him for a moment of Mississippi. But the air was different here, cleaner, fresher, like just taking it in made you healthier.

As he gathered up logs, he thought of the portrait of Pryce back at the station. The irony of his situation was almost too strange. He had landed again in a small town, this time replacing another young cop. A black cop. A black cop who wore size sixteen shirts and spit polished his badge. Louis shivered and started back to the front of the cabin.

He heard footsteps and stopped. He turned and saw a figure out near the shoreline. He strained in the half-light of the moon, but could only make out a silhouette. It was a jogger, a girl. She was short and slender, and her ponytail bounced rhythmically with each stride. He watched her until she disappeared into the pines, then he went back inside. What kind of place was this that a girl could feel safe enough to jog alone at night?

Inside, he dropped the logs on the hearth. Standing to arch his back, his eye caught the photograph of the Pryce boy sitting on the mantel.

A meeting of the minds . . . Well, if Jesse was any indication, Gibralter wasn't happy with the way the Pryce case had been handled so far. Maybe he would welcome a new perspective. Shit, what did he have to lose? He wanted to work the case and there was only one way to get it: come right out and ask.

He glanced at his watch. Just after nine. Jesse had said that Gibralter stayed late at the station. He grabbed his keys and University of Michigan jacket and headed out.

There was no one manning the dispatch desk when Louis got to the station. A steaming mug of coffee, a paperback and a bag of Pepperidge Farm Milano cookies told him Edna had temporarily abandoned her post.

Louis went to Gibralter's door, tapped on the glass and poked his head in. The chief looked up quickly.

Louis continued on in. "Good evening, sir, I—"

Gibralter slammed a drawer shut. "Kincaid, are you a mental deficient?"

Louis stopped cold. "Sir?"

"Why the hell didn't you knock? I told you when I hired you, don't enter without knocking."

Louis looked back at the door. "I did, sir."

"In polite society, people wait for permission to enter."

"My apologies, sir," he said.

Gibralter glared at him and as quickly as it had come, the anger faded. "I don't normally give second chances, but I'm not going to suspend you."

"Thank you, sir."

Gibralter lit a cigarette and blew out the smoke in one blue stream that seemed to fill the room. Louis stifled a cough, afraid it would look as if he was gagging intentionally.

"You're out of uniform," Gibralter said.

Gibralter's shirt and pants were as crisp as they had been that morning. Louis wondered briefly if the man ever sweated, farted or had any normal human body function. "Sorry, sir," he said. "It won't happen again."

Gibralter sat down in the large swivel chair behind his desk. "Now, what did you want?"

Christ, he had forgotten the nice little speech he had rehearsed on the drive over. "Well, sir," he began, "I was thinking tonight—"

"Thinking?"

"Yes, sir, and—"

" 'To him whose elastic and vigorous thought keeps pace with the sun, the day is perpetually morning.' " Gibralter smiled. "Thoreau. You ever read Thoreau?"

Louis shifted slightly, clasping his hands lightly behind his back. "Yes, in college."

"Interesting man, wouldn't you say?"

Louis tried to remember something impressive from his philosophy course. It had been senior year, a three-credit slam-dunk course he needed for graduation and he had slept through it.

"Well, sir, I think his philosophy was admirable."

Gibralter cocked an eyebrow. "Oh? So you're a Transcendentalist, are you?"

A snippet from a forgotten lecture drifted into Louis's head. "Thoreau believed in the basic good of man. And the strength of the individual. I believe in those things, sir."

"I'm sure you do," Gibralter said, leaning forward to snuff out his Camel. " 'Nothing is at least sacred but the integrity of your own mind.' But that was Emerson, wasn't it?"

Louis unclasped his hands, realizing suddenly he looked like he was standing at attention.

"Well, I don't find much to admire in Thoreau's philosophy myself," Gibralter said.

Shit. So much for a meeting of the minds.

"A belief that intuition is better than logic and reason? The idea that man should turn his back on authority and established order?" Gibralter shook his head, smiling again. "The man ran off and lived in the woods, but wouldn't even set a trap or own a gun."

Louis's gaze dropped to the red carpet. How in the hell was he going to turn this around to asking for the Pryce case?

"I understand you were at the Pryce house today," Gibralter said.

Louis looked up. "Yes, it's tragic. Jesse said—"

"It's more than tragic. It's a goddamn outrage. No one kills my cops and gets away with it."

Gibralter reached into a drawer and pulled out a fresh pack of Camels. He slowly peeled off the top and then held the pack out to Louis.

"I don't smoke," Louis said.

Gibralter pulled out one for himself, lit it and sat back in his chair. "You came here to ask for the Pryce case, didn't you?" he said, squinting up at Louis through the smoke.

"Yes, sir," Louis said.

"Why?"

"The house, the scene bothered me," Louis began. He reached in his jacket. "I found this picture—"

"Let me see it."

Louis gave it to him. Gibralter glanced at it and then tossed it on the desk. "Emotions can get in the way in this job," Gibralter said.

"Sometimes they can be powerful motivators," Louis said.

"What did you feel when you saw that?" Gibralter asked, nodding at the photograph.

"Anger," Louis replied.

"What else?"

Louis hesitated. "Frustration."

"What else?"

Louis stared at Gibralter.

Gibralter took a slow drag on his cigarette. Louis watched the tip glow and snap. "So," Gibralter said, "what makes you think you can work this case when none of my other men has been able to come up with anything?"

The office was very warm. Louis felt a trickle of sweat make its way down his forehead. Shit, he didn't want this man seeing him sweat.

"Sir, I wouldn't think to question the ability of anyone here, including yourself," he said. "But I was made aware of the fact that the case isn't going anywhere and that you have not delegated it to anyone in partic—"

"Stop with the bullshit, Kincaid. Why do you want this case?"

Louis wet his lips. "I want to see the man caught."

Gibralter considered him carefully, then smiled. "And you

can't see yourself answering calls for lost dogs and downed geriatrics for the rest of your career here."

Louis felt a small spasm of anger.

"That's all right, Kincaid," Gibralter said. "Ambition is good in a man. I wish all my men had ambition." Gibralter was silent for a moment. "Tell me something, Kincaid," he asked finally. "Do you think a college degree is a help or a handicap for a police officer?"

Now how was he supposed to answer this one? His eyes darted up to the wall with all the framed certificates. No nicely framed diploma from Stanford in all that police stuff.

"I think it makes some people suspicious," Louis said carefully.

"Suspicious? Why is that?"

"Other cops, I mean, sir. They might see it as . . . unnecessary, given the day-to-day demands of the job."

"Clear thinking is unnecessary?"

"That's not what I meant. I meant—"

Gibralter held up a hand. "I know what you meant."

Louis waited, hoping the man wasn't going to ask him why he had decided to become a cop. Sometimes he wasn't even sure himself. When his foster mother had asked him why, just before he went into the academy, he had laughed it off with a crack about girls liking men in uniforms. But what had really triggered his decision? The kindness of the cop who revived the Patterson baby after he fell in the neighbor's pool? Or had it been the meanness of the cop who clubbed his roommate after finding pot in his car?

It was something more visceral. Flickering images on the Zenith. Black smoke, black faces. Orange fires, blue uniforms. Had his eight-year-old mind understood the rioting going on so many miles away in downtown Detroit? Probably not. But something about those uniforms had stuck.

Louis glanced back at Gibralter. A phone rang outside and he heard Edna's nasal voice answering. The wall clock ticked off the seconds. A twig beat against the window. The silence lengthened awkwardly. Louis focused on the window, watching a droplet weave a slow pattern through the condensation.

"I want that cocksucker caught," Gibralter said softly.

Louis looked at Gibralter.

"I want him caught. I want him put behind bars," Gibralter said. "This state doesn't have capital punishment, but I'd like to see him strapped in a chair, hear him scream and see him shit in his pants when the smoke pours off his head and his guts fry." He looked at Louis. "I want him killed for killing my officer."

Louis was locked by pull of the icy eyes. Finally, Gibralter blinked and looked away. "I'm putting you on the case," he said.

Louis nodded. "I'll give it my best."

Gibralter stood up slowly. "You're still green, Kincaid. Two years total as a working officer. And I don't want you neglecting regular duties. You'll still pull patrol, like everyone else."

Gibralter's expression had shifted slightly. His eyes burned like gas-blue flames, but there was something slack, almost weary around his mouth. "When one cop dies, we all die," he said.

Louis nodded once, sensing Gibralter expected no reply.

Gibralter opened a drawer and pulled out a plastic bag sealed with a wide band of orange evidence tape. "You'll need this," he said. Gibralter also picked up the photograph of Pryce's child and handed both items to Louis.

"You're dismissed, Kincaid," Gibralter said. He turned his back, looking out the dark window.

Louis slipped the photograph and the evidence bag in his jacket and started to the door.

"Kincaid."

He turned back. Gibralter was still facing the window. "That other feeling you had when you saw the picture?" Gibralter said. "It was fear."

Louis paused, hand on the doorknob. " 'If a man hasn't dis-

covered something that he will die for, he isn't fit to live,' "
he said. "Martin Luther King, Jr."

Gibralter turned, nodded slowly and turned back to the window.

Louis left, closing the door quietly behind him.

Five

There was something eerie about sitting at Thomas Pryce's desk. The contour of his body was still molded into the worn brown vinyl of the chair. The drawers of the desk he had shared with Ollie Wickshaw were still cluttered with little things that had meaning only to Pryce: paper clips twisted into squares and triangles, a worn tube of Chapstick, gnawed swizzle sticks from endless cups of coffee, and several half-rolls of Tums.

Louis plucked a pen from the plastic holder and chewed on the end as he stared at the ace of spades in the plastic evidence bag. It had already been scrutinized by the experts for prints. There had been none of any use.

Louis turned over the card. It was a Bee card, in the familiar dark blue-and-white pattern with the slightly drunken looking insect. It was from a case mass produced by the U.S. Playing Card Company in Cincinnati and sold everywhere. What made this card different, however, were the black marks on it. The lab had determined the ink was not from an ordinary felt-tip pen; the writer had used a laundry marker. Louis wondered if it had been a conscious choice, to use an indelible pen rather than one that would have easily smeared. He studied the odd black scrawl. It looked as if it had been done hastily, almost like a graffiti. There was a badly drawn skull and crossbones and below it: 1 2 3.

Louis checked his watch. He had been here since 6:00 A.M., unable to sleep once his mind had begun to churn on the investigation. Now it was almost seven-thirty, briefing was in a half hour and he would have to put the Pryce case aside for the day.

The door opened and Dale came in. His blond hair was spotted with snow and his boyish face flushed from the cold. He wiggled out of his coat and walked to the fireplace, stooping to toss logs into the hearth.

"Good morning," he called out cheerfully.

"Morning, Dale," Louis said. He could feel Dale's eyes on him and he looked up. Dale was staring at the evidence bag.

"What are you doing with that?" he asked.

"Chief gave it to me last night," Louis answered. He saw the slight look of distress on Dale's face. "Is there a problem?"

Dale blinked rapidly several times. "No, I just didn't know he had it."

"What? The card?"

Dale nodded. "See, I'm in charge of the evidence room." He jangled the ring on his belt. "Only me and the chief have keys."

Louis nodded.

"I mean, it's not that you can't go in," Dale went on, somewhat apologetically now. "It's just that I keep things straight around here, and if you don't log in and out, things get lost."

Louis nodded again. "I'll keep that in mind."

"I'm kind of the administrative assistant here," Dale said. "The chief never got it officially approved by the city council, so technically, I'm a patrolman, but I don't pull street duty."

Louis looked up at Dale again; the kid seemed to need to explain himself. "Well, every well-run office needs a manager," Louis offered.

Dale smiled. "You aren't kidding. You should've seen this place before I got ahold of things. Now, I do it all, run the computer for the numb-nuts who're too lazy to learn, make the coffee and do all the filing. By the way, Louis, you need anything from the files, let me get it for you, okay? You guys really mess up my system. I mean, no offense."

"None taken." Louis turned back to the card, hoping Dale was finished. No such luck.

"Chief likes things organized, you know," Dale went on.

"I got that impression."

"By the way, he wants all reports typed. Did he tell you that?"

"No," Louis said. "Thanks for the warning."

"Even your daily log should be typed, if you have time. You can type, can't you?"

"Yeah, pretty well."

"Of course, that doesn't apply to Jess," Dale said with a wry smile. "Jess can barely write, let alone type. But then again, not too many rules here apply to Jess."

Well, every department has a golden boy, Louis thought. To his relief, Dale busied himself behind the computer, allowing Louis to turn his attention back to the playing card. The office fell silent, broken only by the crackle of the fire. Dale switched on a radio, tuning it to a treacly "easy-listening" station out of Alpena. He began to hum along to Perry Como warbling the Beatles' "Yesterday." Louis suppressed a sigh, but kept quiet.

"Hey, Dale?"

"Yeah?"

"Where's the other Pryce evidence?"

"There isn't much really."

"I'd like to see it, anyway. And the case file, too."

Dale went to the evidence room, signed the log, unlocked the padlock and went inside the grating. He emerged with another plastic bag bound with orange evidence tape, and a manila file. He handed both to Louis and returned to Windexing his computer.

The bag contained a photograph of the boot print. Nothing special. Louis turned to the report, skimming through it. He stopped at a second photograph. It showed Pryce's body lying on the bottom stairs of his foyer. Louis stared at the gruesome photo, with its tagline date and the photographer's initials, an ironic "O.W." He stuffed the photo back in the file and turned to the witness statements.

The first was from Pryce's next-door neighbor, Leonard Moss, who heard the shots and called the police. The second statement was from a man named Moe Cohick, who lived in the house directly behind Pryce's. He reported seeing a shadowy man running across his yard at 3:15. Louis turned to the last witness statement. It was from Stephanie Pryce. It was handwritten, in bold, sharply slanted strokes that he had a hard time reading.

Statement of Stephanie Pryce
As given to Jesse R. Harrison
December 1, 1984
04:22 hours

Subject Stephanie Pryce stated she woke up when the gun went off. Mrs Pryce stated it was very loud. Mrs Pryce stated "Tom wasn't in bed. There is no phone in the bedroom." Mrs Pryce stated she sat in bed, maybe a minute, then walked to the door. Seeing no one in the hall, she crept to the children's room. They were crying so Mrs Pryce took them back to the master bedroom. Mrs Pryce stated she was too frightened to go anywhere else for several minutes, and called for her husband. There was no answer. Mrs Pryce stated she went back to the hall and saw the hall light on. She stated she could feel a cold breeze. She stated she thought Thomas Pryce might be outside. She stated she walked to the top of the steps and saw Thomas Pryce laying at the bottom. Mrs Pryce stated she wanted to call the police but couldn't. Mrs Pryce stated she could not get to a phone because she would have had to step over her husband's body. NO MORE THIS REPORT.

Jesse had signed the form on the bottom of the page with a sprawling signature boldly underlined twice. Louis closed the file.

"Dale, did Pryce ever mention to you what he was working on in his last few weeks?"

Dale looked up and shook his head. "He never talked about his work. I offered to help, you know, filing, tagging evidence, but he always said no."

"What about his notebook?" Louis asked. Every cop kept a small spiral notebook, and Louis had found nothing in Pryce's drawer.

"Don't know. Maybe the chief has it," Dale replied. He looked up at the wall clock. "Whoa, it's almost eight. Coffee-making time."

"I already made it."

Dale went to the coffee machine, looked at the torn sugar packets on the counter, then over at Louis. "You take three sugars in your coffee?"

"Yeah, why?"

"No reason."

Louis watched Dale as he wiped the counter clean. "What? Pryce took three sugars, too?"

"It's no big deal, Louis. Ollie says it's got something to do with karma trying to correct itself or something."

"Right," Louis muttered. He turned his attention back to the Pryce file on his desk, but his eyes went to the blotter. He hadn't noticed before, but it was covered with doodles. He wondered if they were done by Pryce or his night-shift desk-mate, Ollie. The doodles were tight, intricate, heavily inked. They sprawled over the blotter, paisleys and amoebas curling around numbers and words. He scanned for the numbers 1 2 3. Nothing.

The door flew open, letting in a whirlwind of snowflakes and Jesse, bundled in a hooded parka. Jesse threw back the hood and struggled out of the jacket as he walked across the office. He paused by the mirror and raked his hair with his fingers.

"Damn weather just ruins a good styling," he said, as he headed toward the coffee machine. He poured a cup and came up behind Louis, who was still studying Pryce's blotter.

"What you doing?"

"These doodles . . . You know if Pryce did them or Ollie?"

"Pryce. Ollie was always bitching about it." Jesse took a sip of coffee. "You can tell a lot from doodles, you know."

"Like what?"

"These say that Pryce had an acquisitive mind."

Louis turned to look at him. "What, now you're into hand-writing analysis?"

"I read a book on it once." He pointed at a paisley shape. "Look, see how he tries to contain the numbers with those squiggly shapes? He was trying to organize his thoughts. The guy was a mental pack rat."

Louis shook his head, grinning.

Jesse spotted the Pryce file. "What are you doing with that?"

"The chief gave me the case."

Jesse fell silent. Louis felt an instant chill in the air. Jesse started to walk away, then he turned back. "Sorry. I guess I didn't see the shit on your nose. Blends with your skin."

Louis's head shot up. "What?"

But Jesse had stalked off to the locker room. Louis heard the slam of the door.

"He didn't mean that," Dale said from his desk. "His mouth overruns his brain when he gets upset. Jess has been pissed for weeks. Jess and the chief are kinda close and I think Jess is mad the chief didn't let him work the Pryce case more."

Louis could feel his cheeks grow warm, signaling a slow-burn anger. Damn it, he wasn't going to let this slide. He rose and went into the locker room. There were two other officers in there, both of them looking over their shoulders at Jesse.

Jesse slammed the door of his locker, the clang echoing loudly through the tiled room.

Louis waited until the other men had left. He leaned against the far wall, watching Jesse as he yanked on his uniform.

"All right," Louis said, "what the hell is your problem?"

Jesse glanced at him. "Problem? Who says I've got a problem?"

Louis sighed. "Come on, let's get this over with."

"What?"

"The black-white shit," Louis said evenly.

Jesse let out a nervous chuckle.

"I'm serious, Harrison," Louis said. "I put up with this shit in Mississippi. I'm not going to tolerate it here. Do you understand me?"

Jesse buckled his belt. "Hey, I told you, man. Nobody here is like that."

Louis came forward. "Really? I suppose your little remark back there was just some little test? You want to find out if I can 'lighten up' like Pryce?"

Jesse was silent. Louis waited, watching as he fumbled with his service pin. He dropped the clasp and jerked the bar from his shirt and looked at Louis.

"All right. I'm sorry," he said. "It slipped out."

"Freudian slip?" Louis snapped.

"Give me a fucking break, Kincaid. It's not like I called you a nigger or something."

"Well, actually it *is* like you called me a nigger or something. You'd be surprised how many people don't quite catch that subtle distinction."

Jesse looked away, trying again to force the clasp on the pin under his shirt. His face was red, whether from anger or embarrassment, Louis couldn't tell.

"Look," Jesse said, "I got a real bad habit of using my mouth to hurt people. I didn't mean anything."

"Right."

"Cut me a little slack here, Kincaid. The only black people

in this town are a couple of maids over at the lodge and old Elton at the bait shop. I never worked with a black man before Pryce got here." He dropped the clasp again and bent to pick it up. He still couldn't fix it to the back of the pin. "Christ, my own father used to call black people porch monkeys."

Louis stared at Jesse, but Jesse couldn't look at him.

"I'm sorry, man," Jesse repeated, finally facing Louis. "Okay?"

Louis hesitated, then nodded. "Okay."

Jesse got the last pin on and went to a nearby mirror.

"Look," Louis began. "About this Pryce case. I'm not trying to show anyone up. I think the chief just thought I might bring a fresh eye to it." He paused. "You could help, you know."

Jesse let out a grunt. "The chief doesn't think so. Sometimes I get the feeling he thinks I'm stupid. Well, I'm not stupid. I may not have a college degree and I can't play chess or spout out quotes and shit, but I'm not stupid."

Louis decided to let that one lie. He didn't want to get involved in Jesse's relationship with the chief, whatever it was.

"Jess," Louis said. "I need someone who knows the town, the people. I need your help."

Jesse turned to Louis, studying him. "All right," he said, "what do you want to know?"

"For starters, I need to know more about Pryce. You think he might have kept a case file to himself for some reason?"

Jesse paused, his brows knitting. "Shit, maybe. Pryce hated having anyone looking over his shoulder, that's for sure."

"It's got to be a former perp," Louis said.

"I told you, we looked. We went through every file in his desk."

"Did you ask Mrs. Pryce if he kept any files at home?"

Jesse's face colored slightly. "No. We're not supposed to take files out of here."

Louis leaned against the locker, folding his arms, looking at Jesse.

"You think Pryce might've taken stuff home?" Jesse asked.

"It's possible, given what you've told me about him."

Jesse let out a long sigh. "I guess we're going to have to go to Flint."

"I'll drive," Louis said.

"No fucking way."

They started out of the locker room. Jesse stopped and turned. He patted his pins. "Straight?"

"Damn straight," Louis said.

After shift was over, they made the three-hour drive down to Flint. Stephanie Pryce had moved back to her mother's home, a simple shingled house on the outskirts of the city. When Jesse pulled the Loon Lake cruiser into the drive, the front door opened and a woman came out. She rubbed her hands on her apron as she watched the two officers get out of the car. Louis assumed she was the mother. A small child burst from the door and wrapped chubby arms around the woman's legs. Louis recognized him from the photo. Louis put his cap on and walked to the door, Jesse behind him.

"Mrs. Reanardo?" Louis asked, hoping he had pronounced it properly.

The woman nodded. "Officers. You made good time. Stephanie is in the kitchen. Come on in."

The house was warm and filled with the smell of chocolate chip cookies. The child hopped off to the kitchen and Mrs. Reanardo motioned for them to sit. Both men politely declined and she disappeared into the kitchen.

Louis looked at Jesse, then wandered to the bookshelf. His eyes locked on a frame that encased Pryce's badge against blue velvet. There was a plate with an inscription from Winston Churchill: "The only guide to a man is his conscience; the only shield to his memory is the rectitude and sincerity of his actions. With this shield, however fates may play, we march always in the ranks of honor."

Jesse saw him looking at it. "The chief gave that to Mrs. Pryce at the funeral," he said.

Next to the framed badge was a large piece of lavender quartz sitting on a tripod. Louis picked it up, turning it over in his hands.

"I'm sorry I—" someone said.

Louis turned, the quartz still in his hand. Stephanie Pryce was staring at him oddly, her hand at her throat. The expression on her pale face was so strange Louis couldn't immediately speak.

Jesse spoke for him. "Mrs. Pryce, I'm Officer Harrison. This is Louis Kincaid, my partner."

Louis came forward and she held out her hand. "Is there something wrong?" Louis asked.

She shook her head. "No. It was just . . . just the uniform. From the back . . ."

Louis sighed, thinking he should apologize, but then not knowing what for.

Her eyes went to the crystal in Louis's hand. "Oh, sorry," he said, holding it out.

She hesitated, then took the quartz from Louis, carefully placing it back on its tripod. She walked back to the sofa and sat down. Louis was sure that in better times she was quite lovely. But today she wore an oversize shirt that probably had belonged to her husband. Her straw-colored hair was pulled back in a haphazard ponytail and there were dark circles under her blue eyes. She started chewing on her already bitten-down nails.

"You drove a long way to see me," she said flatly. "What do you want?"

"Do you feel up to talking with us about your husband, ma'am?" Louis asked.

"I don't know what I can tell you." She ran a hand over her hair. "Please, sit down."

Louis waited until after Stephanie Pryce's mother brought coffee. He cleared his throat, edging forward on the sofa.

"Mrs. Pryce, we're looking for some files," he began. "Did your husband ever bring work home from the office?"

"Occasionally," Stephanie Pryce said.

Louis glanced at Jesse.

"Did he ever mention anything specific he was working on?"

She shook her head. "He didn't talk to me about what went on at work."

"Do you ever remember seeing any files like this around the house?" Louis held out a manila case file with a number printed on the front.

She looked at it, then shook her head. Louis handed the file to Jesse. He wasn't sure where to go now; he had been banking on Stephanie Pryce simply handing over a batch of files. He glanced at Jesse, who seemed equally perplexed. Louis thought suddenly of the bits of paper in Pryce's desk and Jesse's comment about his doodles.

"Mrs. Pryce," he said finally, "was your husband the type to keep things, papers, documents and the like?"

She smiled slightly, nodding. "He kept everything. He had one of those minds, you know, always moving. He was always writing notes to himself, stuffing them in drawers, his pockets, then forgetting them. I used to put these little baskets all over the house, trying to get him to throw his stuff in them. It didn't really work."

Great, Louis thought. If there were any missing files, they could be sitting in the county landfill by now.

"What is this about?" she asked, her face clouding.

"Some of your husband's case files might be missing," Louis said. "We were hoping he might have brought them home."

"Did he have a place at home, you know, like a private drawer maybe or cabinet?" Jesse asked.

"Well, there was a file cabinet, but I don't think he used it for work things."

When she did not offer to show it to them, Louis knew he would just have to ask. "May we see it?"

She sighed. Her mother was hovering nearby, and Stephanie looked up at her and then out the window. "What difference can it make now?" she whispered.

Louis knew what she was thinking: *What's the difference . . . ? He's dead and nothing can bring him back.*

"Mrs. Pryce," he said. "There is a possibility that something your husband might have been working on could have played a part in his death. We need to check all leads, no matter how small."

She kept gazing out the window. For a moment, Louis was afraid she was going to cry.

"We were very happy in Loon Lake," she said softly.

Louis felt Jesse squirm, but didn't look at him.

"It was a nice place and we were very happy there."

"Yes, ma'am," Louis said, not knowing what else to say.

Stephanie's mother moved around to sit next to her daughter, a hand on her shoulder.

"We'll find him, Mrs. Pryce, I promise," Louis said. He had no right to say that, but he knew she needed to hear it.

"Show them the cabinet, Stephanie," the mother said gently.

Stephanie wiped at her eyes. She took a deep breath and stood up. "All right. Come with me."

They followed her to a back bedroom cluttered with boxes. She moved a box and exposed a beige two-drawer file cabinet. Louis stepped over a carton and reached for the handle. It was locked.

"Do you have a key?" he asked.

"Somewhere," she said absently, glancing around.

Louis resisted a sigh. They could easily break it open, but he couldn't do that here in her home. They could take the whole damn cabinet back to Loon Lake, but he wasn't sure how she would take that suggestion.

Although she seemed detached, he knew better. She was hurting and her indifference was her only defense. If she had hated her husband's job before he had been killed, she surely had little interest in their motivation now, even if it was to find his killer.

Jesse was the one who asked, "Mrs. Pryce, would it be possible for us take the cabinet with us? We will return it to you later."

Stephanie sighed and brushed back her hair. "I don't know."

"Mrs. Pryce, I understand what you're feeling," Louis said quickly. "I understand that some stranger took away everything, changing your life in seconds. I understand how you want to try to forget it and get on with things. And now we come into your home, bringing it all back again. I'm sorry for that."

Her chin quivered.

"Please, let us try to help you by finding the man who killed your husband."

Stephanie wiped a tear away. The small room was silent and warm. Louis pulled at his fur collar of his jacket.

Finally, she looked up at Louis. "All right, take it. But please mail my papers back to me."

"Yes, ma'am," Louis said.

Six

Louis knelt before the fire, prodding the logs with a stick to renew the blaze. The cabin was cold and there was no heat other than what the fireplace supplied. The rustic charm that had so captivated him when he first saw the place was dissipating as fast as the pile of logs on the hearth.

He stared balefully at the last two logs. There were only a few more left outside. He would either have to go into town and buy some wood or venture outside and cut down a damn tree. Tomorrow, he vowed, he would go to the Sears catalog center in town and order a space heater.

He rose, grabbed the afghan from the back of the worn sofa and wrapped it around his shoulders. He stared at the small television set, knowing there was no sense in even trying. There were only two stations and the last time he tried, all he got was *Hogan's Heros* reruns and a curling tournament out of Canada.

A book, maybe a book. He went to the box in the corner and started sifting through the volumes, mainly college books and a bunch of paperbacks he had already read. He picked up *The Golden Apples*. He ran his fingers across the gold letters, thinking about Grace Lillihouse, the woman who had given him Eudora Welty's book. *Now don't forget to return it to me.* He felt bad that he would probably not make good on his promise. Hell would freeze over before he returned to Mississippi—or he would.

He went back to the sofa, tried to find a comfortable place

amid the broken springs and opened the book. He read a paragraph, and read it again. Finally, he put it aside. It was no use. His mind was spinning too fast.

His thoughts drifted to Thomas Pryce's filing cabinet. After returning from Flint, he and Jesse had spent two hours going through its contents, but had found nothing useful in the paper-crammed drawers. Thomas Pryce had been a pack rat, keeping every bank statement and phone bill he'd ever been issued. But there was nothing about work, and finally, Louis and Jesse had given up, too tired to continue. It seemed like the only thing left to do now was pack up the cabinet's contents and ship them back to Stephanie Pryce.

Louis stared into the dying fire. Stephanie Pryce's face had stayed with him all day. Her expression when she first saw him, as though she had seen a ghost. And the other look, that look of defeat. He had seen it before at the cop's funeral back in Ann Arbor, on the face of the widow. *I give up. You win. I lost. He's yours.*

Cops' wives. He wondered sometimes what kind of women married cops, what kind of women could put up with the life. Sometimes, in locker rooms or in bars after shift, he would listen to the married men talk about their wives. The words were often wrapped in dark humor, but he could sense in them the chasm the job created between a man and woman. He remembered one guy telling about the time he took his wife out for their twentieth anniversary dinner. He spotted a weirdo at the 7-Eleven and jumped out of the car, drawing his gun. She started to cry, yelling that she was tired of being married to John Wayne.

And he had heard the divorced cops talk. It was always the same, about how no one could really understand what it was like. About wives who finally gave up trying to dance in a world of positives when their husbands walked in a world of negatives.

He himself was only twenty-five and had never been with one woman longer than weeks. The women he had dated had no idea what his job was like and he felt no compulsion to share it with them.

Cop's wife. For the first time, he had a picture of what that meant. The picture was Stephanie Pryce's sad face.

Louis pulled the afghan tighter. He couldn't delay any longer. Time to go out for the logs.

He rose and went to the door. He slipped his feet into a pair of old loafers and stepped outside. The air was cold and still, and when he pulled in a breath, it sent knives into his lungs. Quickly, he shuffled around the side of the cabin, retrieved the last three logs and started back to the porch.

He was about to go in when he heard a muffled sound. It sounded like a cat, a soft mewing sound. His eyes searched the darkness. A second sound came to him.

"Shit . . . shit . . ."

Someone was out there, down by the shoreline. The moon emerged from the clouds and he saw her. She was down on one knee, her silhouette clear against the moonlit white lake. She was rubbing her left leg. It was the teenage girl he had seen jogging on other nights. And from the looks of it, something was wrong.

Louis let the logs drop to the porch. Wrapping the afghan tighter around his shoulders, he gingerly waded out through the snow toward her. She heard him and looked up.

"Are you okay?" he asked.

"Yes, fine. I'm fine," she said quickly. "I fell. I'm fine."

"Here. Watch it." He held out his hand.

Her dark eyes glistened up at him from her round face. Her dark hair was wet, plastered to her head like a sleek helmet. Her long ponytail hung limply behind. She hesitated, then took his hand. Louis gently pulled her to her feet and she winced.

"You're not fine," Louis said.

"Yes, I am." She took a step away and winced again. "Shit." Her eyes swept over the lake, off into the distant pines. "Shit," she repeatedly, more softly.

Louis stood, shivering. His loafers were soaked. "Look, you're hurt. Come on inside and we'll take a look."

"No," she said quickly. "I have to get home."

Louis studied her. She wasn't a girl, as he had thought, but a young woman. She was small, only about five-foot-two, with a boyish body, plainly visible in the runner's leggings and close-knit jacket. But her legs and ass were tightly muscled, like a marathon runner's. "How far is home?" he asked.

She frowned. "The other side of the lake."

"Right. You're going to run five miles on that leg? Come on, I'll drive you."

"I'll walk," she said crisply.

Louis shrugged. "Suit yourself, lady. But I'm freezing my ass off here. I'm going in. You can stay out here or come inside." He cocked a head toward the cabin and smiled. "Got a fire going. Or at least I did."

She stared at him for several seconds, then wiped a wet strand of hair off her face. "Okay. Thanks."

He offered his hand but she ignored it, limping ahead of him toward the cabin. He gathered up the logs and followed her inside. She stood by the door watching him as he slipped out of his loafers and went to throw a log on the embers. He poked at the fire until it reignited. When he turned, she was still standing in the shadows by the door.

"Let me warm up a minute and then I'll drive you home," he said.

She nodded.

He wondered how old she was. She looked to be maybe twenty or so. He suppressed a sigh, thinking suddenly of Abby Lillihouse. The last thing he needed was another messy liaison with a starry-eyed young woman like he had experienced in Mississippi. The small surge of anticipation he had felt outside when he first saw the girl was fading fast now. Jesus, protect me from crazy girls.

He glanced back at her. She was shivering. "Here, come over by the fire," he said.

Warily, like a cat in a strange place, she came across the room. As she did, the fire illuminated her face. It was strangely exotic, dark olive-complected and vaguely Asian. But her brow and jawline were more strong than delicate, a contrast to her high cheekbones. Her mouth was large, too large for her small face. Her nose was small, but with a slight flare to the nostrils. And her eyes . . . they were almond-shaped and there were a few lines at the corners and a vigilance inside. Louis stared at her. This was no twenty-year-old. She was at least as old as he was.

She came close to the fire and held out her hands. They were small with short fingers and close-cropped nails, like a boy's hands.

"Feels good," she said.

"I'm Louis," he said, extending a hand. "Louis Kincaid."

She slipped her hand into his. Her hand was soft, warmed from the fire, but the grip was firm. He could feel callouses.

"Zoe," she said. "Zoe Devereaux."

She pulled her hand away and ran it over her hair, down to the end of the ponytail. She looked back into the fire.

"I've seen you jog by before," Louis said.

"I run almost every night," she said.

"In the snow?"

She nodded. "I've been doing it for years. This is the first time I fell."

"Well, I'm glad it happened outside my place."

She looked up at him, then offered a slow, cautious smile. "You're new here," she said. "This place has been deserted for years."

"Yes, just moved here."

"From where?"

Louis hesitated. Mississippi? Detroit? Ann Arbor? "South of here," he said finally. "How about you?" Somehow, he couldn't see this woman being from Loon Lake.

"Chicago," she said. "I rent a cabin up on the north end."

Louis smiled. An East Egger.

"What's so funny?" she asked.

"Nothing."

He came around and sat down on the sofa. He shrugged off the afghan, suddenly aware how he looked in his old gray sweatpants, flannel shirt, tube socks and day-old beard. He wished he had taken a shower. Even in her running clothes and tangled hair, Zoe looked elegant somehow. He felt a stirring halfway between his gut and his groin. Jesus, how long had it been? That woman three months ago. Some nice sex, some good talk, but nothing more. The ache, he realized, was more than sexual. It was plain old loneliness.

Louis glanced at her left hand. No ring. "So you're here with your family?" he asked.

"No. I'm alone."

Thank you, God . . .

"No family at all?" he asked.

"I don't have any family. I come here to get away."

"Loon Lake is a strange place for a woman to spend a vacation alone."

"I'm an artist. I do landscapes, snow scenes mainly. I come here every winter to paint," she said. She seemed to be watching him for his reaction.

"No kidding? I've never met an artist. I've never met anyone really creative before. Except maybe the old woman who knitted this thing." He held up the afghan.

Zoe smiled. She hesitated, then sat down on the far end of the sofa.

"Can I get you a drink?" He gestured toward the small refrigerator. "Haven't got much. Beer? Some bad brandy?"

She shook her head.

He jumped to his feet. "Cocoa," he said.

She hesitated, then nodded. "All right. Cocoa."

He went to the kitchen, pulling out a small pot and the can of Nestlé's from the cupboard. He got out the milk carton and saw it was nearly empty. He poured what was left into the pot and added tap water. As he waited for it to heat, he glanced back at her. She was just sitting there, staring into the fire. He quickly stirred the lukewarm cocoa and brought it back to the living room.

She took the cup, cradling it in her hands, her eyes on him as he sat back down. He took a drink and grimaced.

"It's terrible," he said.

"It's fine." She glanced over his shoulder at the door. He sensed that she was uncomfortable and wanted to leave. He wasn't going to let her, not if he could help it.

"So, tell me about your paintings," he said.

"I'd rather not."

"Why?"

"My work is private. I find it hard to talk to strangers about it." When she saw the look on his face, she shook her head. "I'm sorry. That sounded pretentious."

"No, that's all right," Louis said quickly. "I understand."

"Do you know the Beauman Gallery on Lake Shore Drive?"

"Never been to Chicago."

"Oh . . . That's who handles my work."

The room was silent except for the crackle of the fire. He hesitated, trying to decide whether to tell her he was a cop. He could never tell what sort of reaction that would draw from a woman. Some were intrigued, a few repulsed, as if he had said he was a Nazi or something. Most were just puzzled. Zoe Devereaux, his instincts were telling him, needed only the smallest excuse to bolt and he didn't want his badge to be it. He took a sip of the cocoa, looking at her profile out of the corner of his eye.

Jesus, what a face. Not exactly beautiful, certainly not pretty. She was obviously mixed. But of what? A faint memory came to him in that instant. A memory of himself as a child, sitting on a worn wooden porch. A woman was brushing his hair. His mother? He couldn't see her face. He saw the faces, though, of the three little black girls who stood barefoot in the dirt watching in fascination. Can we touch it? one asked shyly, can we touch his hair? It was the first time he realized he was different.

His eyes traveled to Zoe's hair. It was almost dry now, forming a soft cascade of tight curls around her face. It was neither black nor brown exactly, but the color of the last leaves of fall, wet from the rain.

"You're staring at me again."

He smiled slightly. "I know. I'm sorry. It's just—"

"What?"

He shook his head. "It's personal."

"Go ahead," she said.

He hesitated.

"My mother was Korean," Zoe said evenly. "My father was black. Is that what you wanted to ask?"

Louis nodded. "You were born here?"

"No, in Korea. My mother died and I was in an orphanage for a year. Then, one day, this man showed up, this tall, black American soldier. He told me he was my father. He took me to California." Zoe leaned back against the sofa. "I was ten years old."

"That's incredible," Louis murmured.

"What?"

"That he went back for you."

She nodded, then seemed to drift off to some private place. "I loved him," she said after a moment. She looked up at him, her eyes warmed by the fire.

Louis waited, sensing she wanted to go on. He wanted her to, feeling that if she did, the moment could last, maybe grow into something more. But she remained silent, her eyes suddenly vacant in the waning firelight. It occurred to him that she talked of her father in the past tense. He was dead and Louis had the feeling it was recent. She had the aura of a person in mourning, still tender to the touch.

"He passed away?" Louis asked gently.

She nodded, not looking at him.

Louis regretted asking the question. It had apparently taken her further into some private place.

"He was killed," she said suddenly. "It was during the Watts riot. A sniper bullet."

Louis drew in a deep breath, his brows knitting. "Jesus," he said softly.

"He was a policeman," Zoe said.

"What?" he said.

"He was in one of the riot-control units. They surrounded his car. He couldn't get out." Her tone was matter-of-fact, almost cold. "He was black. It didn't matter," she said.

Louis leaned his head back against the sofa, shutting his eyes. God, a cop, her father had been a cop.

Louis looked at her. She was staring at the fire. He couldn't see her eyes, but her jaw was set, almost clenched. Louis looked away, running a hand over his mouth. Slowly, he rose. He walked slowly to the kitchen, set the mug down and stood there, hands braced on the counter, staring down into the sink.

"It's late," she said softly. "I'd better go."

He turned to face her. She had risen and gone to the door. She slipped on her running shoes, kneeling to lace them up. Louis came over to the door and reached for his jacket.

"I'll drive you," he said.

"It's not necessary."

"I want to."

She looked up at him and smiled slightly, nodding. She quickly slipped on her jacket and waited until he pulled on his boots. They said nothing as they trudged out through the snow to the Mustang, half-buried in a drift. Louis wanted to say something, anything to fill the chill void that had formed between them. He wanted this to move forward somehow. Despite what she had said. Despite what he was.

The Mustang started after several tries. "It's an old car," Louis said. "I never know what will happen. Sorry, there's no heat."

She nodded vigorously and gave him a smile for his small talk. "Take 44 north," she said. "I'll tell you when to turn."

She said nothing after that. Louis made a few weak comments about the snow, the cold, the lake. But she remained silent. Finally, she directed him to turn onto a small side road and stop at the bottom of a hill.

"It's steep. Your car won't make it up. I'll walk from here," she said quickly.

"I'll go with you."

"No," she said quickly. She pressed the door handle, opening the door. Louis grabbed her left hand.

"I want to see you again," he said.

"I don't think that's a good idea."

"Why not?" he pressed.

In the dim glow of the car's overhead light, he could see something anxious cloud her face.

"I don't know who you are," she said. "And you don't know me."

"Okay, but I want to." His hand tightened on hers.

She shook her head slowly.

"Let's just try it," Louis said.

She looked down at his hand. He felt her arm tense as she tried to pull away. He let go.

"I have to go," she said.

"Zoe . . ."

She got out of the car, started to close the door, then stopped. She looked away, up the hill into the dark woods and then back at Louis.

"Do you run?" she asked.

"I used to in college. Cross-country."

"What did you think about?"

Louis had only thought about winning the race, but he knew that wasn't what she meant. "Everything."

She nodded slowly. "I'll think about it tomorrow. When I run."

Seven

Louis pulled the scarf up over his face against the blinding wind. Somewhere in the darkness ahead, he could make out the glow of the station house sign and breathed an icy sigh of relief. It was only one mile from his cabin to the station, but Jesus, what a long damn mile.

He forged ahead, hurrying the last steps. Inside, he fell back against the glass. The warm air filled his lungs, sending a violent shiver through him.

Florence, the day-shift dispatcher, looked up from the desk. "Louis, are you all right?"

He nodded and slowly unwrapped his scarf. He could feel the ice melting off his eyebrows. For a moment he just stood, afraid his bones would snap if he moved.

"Did you walk to work?" Florence asked.

He nodded again and moved stiffly to the fireplace, pulling off his hardened leather gloves. "Car wouldn't start."

Florence went to the coffee urn. "For heaven's sake, why didn't you call someone?"

Louis watched her as she poured a cup of coffee. She was in her sixties, a frizz of white hair topping a willow-thin body. She looked like a Q-tip, a skinny negative to Edna's rotund positive.

"No phone yet," Louis said. He unzipped the jacket and let it drop off his arms.

Florence pressed a mug of coffee into his hands and held her hands over his for several seconds. She smelled like peppermint and her wrinkled hands were warm. "Next time, you radio in and Dale'll give you a jump."

"Yes, ma'am."

Louis sipped the coffee, closing his eyes as the warmth trickled through him. He was pouring a second cup when Dale came through the front door, offering a cheerful "good morning." When Dale returned from the locker room, Louis was waiting at the grating of the evidence room.

"What are you doing here so early?" Dale asked.

"Couldn't sleep. I need the Pryce file cabinet."

Dale snapped the keys off his belt. "Sign the log and note the time."

Louis went to the counter, flipped open the ledger and signed in on December 21.

"You wanna bring it out?" Dale asked.

"Grab me that stool. I'll just stay in here."

Dale slid a rolling stool over to him and Louis wheeled it into the small room. The ceiling-high plywood shelves towered over him, sagging with age and the weight of decades of boxed and bagged evidence. Everything was sealed with orange tape and dated with wrappers' initials. On one shelf were confiscated weapons: broken guns, knives, power tools. Louis stood up to turn on the light. His eye caught a Ziploc bag with a pair of women's panties inside. The tag read CUNNINGHAM RAPE, 69-23119. Jeez, those had to be ripe.

Louis sat down on the stool and pulled open the top drawer of the file cabinet. He and Jesse had gone through it last night and turned up nothing, but he wanted one more look before they sent it back to Flint. He sifted through the folders, pulling out one that said RECEIPTS. It was crammed with bills for gas, dry cleaning, a new holster, boots and other job-related expenses. Pryce must have been saving these for his taxes.

As Louis slipped it back in its place, he noticed another file wedged inside of it. He pulled it out; it was labeled RÉSUMÉ and he knew he had missed it last night. Inside were a dozen crisp copies of Pryce's résumé, clippings of employment ads and a few letters. A familiar letterhead caught his eye: The City of Detroit. He pulled out the letter, addressed to Pryce at his home. *Due to budget cuts, the city is not adding additional officers at this time . . .*

Louis smiled wanly. So Pryce had been trying to make it to the big time, too. He thumbed through the other letters, his smile fading. There were at least a dozen letters of inquiry and almost as many rejections, the oldest dating back to February 1982. Pryce had joined the Loon Lake force in 1981. If this file was any indication, he sure grew bored here quickly.

But that made no sense. Stephanie Pryce said they were happy in Loon Lake. Maybe Pryce didn't tell her he was looking for another job. Who knew what went on between husbands and wives?

Louis set the résumé file aside and continued on through the rest. Forty-five minutes later, in the second drawer, he came across a well-worn yellow legal pad that he also hadn't noticed last night. The top binding was filled with doodles like the ones on the desk blotter. He went quickly through the pages: more doodles amid Pryce's small, hard-to-read handwriting. A few numbers, but nothing that registered.

Slowing down now, he flipped to the last page of the pad, looking for anything relevant to Pryce's last days. He kept going, reading each page, until he got to the top again. It was dated from last summer. It contained brief notes about the burglary of a tourist cabin Jesse had mentioned.

Louis tossed the pad on the floor in disgust. Shit. Nothing . . . absolutely nothing.

He stared at the open drawer of the cabinet, and he kicked it closed. His eyes fell on the legal pad, lying facedown on the floor. Doodles, more damn doodles. The whole back of the pad was one giant paisley doodle that fanned out in elaborate concentric circles. In the center was one number—61829.

Louis wheeled the stool to the room entrance. "Hey, Dale, come here a sec."

Dale looked up from his computer and came over.

Louis held out the pad. "Look at this number. Any thoughts?"

"Too short for a social or phone," Dale offered.

Louis stared at the number. It was probably nothing, but then again, maybe Pryce had drawn this elaborate design around it on purpose, like Jesse giving emphasis to his signature with a double underline.

But cops didn't routinely record notes on bulky legal pads; they wrote important stuff on their pocket notebooks. Pryce's was still missing. He had asked Gibralter about it, but the chief said he had never seen it.

Louis gathered up the legal pad, the résumé file and a few papers he had set aside to be copied. The rest, he was sure now, was useless and he could send it back to Stephanie Pryce. Standing up to stretch, he switched off the light and closed the gate behind him.

"You lock it?" Dale called out.

Louis snapped the padlock closed. "Done."

Going to his desk, he put the materials in his drawer and glanced at the clock. It was past seven. His research time was almost up for this morning. He knew he could work late tonight, but he wasn't sure he wanted to. He wanted to be home in case Zoe jogged by.

He went to the locker room to change into uniform. Normally, he preferred dressing at home, but with the weather as cold as it was and his car on the fritz, he couldn't risk appearing at briefing less than crisp and spit-shined. Yesterday, Gibralter had blasted one guy for having mud on his shoes. Ten inches of snow and Gibralter was worried about mud.

There was a clean uniform hanging in the locker, one of the three he'd received his first day. He wondered when he'd get some more. Surely, they would give him more than three. Shit, he probably had to buy them.

"Good morning," Jesse said from behind him.

"Mornin', Jess."

"You're here early."

"I wanted one more crack at the file cabinet."

"Find anything new?"

"Résumés and letters. Pryce was looking for another job." Jesse didn't look up. "Not surprised. Sometimes I think he felt we weren't good enough for him."

Louis glanced at him, then let the comment go. "I was also going over the case file. There's a statement I'd like to follow up on, a Moe Cohick, lived behind Pryce. He saw a man running."

"He saw a shadow, that's all," Jesse said. "Couldn't give us any description."

"Well, sometimes people remember things later. I'd still like to talk to him. Can you go after shift?"

"Yeah. Remind me to call Julie though. Tonight is taco night and she gets pissed if I'm late."

Jesse pulled off his white T-shirt and opened his locker. "Motherfucker. He didn't bring them."

"Bring what?"

"Pop's Cleaners. They were supposed to drop off my uniforms. Christ," Jesse said, looking at his watch. "Chief is going to rip me apart if I'm not in a clean uniform."

Louis turned to say something but his eyes were drawn to Jesse's bare, brawny back. Across the shoulders and down the spine were faded little scars, like small whip or knife marks.

The door suddenly opened and an old bald man with a fuzzy goatee rushed in, a dozen or so plastic-wrapped uniforms over his shoulder.

"I'm sorry, Jesse. Snowed in this morning."

Jesse took five of the hangers from him. "Damn it, Pop, you know it's tough to work the streets bare-ass naked."

"Cold, too."

Jesse pulled out his wallet. "How much?"

"Forty."

"You greedy old bastard." Jesse slapped the money in the old man's palm.

"You keep talking to me like this, one day I'm going to keep the shit you leave in your pockets."

Jesse sighed. "How much this time?"

Pop held out a handful of wrinkled bills. "What? You think I count it?"

"I know you fucking count it, asshole."

"Five ones and twelve cents."

Jesse took it from him, paused, then stuffed the bills in the old man's shirt pocket. "Can't believe I keep tipping you."

"Can't believe I keep thanking you." Pop grinned. He folded the remaining uniforms over his arm and nodded toward Louis. "New customer?"

"Louis, this is Pop," Jesse said. "He picks up and delivers. Usually, he's on time."

Louis shook his hand. "How do I get in on the pickup?"

"Just leave 'em on that table in your bag every Monday. I come back on Wednesday."

"Sure thing. Thanks."

Pop leaned over to Jesse. "Same size as Pryce, isn't he?"

"Man," Louis moaned.

"Reminds me," Pop said. "I still got three of his. I'll bring 'em to you. And they'll be on the house."

Jesse passed the park and turned left on Fourth Street. It was only five, but in response to the wan winter dusk, the streetlights were already on. Louis craned to look up at the modern poles. They cast the street in a harsh, Martian-landscape light. Forget the quaint old lamps that lined Main Street. Even in a burg like Loon Lake, property owners wanted the brightest, newest lights to protect their homes.

Jesse swung the cruiser into Moe Cohick's drive. Like Pryce's house, it was the last one on the block. To the south was a sturdy twelve-foot wooden fence, which marked the boundary of a small lumberyard beyond. To the north were more homes, each yard partitioned by chain-link fences.

Moe came out on his porch. He was a round little man, with red cheeks and wispy white hairs sprouting from a bald head. He was wearing a brightly striped turtleneck sweater that made him look like a Russian stacking doll. He was eating a bearclaw.

" 'Evening, officers. What brings you about?"

Jesse didn't offer his name and Louis assumed he and Moe knew each other. Louis introduced himself. "We wanted to ask you about the man you saw running the night Officer Pryce was killed," he said.

"Sure, but I don't know what else I can tell you." Moe popped the last of the bearclaw into his mouth.

"Can you show us where you saw him?"

Moe nodded and led them around his garage to the back-yard. A long-snouted dog leapt at them from the neighbors' yard, barking furiously. Moe stopped in the center of his back-yard. He pointed to the back of Pryce's house, then moved his finger along the chain-link fence north, toward the end of the block.

"He was going that way."

Louis opened his notebook, where he had jotted what little description Moe gave the first time. "You said he was big?"

"Well, now, I think I said bigger than me."

Moe was so short Louis could see a birthmark on his scalp. "Can you be more specific, Mr. Cohick?"

"How tall are you?" Moe asked.

"Six-foot."

"Not as big as you. But he could've been bent over, like hunkering down."

Jesse let out an annoyed sigh. The dog behind them was still barking. Moe picked up a snowball and threw it at the dog. "Shut up, you mangy mutt!"

The snowball splattered against the fence, seeming to make the dog angrier. It was growing hoarse.

"Where were you standing?" Louis asked.

"At my kitchen window."

"You're up at three-fifteen in the morning?" Louis asked.

"I own the bakery on Main. I have to be in by four." Moe patted his belly. "I make the best stuff in the county. Always fresh."

"We ain't here to talk about your damn donuts, Cohick," Jesse said. Louis glanced at Jesse. He guessed Jesse had gotten an earful from Julie about being late.

Another bark drifted to Louis. This one was high-pitched, almost shrill. Louis peered over Cohick's head to the house catty-corner. An agitated terrier was straining against its chain, yapping back at the long-snouted dog behind them.

"Mr. Cohick, what direction did the man come from?" Louis asked.

"Well, now, I believe he came around that way and headed that way. Toward Pine, where the park starts."

Louis trudged through the snow to the back fence. He squinted in the fading light at the tall wooden fence of the lumberyard; there was no way a man could scale that. He looked the other way, down the long expanse of chain-link fence that separated all the yards. He could see the pines of the park at the end of the block and in between he counted six backyards that the killer could have cut through on his escape. He was assuming the killer had stayed in the back, under the cover of darkness, making his way across the yards to Pine Street. It was only a guess, but it made sense. A shotgun made a big noise; the neighbor had called it in almost immediately. The killer needed to stay hidden as long as possible. He couldn't take a chance of being spotted in the glare of those streetlights out front. Louis went back to Moe and Jesse.

"Jess, did you talk to everyone on this block?"

"Everyone. Moe's the only one who saw anything, such as it is."

"Hey, at least I saw something," Moe protested.

"Thanks, Mr. Cohick, sorry to bother you," Louis said.

"No problem."

They started back toward the house. The long-snouted dog behind the fence came alive again as they neared, provoking the terrier into action as well.

Jesus, how did these people sleep? Louis stopped and turned. "Mr. Cohick, were the dogs barking that night?"

Cohick rubbed his bald head. "Well, now, come to think of it, they were."

"Damn it, I asked you if you heard anything, Cohick, and you said no," Jesse said.

"You asked me if I heard anything *unusual,*" Cohick said. "Dogs barking their asses off at three A.M. ain't unusual around here!"

"Watch your mouth, doughboy," Jesse snapped.

Louis stepped up. "Mr. Cohick, how many dogs are there on this block?"

"Let's see . . ." He began to count on his hands.

Jesse cut in. "I can tell you how many. The Smiths, the Jessups, and what's his name . . . Haskins. They all got dogs. We're out here all the time giving them leash-law citations."

"Pryce didn't have a dog?" Louis asked.

"No."

"Show me where these people live."

Jesse pointed out the houses. It was every other one and no two butted up against each other. To avoid the dogs, the killer would have been forced to hop the fences diagonally. That's only if he knew the dogs were there. Which meant he probably knew the neighborhood or had scoped it out to plan his escape route.

Louis started back into the yard. The dogs kept up their cacophony.

"Louis!" Jesse called out.

"Come on," Louis answered.

"Christ, now what?" Jesse muttered, trudging after Louis.

Louis hopped the fence into Pryce's yard and headed toward the park. The long-snouted dog charged the fence as Louis approached.

"Louis! Where the hell are you going?" Jesse yelled over the noise.

"Retracing his steps."

They wove their way across the yards, avoiding the ones that Jesse said had dogs. At each fence, Louis would stop and brush off the snow on top.

"What are you looking for?" Jesse said, puffing to keep up.

"I don't know."

It was dark by the time they reached the last yard that bordered Pine Street. Louis's boots were sodden, and his hands were cold as he hoisted himself over the final section of chainlink. Across Pine Street, the park loomed dark and quiet.

Jesse was shaking with effort as he climbed over to join Louis on the sidewalk. His face was red and sweaty. "Now, what the fuck did we do that for?" he demanded, wiping his brow.

Louis ignored him. He was walking slowly along the fence, gently brushing away the snow. Halfway down the length of the last yard, he stopped. He quickly pulled off his glove.

"Jess, come look."

Jesse hurried over. Louis moved so the streetlight fell full on the fence. There, caught on an A-shaped spike, was a small piece of dark fabric.

"Fuck," Jesse whispered, staring at it.

Louis searched his jacket pocket and came up with a paper clip. He used it to pluck the fabric from the fence.

"Jess, go get the car," he said.

Jesse ran off. Louis waited, shivering in the cold, holding the tiny swatch. He turned and looked at the park behind him.

The entrance was marked by a small sign, but it was no more than a two-lane gravel road that plunged deep into thick, snow-covered pines. Not a bad place to conceal your vehicle while you committed a murder. He scanned the neighborhood, wondering where the killer had gone once he left the park. A left turn would have taken him right back to Main Street, exiting close to the station. Not likely. A right turn led him toward the freeway, through a residential area. More logical, but still slow going through unplowed streets.

The cruiser pulled up and Jesse jumped out with a flashlight and evidence bag. They bagged the swatch, and Jesse stared at it in the gleam of the flashlight.

"Green," he said. "Like an Army jacket."

They quickly took some Polaroids and labeled the spot. Jesse was silent as they got in the car.

"I guess I blew it with Cohick," he said finally.

"Witnesses don't always know what they see or hear is important, Jess."

"Well, it's not like I couldn't see or hear the damn dogs, is it?"

"You missed it. It happens."

Jesse said nothing, just slammed the cruiser into gear.

"Jess, pull in the park. I want to check something."

Only one lane of the road had been plowed and there were no lights. The darkness engulfed them and Jesse flicked on the brights to illuminate the tunnel of dense pines. The plowed road led to a parking lot, which was heaped with untouched snowbanks, then continued into the trees.

"People use the park much in winter?" Louis asked.

Jesse shook his head. "Nothing much in here but the baseball diamond. Kids use the hill by the school for sledding."

"I bet this is where he left his car," Louis said.

"And I bet he left that way," Jesse added, pointing to the road.

"There's another entrance?"

Jesse nodded. "It exits on Evergreen, which turns into Highway 44, which is always plowed and usually empty."

Louis looked at him. "What does that tell you?"

Jesse frowned, then blinked. "Shit, it means he knew. He knew there was another exit."

"He probably knew about the dogs, too."

Jesse sat back in the seat, lost in thought. It started to snow lightly and he turned on the wipers. "Whoever killed Pryce knew the town," he said quietly.

"Probably," Louis acknowledged.

The radio gave out a burst of static. Louis turned it down. Edna's voice came on. "Loon-13 and 11. What's your twenty?"

Jesse answered her. "City Park."

"Be advised Loon-1 requests you respond to 181 Lakeside Drive, code three."

Jesse looked at his watch and sighed. "So much for tacos." He clicked the radio on. "Central, what's the nature of the call?"

"Unknown, Loon-13. The caller was a teenager. He said . . ." Edna hesitated. "All he said was there was something 'gross' in the lake."

Eight

The body was facedown, frozen under the ice near the shoreline. It lay in a classic dead man's float position, the upper back and the outstretched arms visible near the surface and the lower torso and legs blurring down into the icy depths.

Even through the milky ice, the green parka and red wool cap were plainly visible. So were the hands, frozen close to the surface, with the tip of the left pinky finger poking out through the ice.

Louis stared at the body. Ollie came up behind him, carrying a 35-mm camera. Without a word, he circled the body and began snapping pictures. Louis recalled the initials "O.W." on the Pryce crime-scene photos. Apparently, Ollie was O.W., the guy entrusted with taking crime-scene photographs.

Louis surveyed the shoreline. There were only a few cabins and most were dark and shuttered on this stretch of the lake. He zipped his jacket up and nestled down into the fur collar. It was getting ball-freezing cold.

"We're going to have to set up some lights," Louis said.

"Electric's bringing them." Jesse started walking around the body. "We might be out here 'til fucking dawn."

Louis sighed loudly. "Damn."

"Hot date?" Jesse asked with a grin.

"In my dreams, man, in my dreams. You call your wife?"

"Yeah, she's pissed. No tacos for *moi* tonight."

Jesse came up to Louis's side. They stood there, staring down at the body. They had already called the coroner and the fire department. The latter had been Jesse's idea when Louis broached the problem of how they were going to get the body out of the ice. At first they had considered trying to chip it out with a crowbar, but had quickly realized how stupid that would be given the foot-thick ice. To say nothing about what damage they could do to the body.

"Any idea who it is?" Louis asked.

"Nope. We're about halfway up the lake. A couple small tourist cabins up here, so it might be an East Egger. They have a habit of getting tanked up, taking out the old Chris-Craft and falling into the lake."

"Not in winter," Louis said.

"Who's to say the guy didn't fall in last summer and just now floated up?"

Louis glanced at him. "He's wearing a parka."

"No shit."

They were getting irritable from the cold. Louis felt his stomach rumble with hunger.

"Well, no matter when he fell in, maybe somebody reported him missing," Louis said. "You remember anything like that?"

Jesse shook his head. "That's what makes me think it was an Egger, maybe somebody who was up here alone. A local would've been missed."

Louis nodded in assent. He was staring now at the pinky sticking up from the ice. He focused the beam of his flashlight on the hand, picking up a flash of metal.

"He's wearing a watch," Louis said. Gingerly, he stepped down from the shallow bank onto the ice and the ice groaned with his weight. Louis squatted and directed the beam at the frozen body's wrist. "Looks like a gold one."

"Figures." Jesse had trudged back up the bank. "What the hell is keeping the fire guys?"

Louis moved the flashlight over the distorted body. He was a large man and from the style of coat, the light gray hair and the thickness of the neck, probably an older man. Damn, why hadn't anyone missed him? And how the hell did he get under the ice when the entire lake was frozen?

"Hey, you know what this reminds me of?" Jesse said suddenly.

Louis jumped. He hadn't heard Jesse come back.

"A movie I saw this past summer," Jesse went on. "Julie and me went down to the drive-in at Rose City. It was about some caveman they found frozen in the ice of the North Pole. Shit, what was the name of that movie?"

Louis looked toward the road, hoping to see headlights. "Didn't see it," he muttered.

"That guy was in it, you know, the one that was in the movie about the kid who drowns and the brother tries to slit his wrists?"

Louis was thinking about Zoe. Maybe she wouldn't run tonight. It was too cold.

"Louis, what was the name of that movie?"

"Shit, Jess, I don't know."

"Mary Tyler Moore was in it. And the guy from *Taxi* was in it. Played a shrink."

"Ordinary People. Judd Hirsch."

"Yeah! That's it. He was in the caveman movie."

"Judd Hirsch was a caveman?"

"No, no, the kid in *Ordinary People,"* Jesse said impatiently. "He was the scientist who found the caveman frozen in the ice. I can't remember how they got him out though."

"Chain saws, I'd bet," Louis muttered.

They fell silent for several minutes.

"Iceman!" Jesse said suddenly.

"What?"

"That was the name of the movie."

They were quiet again. A dog barked somewhere far-off, the sound caroming against the pines surrounding the lake. They stood, staring at the body in its ice coffin.

"Gives a whole new meaning to the word 'stiff,' " Jesse said.

Louis looked up at him. Jesse grinned. Louis started to laugh. Jesse joined in, their cackles echoing in the dark trees. It broke the tension, lessened the irritation. It felt odd, laughing. Louis couldn't remember the last time he had laughed so hard out loud.

"Chief's here," Jesse said.

Louis sobered quickly and looked toward the road. Gibralter's cruiser came to a stop atop the bank. As he was getting out, two other cars and an Oscoda County Electric Company truck pulled up behind. The crewmen began unloading portable spotlights while Gibralter, and a second man Louis did not recognize, came down to the shore's edge. Another man, lugging a Nikon and bag, stumbled behind them.

"Jess, who's that?"

"Delp. Little snot-nose from the *Argus,* the local rag. Thinks he's Geraldo Rivera or something."

"What we got here, Jess?" Gibralter said.

"I'd bet an East Egger left over from hunting season," Jesse said.

"Do we know who it is?"

"No," Jesse answered.

"Who found it?"

"Some kids ice skating. It was hidden by some snow that we cleared away."

Gibralter stared down at the body, his face as hard set as the ice. The thin-faced man with glasses, in a massive hooded parka, pulled out a flashlight and ventured carefully down onto the ice. Louis guessed he was probably the Oscoda County coroner, Ralph Drexler.

"What you think, Ralph?" Gibralter asked.

The coroner looked up and shrugged. "No way to tell anything 'til we get him back to the shop and thaw him out."

"We called the fire department," Louis offered.

"Fire department?" Drexler said.

"Well, we figured they'd have the equipment to chip him out, or chain saws or something," Louis said.

"Well, be careful," Drexler said. "I need the body intact. Don't break off any damn arms. Or fingers. The fingers are important. Be careful with the fingers."

The coroner bent back over the body. The reporter began screwing attachments onto a camera. Louis watched the chief as he trudged back up the bank and toward his cruiser. A moment later, he saw the flick of a lighter and the glow of the chief's cigarette.

"Man, this is going to make a great picture."

Louis turned. The reporter was looking at him, grinning. He couldn't have been more than twenty and his face was flushed from the cold. He wore a red down vest over a heavy turtleneck sweater. Wild blond hair stuck out the sides of his wool cap. He made his way down toward the shoreline and began to take pictures, his strobe sending surreal flashes into the dark night. Louis watched him in disgust. The kid's tongue poked out the side of his mouth with each shot he took. He was obviously enjoying himself. He stepped down onto the ice, aiming his camera straight down at the body.

"Hey, back off a little," Gibralter hollered from the cruiser.

The kid looked up at Gibralter, then at Louis. "I got enough." He retreated to the bank to take pictures of the electrical crew unloading lights.

The six men of the Loon Lake Volunteer Fire Department ambled down to the body and stood gawking, making bad jokes. Louis stuffed his hands in his pockets, growing colder and more irritable. He watched as one man yanked on a chain saw, trying in vain to bring it to life as the others stood silently by, shivering. He looked up at the black sky and let out a long breath, trying to imagine Zoe on the frayed bear rug.

Two hours later, a six-by-six-foot block of ice was unloosed from the lake and hoisted up by pulleys rigged to a tow truck. It hung there, gleaming and dripping in the harsh glare of the lights. Everyone stood in a semicircle, silently looking at it for several minutes. A flash of light made Louis glance over his shoulder. He spotted the reporter a few yards off, recording the grisly tableau.

After a half hour of debate, it was decided to call Noel Wolfe, who ran the granite quarry, to get a truck big enough to transport the ice block. But when the truck arrived, Ralph Drexler stepped forward.

"That body will break into pieces if you hit a bump. We need something to cushion it," he said.

Gibralter looked at Jesse. "Go find a cushion," he said.

"Where the fuck? . . ." Jesse pulled off his cap. "Okay, Chief. It's only fucking midnight. We're in the middle of nowhere and you want a fucking pillow for this stiff? Jesus Christ, in another hour, you're going to have chisel all of us out of the damn ice."

"Harrison!" Gibralter bellowed, silencing the crowd. "I have given you a directive. Now follow it!"

Jesse stared at the chief, his mouth agape. Louis watched, sensing that Gibralter's reprimand was totally unexpected. Apparently, under better circumstances, Jesse was allowed his little fits of temper. But not tonight.

Jesse disappeared into the darkness and Louis watched as he flipped on the lights and ran code three back to town. Again, the men fell silent, a few going back to trucks to turn on heaters and thaw out. Louis went to the truck and ducked under the hoisted block of ice, shining his flashlight on the man's face.

It was distorted by ice, grotesque and pale. The man was Caucasian and chubby, his clean-shaven face clearly visible beneath the crystal pattern of the ice. His eyes were open, two little holes burnt in the ice, with a mild look of bewilderment. His mouth was open, and the upper plate of his dentures had worked its way loose.

A flash of light went off next to him. The damn reporter had ducked under the block with him and taken a picture.

"This one's not so bad," he said, looking at Louis.

"What?" Louis said.

"Pryce. Pryce was still warm when I got there." The young man thrust out a hand. "Delp," he said with a smile. "Doug Delp. *Oscoda County Argus.*"

Louis stared at the man's bare red hand for a moment, then reluctantly shook it.

"You're the guy who replaced Pryce, right?" Delp asked.

"Yeah," Louis said. "Excuse me, will you?"

Ollie was peeking in at them. "Is it worth coming under there to take photos? Or should I wait?" he asked hopefully.

"Wickshaw! Kincaid!" Gibralter yelled. "Get out of there before that damn block of ice falls and kills you both."

Ollie backed off, followed by Louis and Delp. Louis walked up the bank to the cruisers.

Thirty minutes later, Jesse returned with a queen-size mattress tied to the roof of the cruiser. The mattress was placed on the flatbed truck and the ice-encased body gently lowered onto it. Once the block was secured with rope, bungee cords and straps, the electrical crew and firemen began to quickly pack up their gear. No one wanted to linger a moment longer than necessary in the freezing night. Even the reporter had long since hit the road.

"Where will they take it?" Louis asked Jesse.

"Cedar Springs. They have a county lab up that way. It's about twenty miles."

"Thank God. We might get home by dawn."

Gibralter came toward them, tossing aside a cigarette. He watched the firemen finish with the final straps, then looked at Louis and Jesse. "Wickshaw will follow you in the cruiser."

Louis looked at the body, then back at Gibralter, who was walking away. "He expects us to ride with the stiff?" Louis asked Ollie.

Ollie shrugged. "That's what I heard. Isn't that what you heard?"

Jesse was already climbing on the flatbed. Louis started to protest again, but Jesse cut him off, extending a hand.

"Louis, get up here," Jesse said.

Shaking his head, Louis climbed onto the flatbed, over the block of ice and sat down next to Jesse, who had settled into a corner against the truck's cab.

"This is ridiculous," Louis muttered.

"Look at it this way. We're protecting the chain of custody."

The truck kicked into gear and Louis grabbed the edge of the truck. Jesse looked toward the road and watched as the chief climbed into his Bronco. The flatbed pulled slowly up the bank and onto the road. Ollie swung his cruiser in behind.

"Chief seemed kind of tense," Louis said after a moment.

"He's just pissed at me," Jesse said tightly. "I shouldn't have spouted off to him like that."

Louis shivered as the wind began to whip around them. "Not a real smart move."

"He's never yelled at me like that for just mouthing off."

"It's the circumstances, Jess. It's freezing-ass cold. The chief's got a dead body that everyone's making jokes about and all these civilians watching. He was doing a little chest beating, that's all."

"Yeah, I guess."

Louis scooted toward Jesse for warmth. "If I freeze and die out here tonight, tell them I died with honor, okay?" he said.

"You're not going to die. The human body can endure temperatures much colder than this."

Louis nodded toward the body. "Tell that to him."

They quickly fell silent in the biting cold of the open highway.

"Louis?" Jesse said, breaking the silence.

Louis grunted.

"Have you ever been, like, suddenly transported back in time? You know, by something that happens to you now?"

"Déjà vu?"

"No, more like you're a kid again and something that happened to you happens all over again?"

Louis looked at Jesse. In the wind, his voice had sounded

small. And his face, caught in the headlight beam of Wickshaw's cruiser following behind, looked different. The wind whipped his dark hair over his forehead and his eyes were teary from the cold. He looked ten years old.

"My father used to make me ride in the back of his pickup," Jesse said.

"In the wintertime?"

"Winter and summer. Rain or shine."

"Why?"

Jesse blinked. "Said there wasn't enough room in the front seat for me and my uncle both."

Louis shivered and pulled his knees closer. "Excuse me for saying this, Jess, but he sounds like a real ass."

"He was," Jesse said. "But in a way, he made me what I am."

"What do you mean?"

"If he hadn't kicked me out of the house when I was seventeen, I wouldn't have become a cop."

Jesse glanced at Louis and saw he was waiting for more. "I met Gibralter right after that, and man, suddenly it all got clear. I wanted to be a cop. I *had* to be a cop. Know what I mean?"

He didn't, but Louis nodded anyway.

They were quiet the rest of the way to Cedar Springs. The truck pulled into the county morgue parking lot at 1:30 A.M. Louis and Jesse climbed down off the back and went inside to log in the body. A few minutes later, they were walking back to Ollie's cruiser.

"Let's get out of here." Louis opened the passenger door of the cruiser and started to get in. Jesse grabbed his arm.

"Let me ride in front."

Louis shrugged. "Sure."

Louis got in back and closed his eyes. "Don't expect me in 'til later," he muttered. "I'm sleeping in."

Jesse shot him a look over his shoulder through the metal

screen that separated the front and backseats. "At least you got a place to sleep."

"What do you mean?" Louis asked.

Jesse nodded back toward the morgue. "That fucker used *my* bed."

Louis was awakened by the scratchy sound of his radio going off on the nightstand. It was Florence, who informed him it was after eight and he had missed briefing.

Louis fell back on the pillows. Damn, after last night, he expected to get a few extra hours of sleep.

He was zipping up his pants when he heard the squawk of a siren outside. He pushed back the curtain to see Jesse waiting in the cruiser. They went back on routine patrol without hitting the station. Louis sat slumped in the seat, half listening to Jesse's patter, refusing his offer to share his thermos of coffee. Julie, Louis had quickly discovered, made terrible coffee. At noon, Louis suggested they go back to the station.

Inside, Louis went straight to the coffeepot, then sank into his chair, rubbing his bristly jaw. He hadn't had time to shave and he wondered if Gibralter counted that as being out of uniform.

The phone rang and he picked it up. It was the medical examiner from Cedar Springs. Louis waved at Jesse. "Hey, they've identified the stiff," he called out.

Jesse looked over and started toward Louis's desk.

"Uh-huh. Yeah. Got it," Louis murmured, taking notes. After a couple of minutes, he hung up. "The guy was shot."

"You're kidding," Jesse said. "When?"

"They won't know until tissue tests are done."

"I told you, he was probably a hunter," Jesse said. "What kind of gun?"

"Shotgun. Twelve-gauge."

Jesse's expression shifted subtly, his brows coming together.

Louis was about to ask him what was the matter when it hit him. "Pryce was killed with a twelve-gauge," he said.

Jesse nodded.

Louis ripped off a paper from his pad and held it out to Dale. "They found a wallet. Dale, run the guy's name and see if he's reported missing. Run it out of state, too, in case he was a tourist."

Dale took the paper and started back to the computer. He stopped. "Jess," he said, turning.

Jesse looked up at him. "What?"

Dale's face had drained of color. His eyes went from the paper in his shaking hand to Louis and finally back to Jesse. Jesse came forward and took the paper from Dale.

When he looked up, his eyes were glazed.

"Dale, go get the chief," he said quietly.

Nine

The dead man's cabin was located on the west side of the lake in a neighborhood of small bungalows and trailers, about an eighth of a mile north of where the body had been found. It was, Louis guessed, where Loon Lake's less well-heeled lived, the gas station attendants, fishing guides and most of the women who waited tables and changed the motel sheets for the tourists.

His name was Fred Lovejoy. He had been sixty-one years old, single, childless and a former Loon Lake cop.

Now there were two. One old, one young. One white, one black. One with a family, one who lived alone. One active, one retired. But both had worn Loon Lake uniforms.

Jesse hadn't said much on the way over. Louis wanted to question him about local history, possible suspects and anything else Jesse could tell him. But the look on Jesse's face and the subtle shaking in his hands stopped him. Jesse had lost two coworkers in less than a month. The questions could wait.

Jesse swung the cruiser to the side of the plowed road. Louis got out and paused, looking at the cabin. Lovejoy's place looked like the others, a small, dark-green box with a few scraggly evergreens out front. Jesse started up the snowy walk.

"Jess, just a minute," Louis called out. He opened the large metal mailbox. It was crammed with papers. Louis dug it all out and sifted through it quickly. The pile appeared to be nothing but bills, junk mail and one copy each of *Field and Stream* and *Hustler.* There were also three thick newspapers, stuffed in blue plastic bags emblazoned with the *New York Times* logo.

Next to the mailbox was a bright green plastic mail tube with the *Oscoda County Argus* logo on the side, but there were no papers inside. Louis stuffed the newspapers and mail into a bag, tossed it on the seat of the cruiser and followed Jesse to the front door. He noticed a late-model Buick parked in the narrow driveway, covered with a foot-deep layer of snow.

Jesse saw Louis looking at it. "Fred loved his Buicks," he said. "Bought a new one every other year."

"Not bad for a retired cop living on a pension," Louis muttered.

"He drew some big bucks when he retired. Worker's comp settlement to the tune of thirty grand."

"For what?" Louis asked as he shoved gently on the door. He was surprised to find the door unlocked. He had to remind himself that unlocked doors were the norm in Loon Lake.

"Shattered disc or something. Got it taking down a drunk." Jesse's voice trailed off as they surveyed the inside of the cabin.

It was apparent that, other than the Buick, Lovejoy did not spend his money on any other comforts. The place was a dump.

"Jesus, what's that smell?" Jesse said, recoiling slightly in the doorway.

"Garbage, I think. I hope," Louis said. "Just be thankful it's so cold."

He took two steps into the tiny living room. The old yellowed shades were pulled down on the windows, casting the room in a murky gold light. The ancient sofa was half covered with a cheap chenille bedspread. The mismatched end tables were heaped with yellowed newspapers, magazines, dirty dishes and Pabst Blue Ribbon beer bottles. An old Danish-modern Zenith console TV sat in the corner, its top heaped with more papers and trash. Three-foot stacks of newspapers lined the walls, some spilling onto the floor. The green shag carpeting was littered with empty pizza boxes, open tin cans, and what looked to be bones.

Jesse's eyes widened as he noticed the bones. Louis pulled a pair of latex gloves from his pocket and slipped them on as he squatted down. He picked up one bone by the tip, then tossed it down. "Chicken," he said.

Jesse let out a breath and followed Louis into the kitchen.

"Damn, it's cold in here," Louis said.

Jesse stopped at the black potbellied stove. It was dark and cold. "This must be the only heat Fred had."

They made their way to the kitchen. A large plastic trash can lay overturned in the middle of the linoleum floor, garbage strewn everywhere. A box of Cheerios lay on the counter, most of the cereal shaken out. A set of metal canisters had also been overturned, leaving a blanket of sugar and flour over the counter and floor. All the bottom cupboards had been opened, with the pots and pans thrown across the floor.

"Someone was looking for something," Jesse said.

"Doesn't look like he had anything worth a damn," Louis said.

Jesse headed down the hall. Louis continued to search the kitchen, squatting to peer into the cabinets, then standing up. Strange, the upper cabinets were untouched.

"Oh, shit . . ."

"What it is?" Louis called out.

"You'd better come back here."

Louis hurried back to the bedroom. Jesse was staring at something in a corner. Louis went around the rumpled bed and drew up short. It was a dog, a large brown-speckled one, a spaniel of some kind. It was dead, lying on its side, stiff from the cold.

"I forgot Fred had a dog," Jesse said. He ran a hand over his face. "That explains the smell. There's dog shit all over the place."

"It might explain the mess, too," Louis said. "Maybe the dog was looking for something to eat."

Jesse grimaced. "You think it starved to death?"

"Maybe."

Jesse reached down and pulled a blanket off the bed. He carefully laid it over the dog. Without looking at Louis, he hurried out of the room.

Louis looked around the dingy bedroom, but it offered no clues about Fred Lovejoy's death. It was simply a sad testament to a lonely life. He had heard that retired cops sometimes went off the deep end like this. Without the regimen of station or family to give their lives shape, ex-cops drifted into a netherworld of solitary idleness. Louis's eyes drifted over the piles of unwashed clothes. Something on the dresser caught his eye and he moved to it.

It was a holstered gun. Louis slowly pulled it out and turned it over in his hand. It smelled of fresh Hoppes' gun cleaner and the oil left spots on his latex gloves. Even the leather was cared for, like a beloved baseball glove. Louis slipped the gun back in its holster and put it back on the dresser.

He went to the small bathroom. It was filthy, the water in the toilet bowl iced over. Leaving the bathroom, he wandered toward a closed door. He pushed it open slowly. This smell was so strong he drew back. There was a large cage in the corner, with an old blanket in it, layered in dog hair. It was apparently where Lovejoy kept his dog when he was away.

Louis drew his arm over his nose and stared at the cage. It was clear that Lovejoy had not intended to be away from his cabin long or he would have caged the dog. Had his killer come to the cabin? Had Lovejoy been murdered in his own home and then dumped in the lake? Louis frowned. But how did you dump a body in a frozen lake? And where was the blood? Louis had never known of a shotgun blast that didn't leave a drop or two. But if he wasn't killed here, then where?

Jesse came down the short hall. "Hey, Louis, I think I—"

He came to an abrupt stop in the doorway. His eyes locked on the cage. His expression went suddenly dead, his skin ashen.

"Listen, Jess," Louis began, "we're going to have to—"

Jesse bolted from the room.

"Jess!"

Louis stuck his head around the door frame, but Jesse was gone. A moment later, he heard the slam of the front screen door.

"What the hell?" Louis muttered. He went back out into the living room. Through the open front door he could see Jesse leaning against a tree. His head was down and his ragged breath formed white clouds in the cold air.

Louis came up behind him. "Jesse? What's the matter?"

Jesse shook his head. Then slowly, he drew two deep breaths and straightened. His face was sweaty.

"I don't know. I felt sick," he said. "The smell got to me, I think. And that damn dog." Finally, he looked at Louis, his brown eyes glistening. "I'm sorry, man. Don't . . . don't tell the chief, okay?"

Louis stared at him for a moment, then awkwardly patted his shoulder. "No problem. It never happened."

Jesse wiped his brow and stared off toward the lake. "Shit, I just remembered something."

"What?"

"Fred was a fisherman."

"So?"

"An ice fisherman. You know, shanties, holes in the ice."

Louis stepped around the tree and followed Jesse's gaze out at the lake. "Like that one?" Louis asked, pointing to a small, wooden structure about thirty yards out on the frozen lake.

"Yeah. Just like that one."

Louis turned up his collar and started across the snow. Jesse pushed himself off the tree and trailed after him.

"Maybe we should call the chief before we go out there," Jesse said.

Louis pulled his radio out and hailed Florence. He advised her to notify the chief, and on a hunch, the county crime-scene unit. He stuffed the radio back in his belt just as they reached the fishing shanty door. A gray layer of haze drifted over the lake, casting smoky shadows that glittered with light snow. Damn, it was desolate out here.

"You going to open it?" Jesse asked.

Louis pushed open the thin door. The wind whipped in from behind him and he could hear a flutter of papers inside. The shanty was dim and Louis reached for the flashlight on his belt, shining it around the inside.

It was small, about ten feet by ten feet, made of cracked wood. Directly in the center, next to a hole in the ice, sat an old wing-backed chair. Next to it was a TV tray table holding a Coleman lantern. A generator-fueled space heater occupied one corner, a warped Styrofoam cooler another. The ice floor was covered with green Astroturf, littered with cigarette butts, beef jerky wrappers and Pabst cans.

Louis went in, swinging the flashlight up over the walls. They were festooned with fishing gear. There was also a Black and Decker chain saw, an Indian blanket and a sheepskin bota.

"Louis, look."

Louis turned the light on Jesse, who was kneeling by the fishing hole. On one jagged edge there were dark stains.

Louis knelt, shining the light on the hole. It was blood. He trained the light back up on the chair. There was a small stain on the seat, as black as the water in the ice hole.

"This is where he was shot," Louis said quietly.

"Here? But he was found up near the shore," Jesse said.

Louis stood up and pointed the flashlight at the chair and then down at the hole. "See the blood pattern? He was shot sitting in that chair. Then my guess is he was put down that hole."

Jesse stared at the ice hole. "Goddamn," he muttered. "Someone shot him and stuffed him down this fucking hole. Just stuffed him down there. Jesus H. Christ." He turned abruptly and stood at the door, facing outward.

"Jess? What's that?"

Jesse turned in the direction of Louis's flashlight beam. It had picked up an iron bar lying by the chair.

"It's a spud bar. You use it to chisel a hole in the ice."

Louis knelt to examine the bar. Fred Lovejoy had weighed well over two hundred pounds. Chances were the killer hadn't had the patience to use this to hack out a hole big enough for a body. Louis focused the light up on the chain saw hanging on the wall. "And that?"

Jesse glanced at the saw. "Lazy guys use a saw. It's cleaner."

"And faster," Louis said dryly.

Jesse was staring down into the hole. "I don't get it. Why in hell would someone bother to do this? I mean, why not just leave the body here?"

"Maybe to buy time," Louis said. "By spending ten extra minutes cutting the hole, he bought himself enough time for evidence to decay, witnesses to begin to forget. The trail goes cold and the case gets harder to solve."

Louis walked to the door and faced the bloody chair, forming an imaginary shotgun in his arms.

"Think he knew his killer?" Jesse asked quietly.

Louis lowered his arms. "Hard to say. I think the killer walked right up on him just like with Pryce." Louis shook his head. "But Lovejoy was a trained cop. How could somebody get the drop on him so easily?" He paused. "Maybe he did know him."

Jesse picked up a beer can by the small opening. "Or maybe Fred was too drunk to react. Fred did like to drink. And people around here don't expect trouble. Not even us."

"Well, Pryce did," Louis said. "He had his gun drawn."

They were silent for several moments. Then Louis began a slow sweep of the floor with his flashlight.

"What you looking for? A shell?" Jesse asked.

"No, a card."

Jesse stared at him for a moment, then reluctantly began to do the same. For several minutes there was no sound except for their breathing.

"Damn, it has to be here," Louis said softly.

"Maybe it's up in the house," Jesse said.

Louis shook his head. "He left the other one right by Pryce's body."

"Maybe it fell in the hole."

"That would be just our luck." Louis spotted a magazine near the far wall and bent down to look at it more closely. It was the Sunday magazine of the *New York Times,* dated November 24. It was open to the crossword, which was nearly finished.

"He was doing a crossword puzzle when he was shot," Louis said.

Jesse looked over at him. "Fred was a crossword freak. He was always working on those damn things."

Louis knelt and used the end of his flashlight to flip the magazine aside. "Bingo," he said.

The card was lying facedown. Louis guessed it had been swept against the wall with the magazine when he opened the door. Fishing a pen from his jacket, he used it to turn the card over.

"Ten of hearts," Louis said. He rose, his gaze traveling around the shanty.

"There's got to be a connection," he said quietly.

"Connection?" Jesse asked.

"Pryce was an active cop, but Lovejoy was retired. What's the connection?"

"They're both cops," Jesse said.

"It's got to be more than that," Louis said. "We've got to search that cabin, top to bottom."

He turned. Jesse was shaking his head.

"It's there, Jess. All we have to do is—"

"I'm not going back in there," Jesse interrupted him, turning away. He took a deep breath. "I'm not going back in there," he repeated.

The sound of a siren drew Louis's attention before he could reply.

"Chief's here," Jesse said quickly, leaving the shanty.

Louis emerged just as the Bronco pulled up in front of the cabin. Gibralter got out and started toward the front door.

"Chief! Out here!" Jesse called.

Gibralter stopped and turned, peering toward them. He started down the snowy bank and across the ice.

"How long was Fred retired?" Louis asked as they waited.

"About two years," Jesse said. "Fred trained me. I liked the guy. Everybody did. Even the chief."

"The chief?"

Jesse nodded slowly. "They were friends, sort of. After Fred retired, they went fishing together sometimes."

They fell silent.

"Jess, about the cabin," Louis began.

"Drop it," Jesse said sharply, and walked off toward Gibralter.

Louis frowned as he watched him go. What was going on here? What had caused Jesse's reaction in the cabin? And why was he refusing to go back in? Then it came to him. Jesse hadn't been sick from the smell. He was scared. Two of his colleagues had been gunned down. And for all any of them knew, whoever had done it wasn't finished.

Gibralter and Jesse came back to Louis. "What's going on?" Gibralter said, his eyes scanning the shanty.

"This is where Lovejoy was shot," Louis said.

Gibralter's eyes registered surprise. "Here? How do you know?"

But he didn't wait for an answer. He stepped around Louis and looked inside the open door of the shanty. "Kincaid, hand me your flashlight," he said.

Gibralter stepped inside, directing the flashlight over the chair and the jagged hole with its bloody edge. Then he slowly backed out of the shanty and turned to face Jesse and Louis.

"Fred was a good man. I could count on him," Gibralter said tightly. He looked away abruptly, his eyes going back to the cabin, then up at the pines rimming the lake.

Louis watched him carefully, looking for a reaction, not just of a chief for a downed comrade, but for a man mourning a dead friend. But Gibralter's face remained composed and Louis didn't know whether to feel pity or admiration.

"I want this entire area secured and searched thoroughly," Gibralter said. "From the cabin to those trees."

Louis scanned the shoreline. The area had to be at least a mile square. He caught Jesse's eye and knew he was thinking the same thing. Gibralter was grasping at straws.

"Harrison, has Cedar Springs been notified?" Gibralter said.

"Yes, sir."

Gibralter knelt and brushed a layer of powdery snow away from the ice. Visible on the surface were a few dark spots Louis thought at first might be blood. Gibralter stood, took a deep breath and blew it out in a white vapor. He looked at the sky.

"Anyone know the weather forecast?"

"Six inches by midnight," Louis said.

"Well, we damn well better try to preserve something," Gibralter said sharply. "I need these spots intact. Harrison, go get a broom from the cabin. I want the snow around this shanty carefully removed and the ice checked for evidence all the way to the shore."

Louis was going to say that there had been two hard snows in the last week. But judging from the look on Gibralter's face, logic wasn't going to go very far.

"Want me to go get a fucking tent, too?" Jesse said.

Louis glanced at him, stunned by his sarcasm.

Gibralter glared at Jesse. "Do what I say, Harrison."

Jesse trudged off across the ice.

"And watch where you step!" Gibralter hollered, standing and brushing the snow from his hands. He turned and peered back in the shanty's door.

"Was there a card?" he asked after a moment.

"Yes."

"Where was it?"

"Next to his chair, under the crossword."

"What?"

"He was working the crossword puzzle, sir, when he was shot."

Gibralter eyes grew distant. "Crossword," he said softly. He turned away, his gaze wandering out over the lake. Louis watched his profile. Whatever emotion Gibralter was allowing himself to feel, he wasn't going to let anyone else see it.

After a moment, Gibralter turned back to face Louis. "Anything else?" he said brusquely.

Louis hesitated.

"You've got something on your mind, Kincaid. What is it?"

"It's Jesse, sir," Louis said.

"What about him?"

"When we were searching the cabin, Jess got pretty shaken up. I just think he—"

"I know Harrison better than you do, Kincaid," Gilbralter interrupted.

Louis nodded. "I know. It's just that, well, I think he's scared by all—"

"Scared?" Gibralter shot back. "He can't afford to be scared. None of us can right now, Kincaid. There's a fucking cop killer out there."

"Chief, with all due respect, I don't think you can fault a man for being—"

"Two men, two of *my* men are dead!" Gibralter yelled. "I want this fucker found *now!* I don't care what it takes! If it means Jesse gets down on his hands and knees and examines every fucking inch of this ice, or you climb every fucking pine tree in those woods, then you'll do it, you hear?"

"Yes, sir," Louis said quietly.

Gibralter turned and started back to shore. He stopped and turned to Louis.

"Find him, Kincaid," he said.

Ten

It was almost eleven. Still no sign of her.

He had stood out on the porch for an hour, waiting for her to emerge from the fog that covered the lake. Finally, he went in. Now he sat slumped on the worn sofa, staring into the dying fire. A yellow legal pad lay on his lap, filled with notes about Pryce and Lovejoy.

He couldn't get the images out of his head. Fred Lovejoy's face as he lay frozen in the ice. Pryce's face as he lay dead on the stairs, captured in the crime-scene photo.

And Jesse's face. He couldn't shake off that look on Jesse's face after he had run from the cabin. Some cops were lucky enough to go their whole careers without pulling a gun or seeing a corpse, and living in a place like Loon Lake, Jesse had probably never seen a dead man before Pryce. No, not just a dead man—a dead cop.

Louis let out a breath, thinking now of Gibralter. No matter how distraught he was about his friend Lovejoy, he had been too hard on Jesse. Jesse had a right to be afraid. Shit, they all had a right to be afraid.

He stared vacantly at the television. The sound was off, the images throwing flickering shadows over the walls. He pulled the afghan up around his shoulders, but nothing seemed to warm him. The cold came from somewhere inside him. It had started in Lovejoy's cabin when he had seen that dog. It had built in the shanty when he saw the bloody jagged hole in the

ice. And it had finally overtaken him as he stood in the bitter
cold and listened to Gibralter's command.

Find him.

Find *what?* A monster who had murdered two men. A de-
viant who might kill again. A phantom who was as ephemeral
as the fog. Louis tossed the legal pad aside, his feeling of
impotence growing. He didn't know what he was doing, where
to start with this investigation.

Find who . . . find who?

Louis reached for his glass of brandy, but it was empty.
With a sigh, he pushed himself off the sofa to get a refill. As
he trudged back from the kitchen, he spotted the box of books
in the corner. He stared at it, something pricking his memory.

Setting the glass down, he knelt and started rummaging
through the books, pulling out the blue paperback he had
been looking for. The title was *The Criminal Mind* by Dean
Franklin.

Picking up his brandy, Louis returned to the sofa and turned
the book over to the back cover. Franklin's penetrating eyes
stared back at him, transporting Louis immediately back to the
lecture hall at University of Michigan. The elective class was
called "Investigative Analysis," taught by Franklin, a retired
FBI agent who believed that killers could be apprehended by
understanding their psychological makeup.

Louis had taken it because he couldn't get the elective he
wanted, and he remembered thinking, like all the other students, that it was all hocus-pocus bullshit and that Franklin
was a washed-up desk jockey put out to academic pasture. He
had only half-listened to the craggy old agent who droned on
about the brave new world of "criminal profiling."

Louis stopped at a chapter called "Inside the Mind of the
Monster." He skim-read it, digesting its point that a profile of
a killer could be constructed from evidence and tendencies
like an abusive childhood.

Louis closed the book. Shit, so all he had to do was find

some poor, mistreated dirtbag who had mutated into a cop killer.

He tossed the book aside, and his eyes drifted to the television screen. The eleven o'clock news was on, a feed from a station down in Lansing. It flashed a photo of Fred Lovejoy in the corner. Louis jumped up to turn up the sound, but was too late. Great, Loon Lake had made the big time.

He watched listlessly through a series of other news stories, until a familiar graphic caught his attention. It was a blue-and-gold shield, the badge worn by Detroit police officers. Over it were the words "Drug Bust Gone Bad?"

The talking head blabbed on about cops and then cut to film footage of a tall man in a suit emerging from a building. He was stone-faced but strikingly handsome, with reptilian eyes. The type under his face identified him as MARK STEELE, CHIEF CRIMINAL INVESTIGATOR FOR THE STATE POLICE.

Louis leaned forward. He vaguely remembered hearing about Steele during his days in Ann Arbor. Steele had headed an internal affairs case involving Detroit cops accused of brutalizing an innocent couple during a drug raid. The cops had been suspended; the couple settled out of court. But the episode had made Mark Steele's career. The combination of his telegenic looks and the anti-police sentiment in Detroit was too potent for the media and politicians to resist. It was no secret that Steele wanted to be state attorney general, and he was paving his path to the capital with the crushed careers of cops.

Louis stared at the man's flickering face. He suddenly remembered something he had seen in the locker room of the Ann Arbor station. Someone had cut a photo of Steele from the newspaper, smeared it with excrement and hung it on the bulletin board.

Steele's face disappeared. The talking head moved on to a story about a puppy rescued from a drainpipe.

Louis turned off the television and sank back into the sofa.

He reached for the glass of Christian Brothers, raised it to his lips and drained it.

A soft sound behind him made him freeze.

It had come from somewhere outside. He tensed, his ears alert. Nothing. Wind stirring the pines. Man, he was jumpy.

A thump. Out on the porch.

Louis set down the glass and with one quick move jumped up and flattened himself against the wall near the door. His eye darted to his gun, visible on the dresser in the bedroom beyond. His heart hammered as he tried to put the image out of his head of Thomas Pryce opening the door to face his murderer.

A knock on the door. "Louis?" The voice was soft, female.

He exhaled and opened the door. She was standing there in the dark, her slender form encased in a parka, her round face framed in fur. Her eyes searched his face.

"Is something wrong?" she asked.

"No," he said. He hadn't realized it, but his body had been tensed, and now it trembled in relief. "Come in," he said.

Zoe entered in the same wary manner as the first time. Her eyes darted about the room and back to him. "I knew you were here. I saw the smoke from the chimney."

"It's late. You shouldn't be out alone," Louis said.

"It's safe."

He shook his head. "No, it's not safe, Zoe. It's not safe."

"He's not killing women, Louis, he's killing cops."

There was something in her voice, a matter-of-fact tone that stunned him. She hadn't meant it to sound cold; her observation had come from pure innocence. No, it had come from something else, from sheer relief. He could see it in her eyes. *I am not the target. I am safe.* It struck him in that moment that he had seen the same look on other people's faces in town, always women. He had seen it on Florence's and Edna's. He had seen it on the waitress's face at Dot's Cafe. They were distressed that a killer was in their midst, but they were also relieved. *We are safe. For once, we are not the target.*

He shook his head at the irony. Women feeling safe to walk the streets in the dead of night when he and other men—cops—trembled behind locked doors.

"Louis? What is it?"

"Nothing," he said.

She was looking up at him, waiting for something.

"I didn't think you would come back," he said.

She smiled slightly. "I didn't either."

He glanced down at her boots. "You didn't run?"

"No, I drove."

He looked down into her dark eyes. For a second, he saw the dark holes in the ice hut. But this darkness was warm, and he felt as if he could fall into it and drift down to some secret place where he could hide away from the cold.

"Can you stay?" he asked.

"For a while," she said softly.

He helped her out of the parka. She was wearing jeans and a black turtleneck sweater. She rubbed her arms as she went to the fire. He hung up her coat and followed. As she sat down on the sofa, he spotted the legal pad on the floor and kicked it under the sofa. He glanced to the bedroom. His holstered gun was on the dresser. He went to the door and closed it, returning to the sofa to sit by her side.

"Can I get you a drink?" he asked.

"Beer?" she said.

He went to the kitchen and brought back two Heinekens, sitting down next to her. He still felt edgy, like his skin was too tight. She was watching him as she sipped her beer, as if she sensed his tension.

"It's cold," he said, getting up to toss a log on the fire.

"I love the cold," she said.

He looked back over his shoulder. "Well, you're from Chicago so you're used to it. I never seem to warm up."

"Where are you from?" she asked, setting the beer aside.

"Michigan. But I was born in Mississippi." He sat back down, acutely aware of her shoulder touching his. A surge

went through him, electric, magic. Slowly, he felt himself starting to relax.

She turned to face him. She studied his face.

"What are you looking at?" he asked.

"Your bone structure. I'm an artist, remember?"

"Of landscapes, I thought."

"Well, I've taken life-drawing classes."

"Ah, nude men."

"Lots of nude men."

Her gaze traveled over him, down from his face. He held
his breath. It was intimate, more erotic than if she had touched
him.

"You have an athlete's body," she said.

"Used to. Out of shape now."

She smiled, her eyes moving on.

"Your second toe is longer than your big toe."

He glanced down at his feet in their tube socks. "You know
what they say about that, don't you?"

She laughed; then her eyes returned to his face. "You've
got a white relative somewhere," she said.

It caught him off guard. He thought of saying something
flip, but the warmth of her eyes stopped him.

"My father," he said.

Her eyes held his. "Then you know," she said softly. "You
know what it's like."

She raised a hand and touched his cheekbone. She ran her
fingers down his face, under his chin. He closed his eyes at
the excruciatingly light touch.

When he opened his eyes, she was staring at him. The fire
bathed her in gold. Tiny beads of sweat glistened on her high,
broad forehead. The soft tight curls of her hair formed a dark
aureole around her head. She touched his lips. Her own lips
parted.

He kissed her. He held her upper lip softly with his own,
savoring it. When he let go, she leaned into him, placing her
cheek against his. He could feel the fast rise and fall of her

chest against his. Slowly, he raised his hand, brushing his fingers along the small curve of her breast.

"Can you stay?" he asked softly.

"For a while," she whispered.

Eleven

Louis glanced at his watch. Only seven-thirty, still plenty of time before briefing. He got up and went to the coffeepot, pouring his second cup of the morning. Returning to his desk, he looked down at the papers and mail, the stuff he had taken from Lovejoy's mailbox. Gibralter had told him to go through it, see if there might be something, some small clue.

Louis sipped the coffee, struggling to get his blood flowing, his mind working. He hadn't slept more than a couple hours, but for once he didn't care.

Zoe had stayed until nearly three. He had wanted her to spend the night, entwined with him in the afghan on that moth-eaten bear rug. But she had refused. Strange woman. Tender in her lovemaking, but as soon as it was over, she had turned edgy, as if she couldn't wait to leave. Strange, strange woman, unlike any woman he had been with before. The others had all expected things from him after sex—everything from a couple minutes of cuddling to a lifetime commitment. But not Zoe. It had left him feeling a little unbalanced and, he finally had to admit, bruised around the old ego. She wouldn't even give him her phone number. Just the promise that she would return. He couldn't remember the last time he had wanted a woman as much.

He rubbed his hands roughly over his face. Easy, easy . . . Back to the task at hand. He began sorting through Lovejoy's mail.

Lots of bills . . . but nothing from the phone company,

which was what he had been hoping to find. He jotted a note to Dale to have Lovejoy's phone records pulled. Discarding the junk mail and the magazines, he turned his attention to the copies of the *New York Times.*

Pulling off the blue plastic, he saw all three were Sunday editions. Now why would a guy who didn't get the local paper take the trouble to have the Sunday *Times* sent to him every week?

The crossword. Lovejoy had been working on one when he was shot in the shanty. Louis focused on the dates on the front pages. December 1, December 8 and December 15. Louis fished out his pocket notebook and flipped through it. The puzzle found in the shanty was dated November 24. Why was Lovejoy working on an old puzzle when there were new ones in his mailbox?

Louis sat back in his chair, frowning slightly. Shit, maybe it took three weeks for the damn paper to make its way to an outpost like Loon Lake.

He opened the paper and found the circulation number. He dialed it and reached an operator, who politely told him he could get the Sunday edition of "the world's greatest newspaper" mailed to him for $56 a year. But that since he lived in a rural area, it would be a three-day delivery.

Louis thanked her and hung up. He was staring at the *Times,* lost in thought, when Jesse came in. Jesse grunted out a greeting and went to the coffeepot. He stood, still in his parka, gulping down the coffee. He came over to Louis's desk, peering down at the mail and newspapers.

"That Lovejoy's stuff?"

Louis nodded.

"Anything in it?"

"No," Louis said. "No copies of the *Argus,* at least."

Jesse gave a snort of derision. "The *Argus?* Shit, Fred hated that rag. Got mad at it when they endorsed Jimmy Carter and he canceled his subscription."

Louis drummed the pencil on the desk. That explained no

local papers at least. But the untouched *Times* still bothered him. And the dead dog, he realized suddenly. If Lovejoy had been killed recently, the dog would not have starved to death.

"Something doesn't make sense," Louis said.

"What doesn't?" Jesse asked.

"Lovejoy left the papers in his mailbox. The last crossword he worked on was November 24."

Jesse frowned. "So?"

"So, it could mean Lovejoy was killed weeks ago, some time between November 25 and December 4."

Louis watched as Jesse's expression shifted from confusion to trepidation. "About the same time as Pryce," Jesse said.

Louis nodded.

Jesse turned away. Louis couldn't tell, but he thought Jesse was looking at Pryce's photo on the wall.

"Jess."

He turned to look at Louis. "I don't get it," he said.

"Get what?"

"What's he waiting for?" Jesse said. "If it's been three weeks, what's he waiting for?"

Louis didn't know what to say. An undercurrent of fear had been running through the station ever since Lovejoy was discovered, but not one man had given voice to it. Two cops were dead. Who was next? It was the question every man asked, but only of himself.

"Maybe he's finished," Louis said, knowing it didn't sound convincing.

Jesse wasn't listening. "What's the fucker waiting for?" he murmured. He went slowly into the locker room.

Louis thought of going after him, but what could he say? He glanced at the wall clock. Nearly eight, time for briefing. He gathered up Lovejoy's mail and stuffed it back in the bag. This would have to wait. Jesse would have to wait, too.

"Morning, Kincaid."

Louis looked up to see Gibralter coming in.

"Chief," Louis acknowledged.

"I want to see you and Harrison before briefing," he said, as he swept by into his office.

"Right." Louis picked up the bag and deposited it on Dale's desk to be logged back into the evidence room. He was refilling his coffee when Jesse emerged in a crisp uniform.

"Chief wants us now," Louis said.

"He say why?"

Louis shook his head.

Gibralter was lighting up a Camel, standing behind his desk when they went in.

"I've decided to pull you two off regular duty," he said. "I want someone full-time on Pryce and Lovejoy," Gibralter added.

Louis didn't have to look at Jesse to get his reaction; he could almost feel the ripple of excitement arc off his body.

Gibralter tossed a folder on the desk. "The prelims from Fred's shanty are back. The black spots were grease, the stuff they use to lube cars. They found a greasy shoe print, too, size ten. Check to see if it matches the one found on Pryce's porch."

"Is there any doubt?" Jesse asked.

Gibralter ignored him. "They're positive the ice hole was enlarged by the chain saw on the wall. The blood in the chair was Fred's, and they figure he was shot while he was sitting there."

Louis watched for some emotion in Gibralter's face, but there was none. He found himself wondering if he himself could maintain such control.

"From the trajectory angle, they estimate the height of the shooter at five-nine, assuming he held the shotgun at his waist, dead in front of him," Gibralter went on.

"What if he held it at his eye, Chief?" Jesse asked.

"Then the fucker would be about three foot tall, Harrison."

Jesse flushed with color.

"They finish printing the shanty and cabin?" Louis asked.

"Not yet. There's a dozen latents in both places. I doubt we'll find our killer's prints in that shanty, though."

"What about the junk in the cabin?" Louis said.

"Cornwall and Evans are handling that."

Louis started to mention the mail and his theory about the date of death, but the chief pressed on.

"I want you two to talk to every inhabitant on that end of the lake and find out if anyone saw anything. Check with Elton at the bait shop and anyone else out there who might help."

"Chief—"

"Don't interrupt me, Harrison. When you get through with that, I want you to check out every stinking cocksucker we ever busted in this town and find out what he's doing now."

"Case files?" Jesse asked.

Gibralter nodded, grinding his cigarette out in the ashtray. Apparently, the chief had not caught the dismay in Jesse's voice, Louis noted. Jesse was envisioning something more exciting than sifting through dusty file cabinets.

"Has the ME come back with time of death yet?" Louis asked.

Gibralter focused on him. "No, but Fred was wearing a watch, his retirement watch. It stopped at two-thirty, so they figure that's when he was put in the water." Gibralter started rummaging through his drawer for something.

"I have a theory about the date of death," Louis said.

Gibralter looked up. "Theory?"

Louis quickly summarized his thoughts about Lovejoy's mail, his dog and the crossword puzzles.

Gibralter listened as he lit another Camel, blowing out the smoke slowly. When Louis was finished, he waited for the chief to say something but he seemed to have drifted off to some private place. Outside, beyond the closed door, Louis could hear the voices of the day-shift men gathering for briefing.

"Is there anything else, Chief?" Louis prompted.

Gibralter blinked, looking at him. "No, no . . . Just call me if you find out anything."

Louis started to leave.

"Kincaid."

Louis turned.

"You've got a button missing."

Louis glanced down at his uniform shirt. "I'll change, sir."

Louis hurried out the door. The office was empty, the other men already gathered in the adjoining briefing room. Louis noticed a uniformed stranger standing by the door, his cap in his hand. He wore a green nylon jacket and khaki trousers with a brown stripe. The patch on his sleeve said OSCODA COUNTY SHERIFF'S DEPARTMENT. Louis nodded at him. The man nodded back.

"Sheriff Armstrong," the man said, extending a hand.

Louis came forward to shake the sheriff's hand and introduce himself.

"How you doin', Kincaid?" Armstrong asked.

Louis knew the sheriff was asking about the entire department. A cop killing transcended territorial boundaries and Armstrong was there to offer assistance, even if it was just unspoken sympathy.

"Frustrated," Louis answered.

Armstrong nodded. "Well, we got our eyes open for anyone who looks suspicious in the area. You'll let us know if there's anything else we can do, right?"

"Thanks, sheriff," he said, moving to the locker room.

Louis saw, with relief, that Pop had left two fresh uniforms on the pole, tagged with his name. He opened his locker and hung one inside, pulling the plastic wrap off the other.

He felt eyes on him and turned around to see two other officers standing at the end of the lockers, both just finished dressing for shift. He didn't recognize them and he guessed they were night-shift men brought in for extra detail. One was a lean man about forty and the other heavy-set, past fifty.

"Morning," Louis said, glancing at their name badges. Burt Cornwall and Ernest Evans.

"Morning," Cornwall replied gruffly.

Louis pulled off his shirt. The silence lengthened.

"You were on that scene yesterday, weren't you?" Cornwall asked.

"Lovejoy's? Yeah, I was," Louis answered.

"I heard the chief gave you the Pryce case, too," Evans said. The hostility in his voice was undisguised.

"Yeah, he did," Louis replied. Apparently, he was getting a rep as an ass-kisser. But what did he expect? A police force was no different than any other business when it came to recognition and promotions. Those who didn't get them blamed those who did.

Louis turned to face Evans and Cornwall, wanting to tell them simply "tough shit." But he knew he couldn't let himself get cut off from the others, especially not veteran cops who knew the town. It would be Black Pool, Mississippi, all over again, and he couldn't afford that if he expected help.

"So," Louis said, "what can you guys tell me about the local dirtbags? Any suspects come to mind?"

Evans slammed his locker shut. "I give my opinions to the chief," he said.

The men moved away to the door. Louis watched them, his jaw tightening. Cornwall was probably pissed at pulling the duty of going through the garbage hauled out of Lovejoy's cabin. Evans, on the other hand, was more likely just a burnout, angry at being passed over on the biggest case the department had ever seen.

Well, the hell with them. They were expected to do the job they had been assigned. And if that meant rooting through trash to find the damn killer, then that's what they would do. God knows he had pulled his share of garbage searches as a rookie.

He yanked the fresh uniform shirt off the hanger. It felt heavy and he looked at the front, almost expecting to see

Pryce's badge still pinned on it. There was a bulge in the pocket. He unbuttoned it and pulled out a worn spiral notebook.

He flipped it open. Slowly, the crabbed handwriting registered. It was Pryce's notebook. His wife had said that he was always leaving his things lying around. Like leaving his notebook in a dirty uniform.

Louis turned the pages. They were filled, top to bottom, margin to margin, with notes, much of it in a type of shorthand.

He felt a tightening in his gut. There had to be something in here, something he could use to kickstart the investigation. He slipped the notebook in a pants pocket and hurried to get dressed.

"You find anything yet?" Jesse asked eagerly.

Louis flipped through Pryce's notebook as they drove toward Lovejoy's cabin to interview neighbors. Pryce's writing was like hieroglyphics, as inscrutable as his blotter doodles.

"Man, I can't make sense out of this," Louis murmured. " 'C.L. J.L. C.I.S @ 5661. November. Proof. Proof. Proof.' Then at the bottom of a page—'X31.' What the fuck does that mean? And listen to this one: 'Sam Yellow Lincoln 61829.' Who's Sam? What the hell is that number, a plate? You know anybody with a yellow Lincoln?"

"Nobody up here drives a yellow Lincoln," Jesse said.

Louis keyed the mike. "Hey, Flo, would you run a 10-29 on Sam-Adam-Mary 61829?"

A few minutes later, Florence came back on the radio. "There's no such plate, Louis," she said. "At least not in this state."

Louis thanked her and closed the notebook. They were coming up on Lovejoy's place. He would have to go over the notebook more carefully later.

Jesse pulled the cruiser over to the side of the snow-filled
street and cut the engine. He sat there, staring at the cabin.

"Jess?" Louis said.

Jesse didn't respond.

"Jess," Louis repeated.

Jesse looked over at him. With a slight shake of his head,
he got out of the cruiser. They stood in the drive for a moment and Jesse finally suggested they start with the trailer
three lots north and trudged off. Louis trailed him, wondering
just how much help Jesse was going to be on this investigation. Sooner or later, they were going to have to go back
in Lovejoy's cabin.

Louis slowed his step as a sudden realization hit him. Jesse
had not had the same reaction at Pryce's house. Louis remembered the feel of his own stomach turning over when he had
seen the stain on the carpet made from Pryce's blood. But
Jesse had been strictly business.

"Jess!"

Jesse turned. Suddenly, Louis didn't know how to form his
question. "I want to ask you something," he said finally.

"What?"

"Lovejoy's death really bothers you."

"Of course it bothers me. He was a cop."

"So was Pryce."

Jesse stared at him. "What are you saying?"

Louis looked out at the lake and then back at Jesse. "I'm
not sure. It's just that—"

"Are you asking me if I cared more because Lovejoy was
white?"

"What?" Louis said, stunned. "I didn't say that."

"You didn't have to."

"That's not what I—"

"Then what did you mean?"

"Look, I just want to know why you're taking Lovejoy's
death so much harder, that's all."

Jesse shrugged. "Maybe I've had some time to get over Pryce, know what I mean?"

"But you worked with Pryce every day."

Jesse looked away, then took off his cap, running his arm across his brow. He turned away, facing the lake.

"Jess?"

Jesse turned. "I didn't like him, okay?"

"Who? Pryce?"

"Yeah, Pryce. He was kind of a troublemaker."

"What do you mean?"

Jesse looked uncomfortable. "You know, not a team player."

"How?"

"He was . . . Shit, he wasn't one of us, I told you that before."

"In what way?" Louis pressed.

Jesse shook his head. "Well, like he would report us sometimes."

"For what?"

"That's just it. Little shit. Once he even wrote Ollie up for shooting a deer while on duty. Chief didn't care, let us cook up the damn thing for dinner one night. But Pryce wouldn't eat any." He hesitated, then shook his head. "He was a jerk, Louis."

"Why didn't you tell me that before?"

"Fuck . . ."

"Why didn't you tell me before? It's no big deal."

"I didn't want you to think, you know, like I was some sort of bigot."

Louis stared at him.

"I'm not a bigot," Jesse said.

Louis let out a long breath. He needed to change the subject. "Christ, I'm sorry I asked. Let's get this over with." He started toward the trailer.

"Louis, wait," Jesse called out.

Louis turned.

"First, tell me you know I'm not a bigot," Jesse said.

"Jesus . . ."

"I didn't like the guy because he was an asshole sometimes. That's the reason. The *only* reason. I'm no bigot."

Louis threw up his hands. "Okay. Okay. You're not a fucking bigot."

"I mean, a black guy can be an asshole, just like a white guy, can't he?"

Louis let out a sigh. Jesse looked away, and they both just stood there, rooted by the edge of the lake. Jesse slowly began shaking his head.

"Man, that was a dumb conversation," Jesse said.

"No shit."

"It wasn't just Lovejoy himself. I hadn't seen him in years."

"Then what was it?"

Jesse glanced back at Lovejoy's cabin. "It's that there are two now, two dead cops. He's after us, man. It's knowing that this fucker could blow us away at any time. It's affecting everything I do. I can't sleep, I can't eat . . . I can't . . ." His voice trailed off.

Louis didn't know what to say.

"What the hell does he want?" Jesse asked. "Why us? What the hell have we done?"

"That's what we have to find out."

"What do you mean?"

"The case files. Maybe we'll find something."

Jesse nodded slowly. "Maybe," he said. He pulled his cap back on and zipped his coat to the chin. He glanced around at the trailer. "Well, let's get this over with. Maybe we should split up, get it over with faster."

"Good idea. I'll take the shanties," Louis said.

They split up, Jesse going to the trailer, Louis heading out over the ice toward the nearest fishing shanty.

He poked his head inside. A man jumped up from his stool, dropping his pole. "Jesus, you scared the crap outta me, officer," the man said, clutching his coat.

Louis picked up the pole and handed it back to the man. "Sorry," he said.

"I was just reading about that Lovejoy guy," the man said, pointing to the *Argus* on the ice.

Louis introduced himself, saying he wanted to just ask a few questions. The fisherman stuck out a beefy red hand and offered his name as Art Taub.

"I guess you don't see a lot of strangers out here," Louis began, pulling out his notebook. "Are you out here often?"

"Nearly every day, if the wife lets me," Taub answered, dropping his line back into the water.

"What time do you come out?"

"Eight, usually."

"Do you fellows normally fish at night?"

Taub shook his head. "Early morning's best."

"Did you ever see Mr. Lovejoy?"

"Yeah, couple times. Mostly, I heard him."

"Heard him?"

"His generator," Taub said with a grimace. "He'd fire it up around six, six-thirty most mornings. He'd run the damn thing for a while, then turn it off, then run it, turn it off. Drove me nuts."

"So he was out here by six, you think?" Louis asked.

Taub nodded. "You should talk to Elton. He can tell you what time he got his bait every morning. Elton opens at five-thirty."

Louis paused the pen over the pad, thinking now about the *New York Times* in Lovejoy's mailbox. "Mr. Taub, do you remember if you were out here the first weekend of this month?"

Taub frowned. "Yeah, yeah, I was. I remember 'cause the wife went to Grayling to visit her mother so I was out every day."

"Did you hear anything that sounded like a gunshot, maybe around two or two-thirty in the afternoon?"

Taub shook his head. "But I wouldn't have paid attention

because of the hunters. Probably wouldn't have heard it anyway because of that damn generator."

Louis nodded as he wrote. "Were you friendly with Lovejoy?"

"Nah, he was a loner, never bothered to even grunt in passing. One time, I went over there to borrow some line and he told me to go buy my own. I never went back."

"Mr. Taub, did you see anything unusual that weekend, anything at all?"

Taub shook his head.

"Think hard, Mr. Taub."

"Well, wait a minute, there was one thing. There was a red truck driving around over in those trees north of Will Jervey's trailer, like he was lost. Real beat up, lots of rust. It was a Ford pickup, old model. I'd never seen it around before."

"What time did you see it?"

"Ah, little after six. I went in about eight to refill my thermos and it was gone."

"Did you see the driver?"

Taub shook his head.

"Anything else?" Louis pressed.

Taub shook his head again. "Nope. It was a good day, fishing-wise, I mean."

Louis made more notes, then closed his book. He thanked Art Taub and left. There were four other huts. Two were empty, but interviews with the men in the other two yielded nothing useful. Neither men had seen a red truck or heard a shot. As Louis headed back to shore, he saw Jesse coming from the trees near Lovejoy's cabin. They met at the cruiser.

"You get anything?" Jesse asked.

"One guy said he saw a suspicious red truck," Louis said. "What about you?"

"Nothing," Jesse said. "I went over to Elton's. He said Fred bought bait on Sunday the first and didn't see him after that."

"That supports my theory about the crosswords," Louis said. "Unless Lovejoy used old bait."

Jesse shook his head. "Elton says he bought fresh every day."

Louis was frowning, looking out at the shanties on the lake.

"What's the matter?" Jesse asked.

"The watch," Louis said. "Fred's watch stopped at two-thirty. But I just can't see a killer hitting in broad daylight."

"Especially since Pryce was hit at three in the morning," Jesse said.

They were silent for several moments. "Maybe the watch ran for a while," Jesse offered.

Louis shook his head. "In that water? It would freeze up right away."

Jesse turned suddenly and started to get in the cruiser. "Let's go."

"Where?" Louis asked.

"To find out."

"Find out what?"

But Jesse had already started the cruiser. When Louis got in, Jesse was radioing Dale, telling him to pull Lovejoy's watch out of evidence and find out what make and model it was. By the time Jesse swung the cruiser up in front of Red's Drug Store, Louis realized what was up. He waited in the cruiser until Jesse emerged with a bag holding a duplicate Timex. Jesse seemed so excited by his experiment Louis didn't have the heart to discourage him. He would let him play *Columbo*; maybe it would give him some confidence.

Back at the station, Louis watched while Dale scavenged a thermometer from the first-aid kit and Jesse filled the Pyrex coffeepot with ice cubes from the refrigerator. In minutes, the two had their experiment set up on Louis's desk.

"Check the temperature," Dale said, caught up in Jesse's excitement.

"Louis, get the watch," Jesse called out.

Louis unwrapped the new gold-plated Timex and handed it to Jesse. They waited until the water in the pot had dropped below freezing. Louis stepped back, shaking his head.

He watched as Jesse dropped the watch in the water.

"What time you got, Louis?" Jesse asked.

"Five straight up."

The seconds ticked off as Jesse and Dale peered at the watch in the water.

"What the hell are you doing?"

Louis looked to the door. Gibralter was standing there, staring at Jesse and Dale huddled over the coffeepot.

Jesse jumped to his feet. "A test."

Gibralter came over to the desk and looked down at the glass bowl. "What kind of test?"

"We're trying to find out how long this watch will run in ice water."

"Why?" Gibralter demanded.

"Louis thinks Fred—"

Gibralter's eyes flicked to Louis and then back to Jesse. He reached in the coffeepot, pulled out the watch and tossed it on the desk.

"Every minute you waste could cost another officer his life," Gibralter said, leveling his gaze at Jesse. "I told you to go through the case files. Now go do your damn job."

Jesse wet his lips. "But—"

"Do your job, Harrison," Gibralter repeated, enunciating each word, as if to a child. Without looking at Louis, he went into his office, slamming the door.

Louis looked at Jesse. He was just standing there, his face red with embarrassment. Dale and Florence were watching, their eyes wide in sympathy.

"Fuck," Jesse muttered, wandering off.

Louis looked down at the watch. A puddle of water had formed under the gold band and the face was clouded with condensation. He picked it up.

It had stopped at 5:04.

Twelve

The sound of bells tolling. A white meadow, snow, and a stand of pines in the distance. A white church, with a steeple piercing a cobalt blue sky. And a line of blue moving slowly, swaying, emerging from the church. A coffin . . . They were carrying a coffin out into the snowy meadow as the bells tolled.

Louis woke with a start. Bells . . . the phone.

Wiping a hand over his eyes, he turned over and grabbed the receiver. "Yeah," he said hoarsely.

"Louis?"

"Yeah." He reached for his watch and squinted at the dial. Christ, it was after ten. He had slept through the morning.

"Louis, this is Phillip."

"Phillip?" He blinked at the sound of his foster father's voice and pulled himself up on one elbow. "Phillip! Jeez, it's good to hear from you." He reached down to pull the covers over his bare chest. The room was freezing cold.

"You sound strange. Don't tell me I woke you up." The voice on the other end of the line chuckled.

"No, no. Well, yeah, you did. But that's okay. I'm off today." Louis's eyes swept over the crumpled bed. He spotted his chambray shirt crumpled in the blanket at the end. He squinted and saw two glasses on the bureau, half-filled with tawny liquid.

"I know. I called the station. They gave me your number."

Louis suppressed a sigh. He had forgotten to call them and tell them he had finally gotten a phone.

"Look, Louis," Phillip went on, "I won't waste time busting your chops about why we haven't heard from you in weeks."

"Thanks," Louis said softly. Leave it to Phillip Lawrence to cut through the bullshit. He hated talking on the phone more than Louis did.

"But it does make it easier to guilt you into coming down to dinner," Phillip added.

"Dinner?" Louis said, surprised. "Where are you?"

"We're at Higgins Lake. We brought the motor home up for the week."

Louis laughed. "That old piece of shit? I'm surprised it made it this far."

"Oh, I got rid of the Winnebago. Got a brand-new Gulf Stream Super Coach. The galley's bigger than our kitchen. Frances is happier than a clam."

Louis smiled, remembering a trip they had taken to Saugatuck in the Winnebago the summer of his thirteenth year. Frances tried to cook a chicken on the tiny stove.

"So, when can you come?"

Louis rubbed a hand over his face, trying to clear his head. What day was it? He had spent yesterday with Jesse in the station, going through case files. It had been Jesse's day off, but he had come in anyway, desperate to find something after the watch scene with Gibralter. But after hours of going through the files, they had found no one who could be considered a threat.

"Louis? You there?"

"Yeah, Phil."

"How about tonight? Fran's making a Christmas ham."

Christmas . . . It was two days away. He had forgotten that, too. "Sure, I'm off today, I'll be there," he said.

He grabbed a pen off the nightstand and wrote directions to the campsite on his palm. He said good-bye and hung up, rolling onto his back and pulling the blanket up over his naked body.

He shivered, giving in to his mild feeling of guilt. He hadn't called the Lawrences since he left Detroit and he had seen them only three times since his return from Mississippi last February. They hadn't pressed and he was grateful. He knew that they loved him. They had been his parents, without being his mother and father. They had always instinctively honored the emotional buffer he had installed around himself. And he had loved them all the more for that. But right now, he was feeling more than a little shitty. They deserved better.

A snowblower started up somewhere off in the distance. He didn't want to get up. He felt lazy, satiated with the languid energy of a good night's sleep. He pulled the sheet over his cold nose. A smell drifted up to him, the sweet-musky smell of sex.

Zoe . . .

He closed his eyes. Zoe . . . snow . . . glow. He smiled.

Glow . . . go . . . slow.

Slow . . . don't . . . go . . . Zoe.

He flipped over on his stomach, burying his face in the pillow, inhaling her smell, reliving in his head the chaotic choreography of their lovemaking.

Finally, with a sigh, he heaved himself out of the warm bed. He shivered and padded off to the bathroom. It was an hour's drive down to Higgins Lake and he had to stop in town and find something that would pass as Christmas presents.

"So, how's the job going?"

Louis poured himself another glass of brandy and sat back in the kitchen booth. "Good. Not what I expected exactly, but it's a good, honest department."

Phillip smiled. "I guess so. When I called, somebody named Dale McGuire answered. When I told him who I was, he acted like I was his long-lost cousin or something."

Louis laughed. "Dale's very . . . social."

"So they're treating you good there?"

Louis considered the question for a moment. Phillip was asking, without asking, if things were different than they had been in Mississippi. It had always been that like between them, this odd dance they did about race. They were white; he was half white, half black. They had always dealt with it obliquely, a thing seen always from the corner of the eye, never straight on. Sometimes it bothered Louis. Sometimes he was grateful for it.

Like now. He hadn't told Phillip everything that had happened to him down in Mississippi, just that his color had been "a problem." He hadn't told him that for the first time in his life, his color had nearly cost him his life.

Phillip Lawrence, he knew, would not ask either. It was part of the emotional buffer. It was part of their dance.

"It's different here," Louis said finally.

Phillip accepted the answer and took another sip of his brandy. "Thanks for the Courvoisier," he said. "Don't usually get this kind of good stuff."

"I bought it for myself," Louis said with a smile as he poured himself another three-finger shot. Phillip watched him carefully.

"And thank you for the White Shoulders, dear," Frances chimed in from the stove.

Louis smiled up at her. Booze and perfume weren't the most original presents, but then Loon Lake wasn't exactly a Turkish bazaar. "Thanks for the sweater. I needed it," he said.

She smiled and bent to poke her head into the oven. The smell of baked ham filled the motor home. The radio was playing softly, Christmas carols. Frances began to hum along.

"I've been reading about your case in the *Free Press,"* Phillip said. "Tragic."

"Yeah," Louis said, taking a quick drink.

"Are you close to catching anyone?"

"No, not yet," Louis said. He glanced up at Frances. She had stopped humming.

"You're being careful, aren't you?" Phillip asked.

"Of course. We all are." He took another swift drink. He glanced to his left, out the window, unable to meet Phillip's eyes. The window was fogged and he wiped it with his shirtsleeve. He could see out across Higgins Lake. It was much bigger than Loon Lake. To the north, he could see gray clouds moving down toward them. Snow clouds.

Frances set a plate in front of him. He looked down at the careful arrangement of crackers around a crock of bright-yellow cheese. He looked up at her.

"Win Schuler's?" he asked with a smile.

"What else?" she said, smiling back.

He dug a cracker into the soft cheese and took a bite. The tang of the cheese brought back a flood of memories. He had eaten only Velveeta before the Lawrences had taken him to Win Schuler's for his tenth birthday. He had never seen a salad bar before that, never been to a restaurant. He had been paralyzed with the choices. Frances had coaxed him to try the cheese. He loved it. He still did.

"Have you made any new friends, dear?" Frances asked, going back to her post at the sink.

Louis shook his head slowly, smiling. "You mean women."

"Well, okay . . . women," she said, nodding.

"Fran, leave the man alone," Phillip said, scooping a cracker into the cheese.

"It's okay, Phil," Louis said, still smiling. "Fact is, there is someone."

Frances smiled. "Oh, Louis! I'm so glad. What's her name? When can we meet her?"

"Zoe," Louis said. "And not for a while."

"Zoe," Frances repeated. "Is she foreign?"

Louis grinned. "I guess you could say that."

Phillip reached across the table for a pack of cigarettes and matches. Frances saw him and frowned just at the moment he looked up at her.

He let out a sigh. "Come on, Fran. It's twenty degrees out there."

"I don't care. You're not stinking up my new home with those things."

Phillip looked at Louis. "You wanna keep me company?"

"Sure," Louis said, picking up his glass.

They put on their coats and went outside. Louis watched as Phillip lit a cigarette and inhaled deeply. He blew out the smoke in a slow stream, ending almost in a sigh.

"You shouldn't smoke so much," Louis said.

"You shouldn't drink so much," Phillip replied.

Louis looked away out over the lake and then back at Phillip. He leaned against the metal motor home, holding the glass down at his side. They were silent for several minutes.

Louis raised his glass and drained the brandy. He looked over to see Phillip looking at him.

"It's bad, isn't it," Phillip said.

Louis knew he was talking about the murders, but he didn't know what to say in response. As much as he loved Phillip, he had never been able to share his feelings with him easily. Even now, their relationship ripened as it was to adult status, he couldn't bring himself to open a vein and let his fear bleed out for Phillip to see.

"It's hard on the nerves," Louis said finally. "But we'll get him. I know we will." He paused. "They put me in charge of the investigation," he added, a touch of pride in his voice.

"A promotion already?" Phillip asked.

"Not really. Peter Principle more like it."

"So, have you found anything yet?"

Louis told him about the piece of fabric and the other tenuous clues. He told him about the watch experiment and his theory about the timing of the two murders. Before he realized what was happening, he was spilling out all the details of the case, including his doubts about Jesse's stability. It felt good.

He needed to talk to someone outside the department. And as much as he had wanted to, he couldn't share it with Zoe.

Phillip listened attentively. Finally, Louis stopped, noticing that Phillip was standing awkwardly, a slight grimace on his face.

"Something wrong?" Louis asked.

Phillip rubbed his thigh. "Cold makes the leg hurt, that's all."

"You want to go in?"

"Soon as I finish this butt."

Louis watched Phillip as he rubbed his leg again, holding the cigarette between his teeth. Another teenage memory bubbled up into his head, the first time he had seen the long scars on Phillip's leg. Phillip had told him how he had gotten the wound in the Korean War, how the doctor had saved his leg, but left him with a lifelong limp. It was Louis's first indication that the man who had become the most important figure in his life was truly human, less than a god. Not long after that, Phillip had opened a trunk in the attic and shown him his souvenirs from the war. Louis remembered the uniform patch that had caught his eye. It was a soaring eagle on a red background with the words SILVER EAGLES and the numbers of Phillip's company on it. He had let Louis keep the patch. Louis lost it somewhere years ago. He never told Phillip. He wondered idly where it was.

Louis straightened up off the motor home. Something stirred in his brain, a connection being made.

"Phillip, you remember that patch you gave me?"

"What patch?"

"The one from your uniform," Louis said. "The eagle?"

"Oh, yeah. What'd you do with it, by the way?"

Louis felt a surge of excitement. God, the human brain was strange, its synapses firing out to make bridges when you were least expecting it. He was thinking of the cloth they had found on the fence by the park, dark green, like army fatigues.

"Platoons, military units, they all had names like that and numbers?" Louis asked.

"Some," Phillip answered. "Why do you ask?"

"It could be related to one of the things I'm trying to track down in this case," Louis said. "The killer leaves this clue, a drawing of a skull and the numbers '1 2 3.' Does it mean anything? Could it be military?"

Phillip shrugged. "Maybe. The emblems were unofficial, something the guys created themselves."

"What about on a playing card?"

"A card? Like from a poker deck?"

"Yeah. You ever hear of anything like that?"

Phillip shook his head. "Guys painted the emblems on tanks, planes, had patches made. But I never saw them on cards."

"But you had playing cards?"

"Hell, yes. We bought them at the PX, carried them everywhere." He smiled. "I lost a month's pay in Seoul trying to pull an inside straight."

Louis's mind was racing. Could it be that simple? Could it be some sort of military symbol? He had to find someone who knew about the military and what the numbers might mean. Was it a company, a squadron? And which war? It could—

"Louis?"

For a second, Phillip's voice didn't register. When Phillip repeated his name, Louis looked up at him. He saw the concern in Phillip's face.

"It's all right, Phil," Louis said quietly.

"I'm worried about you," Phillip said.

"I'm being careful."

Phillip looked at him for a long time, then took a final, slow, deep drag on his cigarette.

Louis watched the cigarette glow. He was struck suddenly by how different Phillip's way of smoking was from Gibralter's. Phillip's style was deliberate, almost sensual, as though he was surrendering. Gibralter attacked the tobacco, as if he knew it was the enemy.

"My chief smokes unfiltered Camels," Louis said.

"A real man's smoke," Phillip said with a dry smile.

Louis smiled. "Well, that's Gibralter. A real man."

"You like him?"

Louis hesitated, then nodded. "Yeah, yeah, I do. I guess."

"You guess?"

Louis let out a small laugh. "Well, he's not exactly likeable. He's an enigma. Ego the size of Lake Michigan. Smart, strict. Probably ex-Marine and probably overeducated for the job."

"Overeducated. Sounds like somebody else I know," Phillip said with a small smile.

Louis let the remark pass.

"Your chief," Phillip said after a moment, "is he the kind who takes care of his men?"

Louis frowned slightly, unsure of what Phillip was asking. "He's a very dedicated cop," he answered finally.

"But to what?" Phillip said. "Police departments are a lot like the military, Louis. The men who run them understand that sometimes there must be casualties."

Louis knew where Phillip was going with this and he tensed.

"I can read between the lines of the newspaper," Phillip said. "Your department seems to be a target of this maniac. Am I right?"

Louis nodded, looking off toward the lake.

"This man Gibralter, is he taking care of his men?"

"There's not much he can do. We have to do our job."

Phillip paused. He tossed the cigarette into the snow. It fizzed and died.

"I had a C.O.," Phillip said. "His name was Cliff McInerney. We called him Captain Mac. We were driving north near Yongsan and ran into heavy fire."

"Is that where you were wounded?" Louis asked.

Phillip nodded. "We were pinned down for two days. Lost three men. Finally, Captain Mac decided he wasn't going to wait any longer and tried to get us out. He led our squad through heavy fire. At one point, he went back, running across this open field, to rescue Hooper, who went down in a trench. I thought he was nuts."

Phillip looked at Louis. "Maybe he was. But he got us out of there when we were all sure we were going to die."

"What happened to him?" Louis asked.

"He was killed. We were walking through the village. A grenade came out of nowhere. He jumped on it to protect two men walking ahead."

Louis watched the subtle shift of emotions play over Phillip's face.

"A leader believes in himself," Phillip said. "But more important, he gives others the courage to believe in themselves."

Louis lifted the empty glass and looked at it, suddenly wishing there was more in it.

Phillip gently took the glass from his hand, then suddenly grabbed him by the back of the neck and pulled him close.

"Please be careful, Louis," he said.

Thirteen

The sky was the color of sheet metal. Louis looked out at the low-lying clouds, then reached down and turned the cruiser's heater up another notch.

"Smells like it's gonna snow again," Jesse said.

"Which is why I wanted to get an earlier start," Louis said grimly.

Jesse sighed. "I told you, man, we already talked to these assholes."

"You didn't show them the card. Maybe they know something."

"Trust me, they're a bunch of burn-outs. They don't know what year it is."

"I thought you'd be glad to get away from the damn case files for a while."

Jesse reached for his thermos. "Oh yeah, like this isn't a waste of time."

They continued up Highway 33 in stony silence. Louis resisted his urge to lay into Jesse. He had rousted him out of bed with a phone call at five that morning, telling him they had to be on the road by six. It was an hour's drive to Lake Orion, and who knew how long it would take after that to find the veterans' camp?

Louis glanced down at the directions Ollie had scribbled on a scrap of paper. Ollie had warned him the place was tough to find. He had also filled Louis in on what happened the first time the vets were questioned. The day after Pryce's murder,

Gibralter had ordered a sweep of all "organized local weirdos."
It had netted some local members of the Michigan Militia
Corps, two broken-down renegades from the Aryan Nation, a
handful of vegetarian survivalists stockpiling canned goods in
anticipation of a nuclear holocaust, and a local nut who had
once used a sledgehammer to bash all the parking meters along
Main Street.

It had also turned up seven veterans who were living on a
tract of land sixty miles north of Loon Lake. The vets were
brought into the station and "questioned extensively," Ollie
said. Gibralter had been unable to get a search warrant for the
camp. But, Ollie told Louis, Gibralter remained suspicious that
Pryce's killer was among the seven men living in the woods.

Louis gazed out at the dense forest they were about to enter.
The road seemed to be narrowing into a tunnel of gray clouds
and hulking pines. He had a sinking feeling about this whole
thing, that there was no way these men would talk. But after
what Phillip Lawrence had told him yesterday about the emblems, he had to try.

"Turn here," Louis said, spotting a small side road.

"Where?" Jesse asked.

"Stop! Right here. See the road?"

"Road? What fucking road?" Jesse shook his head. "We'll
never get up there without chains."

"Try," Louis said.

The cruiser's wheels spun on the unplowed road, making
slow progress through the thick trees. About two miles in, they
came to a gate that ran across the road. There was a large sign
that said NO TRESPASSING. PRIVATE PROPERTY.

"Now what?" Jesse asked.

"Now we walk," Louis said, getting out of the car.

The road wended its way through the thick pines for another
half mile. Finally, they could see the dark outlines of a building
ahead. As they drew closer, the details of the compound came
into focus. There were at least four well-constructed but spar-
tan buildings, each with its own large generator. One sported

a huge satellite dish on its roof. There was a shed with two Jeeps parked in front. The smell of a fire hung in the damp air.

The quiet was broken by the sharp barking of dogs.

"Jesus, those fuckers better be chained," Jesse said, his hand going to his holster.

They heard a door slam. A dark figure came out of the nearest building. He stood, looking out at them. Louis could see the slender outline of a rifle slung across the man's back.

"Let me do the talking," Louis said quietly as they walked toward the man.

"Better keep it to two syllables or less," Jesse muttered.

The man had not moved. The dogs were in a pen, two German shepherds and something that looked like a rottweiler with a bushy tail. They were barking insanely, bouncing against the chain-link fence like pinballs. The man shifted his M-16 down off his shoulder, letting it dangle at his side. He was wearing a down vest over a heavy navy sweater, fatigue pants and heavy black boots caked with mud. He was tall and burly. His face was hidden on top by a cap emblazoned with the Oakland Raiders logo and below by a thick red beard.

"Stop right there," he said slowly.

Louis and Jesse came to a halt about ten yards away. The cacophony of barking was ear splitting.

"Quiet!" the man shouted suddenly.

The dogs stopped. They circled each other in agitation and then sat, ears pricked forward, snarling at Louis and Jesse.

"This is private property," the man said.

"We know," Louis said. "We just want to talk to you."

Louis became aware of movement from the corner of his eye. He turned slightly to his left. Two men had materialized out of the woods. Both wore the same hybrid outfits of military garb and outdoor clothing. He heard a sound behind him and sensed the presence of others at his back.

"We don't like cops here," the man with the beard said.

Louis nodded. "Fair enough."

Another man came out of the nearest building. He was shorter than the others, wiry, black. He stared at Louis. Louis held his eyes for a moment, then his gaze dropped to the empty left sleeve of the man's jacket. He looked back to the bearded man.

"We're from Loon Lake. We're investigating a murder," Louis said.

"Two murders now," the man said.

Louis stared at him. "Yes, two murders. Two police officers." He waited, but the bearded man said nothing. "We think the killer had some connection to the military. We think—"

"You think," the man interrupted, "your killer is a wacko vet. And here we are, a whole camp of loonie-tunes right under your nose." He smiled and hoisted the rifle up over his shoulder. "Now that's one nifty piece of investigating there, Kojak."

"Look, I just want to show you something," Louis said, reaching into his pocket to pull out the plastic evidence bag. He came closer, holding it up. "You ever seen a card like this?"

The man ignored it. "Look, we don't have to put up with your shit this time. We're not in your fucking jail now. We're on my land. *My land,* officer. And unless you got some search warrant, you've got no business here."

Louis sensed the men behind him moving closer. His eyes flitted up to the black soldier. He was staring at the card. Suddenly, he turned and walked off into the trees. It started to snow.

"Louis, let's get out of here," Jesse said tightly.

"I'd take your partner's advice, friend," the man said.

Louis hesitated. This was going nowhere. He stuffed the bag back in his pocket and brushed the snow from his face. Jesse was right. He wasn't going to get anything out of these head cases.

He turned and started back toward the cruiser. Jesse followed quickly.

"I told you," Jesse said when they were out of earshot.

"Shut up, Jess."

"Christ, look at this shit," Jesse said, gesturing at the snow. "We're never gonna get the cruiser back up that hill. We're gonna get stuck up here and—"

Jesse froze. Louis looked up.

The black soldier was standing a few yards in front of the cruiser. He was holding a large gun of some kind.

"Oh, great," Jesse said through clenched teeth. "If that motherfucker—"

"Shut up!" Louis hissed. He approached the soldier, his eyes going to the gun. With a twist in his gut, he realized it was an AK-47. How in the hell did he fire it with one arm?

From the lines in his face, the soldier looked to be in his forties. He gave off an aura of harnessed energy, his sinewy body a coiled spring, his black eyes snapping. Louis looked at the faded name on his worn jacket. CLOVERDALE. He recognized two patches from Phillip Lawrence's souvenirs: a sergeant's stripes and a CIB, a combat infantry badge. "If you ever see a man wearing a CIB, he's worthy of your respect," Phillip had told him.

"You're lucky Randall didn't blow your head off," the soldier said.

Jesse stepped forward. "Listen, asshole—"

The soldier tensed. Louis's arm shot up against Jesse's chest. He turned his back to Cloverdale and glared at Jesse.

"Goddamn it, Jess," he whispered tightly, "we need this man's help. He knows something."

Jesse's eyes darted over Louis's shoulder to Cloverdale and back to Louis's face. Jesse's neck was red, the flush creeping up into his face.

"Go wait in the cruiser," Louis said. "Please."

Jesse hesitated, glared again at the soldier, then stomped off toward the cruiser. Louis waited until he heard the slam of the door and the start of the motor, then turned to face Cloverdale. He pulled out the card and held it up.

"You know about this?" he asked.

Cloverdale's eyes didn't leave Louis's face. "Why should I talk to you?"

"Because I need help," Louis said.

The man gave a low bitter laugh. "Help? Well, ain't that ironic."

Louis thrust the bag forward. "You know what this card means. And I think you want to tell me about it."

"Why? Because you're black? You think we got some kind of special brother thing going here?" Cloverdale laughed again. "Let me tell you something, *bro*. The only brothers I got are those six white guys back there."

He sobered and looked toward the cruiser, at Jesse sitting sullenly behind the wheel. "That your partner?" he asked.

"Yes."

"Too bad, man."

Louis wiped the snow from his eyes. It was coming down heavy now. But he couldn't leave, not yet. This man wanted to talk, he was sure of it.

"Hey, you got a cigarette?" Cloverdale asked.

"Sorry. Don't smoke."

Cloverdale hoisted the gun up, holding it against his shoulder. He saw Louis looking at it.

"Yeah, it's heavy," he said. He studied Louis's face. "Go on, ask me," he said.

"Ask you what?" Louis said.

"How I lost my arm. It's what you were thinking about."

"No, I wasn't."

Cloverdale smiled. He had beautiful, straight teeth. Movie star teeth. "How old are you?" he asked.

"Twenty-five," Louis said.

"I was twenty-four when I joined up," Cloverdale said. "I grew up in a shithole town in Arkansas . . . Marked Tree. Man, I would have done anything to get out of the South."

"Mississippi," Louis said.

"What?" Cloverdale said, squinting through the snow.

"Black Pool, Mississippi, that's where I was born. Probably makes Marked Tree look like Paris."

Cloverdale stared at him for a moment, then smiled. "You don't strike me as military," he said. "You serve?"

Louis shook his head.

The soldier's smile turned pensive. "I was at Fort Campbell," he said. "They picked me for Delta Company, second battalion, 501st Infantry, 101st Airborne Division. He cocked his head. "You ever see that movie *The Dirty Dozen?*"

Louis nodded.

"We were kind of like that, the leftovers, the guys nobody else wanted. We had guys who liked to steal shit, you know, supplies and equipment. So they started calling us 'The Raiders.' We were tight, a really great unit." Cloverdale's eyes grew distant.

Louis was getting cold, but his muscles were tight with anticipation. He glanced back at the cruiser, hoping Jesse wouldn't do anything stupid to disrupt the soldier's reminiscence.

"So how did it happen?" Louis asked, nodding toward the soldier's missing arm.

Cloverdale blinked, wiping snow from his face. "Firefight near Hue, Valentine's Day, 1968," he said matter-of-factly. "We lost six men, eighteen wounded, including the captain. I lost the arm, but got a ticket back to Marked Tree."

The snow had covered Cloverdale's head, forming a white helmet over his close-cropped hair. He looked suddenly like an old man.

"How did you get here?" Louis asked.

Cloverdale hoisted the gun higher up against his shoulder. "Well, I did my time at the VA hospital, bummed around the country for a couple years. I stuffed all the war shit into a box and tried to build a life." He paused, smiling. "Hard keeping the lid on that damn box sometimes." His eyes drifted to the bag in Louis's hand.

Jesse honked the horn. Louis looked at the car and waved an impatient hand.

"You're gonna get snowed in here, man," Cloverdale said.

"Go on," Louis said. "Please."

Cloverdale looked up the road toward the collection of houses. "Randall was in my unit. His family's from around here. They gave him the land and he decided to make a camp for vets. There's just seven of us now, but we're building houses for more. We look after each other, you know?"

Louis nodded.

Cloverdale's face hardened. "I don't like people who feel sorry for themselves. I mean, what's done is done. But people on the outside, they don't know. They just don't know."

Louis hesitated, his hand gripping the edge of the bag. "Why are you talking to me then?" he asked.

Cloverdale looked back at him. "Because I want you to know that we're not murderers. We're off the grid. But we aren't murderers."

Louis nodded slowly. He held out the Ziploc. Cloverdale took it and looked at the drawing.

"Where'd you get this?" he asked.

"This is one of two. They were found by the bodies of the dead officers," Louis said.

Cloverdale handed it back. He wiped his face. "It's a message," he said.

"Message? What kind of message?" Louis asked.

Cloverdale hesitated, his face twisting slightly. "Your man is military."

Louis waited.

"Some companies had their nicknames printed up on cards." He stopped again, staring out into the trees. "I heard about this, but never really saw it." He paused again. "A company would go in, wipe out a village of Vietcong and then throw the cards down on the bodies. It was a taunt, a kind of challenge to Charlie, letting them know they were there."

He looked at Louis. "They called them death cards."

Louis wiped the snow off the bag and held it out again. "And this one? You recognize it?"

Cloverdale wouldn't take it. "No. The number is probably a company or squadron maybe."

Louis looked down at the bag, then put it back in his pocket. He looked up at Cloverdale's drawn face.

"Thanks," he said.

Cloverdale shifted the gun slightly against his shoulder. Louis started to turn away.

"I know your man," Cloverdale said.

Louis turned back sharply.

Cloverdale just looked at Louis, then he smiled slightly. "I've met him, hundreds of times."

"Look," Louis said quietly, "don't jerk me around."

"I was a counselor afterward," Cloverdale said. "I worked with a lot of fucked-up men, and lot of them who could have done what your killer did, given the wrong circumstances."

"What are the wrong circumstances?" Louis asked.

"You asking me for a profile?"

Louis thought of the FBI agent's book. "Yeah."

"It ain't that easy, officer," Cloverdale said, shaking his head. "Nothing about 'Nam was easy or obvious. It was the camouflage war, and there's no hope of ever flushing it out."

"But you can tell me what kind of man I am looking for," Louis said.

"Yeah, I can." Cloverdale shifted the gun off his shoulder and rested the butt on the ground. "Look for a normal man."

"Normal?" Louis said.

"A guy who tried to be normal and failed."

Louis frowned. "I don't understand."

"He probably enlisted, maybe because his life was shitty up to then and the military makes a lot of big promises about straightening out your life for you."

"Go on, please," Louis said.

"He probably did all right for himself in the military, maybe even had his first taste of success," Cloverdale said. "But something happened and he felt like he was a failure again. He might have had a drug or alcohol problem, and got the quick trip through the VA system." Cloverdale paused. "Now they have a nice name for it, post-traumatic stress syndrome. Back then, we were all just addicts."

"What about after the war?" Louis asked.

"After," Cloverdale said softly. "Well, let's just say nobody was exactly throwing rose petals at your man's feet. Your man went to war, did his job, and then everyone at home told him what he had done was a joke. Not great for the self-esteem."

Louis waited, wishing he had a notebook with him.

"He probably couldn't find a job," Cloverdale went on, "or if he did, it was in some factory that probably laid him off when the recession hit. 'Nam vets earned less, were promoted less, and had more turnover." Cloverdale drew in a breath. "Check homeless shelters, that sort of thing. There's still about a quarter of a million vets on the street."

A horn honked. Louis turned to the cruiser. Jesse was motioning for him. Louis looked back to Cloverdale.

"Can you tell me why?" Louis asked.

"Why he did it?" Cloverdale said. "Shit, who really knows. He might have a hard-on toward authority figures. You know, projecting his frustrations about his life onto any symbol of the establishment." He nodded toward Louis's badge. "Cops would qualify."

Louis shook his head. "A failure at being normal. It can't be that simple."

"Think of it as the blue-collar dream gone gray," Cloverdale said.

Louis held Cloverdale's eyes for a second, then looked up, blinking into the huge flakes. He let out a long sigh. When he looked back at Cloverdale, he was leaning heavily against his gun. His jacket was soaked dark green from the snow. He looked suddenly very tired.

"Your man isn't here," Cloverdale said.

"I know that now."

Cloverdale looked at the cruiser. "You'd better get going up that hill," he said.

Louis nodded, hesitated, then stuck out his hand. Cloverdale stared at it for a moment, then awkwardly shifted the rifle so he could shake Louis's hand.

"Thanks for your help."

"Sure. But don't come back." Cloverdale gave him a final smile, then started back toward the compound. Louis turned and trudged toward the cruiser.

"Hey, Black Pool!"

Louis turned.

"The South," Cloverdale called out. "You ever think about it much?"

"I try not to," Louis said.

Cloverdale gave a low soft laugh. He raised the gun in a salute, turned and was lost in the swirling snow.

Fourteen

"Turn on the defroster."

"It's on."

"Well, then turn it up."

"It's up as high as it goes," Jesse snapped. He rubbed the windshield with his sleeve. "Goddamn it, I can't see a thing."

"Jess, pull over," Louis said.

"What for?"

"I'll drive."

"I can drive."

"Not the way you're acting, you can't. Slow down or we're going to end up wrapped around a damn tree."

Jesse slowed to thirty-five. The cruiser crept along the snow-clogged county road. Louis let out a breath of relief when they turned back onto the main highway. It, too, was snowed over, but at least it was four lanes the rest of the way back to Loon Lake. They drove on in edgy silence for fifteen minutes.

"You get anything useful back there?" Jesse asked finally.

"I'm not sure," Louis replied. He told him what Cloverdale had said.

"So the killer's military," Jesse said quietly.

"Maybe."

"But you don't think he's one of those guys?"

"No, I don't."

"Why not?"

"I don't know. Gut feeling."

Jesse gave a small laugh. "Gut feeling. Right."

Louis stared at Jesse. He was gripping the wheel with his right hand, his left hand bent against his temple. Louis glanced at the speedometer. What the hell was wrong now?

"Jess," he said, "what's the matter?"

"Nothing."

"Then why you snapping at me?"

Jesse didn't look at him. "I'm sorry," he said after a moment. "I'm tired, that's all."

Louis decided to let it go. They rode the rest of the way in silence, picking up the freshly plowed wake of a snowplow just as they turned onto the road at the north end of the lake.

Florence's voice came over the radio, asking for their location. When Louis radioed back that they were on their way back to the station, Florence told them Gibralter was waiting for them at Dot's. Louis acknowledged the call and signed off.

"Now what?" Jesse muttered.

"Probably just wants an update," Louis said.

"Probably wants to chew out my ass for something."

Jesse pushed the cruiser up to forty-five. The gated entrances to tourists' homes flew past. They were coming up fast on a slow-moving red truck and Louis resisted the urge to tell Jesse again to slow down.

"Ford," Jesse said suddenly.

"What?"

"It's a red Ford," Jesse said, peering out at the sludge-encrusted truck ahead of them.

For a second, Louis's heart beat faster. No, it was too new. Art Taub said the Ford was old and rusted. "It's not the one. Let him go, Jess," Louis said.

"No, damn it. His tint's too dark."

Jesse flipped on the lights and squawked the siren twice. The driver's head snapped toward his rearview mirror and he swung to the side of the road. As they pulled up, Louis could see the truck was a new model with not a dent on it, let alone rust.

Jesse was out of the cruiser before Louis could reply. With a sigh, he grabbed the clipboard and followed.

The driver was about thirty, with a thin pale face and a fizz of dirty red hair. He had an old paisley bandana wrapped around his forehead and a small gold hoop in his left ear. On his chin, a sprout of whiskers struggled to form a goatee.

"To what do I owe this honor?" he asked nervously.

Jesse opened the truck door. "Get out."

"Is that a request or an order?"

"Get out of the fucking truck."

The man moved slowly. Jesse yanked him from the car so forcefully he fell to the pavement. The man grabbed the door handle to pull himself up, his eyes wide as he looked at Jesse. He wasn't wearing a coat, just faded jeans and a dingy white T-shirt. Standing there, shivering in the snowdrift, he looked like a cattail stalk.

"Little testy today, are we, officer?" he said.

Louis stepped forward quickly. "Your driver's license, please," he said.

The man's pale eyes darted to the truck. "It's in that bag on the seat."

Jesse reached in and pulled out a blue Crown Royal bag. He retrieved the man's license and thrust it out at Louis. When Louis hesitated, Jesse added, "You gonna run that or not?"

"This license is expired, Mr. Bates," Louis said.

"Dear me, there just aren't enough hours in the day," the man said with a sigh.

Louis glanced at Jesse. Christ, he was bouncing on his toes to nail this guy for something. The best thing to do was get this over as quick as possible. He started back to the cruiser.

"Love the uniform, man," Bates called after him.

Louis heard a clunk and looked back. Jesse had Bates flat against the truck, reaching for his cuffs. Louis keyed the mike and told Florence to run the plate and license. He had to get this over with fast before Bates lost a few front teeth.

Louis leaned against the cruiser and watched as Jesse began

to search the truck's interior. What the hell was he doing now? If he found anything, Bates would scream illegal search. He was just about to call to Jess when Florence came back advising that Bates was free of warrants and priors.

Bates was hollering to Jesse from the rear of the truck. "You going to search *me,* too, officer? I like them full-cavity body searches. You ever done of one of those?" Bates looked at Louis. "What about you, Mandingo?"

"Shut up," Louis said.

Jesse came out of the truck holding a small plastic bag.

"What's that?" Louis asked.

"Looks like grass to me," Jesse said, shaking it in Bates's face. "I asked you if there was any drugs in the truck, asshole. You lied to me."

"Hey, you didn't have any right to search my truck," Bates said. "I've got rights here."

Jesse spun around and grabbed Bates by the back of the T-shirt. "Keep your fucking mouth shut!" He slammed Bates's head down against the side of the truck bed. Louis jumped forward, ripping Jesse's arm from Bates's collar.

Blood dripped from Bates's nose as he staggered backward. Louis caught his sleeve to keep him balanced and glared at Jesse. "That was unnecessary," Louis said.

"I don't have to take lip from any faggot butt-fucker," Jesse hissed.

"Look, cut the macho bullshit. This isn't the time or the place, you got that?" Louis said, his voice low.

Jesse spun away and walked rigidly to the cruiser. Louis took a deep breath and looked back at Bates, who was leaning against the truck fender. Louis uncuffed him. Bates touched his head, his fingers coming away bloody.

"You okay to drive?" Louis asked.

"I oughta sue you," he said, his voice trembling slightly.

"You're not going to sue anyone, Bates," Louis said, picking up the bag of pot. He removed the twist tie and flung the bag in an arc, scattering the pot to the wind.

"Oh, man," Bates moaned. "That was sinsemilla."

Louis stuffed the empty bag in Bates pocket. "Sense this, asshole. You're going to get back in your truck and go home to Alcona County. And all the way, you're going to be telling yourself how lucky you are that it's Christmas Eve and I'm giving you a damn present." Louis leaned closer and held out Bates's driver's license. "Do you understand?"

Bates nodded weakly, took the license and got in his truck. Louis waited until he drove off, then he turned back and walked to the cruiser. Jesse was in the passenger seat, his chin on his chest. Louis got in and put both hands on the wheel. They sat there for several seconds.

"Keys?" Louis asked.

"Cuffs?" Jesse asked.

Louis tossed Jesse's cuffs on the seat. He responded by throwing the rabbit's foot and keys on the dash. Louis reached for them and jammed the keys into the ignition.

"Why'd you let him go?" Jesse said, leaning forward to put his cuffs away.

"He wasn't our man."

"He was holding."

"Half an ounce of grass discovered in an illegal search." Louis paused. "Look, we've got more important things to do than bust potheads." Louis thrust the cruiser into gear. "Come on. Gibralter's waiting."

Dot's Cafe smelled of bacon grease and strong coffee. As he came in, Louis spotted the chief sitting in a booth near the back and he and Jesse went over.

"What kept you?" Gibralter asked, wiping his face with a paper napkin.

Louis slid into the booth, Jesse next to him. "Snow's really coming down, Chief," Louis said. "Plus we had a traffic stop."

Gibralter looked from one man to the other. "Well?"

"I talked to one of the vets, a guy called Cloverdale," Louis said. "He served in 'Nam and he thinks our killer might be military. He also had a theory on what the cards mean."

Gibralter pushed away his plate of half-eaten scrambled eggs. "What did he say?"

"He called it a death card," Louis went on, lowering his voice so the men in the next booth would not hear. "It was a thing some GI's did during the war. A group would go out and wipe out some Vietcong—"

"Not a group, Kincaid. Soldiers are not sent out in *groups*."

Louis suppressed a sigh. "Yes, sir. Afterward, they would walk through the dead and toss cards with their squadron's insignia and number on the bodies. It was suppose to say 'We were here. We did this.' "

"You have the card with you?" Gibralter asked.

Louis fished it out of his pocket. Gibralter took it, examining it through the plastic. "Death card," he said quietly. "The 1-2-3's a squadron number?"

"Probably, sir."

"And this skull thing?"

"Cloverdale said he thought it could be the squad's symbol."

Gibralter put down the card and looked out the window. The snow was coming down so thick Louis couldn't see the shops across the street. The sounds of the diner filtered around them, the clink of glasses and plates, the sizzle of the grill. Laughter drifted over to him, mingling with the faint ring from the Salvation Army Santa Claus out on the corner. Comforting sounds.

The waitress set down two fresh cups of coffee and menus. Louis reached for one.

"What else?" Gibralter asked, pulling the menu gently from his hands.

"He said the killer probably had low self-esteem all his life, making him think everybody was out to get him."

"I could've told you that. It's textbook."

"Cloverdale speculated that whatever problems our perp had

going into the army might have been intensified by drugs. In other words, his brain is fried."

Gibralter's eyes flashed with contempt. "That's crap."

"Chief?"

Gibralter reached for his pack of Camels and lit one. "The poor, misunderstood vet . . . It makes me sick," he said slowly. "These assholes were the same goddamn pussies who sat around smoking pot while the real soldiers were out getting shot. And then they tell the damn VA the war messed up their minds."

Louis glanced at Jesse. He was staring off at some distant point.

Gibralter sat back, laying his arm across the back of the booth. "What else did this Cloverdale say?"

"He said the guy was taking out his anger on the nearest symbol of authority he could find—cops."

"It's more than that," Gibralter said. "If he's military, then he's on a mission, just like 'Nam. And he's not just shooting at any uniform. He's shooting at us."

"What do you mean?" Jesse asked.

"Lovejoy and Pryce were killed in their homes, Harrison. These killings are *personal.*"

The waitress came by to refill their cups and take their orders. They gave them, Louis grateful for the break in intensity.

"So you still believe this is a former perp?" Louis asked.

"There's no other explanation," Gibralter said.

"So what do we do now, Chief?" Jesse asked.

Gibralter leveled his eyes at Jesse. "I already told you what to do, Harrison. You go through the damn case files. Have you done that?"

"Chief, we've gone through hundreds already. We looked—"

"Maybe you didn't look good enough," Gibralter interrupted.

Jesse looked away, his jaw twitching under a flush of color.

Gibralter ground his cigarette out in the eggs. "I expect a

full report on this man Cloverdale on my desk by end of shift today. Do you understand?"

Louis looked at the clock over Gibralter's head. It was almost 9:00 A.M. They had already been at it three hours and they still had boxes of old case files to wade through.

"Yes, sir," Louis said. He reached for the evidence bag with the card, but Gibralter snapped it up.

"I'll take it, Kincaid. I know a colonel over in Grayling. Let me see what I can find out about this. If we go through normal channels, it will take weeks."

Louis glanced at Jesse. He was still staring out the window at the snow.

Gibralter rose and tossed a twenty-dollar bill on the table. "Breakfast is on me. Good job, Kincaid," he said.

"What time is it?"

"You don't want to know."

"Yeah, I do. What time is it?"

Louis looked at his watch. "Eleven-thirty."

Jesse laid his head on the desk. "Wake me up at roll call."

Louis rubbed his face. They had been at it for hours and were no closer to finding a legitimate perp than they had been two days ago. What a way to spend Christmas Eve.

He glanced over at the dispatch desk, where Edna sat, immersed in her latest romance novel. The radio was quiet. The only sound was the occasional crunch of a cookie. Silent night, holy night, all is calm, all is bright. Damn, he was tired.

Louis looked at the pile of folders spread on the desk between him and Jesse. They had gone through at least a hundred case files since leaving Dot's that morning and the best suspect they could find was an ex-sergeant who was busted in 1981 for armed robbery, served three years and was out since 1980. When they called to check on his current status, they were told he was in a wheelchair.

Louis reached over the files and grabbed the computer printout he had asked Dale to run several hours earlier. It was a half-inch thick, listing all the red Ford trucks in the state. All thirty-five hundred of them. They had begun cross-checking the owners with local ex-cons, but so far, had no matches.

Louis dropped the printout. How come nobody knew this guy? And why the hell was he after Loon Lake's cops? Why pick an innocuous nine-man force in the middle of nowhere?

He's on a mission. These crimes are personal.

Louis rose and went to the coffeepot. Maybe it wasn't a local. Maybe it was a relative of someone exacting revenge for a family member. But as he realized how many more suspects that gave them, he felt even more depressed.

The door opened and Ollie Wickshaw came in, carrying a bag. He was sprinkled with snow and he shook it off like a wet greyhound. Ollie greeted Edna, who gave him a grunt from behind the book, and he went to his desk.

Louis poured a second cup of coffee and took it over to Ollie. Ollie looked up, blinking his pale gray eyes.

"Thank you," he said, taking it.

"No problem."

Ollie wriggled out of his jacket and as he did, a small prescription bottle tumbled to the floor. It rolled to a stop at Louis's feet and he picked it up. He held it out to Ollie, but couldn't miss the label on the front: VALIUM.

Ollie mumbled a thanks, averted his eyes and slipped it back into his pocket. Then he reached down and pulled a bright new Hot Wheels bike from behind a desk. When he saw Louis looking at him, he smiled wanly.

"Grandkids."

Louis nodded. "How many?"

Ollie pulled a bow from the drugstore bag and stuck it on the bike. "Three."

"How old?" Louis asked.

"Five, three and two. This is for the two-year-old, Joshua."

"Nice."

"You got kids?"

Louis shook his head. "Need a wife first."

Ollie looked at him blankly. "I guess that would help."

Ollie picked up the paper bag and rose, going to the mailboxes on the wall. Louis watched as he reached in the bag and deposited little gifts, wrapped like candy kisses, in each officer's mailbox. He came back and held one out to Louis.

"Merry Christmas," he said.

Louis hesitated, then took the little package. "Hey, thanks, man," he said, surprised.

Ollie nodded and moved back to his desk.

Louis unwrapped the gold foil paper. It was a rock. A pretty, polished black rock with little white flecks, but still a rock. He looked up at Ollie, who was watching him.

"It's a snowflake obsidian," he said. When Louis didn't reply, Ollie gave him a small smile. "You don't believe in the power of crystals, do you."

Louis shook his head. "Sorry."

"The snowflake is the stone of purity, balances the mind, body and spirit," Ollie went on. "It brings the wearer strength and protection." He pulled a chain out of his shirt. "I've been wearing one for ten years."

Louis rubbed the rock between his fingers. He watched, in mild amusement, as Ollie went about his routine of putting his desk items away for the night. He was about to stick a geode of lavender quartz in his drawer when Louis realized he had seen the same quartz in Stephanie Pryce's home.

"Pryce had one of those," he said.

Ollie looked up, holding the quartz. "Yes, I gave it to him. About a year or so ago."

Odd, Louis thought, considering Pryce didn't have friends in the department. "Christmas present?" he asked.

Ollie shook his head. "No. I thought it might help him."

"With what?"

"With whatever was troubling him. Amethyst brings serenity, peace of mind, forgiveness."

"You think Pryce was troubled?"

Ollie gave him a wry smile. "We all have demons, don't we?"

Louis resisted the urge to say what he was thinking, that if the damn serenity crystal worked so well, why was Ollie chucking down Valium?

Ollie gently placed the geode in the drawer, closed and locked it. He looked at Louis. "It's all yours," he said.

Louis nodded.

"Oops, forgot," Ollie said. He opened the middle drawer, retrieved Louis's reading glasses and placed them carefully on the pencil holder where Louis had left them hours ago. "I'm sorry I moved them," Ollie said. "I didn't know you'd be here tonight."

Louis walked over and picked up his glasses. "I thought Florence was the one who cleaned up my desk every night."

"I'm something of a neat freak," Ollie said, almost apologetically. "Hope you don't mind me straightening your stuff. Pryce didn't like it much."

"Hey, knock yourself out, man."

Louis went back to the desk where he had been working on the files. Jesse was hunched over, snoring lightly. Louis sat down and picked up another file. Moments later, he felt someone behind him and looked up to see Ollie.

"Lots of bad karma here," Ollie said, nodding at the case files.

"But no murderers," Louis said. "This town doesn't seem to breed weirdos. Must be something in the water supply."

Ollie smiled weakly.

"How long you been on the force, Ollie?" Louis asked.

"Twelve years," Ollie replied. "Only eight years and forty-five days 'til retirement. But who's counting?"

"When's the last time you had a homicide? Before Pryce and Lovejoy, I mean."

Ollie's wan face creased up in thought. "Ah, the Swope brothers . . . 1973, no, '74. Got drunk and one stabbed the other."

Louis shook his head, stacking a pile of folders. "But nobody pissed off at the local cops. Hard to believe."

"Well, Jesse has had his run-ins. But I can't think of anybody who would, I mean, to cause this kind of . . . retribution.
It, this isn't normal, it isn't . . ." Ollie's voice trailed off. He
caught Louis's eye and looked away. He went back to his desk.

Louis glanced at Jesse, envying his deep sleep. Man, he was
tired. He was tired of thinking. His brain actually ached.

"Shit, this is nuts," he said, more to himself than anyone.
"We're never going to find him this way."

Ollie looked over. "Why not?"

"Whatever it was that pissed the guy off could have happened ten, twenty years ago."

"But then why did he wait?" Ollie asked.

"What?"

"If it's an old crime, why would he wait so long to kill?"

Ollie had a point. Hatred usually didn't wait to go unvented.
Murder was almost always a violent and immediate reaction
to something. What could have forced the killer to wait so
long?

Louis sat forward, planting his feet on the floor. "Prison,"
he said softly.

Ollie looked over at him blankly.

Louis stood up, nodding. "He's been in prison. I'd bet on
it. That has to be it." He turned to Ollie. "Think about it.
Some jerkweed's sitting in jail, stewing about something the
cops did to him. Every day, every week, every year, he gets
madder and madder and he thinks of a plan. I mean, what else
does he have to do? He plans and waits." Louis took a few
quick steps toward Ollie. "Then when he gets out . . . bang."

Ollie took a step back, blinking rapidly. His slack face
looked gray in the harsh fluorescent light. Louis suddenly
wished he could take back his vivid image. For several seconds, they just stared at each other.

Then Ollie turned away, busying himself with packing up

the Hot Wheels and putting on his coat. Clutching the bike, he hurried to the door. But he paused, turning.

"Louis," Ollie called.

"Yeah?"

"Merry Christmas."

Louis nodded. "Same to you."

Ollie left and the office was quiet again. Louis rubbed his eyes, focusing his thoughts. He needed to get a list of prison releasees. He quickly scribbled a note to Dale, asking him to run a list of every state prisoner released after November 30, 1984. He taped it to Dale's phone.

"Edna?" he called out.

No response.

"Edna!"

Her round face appeared over the book. "Edna, when Dale comes in, would you tell him to leave these files out? He'll refile them if you don't. I'm heading home."

Edna popped the last bit of cookie in her mouth. "Ten-four, Louis." She nodded to the snoring Jesse. "What about Jess?"

"Let him sleep, I guess."

Louis yawned and rose, stretching. His thoughts drifted to his cold cabin with its cold bed. He wondered what Zoe was doing tonight. He hadn't seen her in three days; she had told him she was going home for Christmas. His mind shaped a sudden image of her sitting in a fancy high-rise on Lakeshore Drive, unwrapping a gift of lingerie from some faceless boyfriend. Christ, where had that come from? He let out a frustrated sigh, wondering if she was going to be gone all week. He had been hoping to spend New Year's Eve with her. Especially since he was obviously going to spend Christmas Day by himself.

He slipped on his jacket. The phone on Jesse's desk rang and he grabbed it before it woke him up.

"Loon Lake Police, Officer Kincaid."

"Is Jesse there?" a feminine voice asked.

"Julie?"

"Yes." She sounded very young.

"Hold on, I'll wake him."

"He's sleeping?" Julie asked. "Where?"

"On his desk."

"Wait, don't wake him up."

Louis frowned. He couldn't let Jesse sleep in the station on Christmas Eve. "Julie—"

"Let him sleep, please," she said quickly.

Louis sensed something anxious in her voice and he wondered if they were having problems.

"Julie," he said, "I can bring him home."

"No, he's safe there," she said softly. "Let him stay. He's safe there. He's safe."

Fifteen

Dawn. Christmas Day. The world had stopped.

Louis walked slowly down Main Street, past the dark store-fronts, past the pillared First National Bank and under the silent marque of the Palace Theater. His eyes caught sight of the barechested Sylvester Stallone holding the machine gun above the type: *Rambo: First Blood II.* He hurried on.

The Mustang had refused to start again, but this morning the idea of walking to the station hadn't bothered him. After a night of restless sleep, he needed time to think. He could almost feel his brain cells gulping in the chilly air.

He had to walk slowly, slogging through the foot of new snow that had fallen since yesterday morning. The streets were empty, blanketed in white. No cars, no people, no sounds, no sign of human life. Just the crunch of his boots and rush of his blood in his ears.

He felt stiff, fragile somehow, as if his bones might snap. Funny what lack of sleep did to a body and a mind. His whole body ached, from the constant tension of keeping muscles and senses on alert. Alert for what? The clues that might be lurking somewhere in those piles of case folders, in Pryce's notebook or in the blotter doodles? Alert for what? A bullet that would come out of nowhere some morning when he opened his door?

Ahead, he saw the glow of the station sign and increased his pace. There was a faint pink in the eastern sky. Above, a few errant flakes floated down in the amber light of the antique street lamps.

He crossed the street, climbing over the bank of snow lining the curb. All through the night, between bouts of jagged sleep, his mind had worked. Pieces. Nothing but pieces of a puzzle whose whole he could not yet see.

Lovejoy . . . A test watch that stopped three minutes after it was submerged in water. A murder probably committed in the afternoon, but unnoticed by fishermen. Or committed before dawn when no one went out on the lake to fish.

Pryce . . . A smart, experienced detective who kept unintelligible notes, scrawled senseless doodles on a blotter and was peppering the state with résumés.

Nothing fit. What was the big picture? What did the puzzle even look like?

Louis tipped his head back, up into the lazy fall of the flakes. They settled gently on his face and melted.

Someone had already shoveled the station walk. He stamped his boots on the concrete and went inside. Dale was at the coffeepot, setting out a box of donuts.

He looked up at Louis. "Do you ever sleep?"

Louis shook his head. "Doesn't feel like it."

Dale filled a cup, plucked a sprinkled donut from the box and set them on Louis's desk. "I got your note. Request for the ex-cons is already sent. I told them I needed it ASAP. They said they'd try, but with the holiday and all, they couldn't promise anything."

Louis thanked him and slithered out of his coat. He saw the stack of case files still sitting on the desk where he and Jesse had left them the night before. He couldn't face them right now. It could wait until the report came back of newly released prisoners and they could compare names.

Louis dropped down into his chair, sipping his coffee. His gaze strayed to the desk blotter with its doodles and nonsensical numbers. Christ, didn't Pryce have a Rolodex? He focused finally on several sets of numbers. Seven digits, no hyphens but possibly a phone number. He called Dale over and asked him if he recognized them.

"That's Ollie's home phone," Dale said, pointing. "And that one there is the chief's."

Louis pointed to the third, almost obscured in the doodles. "What about this one?"

"Don't know."

Louis dialed it. He got a recording that said he needed to dial a "1" for long distance. He tried it again and a woman answered.

"Michigan State Police."

"Uh, sorry, wrong number." He hung up.

"What was it?" Dale asked.

"The state police."

"Figures. They had an ad in the Lansing paper last month for officers."

Louis pulled open a desk drawer and got out Pryce's RÉSUMÉ file, the worn legal pad and a few papers he had pulled out of Stephanie Pryce's cabinet. He opened the RÉSUMÉ file, looking for something from the state police, but there was nothing.

"Hey, Louis?"

He looked over at Dale.

"I almost forgot. Mrs. Pryce called yesterday. She asked when you were going to send her file cabinet back."

Louis picked up the papers. "I'd better pack it up."

Dale opened the evidence room to let him in. Louis went to the file cabinet, opened a drawer and stuck the RÉSUMÉ file back in. He was about to stick the legal pad in when he paused. There it was again—that giant, sprawling doodle on the back with the number in the center: 61829. Shit, where had he seen it before?

The notebook . . .

Taking the legal pad, he went back to his desk and retrieved Pryce's pocket notebook from a drawer. Sitting down, he flipped slowly through the pages, searching for the number.

There it was—61829. But this time with the words in front of it: SAM YELLOW LINCOLN. Sam . . . Yellow . . . Lincoln.

Damn, Pryce wasn't referring to a car or a plate; he was using standard radio code: SYL61829. Was it a serial number for a gun? He jotted it on a paper and went over to Dale's computer.

"Dale, I need you to run a gun check."

"Sure. No prob."

Louis glanced at his watch. Shift was starting soon; he had to get into uniform. He hurried off to the locker room. Dale was watching the report print out as Louis came back into the office, buckling his belt.

"It's a Beretta 9-millimeter," Dale said, ripping off the print-out. "It's registered to Calvin Hammersmith, 4578 Pine Bluff Road, Kalkaska, Michigan."

"Check an arrest record," Louis said, his heart quickening.

Dale started punching in numbers. Louis sat down at his desk and stared at the name on the printout. Who the hell was this guy? And why did Pryce care about his gun?

"Hammersmith was arrested a bunch of times," Dale called out a few minutes later. "The last time was in 1975 for assault. And it was right here in Loon Lake."

Louis jumped up from his chair. "Here? You're kidding."

"He served two years."

Louis came over to the computer to read the report. "Nothing after that? Nothing since '77?"

Dale shook his head.

Louis began to pace. "I need to know more about this guy."

Dale picked up the phone. "I'll call the sheriff over there."

Louis returned to his desk and picked up Pryce's notebook, staring at the gun serial number. The radio crackled and he listened while Flo gave directions to a traffic accident.

Dale hung up. "Well, I have some bad news and some good news," he said. "Hammersmith was a badass. Disabled vet with a history of violence and alcoholism."

Louis's heart skipped. "And?"

"He died in 1980. Motorcycle accident."

Louis tossed the notebook on the desk. "Shit!"

"What's the matter?" Dale asked.

Louis looked over at him, shaking his head. "I was just hoping for a nice Christmas present, Dale, that's all."

He picked up the notebook again. Damn, Pryce had written the number down twice. It had to mean something. Or did Hammersmith, even though he was dead, have some connection? He stared at the number, locking it away in his memory. It had to mean something.

Sixteen

"Did you get anything for Christmas?"

Jesse looked at Louis from behind his sunglasses. "I got laid."

"I meant presents. What the hell's wrong with you?"

The light changed and Jesse moved the cruiser down Main Street. "Sorry. Julie's on my ass. Says she's scared for me. Neither of us is getting any sleep."

"Well, it seems you found an acceptable substitute."

Jesse smiled weakly. "Right. Actually, she got me a cool present, a compact disc player. You ever seen one?"

"This year's quadrophonic. What kind of music you like?"

"Good old-fashioned rock and roll, man. I like the Stones best. How about you?"

"I like lots of different music."

"But what do you listen to at night, you know, when you're alone?"

"Rhythm and blues . . . Chuck Willis, Sam Cooke, Clyde McPhatter. You know them?"

Jesse shook his head. "Don't like that old shit."

"You should try it. The Stones are really just repackaged R & B."

"The Stones are rockers, Louis."

"You know their song 'Time Is on My Side'?"

"Sure. *12 X 5,* fifth cut, first side. Great album."

"It's an old blues song by Irma Thomas." Louis smiled. "Your boy Mick is rock's blackest white boy."

Jesse frowned, digesting the information as Louis laughed.

Louis reached for the computer printout on the seat between them. It listed the seventy-one red Ford pickups in the tri-county area, but when cross-referenced with felons, they still had eight names to check out. They had already done two with no results.

"Who's next?" Jesse asked.

Louis read off the address, and Jesse took a right at the next corner and they headed out of town. They passed the Sunoco station and rounded a curve. Ahead of them was a log building set in the shade of thick pines. Louis had seen Jo-Jo's Tavern once before, on a drive during a sleepless night. He had considered stopping in for a drink, but the place had such a foreboding aura that he had passed it by and gone home. He scanned its exterior now. It seemed more benign in the daylight, with its red Budweiser signs in the windows, smoke curling from the chimney and scattering of cars in the muddy lot.

Jesse hit the brakes.

"What the—" Louis spat out, bracing against the dash. Jesse slammed the cruiser into reverse, backed onto the shoulder and turned around. "There's a red Ford. An old one."

As Jesse swung in the parking lot, Louis squinted at the truck. It was an older model, the paint fading, the lower sides pocked with rust. They parked behind the truck and got out. Louis circled the truck, peering in the dirty windows while Jesse ran the plate.

"It returns to a Mildred Cronk of Dollar Bay, Houghton County," Jesse said, coming up to his side.

"Where's that?" Louis asked.

"Upper Peninsula."

"Long way from home."

"No warrants."

Louis looked at the bar. "Well, guess we better go find Millie."

Inside Jo-Jo's, a fetid brew of smells greeted them—beer, cigarettes, fried fish and urine. From a dark corner came Freddie Fender's twangy basso singing "Wasted Days and Wasted Nights." Jesse plunged into the murk, heading toward the bar. Louis stood just inside the door, blinking to get his pupils dilated enough to see.

At first, he saw only spots of color. A flicker of purple neon over the bar. The green glow of the pool table lighted by the plastic stained-glass Stroh's sign above. The rainbow of the jukebox. And the orange glow of a cigarette. Shadows gradually turned into men. The burly bartender, three men standing around the pool table, a cluster huddled at a table. They were all standing motionless and mute, watching, waiting.

Jesse's footsteps on the warped wood planks drew Louis's attention. He felt his heart quicken. Something felt weird about this.

"Turn off the music," Jesse called out.

The shadow behind the bar didn't move.

"Turn off the damn music," Jesse repeated.

The bartender still didn't move. Jesse went to the jukebox and gave it a sharp kick. The needle ripped across the record and stopped, plunging the tavern into silence.

"Who's driving the red Ford pickup outside?" Jesse demanded.

No one moved.

"Look, you stupid motherfuckers, I asked you a question."

A soft rumbling came from the men at the pool table. Jesse started slowly toward them and Louis suppressed a sigh, his muscles tightening in anticipation. A crazy image flashed into his head: Dean Martin in *Rio Bravo,* just before he shot a guy hiding in the rafters.

"Anyone in here named Cronk?" Jesse asked, his voice rising. When no one answered, Jesse turned to Louis and started to say something, but he stopped. Louis saw Jesse's eyes flick to something behind him.

Suddenly, Jesse bolted past him and disappeared into a dark hallway.

"What's down there?" Louis yelled to the bartender.

"Just the can," the man said. "And the back door!"

Louis ran down the hall. He heard a crash and knew Jesse had kicked open a door. He came to a stop as a rush of cold air hit him in the face. The rear door hung open. Jesse and a man were slogging through drifts, heading toward the woods on the far side of the field. Louis ran after them, grabbing his radio from his belt.

"Central! Central! This is L-11. We are in a foot pursuit of a white male—"

The suspect was heading toward a barbed-wire fence that ran the length of the field. No way the man could get away now. But then Louis watched in dismay as the man hurdled the fence and kept going toward the woods. Jesse tried to jump the fence, caught his pant leg and tumbled to the snow on the other side, his feet tangled in the wire.

Louis caught up, grabbed the top wire and swung his legs over. The man was almost to the woods. Louis drew his gun.

"Stop!" he shouted. "Stop or I'll shoot!"

The suspect froze and threw his hands in the air. Louis hurried over to the man. "Don't move," Louis ordered.

Jesse trotted up, limping and panting. He grabbed the man's raised hand to cuff him and he tightened against his grasp.

"Don't fight me, asshole," Jesse said, twisting his arm.

"I'm not."

An army jacket hung loosely on the man's small frame. He had stringy yellow hair and tight, leathery skin lined with fine wrinkles. Narrow, pale gray eyes stared back at Louis.

Jesse shoved him and the man fell. "Who are you?"

The man stared up at Jesse coolly.

"Answer me!"

"Jess, check for a wallet," Louis said firmly.

Jesse patted him down. He pulled out a paper and a set of keys but no wallet. He handed them to Louis.

Louis unfolded the paper. It looked to be a letter. Louis stuck it in his back pocket with the keys.

"Where's your ID?" Louis asked.

"Don't got one," the man mumbled.

"What's your name?" Louis asked.

"Maybe I ain't got one of those either."

"Don't play games!" Jesse said, reaching for the man's collar.

Louis quickly stepped between them. Louis's radio went off. Florence calling for a status check. "Jess, answer that," Louis said.

Jesse reluctantly called back that they had the subject in custody and clicked off. Louis had the man firmly by his arm and was guiding him toward the cruiser. He noticed Jesse's ripped pants.

"You're bleeding," Louis said, nodding toward Jesse's thigh.

Jesse looked down at the six-inch gash in his pants. It was soaked dark red. Suddenly, he hit the man's shoulder, sending him stumbling forward out of Louis's grasp and down into the snow.

"You asshole! See what you did?"

"Jess!" Louis grabbed the suspect's arm and pulled him to his feet. He could feel the man's arm through the jacket, sinewy with muscle.

"What's your name, you stinkin' piece of shit?" Jesse demanded.

"Harrison!" Louis said sharply.

Jesse turned and glared at Louis.

"You're bleeding," Louis said slowly, enunciating each syllable. "Go back to the car."

Jesse didn't move.

"Now," Louis said.

Jesse held Louis's eyes for a second longer; then he turned and limped off through the snow.

Louis gave the man's arm a jerk. "Name," he demanded.

"John Smith."

Louis sighed and shoved the man toward the parking lot. "Okay, 'John Smith.' Let's go."

Jesse was in the cruiser, trying to wrap his leg with a roll of gauze from the first-aid kit. Louis put the suspect in the back and got in, starting the car. He looked down at Jesse's leg. The barbed wire had left a deep gash several inches long in his thigh. Jesse was sweating.

"You want me to call EMS?" Louis asked.

"Fuck no," Jesse said, not looking up. "Just get me to the damn emergency room."

Louis pulled out of the lot, radioing they were coming back with the suspect. Jesse sat stone-faced, occasionally pulling off new sections of gauze to dab at his cut. Louis looked in the rearview mirror and caught the eyes of the suspect. The man's face was dirty, his hair wet from the snow.

"Whyda hell you arrest me?" he demanded. He had a weird accent, even stranger than the usual Michigan twang.

Louis didn't answer.

"I ain't done nuttin'."

Jesse turned to glare at him. "Listen, you stupid Yooper, you shut that fucking trap of yours or you're gonna be eating those teeth."

Louis watched the man's face in the mirror. The man stared at Jesse for several seconds, then slumped down in the seat, turning his face away to stare blankly out at the snow.

Louis dropped Jesse off at the emergency room entrance of the hospital. When he reached the station five minutes later, Dale was waiting for him just inside the front door. He watched as Louis helped "John Smith" out of the cruiser and trailed behind as Louis led the suspect inside.

"Who is it?" Dale asked.

"I don't know yet." He told him to send someone out to retrieve the red Ford truck in Jo-Jo's parking lot.

"Red truck?" Dale asked. "You think—"

"Don't know yet," Louis said.

"What do I book him on?" Dale asked, his gaze sliding uneasily over the suspect.

"Attempting to elude, for now."

As Dale led the man to the back, Louis wriggled out of his

jacket and went to his desk. He fell into the chair and took a deep breath. The idea that they had lucked into finding the right truck was too much to hope for. But the description fit, and the man was about five-foot-nine, the estimated height of Lovejoy's killer.

Louis glanced toward the glass that separated the booking room from the office. Smith had taken off his army jacket. Louis was surprised to see how small he was underneath. He looked like someone had placed a hand on his head and squashed him down a few inches. His legs bowed outward, but his chest and shoulders, outlined beneath his thin T-shirt, were rock hard with muscle.

Louis rose and went to the booking room door, crossing his arms. Smith glanced at him as Dale took his prints.

"I ain't done nuttin'," he said.

"Then why'd you run?"

Smith shrugged.

"You're not scoring very high on the brain meter here," Louis said. "Why won't you tell us who you are? You got warrants?"

Smith shook his head as Dale rocked his inky fingers on the print card.

"We're going to find out anyway."

Smith sighed. "Okay, okay. Can we talk alone?"

Louis nodded to Dale to leave. "Okay, talk," Louis said, closing the door.

"My name is Duane Lacey. I'm on parole. I'm not supposed to be outta Houghton County without permission."

"Who owns the truck?"

"My mother." He wiped a strand of dirty blond hair off his forehead. "I thought you guys wanted me for parole violation."

"What are you doing down here?"

"Seein' my kid."

"Where's he?"

"Red Oak juvie center. That's a few miles—"

"I know where it is. When did you get here?"

"Yesterday. I was heading there this afternoon. They only let you visit afternoons." Lacey moved to the bench and sat down. "I ain't seen him in years. His mother took him."

"Sad story," Louis said.

"Look, I'm tellin' ya the truth. Look at that letter you took off me. It's from my kid."

Louis reached in his back pants pocket and took out the letter Jesse had given him back at Jo-Jo's. It was written on a page of lined loose-leaf paper and began: *Dear Dad.*

Louis opened the door to look for Dale, wanting him to run Lacey's name for warrants. Dale was nowhere to be seen.

"Who's your parole officer?" Louis asked.

"Bill James," Lacey answered.

Louis pulled a pen from his pocket. "All right, Lacey, give me your social security number." Lacey rattled it off and Louis started for the door.

"You ain't gonna reach James at his office," Lacey called after him. "It's the holidays, you know."

Louis picked up Lacey's army jacket and left, locking the door. He gave Lacey's number to Florence to run for outstanding warrants, then went to his desk and dialed Dollar Bay information to get a home phone number for William James. Louis called him, and after apologizing for bothering him on the day after Christmas, he told him about Lacey.

James gave a short bitter laugh. "He ran on you? Doesn't surprise me."

"Why?"

"He's paranoid. Tells me all the time everybody's out to get him. Hold on, gotta turn down the TV."

Louis waited until he heard James pick up the phone again. "So, what did he do now?" James asked.

"Ran a light," Louis said, deciding not to involve James until he had reason to.

James sighed. "Idiot's not supposed to be out of Houghton. What's he doing down there?"

"Says he's visiting his son," Louis said.

"Son? Oh, right, forgot. Lacey's new to me so I don't have all the background. I can tell you, though, he's been a model citizen since he got out of prison."

"When was that?"

"Real recent, but I'd have to check." Louis sensed impatience in James's voice, as though he wanted to get back to his television.

"What was he sent up for?" Louis asked.

"Tell you what. I'll call the local P.D. and have them send you his sheet. The chief's my cousin. What's your fax number?"

Louis gave it to him. "One last question. Is Lacey dangerous?"

"Well, he's weird," James said, "but he's always been polite to me. It's Christmas, he probably just wanted to see his kid."

Louis thanked him and hung up. He glanced at the letter in his hand and then looked back at Lacey, sitting quietly in the booking room. Turning his back, he unfolded the letter.

Dear Dad,
I know you haven't probaly gotten no letters from me since you went up but I was thinking maybe now that you was out maybe you might want to come and see me. I don't know where mom went to. The last time I saw her she said she would give grandma her address so when I got out I could maybe come there. She said something about Florida. But I ain't heard from Grandma neither. I understand maybe you won't want to come all the way down here because its such a long drive and that's cool if you don't. Grandma never wanted to come neither and I'm really doing okay here. I mean I'm still alive so far. It sucks bad though.

Louis refolded the letter. While he waited for the fax, he carefully examined Lacey's jacket for any tears. It was old but intact.

The fax machine began to purr and he went to it, pulling off the papers as they dropped off the end.

Duane Herbert Lacey had been a criminal from the age of eighteen. Shoplifting, grand theft auto, joyriding, burglary, possession and assault on his wife. In February 1977, he was arrested for assault with a deadly weapon and sentenced to twelve to fifteen in Marquette State Prison.

Louis glanced back at Lacey. What the hell was he doing out after only seven years? Then he saw it. Duane Lacey had been paroled on the governor's early release program earlier in the month, on December 10, 1984.

Louis lowered the paper slowly, a wave of disappointment washing over him. Pryce and Lovejoy had been killed on or around the first. This guy could not be their killer.

He went back to the booking room. Lacey's head jerked up when he unlocked the door.

"You reach James?" he asked.

Louis nodded. "The assault. What happened?"

Lacey looked away, shaking his head. "It was a bar fight. I drew a knife."

"You were just defending yourself, right?" Louis said flatly.

"That's right," Lacey answered, meeting his eyes.

Louis stared at Lacey, at the man's pale gray eyes. They were like water, colorless and shallow, as though nothing stirred beneath. Finally Lacey looked away.

James was right, there was something weird about the guy. But no more than a hundred other lowlifes who were wound a little too tight. It would be easy to call Red Oak to verify Lacey's story about his kid, but why bother? Duane Lacey had been five hundred miles away, behind bars, when Pryce and Lovejoy were killed. Besides, if he booked him now for running, the guy would go right back to Marquette on parole violation.

Florence called to him. "No warrants, Louis. He's clean."

Louis watched Lacey's watery eyes for a reaction. But nothing registered, not even relief.

Louis tossed the fatigue jacket at Lacey. "Go on. Get out of here," he said, holding out the letter and the keys to the truck. "Get your ass back to Dollar Bay."

Lacey rose slowly, took the letter and keys and put on his jacket. "You don't know how much I appreciate this, officer, I really do," he said quickly. "I don't wanna end up back in jail just 'cause I wanted to see my kid."

Louis turned away, and on his way to the locker room, asked Florence to cancel the truck's tow. He pushed open the locker-room door.

It was cold inside and he shivered as he passed the first row of lockers. God, he was discouraged. So damn close. First Hammerstein or Hammersmith or whatever the hell his name was. Now this pathetic jerkweed who risked jail to see his delinquent son on Christmas.

He was pulling on a sweatshirt when the door slammed open with a bang. Louis looked up. Jesse rushed in, waving a paper.

"Where is the motherfucker?" he shouted.

Louis frowned. "Who?"

"Lacey!" Jesse said, jabbing at the fax. "Lacey. Fucking Lacey. I don't believe this! We got him! Where is he? Where's Lacey?"

"I let him go," Louis said.

Jesse's mouth dropped open. "What? You let him go? Why?"

"Because he was in prison," Louis said.

Jesse stared at Louis. "What? He couldn't have been!"

"Read the release date from prison," Louis said.

Jesse read the fax. Slowly, the information registered and Jesse blinked rapidly. "Fuck," he whispered. He crumpled the paper in anger and dropped down onto the bench.

Louis sat down next to him. His own disappointment prevented him from saying anything of comfort.

Jesse uncrumpled the paper and stared at it again. "This has to be wrong," he said.

"Jess . . ."

Jesse jumped up. "I'm going after him. This has to be—"

Louis grabbed Jesse's arm. "Jess, listen to me," he said firmly. "I talked to his P.O. Lacey was in Marquette when Pryce and Lovejoy were killed. It's not him!"

Jesse's face went slack, the mix of fatigue and bitter disappointment finally taking hold. Louis glanced at his pant leg, which had been cut off at the knee. A six-inch-long track of small black stitches was outlined against the fresh gauze wrapping.

"How's the leg?" Louis asked.

Jesse didn't seem to hear him. He was staring at the fax again. Suddenly, he spun away and kicked the locker. He grabbed his jacket and headed toward the door. Dale opened it just as Jesse reached it. Jesse brushed past him, knocking him against the door frame.

Louis watched him go, a slow anger rising in him. Goddammit, he was sick and tired of this. He was tired of dead ends and dirtbags. He was tired of dead cops. And he was really tired of Jesse's moods.

Dale came forward. "You need to sign this, Louis."

Louis pulled his eyes from the door and took the paper from Dale. He signed it and gave it back. He noticed Dale was rubbing his arm.

"You okay?"

"Sure. What's wrong with Jess?"

"I don't know," Louis said. Damn, he *did* know. Jesse was out of control, and in his state of mind he was useless on this investigation. There was no way to put it off any longer. It was time to talk to Gibralter about him.

"Is the chief back yet?" Louis asked Dale.

"Just got in."

"Thanks." Louis left the locker room and went to Gibralter's door, knocking. The chief called him to come in.

"Well, what is it?" Gibralter said, looking up from some papers.

"I need to speak with you, sir," Louis said.

"Can it wait?"

"Not really, sir. It's about Jesse."

Gibralter set the papers aside and picked up his cigarette from the ashtray. "What about him?"

Louis drew in a breath. "I think he might need to be relieved of duty for a while."

"Explain."

"We arrested a guy today who we thought might be our killer but it didn't pan out," Louis said. "Jesse lost control, sir, lost his temper. I think he's . . . losing it."

"Explain."

"I think he's afraid, sir, too afraid to function. I think he will hurt himself, or someone else, if he doesn't calm down."

Gibralter took a drag from the cigarette and slowly snuffed it out in the ashtray. "We're all a little tense right now, Kincaid," he said.

"I know," Louis said. "But Jesse can't control himself. The other day, during a traffic stop, I had to back him off a guy."

"Back him off?"

"He slammed the guy's head against the truck."

"What did you do?"

"I pulled him off him."

Gibralter rose and came around the front of the desk to stand in front of Louis. "Did this man see you do this?" he asked.

Louis nodded.

Gibralter slapped him, lightly but sharply on the cheek. Louis blinked in shock.

"Humiliated?" Gibralter asked.

Louis refused to even nod.

Gibralter went back around his desk. "I did that only so you'll know how Jess felt when you stepped in between him and that man. Don't ever do it again."

Louis's jaw flinched.

"You got something to say, Kincaid?"

He had plenty to say, but he held it in.

"Sit down, Kincaid."

Louis looked up, surprised by the sudden softening in Gibralter's voice. Gibralter was standing by the credenza now, holding one of the pieces from the chessboard. Louis sat on the edge of the chair across from Gibralter's desk.

"I worked in Chicago before coming here," Gibralter said. "I worked my way up through the force to captain. I was the youngest man ever to make captain in the city's history. Before that, I was in the army, a first lieutenant, leading a platoon in Vietnam."

Louis wondered where this was going.

"Both experiences taught me a lot about commanding men in a unit," Gibralter continued, fingering the chess piece. "I learned that each man has his strengths and that it is the leader's job to exploit them for the unit's success."

Gibralter held out the chess piece. Louis saw it was a pawn.

"Some men are foot soldiers," Gibralter said. "They are the lifeblood of the game, but they have no power on their own."

Gibralter picked up a rook. "Other men are like rooks, limited and plodding, but valuable if you know how to use them."

He exchanged the rook for another piece. "And then there is the knight," he said, holding up the pewter piece. "Now, the knight is the attacker, always ready to charge into battle in service of its king, but you have to be careful with it because it is hard to control."

Gibralter tossed the piece at Louis. He caught it and looked up at Gibralter.

"Jesse is my knight," Gibralter said.

Louis turned the piece over in his fingers, trying to figure out a way to say Jesse was acting more like a horse's ass and that he was getting fed up with Gibralter's metaphors.

"Has Jesse told you much about his background?"

Louis looked up at Gibralter. "No."

"That doesn't surprise me."

Gibralter came forward and took the knight from Louis. He

set it back in its place on the board and returned to sit behind his desk.

"There are some things you should know about him," Gibralter said. "I don't normally do this, but I'm going to tell you because you seem eager to judge people sometimes, which is not a good quality in a cop. And I don't think Jesse deserves it."

Louis stared at Gibralter.

"Jesse's childhood was hell," Gibralter began. "His mother was a drunk and his father Len . . . Well, he was just a bastard."

Lila Kincaid floated into Louis's mind, and her smell: Evening in Paris and booze. Shit, he had no memories of his father, not even bad ones.

"I met Jesse when he was seventeen, just after he had run away from home. He didn't tell me every detail, but I know Len used him as a punching bag from the time he was about ten. Once, when Jess was about twelve, he tried to stop his father from beating his mother and the father attacked Jess with his pocketknife. That's how he got the scar on his neck."

Louis thought of the crosshatch of scars on Jesse's back.

"But the worst thing was the cage," Gibralter said. "Whenever Jess acted out, Len would lock him in the dog cage in the backyard and leave him there for days."

Louis felt his stomach turn. Jesus, the cage in Lovejoy's cabin.

Gibralter paused, watching Louis's face. "There's more. Want to hear it?"

Louis drew in a breath. "No."

"Jesse has a temper. I know that," Gibralter said. "But I've seen him come a long way to become a decent man and a good cop. I can count on him, Kincaid. I wish I could say that about every man who has worked for me."

Louis nodded. Christ, this man was something. One minute talking about Vietnam, the next minute opening up a vein over Jesse's childhood.

"You can go now," Gibralter said quietly.

Louis rose and left the office. He stood outside the door for a moment, his head swimming. He felt anger—at Gibralter for making excuses for Jesse and at Jesse for needing them. He felt humiliation, the sting of Gibralter's hand still fresh on his face. But more than anything, he felt a suffocating disappointment over losing Lacey as a suspect.

He felt eyes on him and looked up to see Ollie watching him. Ollie . . . rook or pawn? Jesus.

With a glance at his watch, he went to his desk and snatched up his jacket. He paused, then jerked open a drawer and pulled out the legal pad with his notes on the Pryce and Lovejoy cases. There was half a bottle of Christian Brothers in the cupboard back home. Maybe after it was gone, he could face looking at the cases again.

Seventeen

She was there, standing on the porch, when he got to the cabin. He hurried to her, pulling her to his chest.

"You're here," he said.

Zoe fit her body against his, holding him tightly. "I just got back. I came right here."

He kissed her. Her lips were cold and chapped. He cupped her small face with his hands. "I missed you," he whispered.

He crushed her to his chest again and closed his eyes.

She pulled back to look at his face. "Something's wrong?" she asked.

"Things are tense at work," he said.

She smiled again. "Trees make you tense?"

He laughed, but it was to cover his guilt more than anything. He had lied to her about what he did, the second night they were together. The lie had come to him one morning when he saw a sign for the Huron State Forest. He told her he was working for the Forestry Office, a temporary assignment connected with the University of Michigan.

"My boss is a prick," he said.

"You need to reduce your stress level."

"Oh yeah? Got any ideas?"

"Well, in fact, I do. You own a pair of running shoes?"

"What?"

"You can come run with me."

He smiled to hide his weariness. "I had a different form of exercise in mind."

She laughed again. "Go get dressed. We'll run to my place."

They went into the cabin. He was bone tired and didn't really want to go anywhere, but played along, dressing quickly.

They struck off through the snow. Louis was chagrined that Zoe slowed her pace for his sake, but as they rounded the east end of the lake, he slowly forgot his discomfort. He forgot, almost, about Gibralter, about cops, about the cases, about everything, losing himself in the simple pleasure of running. He had forgotten how exhilarating it felt to run. He glanced at Zoe. And how good it felt to be in love. The realization struck him like a laser. Jesus, how could he be in love after only a few weeks? No, he told himself quickly, it wasn't love. It was lust, pure and simple. But then, why had he missed her so much?

After an hour, they came to a hill and walked up to a small log cabin set down in a stand of tall pines. Below, the lake was an opaque white expanse in the moonlight, rimmed with the yellow lights of cabins and a cluster of brightness where the town sat, down on the south end.

"You're really isolated here," Louis said.

She held open the door for him. "I like it that way."

Louis stepped inside. He was struck immediately by the smell, something sweet that transported him immediately back to college. Patchouli incense.

"Leave your shoes there," Zoe said, pulling off her jacket and shoes. "I'm going to go change."

Louis slipped off his sodden Nikes and jacket, his eyes taking in the small room. From the outside, it was a log cabin, much like his. But inside, it looked like an exotic brothel. The log walls were draped with swags of gauze in peach and orange. There were brass candlestick holders on the mantel, the windowsills, the tables, the weeping wax of their candles puddled down onto the wood floor. A large rough-hewn wood coffee table dominated the room, filled with more candles and flanked by a Victorian sofa, upholstered in paisley. The floor was covered by an Oriental carpet and dotted with dozens of pillows, all in a riot of colors, fabrics and patterns.

Louis's gaze traveled around the incredible room. There were no pictures, except for one large print in a heavy gilt frame above the fireplace. It showed two men and a woman having a picnic in the woods. The men wore formal nineteenth-century dress and the blissfully blank expression of cows. But the woman was nude, gazing out nonchalantly at whoever looked at the painting.

Louis was staring at the painting when Zoe came back in. She was barefoot, wearing a red caftan and carrying two brandy snifters. She smiled as she handed one to Louis and then set about lighting the candles.

"I've seen this painting before," he said.

"Manet. *Le Dejeuner sur l'herbe,*" she said, going to sit on the sofa.

" 'Lunch' . . ." Louis began, then shook his head.

" 'On the lawn,' " she finished.

"Can't run anymore, can't remember my college French," he said, coming to sit next to her.

She smiled and took a sip of brandy. "The real one is in the Louvre. I want to go see it someday. It's one of my favorite paintings."

"Why?"

"The woman," she said, nodding at the painting. "Look at her. She's naked, but she's obviously the one in charge."

Louis took a deep drink of the brandy, tilting his head and closing his eyes. He let the soft, warm liquid trickle down the back of his throat. He heard a gentle tinkling sound and looked back at Zoe. She had shifted to face him, folding her legs up under her on the sofa. She was wearing earrings, intricate little gold things with tiny bells.

"I like your place," he said. "It's very . . ."

"Overwrought?" she said with a smile.

"Romantic."

"If you like early Turkish brothel."

"I feel like I should be listening to 'White Rabbit' and stuffing towels under the door."

She laughed. He felt so good, as if he were drifting in a warm ocean somewhere, surrounded by the smell of flowers. It was the patchouli and her perfume. She had moved closer to him, leaning back into the pillows, swirling the brandy in the glass.

"Well, I'm just an old hippie at heart," she said.

"How old?"

"Thirty-five."

He cocked a brow. "I've never been out with an older woman before."

A black cat jumped up on the sofa and settled into Louis's lap. Zoe reached to brush it away, but Louis stopped her.

"It's okay. I don't mind," he said. The cat began to knead his belly, stretching its paws and purring loudly.

"She likes you," Zoe said.

"I have that effect on women." Louis rubbed the cat's head. "What's her name?"

"Isolde."

"Come again?"

"Isolde." She pointed to a white cat cowering behind a chair. "That's Tristan. You know, Wagner?"

Louis gave her a puzzled shrug.

"Tristan and Isolde. It's an opera about two doomed lovers." She paused, smiling. "Louis, don't tell me you've never heard Wagner."

"Sure. He wrote that music in *Apocalypse Now,* the part where Robert Duvall is in the helicopter talking about how much he loves the smell of napalm in the morning." He sobered. Shit, for all he knew, her mother had been killed by some soldier in Korea.

But to his relief, she didn't seem to get it. She rose and went to the stereo, putting on a tape. Moments later, the music began, so softly he barely heard it. Zoe came back, fitting into the crook of his arm, laying her head back on his shoulder.

"This is *Liebestod,*" she said.

"Nice," Louis murmured.

"It means 'Love Death.' It's Isolde's song of ecstasy, just as she's getting ready to jump into the fire to meet Tristan in death."

"Oh, those wacky Germans . . ."

Zoe closed her eyes. "Now, just listen to it. It starts out so slow, so sensual."

Louis set the brandy aside and shut his eyes.

"Listen," she whispered. "Hear how it builds?"

"Hmmm."

"This part . . . Listen to this. Louis? Are you listening?"

The music was growing louder. Zoe's voice was at his ear. "Here," she said. "The climax begins. It comes in waves, hear it?"

"Yes."

"And now, just when you think it is over—"

"Zoe . . ."

"It builds again."

"Zoe . . ."

"Hang on, it's only seven minutes long."

"That's not the problem."

The music came to a crescendo, then became quiet again, trailing off as it had begun. It ended with a tremulous climb of notes. The only sound was the cat purring in his lap. Zoe kissed his cheek and he opened his eyes.

"I like opera," he murmured.

"I knew you would."

"But I don't think I should stand up just yet."

She laughed and went to put on another tape. It was Billie Holliday. He listened to "Trav'lin' Light" and "Gimme a Pig-foot and a Bottle of Beer," a small smile tipping his lips. Zoe was tapping out the tempo lightly on his thigh. It turned to a caress as Billie Holliday moved on to "What a Little Moon-light Can Do."

The next song began, "Strange Fruit." Zoe's hand stopped

moving. They sat motionless through the brief song with its chilling images of magnolias and black bodies hanging from trees. Neither moved until the tape moved on to the next cut.

"When I was living in Mississippi, I started listening to her stuff a lot more," Louis said slowly. "But I couldn't listen to that song. I used to advance the tape when it came on."

Zoe leaned in and kissed him, her hand cupping his cheek. She pulled back, her dark eyes locked on his.

He wanted suddenly to tell her. To tell her the truth about himself, about what he was. He wanted to tell her everything, about what had happened down in Mississippi, about the bones of the black man he had found in that grave under the tree, about how he had felt when he finally found the man's murderer. He wanted to tell her about the terror he had felt in that cell when Larry Cutter put that rope around his neck and pulled it tight. He wanted to tell her about the dark things that cluttered his brain and kept him awake. He wanted to tell her because something told him she would listen.

She kissed him again, more deeply. He returned her kiss, then gently pushed away from her. He rose slowly, picking up the brandy glass. He took a deep drink and went toward the fireplace. He stared at the painting, unable to turn around and face her.

After a moment, she came up and put her arms around his waist, leaning into him.

"What would you like to do now?" she said softly.

What he wanted to do was make love. But he couldn't look at her. Not just yet.

"Can I see your paintings?" he asked.

"All right," she said. "They're in the other room."

He followed her into an adjoining room. She switched on a small lamp. In contrast to the living room, this room was barren. There was no furniture except for a table and one old chair. The table was covered with tubes of paints and cans holding brushes. In one corner stood a large easel, which held a bare white canvas about four by three feet. The north wall of the room was given over entirely to two huge bare windows. Outside, in the moonlight, Louis could see that all the trees within ten yards of the cabin had been cut down. Zoe saw him staring at the stumps.

"I had to take them out. I needed the light," she said. "You won't arrest me or something, will you."

He turned sharply, then realized she was joking about his "job" with the forestry department. He shook his head.

He went to the table, touching the tubes of paint. Zoe hovered behind him. His eyes went finally to the canvases stacked in the corner against the wall and he picked one up. It was a landscape of the lake in winter, a stark study in grays, whites and blacks. He put it back and looked through the others. They were all variations on the same theme: somber-toned studies of nature caught in its coldest moments.

He turned to look at her. "They're good. But . . . bleak. Why no people?"

"I don't know."

She was looking up at him. She seemed suddenly self-conscious, vulnerable, in a way she never did, even when they made love. "I've never let anyone in here before," she said.

He couldn't think of anything to say.

"I'd like to paint you," she said.

"What?"

"I've been thinking about it all night. I want to paint you." She hurried to the table.

Louis stared at her back. "Right now?" he asked.

She turned, smiling. "Why not? Take off your shirt."

"Zoe—"

She had pulled her hair back in a ponytail and was rummaging through a box of charcoal. She turned and saw that he hadn't moved. "Come on, it'll be fun," she said with a smile. "I'll turn on the space heater for you."

She went to the easel and set up a small canvas. He hesitated, then pulled his sweatshirt off over his head.

"Just sit down in the chair," Zoe said. "However you're comfortable."

Reluctantly, he sat down in the overstuffed chair. Zoe studied him for a moment, then repositioned one of his arms on the back of the chair. She took her place behind the easel.

"Don't move," she said.

"For how long?" he asked.

"Until I get you sketched in."

The room grew quiet. Louis sat motionless, watching her as she made swift arcing movements over the canvas. She frowned slightly in concentration as her eyes moved back and forth from the canvas to him, her gaze intense yet oddly detached. He could feel the heat of her regard moving over his body, but it was different than how she looked at him when they made love. He felt a surge move through his body and knew he was starting to get erect again.

She noticed it and laughed. She kept sketching.

His eyes drifted toward the windows. It had started to snow and the windows were starting to fog up from the space heater. He didn't realize until she spoke that he had closed his eyes and that a half hour had passed.

"You have a good face," she said, sketching.

"Good?" he said.

She nodded. "I had forgotten how it all comes out when you draw people. Their characters, it comes out." She wiped a strand of hair back from her face, leaving a black smudge of charcoal on her cheek. "I can see things in your face," she said. "Things that I try to put in my painting."

"What things?" Louis asked.

"Goodness," she said. "Grace, kindness, honor."

He looked away, out the windows. He shook his head slowly, letting his arm drop from the back of the chair. She was concentrating and didn't notice.

"Zoe . . ."

She looked up.

"Zoe, there's something I have to tell you," he said.

"What?"

He brought his arms down to rest on his knees, bowing his head.

"Louis? What is it?"

He looked up at her. "The first night, when you were talking about your father. Remember that?"

She nodded slightly, the charcoal poised above the canvas. Louis ran a hand over his head.

"For God's sake," she said with a small laugh. "What is it?"

"I lied to you. When I told you what I did for a living. I lied to you." He let out a deep breath. "I'm a cop, Zoe."

For a moment, she didn't move. Then she blinked, turned her back to him and went to the table.

"Here?" she asked.

"Yes."

Suddenly, she picked up a can of brushes and hurled it at the wall. It caught the edge of the easel and knocked it over, splashing colored water across the walls. The canvas fell to the floor. Louis reached to pick it up.

"Leave it!" she said. She was holding a hand over her eyes. It was shaking.

"Zoe," he said, taking a step toward her.

She turned abruptly. "Get out of here," she said.

"Zoe, let's talk—"

"Get out!" she yelled. She snatched his sweatshirt from the floor and threw it at him. "Get out!" She went stiffly to the windows, holding herself as she stared out at the snow.

Louis watched her for a moment, then slowly went back out into the living room. He dressed quickly, stopping at the door to pull on his running shoes. He paused, his hand on the door-knob, listening. He could hear nothing from the other room. Finally, he opened the door and stepped out into the cold.

It was snowing hard. He could barely make out the lake down below and the lights of the town far beyond. He took a few steps off the cabin's porch and down the hill, then stopped.

He turned to look back at the cabin. His chest, the entire inside
of his body, felt hollow, as though everything had been
scooped out. It burned, almost like when he had been shot.

He had fucked it up. And there was no way to go back and
change it. He pressed his hands against his gut, but the burning
wouldn't stop.

"Goddamm it," he whispered. Then louder. "Goddamn it!"
He swung and slammed his hand into a tree.

Eighteen

Louis pushed open the door of the emergency room and paused, holding up his right hand to examine the gauze wrapping. What an ass he was, ramming his fist into a tree. The pain had kept him up most of the night—that and the memory of Zoe's face. Finally, at five-thirty, he had gotten up, dressed and walked to the hospital. Just a sprain, the doctor had told him, don't use it for a couple of days.

He glanced at his watch. Seven-fifteen. Now what? He pulled up the collar of his jacket and started down the walk toward the station. There was nowhere else to go.

How could he have been so stupid? He should have told her the truth that first night. He should have been different with her than he had been with other women. Different because *she* was different, *this* was different. Even though they had known each other only a few weeks, he had felt this relationship was special, that it had the hope of going somewhere. But not now. He had blown it big time.

He turned the corner onto Main Street. The town was just starting to come to life. A couple of shop owners were out shoveling walks. The lights were on in Moe Cohick's Bakery, the smell of fresh bread wafting out on the cold air. What day was it? He wasn't even sure. Worse, he didn't care.

Deep in self-pity, he didn't hear someone calling his name. Finally, it penetrated his funk and he turned. A rusty brown Honda Civic slid up to the curb. The passenger window rolled down and a pink face peered out. "Hey, you need a lift?"

Louis stared at the guy dumbly.

"Delp," the man said. "Doug Delp. Reporter, *Argus?*"

Louis turned and trudged on.

The Civic followed slowly. "Where you heading?" Delp called.

Louis didn't turn around.

"Officer? Officer Kincaid? Hey, we should talk."

"Nothing to talk about, man," Louis shot back over his shoulder without stopping. The last thing he needed now was some punk reporter gnawing on his ear.

"How about Duane Lacey?"

Louis stopped and stared at Delp, who had leaned over to look out the passenger window.

"What do you know about Lacey?" Louis said.

"Just what I hear," Delp said, nodding toward the police scanner mounted to his dashboard.

"Get lost," Louis said, turning away.

"I heard you let him go. That true?" Delp said.

Louis came back to the car. He pointed a finger into the open window. "Stay out of my face, Delp," he said slowly.

Delp put up his gloved hands. "Hey, just doing my job, just following up. Always a good idea, following up."

Louis started walking again.

"I found these clips about Lacey," Delp called out.

Louis turned. Delp was holding a manila envelope out the window.

"Strange, isn't it?" Delp said. "Why would my newspaper have a file full of old articles about some dirtbag from the U.P.?"

Louis came forward. "Let me see that."

Delp pulled the file back quickly. "Quid pro quo."

"What?"

Delp smiled and opened the door. "You show me yours, I'll show you mine. Come on. I'll buy you breakfast. You look like you need it."

Five minutes later, they were seated in a booth in the back

corner of Dot's. Louis waited until Delp had ordered breakfast and the waitress had left.

"What you do to your hand?" Delp asked.

"Nothing," Louis said, putting his hand below the table. "Now what do you have on Lacey?"

Delp smiled and held up the envelope. "This is hot, man, it's so fucking hot."

It took all of Louis's patience not to reach over and snatch the envelope from the asshole's hand. "Show me," Louis said.

Delp leveled his brown eyes from beneath the brim of his Lions cap. "First tell me why you let Lacey go," he said.

"I can't share the details of an ongoing investigation."

"Bullshit."

The waitress appeared with two steaming mugs. Louis dumped in a stream of sugar and awkwardly picked up the spoon with his bandaged hand to stir it in.

"That much sugar's bad for you," Delp said.

Louis set down the spoon. "Look, are you going to show me what you have or do I have to go over to that rag or yours and pull this myself?"

"You can't. Closed 'til tomorrow," Delp said with a smile. "But I can save you a lot of time. It's all in this envelope."

Louis took a drink of coffee. "What do you want from me?"

"Just information."

"I can't tell you anything without clearance."

"I know that. I just want to be in on everything you get." Delp's smile faded. "Because when this comes out, the big papers are going to be on this like stink on shit, and I want it first."

Louis studied the young reporter. What did it matter? The kid was an idiot and Lacey wasn't a suspect anymore.

"Why'd you let Lacey go?" Delp pressed.

"Because he was in prison at the time of the murders."

Delp frowned. "Man, that doesn't figure."

"What do you mean?" Louis asked.

Delp sifted through the clips and held one out. Louis patted his shirt and let out a sigh. He had left his glasses at work. "Just tell me," he said impatiently.

"Duane Lacey had good reason to be pissed at you guys," he said.

"Why?"

"You killed two of his kids," Delp said.

Louis stared at him. "What?"

"Well, not you. You weren't here."

"Where?"

"Right here in Loon Lake. Nineteen seventy-nine."

"What do you mean, 'killed two of his kids'?"

"It's right here, man."

Louis took the clipping. He couldn't make out the small print of the story, but the headline made him pull in a breath.

TEENS KILLED IN LOON LAKE RAID
BY ARNOLD ROGERS

There were two thumbnail black-and-white photos of the kids, probably high school yearbook pictures. Louis squinted to make out their features. Jesus, one was a girl.

"What happened?" Louis asked.

"Apparently, the kids broke into a tourist cabin up on the north end," Delp said. "At least one of them was wanted by the cops for gang stuff and they tracked them to the cabin. The cops called them out, but the kids had guns and fired back. Cops threw in gas, but two of the three kids were killed."

"Two?"

"Yeah. The twins. The youngest survived."

Louis took a slow drink of coffee, thinking of the letter from Lacey's son at Red Oak. "How'd you find out about Lacey?"

"Well, I wasn't working here then, but when I heard Lacey's name on the scanner yesterday, I mentioned it to my editor and he kinda vaguely remembered hearing the name before.

So I ran it through the morgue and came up with all these clips."

"Can I have this?" Louis asked.

Delp pushed the envelope across the table. "Go ahead. There are plenty of copies."

"I'll need to talk to Rogers."

"Can't. He croaked last winter. Heart attack. Guess that's what twenty years covering cops will do to you."

Louis was staring at the photographs of the Lacey twins.

"Too many guns, that's what I think," Delp said, shaking his head. "People here love their guns. Kids here get rifles when they lose their baby teeth."

Louis looked at Delp. "You're not from here, are you?"

"Hell no," Delp said. "I'm from Detroit, and I'm just trying to get back there as fast as I can."

Louis stood up and pulled on his jacket, picking up the envelope.

"So, what you going to do about Lacey?" Delp said quickly.

Louis didn't answer as he started for the door.

"Hey! You let me know!" Delp called out.

Louis hurried back to the station. In the locker room, he quickly changed into his uniform and went right to the files. He tugged at the drawer labeled NOVEMBER 1979. It was locked. He would have to wait for Dale.

He went to his desk, taking the envelope Delp had given him. He spotted his glasses, hanging from the pencil holder where Ollie had left them. He put them on and opened the folder.

There were only four articles. The longest was the one he had looked at in Dot's with the headline and two photographs.

BY ARNOLD ROGERS
Argus Staff Writer

LOON LAKE—Two teenagers were killed and a third taken into custody after a routine raid on a tourist cabin by city police here Wednesday.

John Andrew "Johnny" Lacey, 16, and Angela Lee Lacey, 16, of 476 Manetta Dr., were shot by police after the teenagers fired on the officers who had tracked them to a remote cabin on north Loon Lake, owned by David and Glenda Eden of Dearborn, Michigan.

Police had been searching for the teens who were believed to be involved in a gang terrorizing tourists in the resort town. It is believed the teens were using the cabin as a hideout.

According to Chief Brian Gibralter, officers ordered the teens to surrender and after firing tear gas into the cabin, the teens opened fire on the five officers outside.

Chief Gibralter added that John Lacey ran from the cabin and was killed during a scuffle with Officer Jesse Harrison, when Harrison's gun accidentally discharged. Lacey's sister, Angela, was shot and killed when she fired on the officers.

Cole Lacey, 12, was found hiding in a closet and was taken into custody. John Lacey, according to Chief Gibralter, was the suspected leader of a teenage gang, centered in Oscoda County, that has been responsible for a series of burglaries of tourist cabins in the area.

Police are investigating whether the gang was also involved in the robbery of a convenience store July 24. During the robbery, the store clerk, Denise Lawicki, 22, was beaten.

"The outcome of this episode is very distressing for all involved," said Chief Gibralter. "The deaths of the two young people were tragic and unfortunate."

Chief Gibralter added that there will be an internal review of the incident to assess that the officers involved acted within normal procedure.

"However, all evidence points to the fact that these men had reason to fear for their lives and acted out of self-defense," the chief added.

Helen Lacey, the mother of the three teenagers, refused
to speak with this reporter.

Louis set the article down. No mention of dear old Dad. He
went through the remaining three articles. One was a follow-up
that offered no new information. The second was a short story
saying the "internal investigation" revealed no wrong doing
on the part of the Loon Lake officers. The fourth article was
an overwrought feature on teenage gangs, pegged to the Lacey
kids. The headline was WHEN GOOD KIDS GO BAD. It was
written by a woman reporter and was filled with stock quotes
from psychologists and juvenile authorities speculating on the
sources of teen violence. But the reporter had taken the trouble
to track down Duane Lacey and ended her story with the neat
coda: "For the Lacey children, the seeds of violence were sown
in the home. Their father, Duane Lacey, is currently incarcer-
ated in Marquette State Prison, serving the seventh year of his
fifteen-year sentence for assault with a deadly weapon."

Louis felt a tightening in his chest. Christ, why had no one
told him about this? Gibralter had directed him to go through
the case files, but why in the hell hadn't he thought of Duane
Lacey as a potential suspect? And Jesse . . . He had been at
the raid. Why didn't he say anything?

Louis read again the last paragraph of the feature story. All
right, it said Lacey was in prison. So had the fax from the
department of corrections. But the fax could have been wrong.
He knew prison records were routinely screwed up, especially
computer records, which were often inputted by clerk convicts.

He had not double-checked it. Shit, what if the record was
wrong?

He felt a trickle of sweat make its way down his back under
his shirt. He glanced up at the clock. It was still too early. The
DOC wouldn't open until eight.

"Morning, Louis."

Louis turned to see Dale coming in from the locker room.
Dale started to the coffeepot. "Hey, how come you didn't make

the coffee yet?" he said amiably. "But then again, you don't do such a great job anyway, no offense."

Louis was silent. Finally, Dale looked up and saw Louis's stony expression. "Something wrong?" he asked.

Looking into Dale's pink face, Louis realized suddenly he was angry. He was angry at Dale. He was angry at Jesse and Gibralter. He was angry at all of them for not telling him about the raid on the cabin. And he was angry at himself for not double-checking.

"Louis? What is it?" Dale asked.

"Nothing," he said, turning back to his desk. "I need a file," he said tersely.

"Sure, no problem," Dale said cautiously, "just let me get the coffee—"

Louis spun around. "Just give me the keys. I'll get it."

Dale stared at him for a moment, then reached in his pocket for the keys. Louis came forward to get them, almost grabbing them from Dale's hand. He unlocked the cabinet and started sifting through the files. He couldn't find the one for the raid.

"Where the hell is it?" he muttered.

Dale came up behind him. "Let me find it. What do you need?"

Louis turned to face him. "November, 1979. John and Angela Lacey. Those names ring a bell?"

Dale looked confused. "I'll find it." He held out a mug of coffee. "Three sugars. Hey, what happened to your hand?"

Louis ignored him, took the coffee and went back to his desk. He felt a small wave of guilt as he watched Dale hunt through the file drawer. He probably had nothing to do with the raid. But right now, he was lumped in with the rest of the department. What the hell was going on here? Was it just the ineptitude of a small-town department? He couldn't believe that; Lacey was too logical a suspect, in prison or not.

Dale came over and handed him a thick file. It was labeled LACEY, JOHN. A. #79-11-543.

"I brought your mail, too," Dale said, dropping some enve-
lopes on the desk and backing away.

Louis put on his glasses and opened the file. On top was
the three-page crime report that listed suspects and victims
along with their personal information. The reporting officer
was listed as Chief Brian Gibralter, #1. Louis began to read.

*On November 23, 1979, at 16:05 hours officer Pryce
(see supplemental report #2) observed suspect #1, a
twelve-year-old white male juvenile, identified as Cole
Lacey walking along the 1400 block of Lakeside drive.
When Officer Pryce attempted to stop Lacey, the suspect
ran south approximately one hundred yards to an unoc-
cupied cabin located at 1387 Lakeside Drive. Suspect entered the cabin.*

*Officer Pryce approached the cabin and at that time
heard activity, leading officer Pryce to believe the cabin
was occupied by more than the suspect. Officer Pryce
verbally advised the suspect to vacate the premises. At
this time, unknown suspect inside the premises yelled,
"Fuck you, come and get me."*

*At this time officer Pryce called for backup, advising
Central he was involved in a foot pursuit that had con-
cluded with a challenge to enter. Chief Gibralter, #1, and
Officers Harrison, #13, Wickshaw, #8, and Lovejoy, #10
(supplemental reports #3, #4, #5) responded to the scene.
Upon arriving at the scene, I observed officer Pryce positioned by his patrol car. Officer Pryce advised that he
had made numerous attempts to persuade the suspects to
vacate the premises and that an unknown number of suspects had responded with verbal threats.*

*I assumed command of the situation and directed offi-
cers Wickshaw, Lovejoy and Harrison to secure the cabin
by taking positions at the cabin's corners. Positioned in
front of the cabin, I attempted again to persuade suspects*

*to surrender. They responded with numerous verbal ob-
scenities.*

*At approximately 16:20 hours I ordered tear gas acti-
vated. Tear gas was launched through both front windows.
Unknown suspects began to shout from inside the premises.*

*At approximately 16:28 hours, suspect #2, John A. La-
cey, white male juvenile, exited the premises through the
rear door. Suspect attempted to elude officer Harrison,
who radioed for assistance. Suspect J. Lacey ran south
toward the property's rear perimeter approximately
twenty-five yards. Officer Harrison tackled suspect and
attempted to subdue him. Officer Harrison's shotgun discharged, hitting subject on the left front facial area. Suspect died at the scene.*

*Officers Wickshaw, Lovejoy and myself abandoned our
positions to assist officer Harrison. At this time, suspect
#3, Angela L. Lacey, white female juvenile, exited the
premises through the rear door, armed with a small cali-
ber handgun. She positioned herself on the deck and an-
nounced she intended to shoot the officers unless they
allowed her to leave the scene.*

*Officers Wickshaw and Lovejoy ordered the suspect to
drop her weapon. Suspect refused. Suspect then raised
her weapon and fired at officers. Officer Wickshaw discharged his weapon, fatally wounding her in the chest.
Officers Lovejoy and Wickshaw then entered the premises
through the rear door to secure them. Suspect #1, C. Lacey was found hiding in a closet in the rear upstairs bedroom. After threatening officers with a gun, suspect
surrendered without incident.*

No officers were injured in this action.

Louis closed his eyes, his face burning with anger. "Goddamn it, goddamn it to hell," he muttered.

Dale looked over, but said nothing.

Louis ran a hand over his face, and went on through the file. He was stopped cold by a photograph. It was of Angela Lacey. She was slumped against the wood exterior of the cabin, her Mackinaw Island sweatshirt drenched in blood. There was a gun near her open palm.

A girl, for chrissakes, a girl who should have been going to a prom, but was holed up in a cabin with a gun shooting at cops.

Louis looked at the clock. It was eight, straight up. He redialed the Department of Corrections. For a second, he hoped no one would answer.

"Department of Corrections, Ms. Meyers speaking."

Louis explained what he needed.

"It'll take me a few minutes, officer," she said, "the computer this morning is—"

"No," Louis interrupted. "No computer. I need you to pull the hard copy."

"Well, that's not really necessary—"

"Yes, it is," Louis said sharply. "It is very important that I verify this information. Please."

The woman sighed. "This will take a while. Why don't you give me your—"

"I'll hold."

While he waited, Louis sifted through the other reports. First Jesse's, then Ollie's, then Lovejoy's, but they offered no new information. He went back to the photos.

The first dozen were routine crime-scene photos, and he went through them quickly. Bloodstained snow, broken windows, tear gas canisters and Pryce's patrol car. There were two photos of Johnny Lacey. One was a mug shot showing him as a handsome kid with chopped blond hair and an arrogant smirk. The second was a closeup of him after he had been shot. The entire left cheekbone area of his face was gone, leaving a gaping dark hole.

"Officer Kincaid? Are you still there?"

"Yes, I am," Louis said, shifting the phone.

"The file says this man was released November 10, 1984, on the governor's early release program."

"November? Are you sure?" Louis asked.

"That's what I said."

Louis hung up and for several seconds couldn't move. November 10, not December 10. *Double-check. Double-check.* How could he have been so careless? How could his instincts have been that bad? He had fucked up. But so had they, all of them, every man in the goddamn department who knew about the raid and didn't talk about it.

"Louis, you okay?" Dale asked.

"Why didn't someone tell me about this case?" Louis asked tightly.

Dale hesitated, seeming to measure his thoughts carefully. "It was a bad time around here," he said quietly. "Jesse took it really bad."

Louis wasn't listening. His anger wouldn't let him. He glanced at his watch. Jesse and the chief were both due in soon.

"I was here when Jesse came back in after," Dale said. "He still had . . . He had blood in his hair, you know? He was in bad shape. He wouldn't talk about it."

Louis shook his head in disgust. He was tired of everyone making excuses for Jesse. Jesse had withheld information about the raid because he couldn't bring himself to talk about it?

"Louis," Dale said, "it doesn't matter. I mean, this Lacey guy was still—"

"Dale," Louis said sharply, "Lacey was out in November. He was an early release. The printout had a typo. A fucking typo."

For several seconds, Dale just stared at him. Then, he turned and walked slowly back to his desk. The silence was broken by the squeak of Dale's chair. Louis looked over at him. Dale was pale, his eyes locked on Pryce's and Lovejoy's photographs hanging on the wall.

Louis closed the file. "Dale, make me a copy of this, will you?" Louis said.

Dale nodded slowly, taking the file.

Gibralter's voice broke the silence as it came over the radio. "Loon-1 to Central," Gibralter said, "I'm going to be 10-6 for a while. Hold the briefing until I arrive."

Dale didn't move.

"Dale," Louis called out. "The radio."

Dale grabbed the mike and acknowledged.

"Tell him I need to talk to him—that it's important," Louis said.

Dale nodded woodenly and relayed the message. Louis heard Gibralter come back that he'd see him after briefing.

"No," Louis said sharply. "Tell him it can't wait."

Nineteen

Louis glanced again at his watch. Eight-twenty. Where the hell was Gibralter? The man was never late for briefing.

Louis's eyes went to Jesse, sitting across the room. He felt a new spurt of anger, but forced it back. When Jesse had come in, he had wanted to confront him right there with the raid file, throw the damn thing in his face. But he knew he had to keep a calm head right now when he talked to Gibralter.

A blast of cold air filled the room. Louis turned to see Gibralter come in. He quickly turned away to avoid eye contact.

"Kincaid, in my office," Gibralter said, handing his parka to Dale.

Jesse looked up questioningly. Louis didn't look at him as he passed.

"Shut the door."

Louis closed the door and turned to face Gibralter.

"Now what was so damn important?" Gibralter demanded.

"We picked up a suspect yesterday," Louis began.

"Duane Lacey," Gibralter said.

Louis nodded. "He looked good, but his sheet said he was in prison until December 10. So I cut him loose."

"And?" Gibralter said.

"The release date was wrong. It was a typo," Louis said. "I called the DOC this morning. Lacey was released November 10."

Gibralter didn't move, not a muscle, not an eyebrow, nothing. From outside came the sounds of the other day-shift men waiting for briefing. The smell of brewing coffee drifted in. Louis realized he was holding his breath and let it out. The red carpet beneath his feet seemed to be moving, undulating.

Gibralter turned away, going to the window.

"Why didn't you tell me about his dead kids?" Louis asked.

"Lacey wasn't a suspect. He was in prison."

"You should have checked," Louis said.

Gibralter turned to face him. "We did, Kincaid. I assigned it to Jesse."

Louis's gaze dropped to the carpet again. Jesus, Jesse had relied on the written record instead of calling, just like he had.

"Jesse fucked up," Gibralter said. "But that doesn't make what you did any less stupid. You had a description of the truck and you had Lacey in custody. You should have held him."

"On what?" Louis shot back.

"Anything," Gibralter said, raising his voice. "You had him, Kincaid, and you shouldn't have let him go."

Louis bit back the angry words forming in his head. Lacey was on the loose to kill again. He himself was willing to take some of the blame, but he wasn't going to let Gibralter crucify him alone.

"Am I dismissed, *sir?*" he asked, the last word taking on an edge.

"Yes. But before you show your face at briefing, I want an APB put out."

Louis nodded, turned and left. The outer office was deserted, the other men waiting in the briefing room. Louis went quickly to his desk, scribbled down the particulars on Lacey and went to the dispatch desk.

"Flo, put this out, ASAP, please," Louis said.

She took the paper and read it, her eyes widening. Louis could hear her soft voice going out over the airwaves as he headed to the briefing room.

He paused outside the door to take a calming breath, then

went in. Gibralter was standing in his usual place behind the lectern. Five officers sat in folding chairs, including Dale. There were no other chairs, so Louis stood at the back of the room. Gibralter was staring at him. Suddenly, he knew what was going to happen. He was going to get lectured, right there in front of everyone.

"Stay where you are, and introduce yourself, officer."

Louis forced himself to look at Gibralter. He focused on a small white mark on his jaw, the white smudge of a styptic pencil.

"Let me help you," Gibralter said, moving around in front of the lectern. "My name is Kincaid and I am a bleeding heart pussy who feels sorry for cop killers and I have no concept of what it means to wear a badge like the rest of these fine men."

Louis felt his body go tight. The room was dead silent and the five faces became a blur.

"Explain to your fellow officers why you let a cop killer go."

Louis kept his eyes on Gibralter. "The computer report said Lacey was still in prison. We didn't—"

Gibralter cut in sharply. "Take responsibility for your own actions, officer. There is no *we* in this scenario."

Louis glanced at Jesse, but he wouldn't look at him. "I had no reason to hold him," Louis said slowly.

Gibralter picked something up off the lectern and held it up to the room. It was a photograph of Thomas Pryce, spread-eagled on his staircase, his pajamas covered with his blood.

"Is this not a good enough reason, officer?"

Louis felt his face grow hot.

"What about this?" Gibralter asked, holding up another photograph. It was a close-up of Lovejoy's face, his eyes open, his hair forming a halo of little icicle spikes around his face.

"I made a mistake," Louis said stiffly. "But I put out the APB, we can still find him—"

"He's gone!" Gibralter yelled. "He's fucking gone! Do you think he's as stupid as you are?"

The room was silent as a tomb. Gibralter came forward, pausing inches in front of Louis. He reached up suddenly and pulled off Louis's tie, ripping the collar open. Louis stumbled back, then steadied himself, glaring at Gibralter.

Fired! He was being fired. A flash of shame came over him, followed by a wave of relief. Gibralter reached for his shirt again and Louis tightened, expecting Gibralter to rip his badge off his pocket. Gibralter stuffed the two photographs down Louis's shirt.

Louis went rigid, his jaw clenching in anger.

"Tell them," Gibralter said softly. "Tell these men how sorry you are."

Louis kept his eyes locked on Gibralter's face.

"Tell them!" Gibralter shouted.

Louis pulled the photographs from his shirt and looked at the other men. He saw Cornwall and Evans, their faces charged with contempt. His eyes settled on Jesse, who was staring at his shoes.

"I am sorry," Louis said hoarsely.

A phone rang out in the office. Someone coughed. Louis could not stand it any longer and dropped his gaze to the floor.

"All right, listen to me," Gibralter said, going back to the lectern. "Here is where we are going to begin."

When Louis looked up, he saw that Gibralter had gone to a map that had been put up on the bulletin board. Louis stared at the map. It was nothing but a patchwork of colors and he struggled to bring it into focus, struggled to bring himself back into focus.

He took slow, careful breaths, trying to quell his anger. He wasn't going to let Gibralter win, not this way. He wasn't going to let Gibralter humiliate him, blame him, and then drive him out. He would stay until that fucking bastard Lacey was caught.

Gibralter was giving assignments for a search, and Louis concentrated on the map on the wall. The county was a large square with a grand total of five towns big enough to merit dots. About a third of the county was given over to the Huron National Forest. The rest was sheer wilderness. Thousands of square miles to hide in.

Louis shook his head. Nine men . . . Jesus Christ, they would never find Lacey. They would need help from the state police. Why wasn't Gibralter talking about that?

Finally, Gibralter dismissed the men. They filed past Louis, no one making eye contact. Louis waited. He knew this wasn't over. Gibralter leaned on the lectern, his eyes locked on Louis. He drew a cigarette out of his pack of Camels and slipped it between his lips. Slowly, he lit the cigarette. It sizzled in the quiet room.

"What do you think I should do with you?" Gibralter said.

"Suspension would be in order," Louis said tightly.

"No."

"Am I fired?"

"No."

"Then what will be my exact assignment during the search?"

"You think I'm going to put you out there with the rest of the men?"

Louis decided not to answer.

"First of all, you don't *deserve* to be with them," Gibralter said, pointing the cigarette. "And second, the way they feel about you right now, I wouldn't put it past someone to take a shot at you."

Louis felt the knot of anger reforming in his gut.

Gibralter straightened off the lectern and went to the map, his back to Louis. "Right now, if we're going to find this motherfucker Lacey, I need every man I have. If I didn't need you, you'd be gone. You understand?"

I understand that we need outside help, damn it, Louis thought.

"But I don't want you around here right now, Kincaid," Gibralter said, turning to him. "I don't want to see your face. You're going to Dollar Bay."

"Excuse me?"

"Lacey lives in Dollar Bay. I want you up there to find out anything you can. Take the Bronco unit number three. The keys are in the box. Pack what you have in your locker, get a few personal things from home and get the hell out of here." Gibralter turned away. "Dismissed."

Louis stared at Gibralter's back. Shit, he was being exiled. Lacey wasn't going back to the U.P. now. He was still here, hiding and waiting until he could kill the rest of the men who had been at the raid that night. Lacey was here. And Louis was not going to be allowed in on the real work of finding him.

Louis left the briefing room, closing the door. The outer office was deserted, except for Florence, who gave him a quick look of sympathy, then averted her eyes.

He went quickly to his desk, threw some things into a large manila envelope and headed to the locker room. It was empty and as he approached his locker, he slowed. The locker was ajar. He never locked it; no one here did.

He opened it slowly. Hanging from the hook was a used Kotex sanitary napkin with a note that had one word: *Pussy.*

Twenty

There was too much empty road and too much time to think on the way to Dollar Bay.

About Pryce, Lovejoy and Lacey. About watches that ran in cold water, serial numbers on meaningless guns. About dead teenage girls and Jesse's hair-trigger temper. About Gibralter. About Zoe. About himself.

Keeping his left hand on the wheel, Louis used his thumb of his bandaged right hand to ease the lid off the Styrofoam cup. He took a sip of the hot coffee and carefully set it back in the cupholder. His stomach was sending up groans of hunger, despite the greasy 7-Eleven muffin he had already downed. He glanced at his watch. Back at the 7-Eleven he had called Dollar Bay and was told Sheriff Bjork would meet him at twelve-thirty at a local tavern. He was running late and he pressed the gas pedal, easing up over the fifty-five-mile-per-hour speed limit. No matter. The road was empty. It pretty much had been that way since he crossed the Mackinaw Bridge about an hour back.

The stunning scenery flew by, but he didn't really notice it. It occurred to him that he was becoming immune to the vistas of pristine snow with their black-green frames of pine forest. He no longer saw the beauty in it, no longer found anything of charm in the stark serenity of the Michigan wilderness. Now, it all looked just . . . lonely. So incredibly, terribly lonely.

He passed through a tiny town, some speck called Little Bear, and didn't slow down. It was like the countless others he had seen as he made his way north up the peninsula. Not a human being in sight. He pressed on.

A half hour later, he came to a sign announcing the city of Houghton. He glanced down at the map open on the passenger seat. Dollar Bay was just beyond.

He had half expected Houghton to be like some Siberian tin-shack outpost, but it turned out to be a pretty town, handsome redbrick buildings built on snowy bluffs overlooking the river below. The streets were freshly plowed, lined with towering drifts. As he drove along the river, he passed the modern buildings of Michigan Tech. On the other side of the river, he could see the colorful parkas of skiers racing down a steep hill. The town had the cozy bustle of any college town, and it reminded him a little of an arctic version of Ann Arbor.

He headed the Bronco to the center of town, slowing to look for King's Tavern, where Bjork had said he would meet him for lunch. He would have preferred to conduct business at the sheriff's department, but he knew how these small-town sheriffs could be. Long on down-home wisdom but short on the kind of technical know-how that solved murder cases.

King's Tavern was a small log building set down between an antique shop and a bookstore. Louis passed it and had to do a quick U-turn. He parked, fed a couple quarters into the meter and went in.

It took him a few minutes to adjust to the dim light within, but he soon picked out the requisite mahogany bar, jukebox, pool table and booths. It looked like Jo-Jo's, but cleaner, with a pleasing hickory smell coming from a black potbellied stove. His nose also picked up a delicious meaty smell.

His eyes swept the flannel-clad patrons. Great, so where was Dudley Do-Right already?

"Kincaid?"

Louis turned at the sound of the soft voice. A woman's face poked out from the last booth. She was wearing a brown shirt. Louis stared. There was a badge pinned to it.

"Over here." She waved him over.

He went slowly to the booth, taking off his hat. She stuck out her hand.

"Sheriff Bjork," she said.

He stared at her, dumbfounded.

"Sit down, please," she said.

Louis slid in across from her. She was about forty, with a strong, square-jawed, sun-freckled face. Lines fanned out from her lively blue eyes, framed by sprigs of red hair that sprouted from her heavy braid. Christ, a woman sheriff. Louis could almost feel the gears shifting as his brain tried to digest this.

A small smile played on her lips. She was enjoying his confusion and wasn't going to give him an easy entrée into conversation by apologizing for her gender.

"I hope you don't mind, but I went ahead and ordered for us," she said.

"No, no, that's fine," Louis said.

"What'll ya have to drink?"

"Ah, Dr Pepper, if they've got it."

"Dave!" Sheriff Bjork yelled out.

"Yeah, Liddie?"

"You got Dr Pepper back there?"

"Got Coke, Vernor's, 7-Up, Faygo Rock and Rye. That's it for pop."

Bjork looked at Louis.

"Coke," Louis said.

Sheriff Bjork settled back in the booth. Louis found himself staring at her badge. And at her breasts. They were big and healthy, like the sheriff herself seemed to be. He was grateful when Dave brought over a Coke and glass, and he immersed himself in the process of pouring it.

"So, how was the drive up?" Sheriff Bjork asked.

"Fine. Roads were pretty clear."

"You have trouble finding King's here?"

"No, not at all."

"Saw that little U-ey you did out there. That's illegal here."

He managed a smile. "Professional courtesy?"

She returned the smile and nodded. "So, where you want to start with Lacey?"

"Well, with any records you might have on him."

She set a thick folder on the table. "I could have faxed you this stuff. You didn't have to make the trip."

"My chief thought it would be better this way," Louis said. "Plus, I want to talk to his mother."

"Millie?" Bjork slowly shook her head. "I don't know how much help she can be to you."

"Why?"

"She's not exactly Donna Reed."

Louis nodded. "Just the same, I need to see Lacey's home."

Bjork shrugged. "It's after noon. She might be sobered up by now."

Dave came to the table and deposited two plates between them. Louis looked down at the steaming, fragrant pielike concoction.

"It's a pastie," Bjork said. "Kinda like a Swanson's pot pie, only better." She smiled. "It's the *ne plus ultra* of Yooper cuisine."

Louis took a bite. It was delicious. "May I?" he said, pulling over the file.

Bjork nodded, digging into her food. Louis quickly scanned the contents of the file. It was filled with detailed reports: Lacey's arrest records, including copies of every incident report, judicial files, fingerprints, even high school transcripts. Louis focused on the military record. It took him a moment, but he found it: Lacey had been attached to the 123rd squadron in Vietnam. He closed the file.

"This is very complete," he said.

Bjork gazed at him over the frosty glass. "You sound surprised."

"No, I just . . . well—"

"We run a very professional department here, Officer Kincaid," Bjork said.

"I didn't mean—"

"Do you know how many Yoopers it takes to screw in a lightbulb?"

"Pardon?"

"None. We don't have electricity here."

Louis smiled weakly.

"You hear about the Yooper who saw the billboard that said 'Drink Canada Dry'? He's been trying to ever since."

Louis gave a chuckle.

She smiled. "We know what you think of us up here. We know you think we do nothing but hunt deer, drink and go bowling. That's how you trolls see us, right?"

"Trolls?"

"Yeah, all you folks who live 'under the bridge.' "

Louis laughed.

"Eat up, Officer Kincaid," Bjork said. "And I'll take you to meet Millie."

"Call me Louis, please."

She gave him a curt nod. "Only if you call me Bjork."

They rode in Bjork's Jeep. Leaving Houghton, they passed over an old iron bridge that spanned a partially frozen river. Abandoned shipping berths loomed to the south, framing the river like a giant rusty chain. Hancock on the other side was not nearly as pretty as its sister-city Houghton and faded quickly as Bjork steered her Jeep up a hill and out of town. Five or six miles later, they saw the state-issue, green metal sign for Dollar Bay.

The town itself had a haphazard look, as though it had come together out of plain bad luck rather than some neat chamber of commerce design. Even the streets seemed an after-thought—no names, just numbers that intersected letters. The town's core was a clump of buildings: a general store, a beauty parlor, a bar and further on, a ramshackle lumberyard.

Louis stared at the rows of shingled houses that made up Dollar Bay's residential area. Gray . . . Everything here was gray. Even the damn snow. The place smelled of dirt, rust and defeat. Cloverdale's profile came back to him in that moment. "The blue-collar dream gone gray."

They passed a two-story school of old brick and just as Louis was wondering why they needed a school so large, Bjork told him that it drew students from all around the area.

"So Lacey went there?" Louis asked.

"Me, too."

"Did you know him?"

She nodded. "There were only ten in my graduating class. So yeah, I knew Duane."

"What was he like?" Louis asked.

"Quiet. Skinny. Skipped school a lot, ya know? I never took him to be dangerous, though. He was just one of those weird guys who took shop class, smoked in the john and lurked around the edges of everything." She reached down and pulled out a thin blue book. "Here's our yearbook. Make sure you get it back to me."

Louis took it and opened to the seniors. He quickly found Lacey's picture. He was thin faced and unsmiling, his odd watery eyes unsettling even then. He looked like some kind of feral animal, like a stray cat or ferret. There was nothing listed under his name except "Audio-Visual Club." The yearbook editors had used popular song titles for future predictions, and in a stroke of cruelty some smartass had stuck Lacey with Chuck Berry's "No Particular Place to Go."

"Duane wanted to go to college," Bjork said.

"College?" Louis said.

"Yeah. He applied to Tech, but didn't get in. Couple months later, he got arrested, joyriding with some older kids in a stolen car. Judge told Lacey to shape up or he was headed for jail. Recommended he join the service."

"Lacey have a juvenile record?"

"Yeah, but it's sealed."

Louis nodded. "Judges think if parents can't straighten a kid out, the service will."

"Well, all I know is we were glad he was somebody's else's problem for a change," Bjork said, swinging the Jeep down a side street. "He was gone for eight years, on and off. Then one day, I saw him in town, standing outside the Rexall. He was discharged, but still wearing his uniform, boots, the whole shot. He wore his fatigues and hair shaved off for months."

"Lots of vets were raw around the edges," Louis said, remembering what Cloverdale had said.

Bjork shook her head. "It was more than that. Duane was always weird, but he was downright creepy when he got back. Always talking about how the government was screwing everybody over." Bjork glanced over at him. "I mean, lots of folks around here feel the same way, that their freedoms are being chipped away and they want authority off their backs."

She shook her head again. "But Duane seemed to take it personal. I remember one day, he walked into the post office, cut up his driver's license and social security card and threw the pieces at the poor woman behind the desk."

"Was he ever involved in any organized antigovernment groups?" Louis asked.

"He joined the Michigan Militia. But we keep an eye on them and they're pretty harmless," Bjork said. "They sit in their trucks, get tanked up on beer and bitch a lot. But next morning, they go back to work with a hangover and forget about it."

"And Lacey?"

Bjork shrugged. "Not enough action for him. He dropped out after six months." Bjork slowed the Jeep. "This is it."

Louis looked up. It was a narrow, two-story, gray-shingled house, just like all the others. There were crackled wooden flower boxes beneath the front small windows, tendrils of dead plants snaking out through the snow. As he got out of the Jeep, Louis peered around the side. No red truck.

"We checked the house this morning when we heard the BOLO, but Lacey wasn't here," Bjork said, getting out of the

Jeep. "Since then, we've had Dennis down there keeping an eye out. Lacey hasn't shown up."

As Louis closed his door, he saw a Jeep sitting a block down the snowy road.

Bjork trudged to the porch through knee-high drifts and knocked hard on the door.

"Have you spoken to his mother?" Louis asked, following.

"Usually she's three sheets to the wind. Maybe we'll have better luck hitting her this early in the day."

Bjork banged again and the thin curtain in the small window moved slightly. "It's okay, Mrs. Cronk, it's just me," Bjork called.

The door cracked and a pale single eye, embedded in shriveled skin, peeked out at them.

"Cops again?"

Bjork opened the screen and gently pushed against the wood door. Millie Cronk moved backward and let them enter.

The house was dark as a cave and smelled of stale liquor and cigarettes. Dust and smoke floated in a ray of yellow light from a torn window shade.

Millie was small, a humped shadowy figure huddled near the bottom step of a long, steep staircase. The top disappeared into darkness. Bjork reached in front of Louis and flipped on a switch. A weak overhead lamp lit up the foyer. Millie withdrew like a mole unused to sunshine.

"You sober today, Millie?" Bjork asked. "I need to talk to you about Duane."

Millie's lip curled and she shuffled off toward the living room, her hand on the wall. They followed her, and Bjork flipped up the torn shade, flooding the room in sunlight.

Louis glanced around. The tables were old mahogany stuff that almost looked valuable, except for the glass rings and dust that covered them. Millie's couch was, what, green, maybe? It was covered in frayed afghans and doilies, yellow with nicotine stains.

Louis forced his attention back to Millie. She had slumped

down on the couch, her hands clasped between her knees. A cotton housedress, splashed with ugly daisies, hung over her knees. She had on calf-high stockings and dirty pink fur slippers with little pig snouts and plastic eyes.

She combed her bleached hair with shaking fingers. She looked up, her eyes slithering to Louis's face. "Who's he?"

"He's from down under, Millie. He's looking for Duane."

"What's he done now?" she asked. Her voice was husky, scarred with years of smoke and booze.

"Officer Kincaid thinks Duane might have caused some trouble there and he just wants to ask you some questions, ya know?" Bjork said.

Millie raked her hair. "I don't like cops. Never did."

"Millie . . ." Bjork said.

"Why can't you just leave him alone? Why ya always gotta cause him trouble?"

Louis tensed involuntarily and he had to remind himself this was Lacey's mother. She was entitled to believe he was harmless.

"Mrs. Lacey—" Louis started.

"Cronk!" Millie spat. "My name is Cronk. I ain't been a Lacey in years."

"I'm sorry. We need to find your son. If we can locate him peacefully, no one will get hurt."

"Peaceful . . . right," Millie said with a sneer. She turned and reached for a pack of Pall Malls on the end table. A book of matches slid to the floor and Bjork picked them up. She took one look and passed them to Louis. The front said: Jo-Jo's Tavern, Loon Lake, Mi.

"When's the last time Duane was home, can you tell us that?" Bjork asked.

Millie drew in on her cigarette, her gray skin pulling over her high cheekbones. "Last Tuesday or Wednesday," she said, smoke drifting from her mouth as she talked. "It was, no, wait, about a week before Christmas. He came home 'bout the first of the month and stayed 'til . . . hell, I don't know. Days get mixed up, ya know?"

"He left around the first of December?" Louis asked.

" 'Round then, ya."

"Where did he go?" Louis asked.

"Don't you know?" Millie asked.

Louis stared at her. She had the same weird eyes as Lacey, only hers were clouded with cataracts, more milky than watery.

"He don't tell me things, ya know?" Millie went on. "He was gone a coupla days. When he got back, he started drinking and talking about things that made no sense, ya know?"

Louis stepped forward. "What did he say?"

Millie glanced around the room. Bjork watched her, then went to the tiny kitchen, returning with a bottle of Beefeater's Gin. She set it loudly on the end table.

Millie picked it up and twisted off the cap. She looked back at Bjork. "What? Ya think I got no class?"

Louis saw a glass on the coffee table and reached down to take the bottle from Millie. He poured her half a glass and handed it back.

Millie looked up at him. "I ain't never had no black man in my house before."

Louis glanced at Bjork, who rolled her eyes.

"Mrs. Cronk, did your son say anything when he got back from his trip?" Louis repeated.

"He was talking about things not goin' right. He said it was all fucked up. All fucked up."

Louis frowned. "Did he say anything else? Mention any names?"

"No, no, said he needed to think things out." She gave a little snort. "Like he could think straight. He ain't been right in the head since . . . since, shit, who knows."

"Did he take anything with him when he left?" Louis asked.

Millie's eyes were closed.

"Mrs. Cronk?" Louis said loudly.

"What?"

"Did your son take anything with him when he left here?"

She shrugged. "Clothes and food. Cleaned out the kitchen, took all the Dinty Moore and Spaghettios. Took my truck, too." She puffed furiously on the cigarette, apparently upset about the truck.

"Anything else?" Louis pressed.

"His guns. And snowshoes. I 'member he went down and got 'em out of the basement."

Louis glanced at Bjork, then back at Millie. "Mrs. Cronk, may we look at Duane's room?" he asked.

"You need a warrant for that, eh?"

Bjork pulled a paper from her jacket. "Got it right here, Millie."

"Well, just don't tear anything up," Millie said, falling back into the couch.

Bjork led Louis up the gaunt staircase, pushing open several doors as they walked the narrow corridor. There were only two bedrooms and a tiny dingy bath. Bjork stepped aside so Louis could enter Lacey's room.

Louis stopped at the door. It was a small room, smelling of soiled clothes and cigarettes. The wallpaper was a drab yellow with what looked like flowers, but were little figures of cowboys and bucking horses. The furniture seemed undersized: a narrow single bed, with a tiny nightstand, a small desk and an old four-drawer bureau with DUANE carved prominently on the front. It was kid's furniture, a little boy's room. Until you looked more closely.

Louis's eyes went from the taut army blanket on the bed to a framed photograph hanging above the desk. It was of three bare-chested soldiers.

He went to the desk. It was covered with junk—papers, a few books, beer cans, an overflowing ashtray and several *Soldier of Fortune* magazines. Louis carefully sifted through the papers.

There were brochures from gun shows, including one flyer that shouted "Get Yours Before It's too Late." There was an ad for fully dressed AK-47s, "VISA and MasterCard Accepted," and another for flak vests and rifles with infrared scopes. A flyer hawked burial tubes to hide guns and food in preparation for "The New World Order."

Louis turned his attention to the small stack of books. There was a paperback called *How to Create a New Identity* and a guide to Third Reich daggers. Another was a poorly bound paperback that detailed homemade bombs. Louis picked up the last book, titled *The Turner Diaries,* by a man named William Pierce. His gut tightened. He had heard about the book before. It was a novel set in the future, the late 1990s, about a race war in the United States. The hero, Earl Turner, leads a group of Aryan warriors who dole out justice by lynching or shooting Jews, blacks, journalists, politicians, feminists and race-mixers.

"What's that?" Bjork asked, coming up behind him.

"His bible," Louis muttered, tossing it back on the desk.

Louis looked back at the photograph of the GI's and spotted Lacey immediately. He took the photo off the wall. He felt suddenly lightheaded in the stuffy room and went slowly to the bed and sat down on it.

"You okay?" Bjork asked.

He looked up. Bjork was standing at the closet. He nodded, staring at the photograph. It was quiet, except for the scrape of wire hangers against a metal closet pole as Bjork sifted through Lacey's clothes.

Louis's glance fell on the small nightstand. He reached over and pulled open the single drawer. It was a mess of papers, nothing that looked important. He pulled out a printout from a Radio Shack store in Houghton. It was an instruction sheet on how to program something, followed by a printout of numbers.

His gaze drifted to the top of the nightstand. Its scarred top was filmed with a heavy layer of dust except for one small area about two by three inches. Louis stared at it for several seconds, then looked back at the Radio Shack printout in his hand. The spot on the nightstand was exactly the size of a portable, battery-powered scanner. The printout, he realized suddenly, showed the police frequencies for Oscoda County.

"Louis, look at this."

Bjork came over to the bed and handed Louis an envelope. It was addressed to Lacey in prison, in a childish scrawl. Louis pulled out the letter. It was from Cole, dated December 5, from the juvenile center.

Dear Dad,
I saw it on TV! I am proud of you. I can't wait until you come see me Sunday. Man, that was so cool. Everyone here was talking about how that nigger cop got blowed away. I bet that fucking Gibralter guy is pissed. And scared too now. Right? You must be feeling real good right now.

Louis handed her the letter. She read it quickly. "Bastard," she whispered, moving away.

Louis felt a tightening in his stomach. He had known when he set out for Dollar Bay that Lacey was the killer. But being here, in his room, breathing his air, made things different. It made Lacey real, more real even than he had been that day in the bar. He slipped the letter into his pocket with the Radio Shack paper.

"So, what's your area of search?"

Louis looked up at Bjork. She was leaning against the door frame, arms folded over her chest.

"What?" Louis asked.

"Where you looking for him?" she asked.

"I don't know exactly," Louis said. He looked away, not liking the question he saw in her eyes, namely, "Why the hell aren't you down there looking for him?"

"I'd bet he's holed up in the woods somewhere," Bjork said, pushing off the door.

"He'd freeze," Louis said.

Bjork shook her head. "Lacey lived outdoors all his life. When he was a kid, he built a shack out in the woods. He used to hide in there when Millie went off the deep end on one of her binges."

"You check it?"

"First thing. No sign of life."

Louis rose slowly from the bed. He glanced around the room, unsure where to go next. "I don't get it," he said softly.

"Get what?" Bjork said.

"How'd his kids get to Loon Lake? Lacey never lived there."

"His wife did. She was from there." Bjork frowned. "Shoot, can't remember her name. . . ."

"But Lacey never lived there?" Louis pressed.

Bjork shook her head. "No, but after his wife finally got fed up and put him in jail for battery, she went back down there to stay. That was in early '77, I think. Then when Duane went up for the assault, she left here for good."

"Any idea where she is now?"

Bjork shook her head. "I had my men check, but we can't find her."

"Think she'll come back?"

"Would you?" Bjork paused. "I feel sorry for Cole. My daughter went to school with him."

Louis gave a derisive sigh. "Oh yeah, Cole's a real upstanding young man. Real proud of his dad for blowing away a nigger cop." Louis shut the drawer of the nightstand roughly.

Bjork said nothing. She turned and went to the window. "I was here that first time we came out on the child-abuse complaint," she said. "I was a rookie."

Louis turned to looked at her. She was staring out the window.

"Cole was only five," she said. "He had all these little red circles on his back. He was crying and I remember thinking it was chicken pox. Turned out to be cigarette burns. Duane burned him because he wet his bed."

Louis waited, not knowing what to say.

"The doc said that he thought Cole had been sodomized, too. Probably with a broom handle. But Cole refused to tell us. The doc wouldn't swear to it in court and we had no proof. Social Services refused to act. Cole was returned to Duane after six months in the system."

Louis let out a sigh. The room was very still for a few moments.

"Helen," Bjork said finally. "That was her name. The mother . . . Helen."

She turned to face Louis. He had expected tears. She was dry eyed, her mouth pulled into a line. "Let's get out of here," she said.

He followed her down the staircase. Bjork went quickly out the front door without a word to Millie, but Louis paused at the living room, trying to think if there was anything else to ask the old woman.

She had pulled the shade back down and turned on the television. She sat hunched on the couch, backlit by the muddy amber light, puffing on her Pall Mall. Her hair spiked out around her head and her face was hid in shadows.

"Mrs. Cronk," Louis called. "Thank you for your cooperation."

Millie turned her attention away from *The Newlywed Game* to look at him, all milky eyes, smoke and Medusa hair.

"You see Duane, you tell him to call me," she said.

Louis stared at her.

She took a deep sucking drag on her cigarette, squinting back at the television through the smoke. "You talk to him, tell him I want my truck back, you hear?"

"I'll tell him," Louis said.

"Damn kid," she muttered. She turned away and punched the remote-control button, filling the fetid room with canned laughter. Louis backed out, closing the door behind him.

Twenty-one

Louis put on his glasses, crossed his legs on the bed and opened Lacey's ID file. It was several inches thick. Bjork's department had done a thorough job.

Lacey's mug shot was on top. Louis stared at it but didn't touch it. Finally, he brushed it aside and turned to the lengthy general report.

Lacey was born March 1, 1940, in Houghton, Michigan. He graduated from Houghton County High in 1959, held back a year in junior high. He was arrested in July of 1959 for joyriding and failure to stop for a police officer. The judge recommended the armed services. Lacey joined the army on August 5, 1959.

Louis paused, wiping his brow. The hotel room was hot and stuffy. He glanced at the heater, a long metal contraption under the window that seemed to have two settings: high and stifling. He rolled off the bed and went to crack the window. A stream of cold air slithered in. Louis reached out to the snowy window sill and snagged a can of Dr Pepper from the six-pack he had set out there earlier.

He returned to the bed, taking a long swig, then pulled out Lacey's military record.

After basic training, Lacey spent an uneventful couple of years in the army, returning home to Dollar Bay in 1962 only long enough to marry Helen Scully and father Johnny and Angela. He reenlisted before they were born, and Helen and the infant twins stayed with Millie.

In 1964, Lacey was shipped off to Vietnam where he was assigned to something identified only as LRRP. He had a special medal for marksmanship and he volunteered for a second tour of duty.

Lacey had achieved an E5 rank, buck sergeant. But by the time he left the army, he was an E4, a corporal. Louis searched through the rest of the information, but there was nothing to explain it, just a notation that Lacey had been issued an Article 15 and got out on a general discharge in 1967.

Louis set the Dr Pepper aside. General? He thought there were only two ways out: honorable and dishonorable. Louis rubbed his chin in irritation. He was ignorant about the military and wasn't sure who he could ask. Phillip . . .

Louis reached for the phone and dialed. Phillip Lawrence answered the phone after two rings.

"Hey, Phillip, it's me," Louis began. "I'm glad you're home."

"Came back early." Phillip paused. "So, what do you need?"

"Why you think I need something?" Louis asked.

"A visit and a phone call in the same week?" Phillip laughed. "Not your usual M.O."

"Okay, okay, cut the sarcasm," Louis said, laughing softly. "I'll call more often, I promise."

"Just busting your chops. How are you?"

Louis shifted the phone to his other ear, looking at his bandaged hand. "Fine. Getting a cold, I think."

"I won't tell Fran."

"Good."

Louis closed his eyes. For a second, he considered telling Phillip Lawrence the truth, that he was drinking too much, putting his fist into trees, finding Kotex pads in his locker, and jumping every time he heard the snap of a tree branch. But he couldn't. And Phillip Lawrence knew he couldn't.

"Listen, Phillip, I was wondering if I could pick your brain about something," he said quickly.

"You asking me for help? That's a switch."

"It's about the case. Remember I asked you about my suspect being military? Well, it turns out I was right. I have his military record and a couple things don't make sense."

"I'll help if I can, Louis."

Louis picked up the top paper. "What's LRRP?"

"It stands for Long Range Reconnaissance Patrol. We called them lurps. Your guy was in Vietnam?"

"Yup."

"The lurps were the guys dropped by helicopter behind enemy lines to scout, not kill. They were usually left in there a week, ten days, before being picked up. Real testosterone cases."

"Tough on the nerves," Louis said.

"You had to be half nuts to be a lurp. If you made it out alive, you were completely nuts."

Louis was making notes on the margins of the report. "This guy made sergeant, but was a corporal by the time he got out."

"On a general, right?"

"How'd you know?"

"You're never promoted to corporal, you're demoted," Phillip said. "He probably did something to piss off a superior."

"He got something called an Article 15."

"That's a non-court martial punishment. Probably a refusal of orders. I knew a guy like that in Korea. He was a good soldier, but he was getting short—near his discharge time— and one day, we were ordered to go into this village. Well, the guy refused. Just put down his gun and refused."

Louis shook his head slowly. "But this man, he looked to be on a straight track. He made sergeant, got some citations. . . ."

"The military changes men, Louis," Phillip said. "Often for the good, but sometimes for the bad. Some guys just finally flip out. My C.O. called them cracked jugs. They're okay, except for a tiny crack that you can't see. You kept filling them up, pouring in more water and everything's fine. Then, one day, without warning, the crack gives way." Phillip paused. "You still there?"

"Yeah, I'm here."

"Louis, are you sure you're all right up there?"

Louis leaned on the nightstand. "I'm okay."

There was a pause.

"Louis?"

"I gotta go, Phillip."

"Louis . . . be careful," Phillip said.

"I will." He hung up the phone and sat there for a moment. He took off his glasses and rubbed the bridge of his nose. A cracked jug.

A sudden vision of the advertisements in Lacey's room came back to him. The infrared scopes. Long-range rifles. Had Lacey progressed from a shotgun to more sophisticated weapons? Were his days of walking up to his victims and killing them face-to-face over?

He felt a trickle of sweat run down his back. Louis got off the bed, grabbed a shoe and went to the heater. He banged on the gauge several times. The heater gave out a wheeze and a blast of hot air. Louis crawled back on the bed, turning back to Lacey's personal history.

After his discharge, Lacey returned to Dollar Bay. Cole was born a year later. Here, Bjork had inserted her own notation: that Lacey couldn't find work and moved in with his mother, Millie. Louis thought of Millie's gloomy little two-bedroom house in Dollar Bay. Jesus, three adults and three kids crammed into that dump. Who wouldn't go crazy?

Louis read on, his depression deepening. Back in Dollar Bay, Lacey resumed his criminal history. An arrest in a Houghton bar fight; an arrest for vandalizing the office of a Veteran's Administration agent. Two years later, he assaulted a doctor at a VA hospital in Marquette. He served three days when charges were dropped by the local DA; the judge directed Lacey to remain on lithium.

Louis glanced at Lacey's mug shot. Lacey's eyes stared back, with the flat sheen of ball bearings. Louis went on reading.

There it was: the first domestic violence report. Christmas Eve, 1970. A drunken Lacey had thrown all the Christmas presents out into the snow, smacked Helen, and then passed out on the sidewalk. Bjork was the responding officer. In June 1972, Lacey put Helen in the hospital with a smashed jaw and two broken ribs. She, in turn, finally put him in jail. He served sixty days.

A year later, Lacey was arrested again, this time for child abuse. Louis picked up the small Polaroid attached to the report. It was a closeup of a Cole's thin shoulders with six small red marks. The cigarette burns. Louis tucked the photo back into the file. He read a brief synopsis of the unsubstantiated sexual assault charge. As Bjork had said, Social Services had removed Cole Lacey from the home, but he was returned six months later.

Up to this point, Lacey had kept to beating up women and kids. What had finally turned him into a murderer? What had finally caused the jug to break?

Louis returned to the rap sheet and finally reached February 1977, and the assault that had resulted in Lacey's prison sentence.

Lacey had said it was a bar fight where he had just pulled a knife. Lacey had pulled a knife, all right, slicing open an old man's abdomen five times. He was sentenced to twelve to fifteen years in Marquette State Prison. Bjork had included a brief report on Lacey's prison record. It was surprisingly unremarkable.

Louis drained the Dr Pepper and leaned back against the headboard. But Lacey had been busy in prison, real busy. Somehow, he had found out about the raid. Maybe Cole had told him, maybe his mother. But Lacey had found out that his son and daughter had been killed by Loon Lake cops. And for two years, he just sat in his cell, with nothing to do but wait and plan his revenge.

Louis closed the file. There was a knot in his stomach, the same one he had felt earlier back in Lacey's room, but with a slight nausea creeping in. He knew Lacey now. And Lacey knew them. Lacey knew who he wanted to kill, knew where they lived, when they were on duty, even their call numbers. All Lacey had to do was pick his time.

Louis slipped off the bed and walked to the window, throwing it wide open. The sound of laughter drew his eyes down to the street. His room overlooked downtown Houghton. The snow was heaped in eight-foot drifts along Main Street, more falling now. But the town was alive with activity, mostly college kids, he guessed. He watched a couple stroll under the window. The woman's laugh drifted up to him again. They paused to share a kiss.

He moved back to the bed, staring down at the files spread over the rust-colored spread. He had to get out.

King's Tavern was quiet, except for a jukebox near the back that was playing "All My Ex's Live in Texas." A trio of coeds sat at the bar, heads together, giggling softly. Louis slid onto a stool, laying his coat on the stool next to him.

He ordered a Heineken and when it came, he ignored the glass and gulped it quickly. The beer dripped onto his chin. He started to reach for a bar napkin but one appeared in front of his face.

Louis looked to see Bjork standing next to him. He accepted the napkin and wiped his chin.

"Thanks," he said.

"I was sitting in the back and saw you come in," she said. She wasn't in uniform. She was wearing jeans and a heavy, cream-colored sweater.

"Join me?" Louis asked.

"You buying?"

"Sure." He pulled his coat into his lap and Bjork slid onto the stool. She looked different, softer. Her braid was gone and her hair was a red washboard of ripples down her back. She reached up to tuck her hair behind her ears and gold earrings glimmered in the neon lights of the bar. It took Louis a moment to realize they were tiny handcuffs.

Bjork saw him looking at them. "A gift from my ex," she said.

"Was he a cop, too?"

She shook her head. "Lumber worker."

Louis hesitated, wondering if he should get personal. There had been only one woman back at the academy and he never worked with one.

"What did he think about you being a cop?" he asked. He didn't know what had prompted the question. Maybe the idea that something in Bjork's experience could give him a clue about Zoe.

"Wasn't crazy about it," Bjork said. "Guess that's why he finally split." She fingered the earrings, smiling. "He got these for me one Christmas. It was a hint after the black nightie didn't work." She waved at the bartender. "Ed was not the most subtle guy in the world."

Louis stared at her, questions swimming in his head. He looked away, finished off his beer and set it out in the well. Another appeared, along with a Stroh's for Bjork. She held up her bottle.

"To catching the son of a bitch."

Louis clinked his bottle and took a sip.

"You finish reading the file?"

"Almost. I got hungry," Louis said.

"Looks to me like you're drinking your dinner."

Louis covered up his mild annoyance with a smile. "Occupational hazard."

Bjork let it go. "Want to bounce a few things off me?" she asked.

"Like what?"

Her face grew serious. "Two dead cops. Maybe I can help."

Louis hesitated, then looked around the tavern. There was

an empty booth and he picked up his beer, motioned for her to follow. He slid in one side; Bjork across from him. Neither said anything for several long seconds. The jukebox launched into Artie Shaw playing "Summit Ridge Drive."

"So, tell me about how they died," Bjork said.

"Both surprised by a shotgun to the chest, both off duty," Louis said.

"Ballsy little bastard, isn't he?"

Louis nodded. "One was an easy target, a retired old fart who drank a lot. He was out fishing at six A.M. The other was active duty, young, alert and experienced. He carried his gun to his own front door. Lacey was on his porch and blew away the door with him behind it."

"Christ," Bjork said.

"It gets sicker. He leaves these cards."

"What kind of cards?"

"A military thing, death cards. A sign that was supposed to tell us: 'I was here.' "

Louis caught the bartender's attention, circling a finger to indicate another round.

"Kincaid, what is Lacey after?" Bjork asked.

"What do you mean?"

"I mean, why is he targeting your cops?"

Louis hesitated. "Revenge. Two of his kids, teenagers, were killed by us in a barricade situation five years ago. They fired on the cops and refused to surrender. The girl drew on one of the officers."

Bjork took a sip of her beer, digesting his words. "What about Cole?"

"He's at Red Oak until he's twenty-one."

"Stiff sentence for a kid."

"He pulled a shotgun when they took him into custody." Bjork shook her head. "Well, pardon my bluntness but given what you just told me, why did it take you guys so long to name Lacey as a suspect?"

Louis was glad it was so dark; she couldn't see his embarrassment. Over what? That Jesse had fucked up? That the DOC was filled with incompetents? That no one bothered to bring up the raid? That Gibralter was too pigheaded to ask for outside help? That he himself had let Lacey go?

Her question hung in the smoky air, waiting to be answered. Maybe he was embarrassed because he had no idea how to answer. Hell, maybe he was embarrassed because he didn't know what in God's name to do next.

He met her eyes, seeing again the spread of fine wrinkles at the corners, seeing for the first time the depth on the inside. All right, she was a woman. But she was also a cop. A cop with decades more experience than he had. If anyone could understand about his letting Lacey go, she would.

"We had him once," Louis said.

"Lacey?"

Louis nodded. "Day after Christmas. We picked him up for running from us when we walked into a bar."

Bjork waited for more.

Louis sat back. Just say it. "I cut him loose."

"You didn't check on him? You didn't put two and two together?"

"I didn't know who he was. The name meant nothing. And the DOC had him listed as being in prison. It turned out to be a typo." Louis let out a breath. "A damn typo."

Bjork studied him.

Louis stared into his beer. "It was Christmas. I tried to do something decent."

"Well, Louis, there is decent and then there is dumb."

"Thanks," Louis mumbled.

"Did you expect sympathy from me?"

He met her eyes briefly, then looked away. "I don't know what I'm expecting anymore."

"How come nobody in the department thought of him, thought the barricade situation would—"

"I have no idea," Louis interrupted. He stared at a set of carved initials in the tabletop, listening absently to the music.

"Louis," Bjork said. "You will get him."

He looked up at her. "Right."

She shook her head and glanced at the bar. Her eyes lit up and she waved to someone, who hollered a friendly hello across the room.

Louis stared at her. "You like it here, don't you?"

"I love it. It's my home," she said with a smile. "I mean, I've traveled some, lived below the bridge for a year even. But I always come back. I belong here."

He could almost feel his mind slowing, slowing as it approached this strange bend in the road. Home. That's what he had thought Loon Lake would be. A safe place that he could settle into. But it was not as it had first seemed. Nothing was as it first seemed. Loon Lake wasn't a postcard paradise; it was a place of death. Jesse wasn't a partner he could count on; he was a coward, his judgment clouded by blind loyalty to Gibralter. And Gibralter, what was he? Certainly not the great, perfect chief.

And Zoe . . . what he had felt with her. What was that?

"Louis?"

He glanced at Bjork. "What are you thinking?"

"About Loon Lake, the job. My chief."

"I talked to your chief today. Strange man."

"He called you?"

"Ya, wanted to make sure you arrived okay."

"Christ," Louis said under his breath, looking away.

They were silent, the laughter and music of the tavern floating around them.

"What else did he have to say?" Louis asked finally.

Bjork fiddled with the neck of the Stroh's bottle.

"What else?" Louis pressed.

"He said he was concerned because you, quote, 'Couldn't find your ass with two hands,' unquote."

Louis felt the heat creeping into his face, but he didn't look away.

"Sounds like a hard-ass," Bjork offered.

Bjork reached across the table and touched his hand. Louis looked down at her hand. Her nails were short with chipped, rose-colored polish. There was one of those mother's rings on her finger, with three little gemstones. He withdrew his hand and dropped it in his lap.

Bjork sat back, looking at him. Then she quickly raised her bottle and drained it, setting it down loudly.

"Well, I need to call it a night. How about you? You okay?"

"I'll be fine."

Bjork stood up, looking down at him. Her eyes were watery in the neon light and he wanted to believe it was from the booze, not veteran-to-rookie sympathy. Or worse, some woman-to-man thing. Christ, he had started the night thinking about what Bjork might look like handcuffed to a bed and now she was looking at him like he was her kid.

"Lieutenant Byrd will have your evidence ready for you tomorrow morning," she said. "Swing by and pick it up."

Louis nodded.

Bjork hesitated, then extended a hand. "It was a pleasure, Officer Kincaid."

Louis took her hand. "Thanks, Bjork," he said softly. "Thanks for everything."

Twenty-two

No doubt about it. He was drunk.

On the ride home from Dollar Bay, he had stopped off at the grocery to picked up a six-pack of Heineken. It had taken only two hours to go through that, and then he had moved on to the Christian Brothers.

Now, he was sprawled on the sofa, staring into the dying fire in the hearth. Something in his fogged brain was telling him to go outside and get more logs, but he was too tired to move.

With a grunt, he turned and reached for the bottle on the floor. He brought it up to his eyes, squinting. Empty. He stood and stumbled to the kitchen, jerking open the cupboard. Empty. No booze, no food, no woman, and soon, probably no job. What a shitty week.

Going back to the sofa, he grabbed a hooded sweatshirt, jerked open the door and headed to the lake. He wasn't sure why. Maybe to just cut a hole in the ice and jump in. Hell, they wouldn't find him until spring, unless, of course, he floated up under some kid's ice skate like Lovejoy had. That would be just his luck.

He was halfway to the shoreline when it occurred to him that he could be a walking target for Duane Lacey's rifle. At least he was too drunk to feel the bullet.

Leaning heavily against a tree, he stared blankly out at the dark lake. He had to stop this. He had to stop drinking so much. An image flashed into his head, his mother's sunken face, leathery against the white pillow of her deathbed. For the first time, he was beginning to understand how people could drink themselves to death. He ran a shaky hand over his face. No, he was just, what? Stressed out? Under pressure. Shit, all cops drank too much, didn't they? He wasn't like her. He wasn't going to die like she did, liver eaten away, alone and scared.

He looked up. The moon was a silver scythe in the black sky. Louis squinted across the lake, trying to make out the specks of lights, wondering which was Zoe's cabin, thinking about Jay Gatsby. Gatsby, the stupid putz who stood around mooning out at Daisy's dock.

"Kincaid," he said, "how in the hell could you be so stupid about so much?"

He heard a noise and spun around, trying to focus on the cabin. He saw a car and wondered why he hadn't heard it pull up. He let out a breath when he saw Jesse heading to the cabin's porch. Fucking traitor.

Jesse knocked, waited, knocked again. He started back toward his truck.

"Hey!" Louis called.

Jesse turned and Louis stepped out of the shadows. Jesse trudged out to him. "What you doing out here?" he asked.

"Looking for UFOs," Louis mumbled.

Jesse looked up, stuffing his hands in the pockets of his beige parka. Louis watched him from the corner of his eye. He was wearing a turtleneck and jeans, and his hair blown down across his forehead. Out of uniform, he looked like a teenager.

"What are you doing here?" Louis said.

Jesse shrugged. "I just wanted to know how it went in Dollar Bay."

Louis eyed him coldly. "You can read the report."

Jesse's sigh came out in a long white vapor. "Look, Louis, I came here . . . Shit, I guess I wanted to apologize."

"For what?"

"The chief was kind of rough on you the other day."

"Aw gee, thanks for your support," Louis muttered, starting back to the cabin.

Jesse hesitated, then followed. "Maybe I should have said something, Louis, but it's hard with the chief, the way he is about things. I mean, it's a small department and I—"

"You left me hanging out there by my balls."

"There was nothing I could do!"

"Bullshit."

"What?" Jesse asked, throwing his arms up. "What was I supposed to do?"

Louis faced him. "You could've told me about the raid. You could have told me about those kids. You could've told me about their fucking *father!"*

"I didn't know he was out!"

"You should have! It was your job to know."

Jesse spun away suddenly and started toward his Bronco. Then he stopped and turned, looking down at the snow. For several seconds, he said nothing. "All right," he said finally. "I should have known. I should have double-checked the fucking record."

Louis shook his head in disgust. "Get out of here. I'm done listening to your bullshit excuses."

Louis staggered past him to the porch. Jesse hesitated, then caught up, grabbing Louis's arm. Louis jerked away and pushed open the door. Inside, he kicked off his wet shoes and went to the sofa, dropping down onto it. He heard the door close and knew Jesse had followed him.

"Look," Jesse said slowly, "I know I should have said something in your defense, but if I had opened my mouth, Gibralter would have canned me. And I couldn't take it if I couldn't be a cop anymore."

Louis looked up at him. "What makes you think you ever were one?"

Jesse stared at him. "You know, I've had about enough of your shit," he said.

"That makes two of us."

"Come on, man! Cut me some slack!"

"You fucked up!"

"So did you!" Jesse yelled.

Louis closed his eyes. It was quiet. He heard a squeak of the floorboards and opened his eyes. It took him a moment to focus on the bottle in front of his nose. His eyes went up to Jesse's face above him.

He took the bottle of Jack Daniel's from Jesse, unscrewed the cap and took a swig. He grimaced and handed it back to Jesse. Jesse retreated three feet to perch cautiously on the arm of a chair. In the long silence, Louis felt the whiskey burn a path down his throat to his empty stomach. For a moment, he thought he was going to vomit. He opened his eyes to see Jesse holding out the bottle again. He waved it off.

"Why didn't you quit?" Jesse asked quietly.

Louis shook his head. "Can't . . ."

"Why?"

"He's still out there."

They fell silent. Louis shivered and reached down to pull the afghan over his chest.

"You got any wood?" Jesse asked, glancing at the cold fireplace.

Louis shook his head. Jesse waited for Louis to say something. Finally, he rose. "I gotta go," he said. "Julie's waiting up."

Louis looked up at him, frowning. "Huh?"

"Julie. She was the one who told me to come over here, said she was tired of listening to me bitch about it."

Louis squinted at Jesse. "Any more of that shit left?" he asked, nodding toward the bottle.

Jesse handed him the Jack Daniel's. Louis took a drink and handed it back. Jesse took a swig.

"Whiskey'll kill you," Louis mumbled.

"Better than that cough syrup you drink," Jesse said, nodding toward the empty Christian Brothers on the floor.

Louis pulled the afghan up to his chin and shivered. From outside came the call of a loon.

"I hate the sound of those fucking birds," Jesse murmured.

"Lonely," Louis said.

"What?"

"They sound lonely."

Jesse nodded. He slid down again onto the arm of the chair, waiting, watching Louis's face.

"Julie . . ." Louis said. "She like you being a cop?"

Jesse wasn't sure how to answer. There was something in Louis's voice, something unspoken and unprotected in the question. Jesse shifted on the arm, vaguely uncomfortable. "I guess," he said. "I met her giving her a ticket. The first time we did it, she made me leave my uniform shirt on. Said it made her feel like she was doing something criminal."

Louis laughed softly.

"Why'd you ask that?" Jesse ventured.

"No reason."

"Shit, everything you say or do has a reason attached. You seeing someone?"

Louis shook his head. Jesse took another drink and held out the bottle. Louis waved it away.

"Can you talk to her?" Louis asked. "About the job, I mean."

Jesse paused, then nodded. "Yeah, most of the time."

They fell silent again. Louis knew the booze had pushed him past his limit and that he was dangerously close to getting sloppy. But as much as he needed someone to talk to, he wasn't about to let Jesse see him that way. As much as he needed to talk about Zoe, he wasn't ready to tell Jesse. He closed his eyes, drifting, drifting down . . . to sleep, he hoped, to blessed sleep.

He heard a sound, the door opening and closing. Jesse had left. But after several minutes, there was a thud. Louis opened his eyes to see Jesse kneeling to dump an armload of logs onto the hearth. He watched as Jesse stuffed newspapers into it and slowly prodded a fire to life.

The warmth curled slowly toward him and Louis extended his legs toward it. "Thanks," he muttered.

"I wasn't going to let you sit here in the dark and freeze to death, and you're too shit-faced to go outside and get some wood," Jesse said.

"Yeah, why make Lacey's job any easier than it is?" Louis said.

Jesse stared at him for a moment, then laughed. Louis joined in. Finally, they stopped.

"You're one sick mother," Louis said.

"You're the one who said it," Jesse said, falling into the chair and uncapping the Jack Daniel's. Louis watched him as he drank.

"You scared?" Louis asked softly.

Jesse didn't look at him. He nodded, then took another drink.

Louis rubbed a hand roughly over his face. "I found out some good stuff up in Dollar Bay," he said.

Jesse looked relieved to talk business. "Like what?"

"He's got survival skills, learned them as a lurp."

"A what?"

"Long Range Reconnaissance Patrol," Louis slurred. "They dropped the suckers from choppers in 'Nam and they had to find their own way out of the jungle."

"What, like some kind of test?"

"No, in combat," Louis said, struggling through the booze haze. "Phillip said they were nuts and—"

"Who's Phillip?"

"My foster father. He said—"

"You were a foster kid?" Jesse asked.

Louis yawned. "Bjork said that Lacey was a natural—"

"Who's Bjork?"

"Sheriff in Dollar Bay," Louis murmured. A small smile crept to his lips. "Great hair, little gold earrings . . ."

Jesse stood up, palms up. "I don't want to hear this. You can tell me tomorrow."

Louis tried to push himself up from the sofa. Jesse put a hand on his shoulder. "Stay there. And get some sleep. You're gonna feel like shit tomorrow."

Louis nodded, closing his eyes.

Jesse reached over and pulled the afghan up over Louis. "See you in the morning, partner."

Twenty-three

Louis pulled the page out of the typewriter, his report on Dollar Bay finished. As he read it over for typos, he realized that his hand was shaking.

He let out a slow breath. That was it, no more heavy drinking like last night. He couldn't afford to be off his game right now. He started to reach for his coffee, but instead went to the water cooler and gulped down his third Dixie Cup of water.

He was crumpling the cup when Gibralter came in, unzipping his parka. Gibralter spotted Louis, gave him a curt nod and headed toward his office.

"Chief?" Dale called out.

Gibralter turned.

Dale hurried forward, holding out several pink slips. "Mr. Steele called again, twice this morning."

Gibralter took the slips, crumpled them and tossed the wad to the trash. It missed and bounced to the floor. "Jesse here yet?" he asked Dale.

"In the locker room, sir."

"Tell him I want to see him." Gibralter looked at Louis. "You, too, Kincaid." He disappeared into his office.

Louis poured a fresh cup of coffee. His eyes went to the pink paper on the floor and he picked it up. He unfolded it and stared at Mark Steele's name, wondering what the calls were about. Was Steele trying to offer help in the investigation? Louis tossed the papers in the trash. Shit, any help would be welcome at this point, even from an asshole like Steele. Picking up his coffee, he went to the mailbox, pulling out the single paper from his slot. It was Lovejoy's phone record. It must have come back while he had been in Dollar Bay.

Going to his desk, he put on his glasses. Most of the numbers appeared to be local, but two stood out. The first was 578-7770, which Lovejoy had called every day at nearly the same time, 6:35 A.M. The last day he called it was on Sunday, December 1. The other number was 578-3482, a call made at 10:30 P.M. on November 30.

"Dale," Louis called out, "Could you run these for me?"

Dale came over to peer at the two numbers Louis had underlined. "Don't have to," he said. "The first one's the weather. The other's the chief's house."

"The chief?" Louis said, frowning. "Lovejoy was retired. Why would he call the chief?"

Dale shrugged. "They were kinda friendly."

He had forgotten; Jesse had told him the chief and Lovejoy went fishing together occasionally. But any cop knew that the last person a dead man talked to was important. Why hadn't Gibralter mentioned it?

Louis sat back in his chair. Well, at least the call to the weather made sense. It was more evidence that Lovejoy fished in the morning, not at night. But it still didn't make sense that Lacey had risked killing him in broad daylight.

Louis sat forward suddenly. Unless . . . Lovejoy was not put in the water at the same time he was killed.

Louis slipped off his glasses, his mind working on this new possibility. Had Lacey shot Lovejoy at night, like Pryce, then returned the next afternoon to stuff him in the ice hole? That fit Lacey's M.O. at least. But why did he feel he had to conceal Lovejoy when he had left Pryce's body in the open?

His eyes went to the Dollar Bay report sitting on his desk, and something Millie Cronk had said nagged at his brain. He got out his notebook and flipped to the notes of their conversation. She had said that Lacey came home after his first visit to Loon Lake, that he seemed upset about something. He had told her that "everything is fucked up."

What had he meant? Had something gone wrong for Lacey? Had he planned a third hit that didn't come off? Is that why, in the last four weeks, he hadn't struck again?

"Hey, you're alive."

Louis turned to see Jesse coming from the locker room. "Barely," Louis said, closing his notebook. "Chief wants to see us."

"Before briefing? He say why?"

"Not a clue." Louis picked up the Dollar Bay report as he rose. Several other men were heading toward the briefing room and eyed Louis as they passed. Jesse saw it.

"Let it go," he said to Louis quietly.

Jesse knocked on the chief's door and Gibralter called for them to come in. He was standing at the window, back to the door, and turned.

"Anything new on Lacey?" Gibralter asked Jesse.

"We found the wife," Jesse said. "She's in Texas, some berg near Austin. Been there for the last three years. Cops down there questioned her, but she said she hasn't heard from Lacey since '77."

"That it?"

"We also found out Lacey checked into a motel down near Rose City on November 30, but the search turned up nothing."

"And since then?" Gibralter asked.

"No sign of him."

"He's trained in wilderness survival skills," Louis ventured.

"How do you know?" Gibralter asked.

Louis quickly summarized Lacey's military record and the other information from Dollar Bay. "It's in my report," he said, holding it out.

Gibralter took it, scanned it, and tossed it on the desk behind him. He went to the wall map, studying it. "Lacey isn't from here. He doesn't know this area," he said. "If he's holed up somewhere, he has help."

Louis's eyes went to the county map on the wall behind Gibralter, to the large, amoebalike blob of green that was the Huron National Forest. Lacey was in there somewhere, and they would never find him. To them, it was a foreign and hostile place; to Lacey it was shelter.

"What about his son?" Louis asked. "He's lived here, and Lacey visited him at Red Oak. The kid wrote to him too."

"Then that's where you go next, the kid. I want you two up there today to question him."

Louis's eyes flitted to the map again. Even if Cole Lacey did know something, nine small-town police officers didn't have a prayer of finding Lacey without help.

"Chief, I have a question," Louis said. "Are you going to request assistance from the state?"

Gibralter gazed at him through the cigarette smoke haze. "We'll handle this ourselves," he said. "That's what good departments do, they take care of their own problems. They don't need outsiders."

Louis could feel a faint pounding in his head, the lingering effect of the booze and the beginning of a headache. He resisted the urge to rub his temples and the urge to say what he was thinking, that this was no time for a territorial pissing match between Gibralter and this guy Steele. Unconsciously, he let a sigh slip.

"Do you have a problem with what I just said?" Gibralter asked.

"No, sir." Gibralter's icy stare seemed to drill into his head, hitting the pounding place in his brain.

"There's something else on your mind, Kincaid. What is it?"

Louis hesitated. "Lovejoy's phone records came back."

"And?"

"They show he made a call to your home at ten-thirty P.M. the night before he was killed."

"So?"

"So," Louis said carefully, "I was curious about why you didn't mention it."

Louis heard Jesse draw in a slow breath.

"I didn't mention it because I never got the call," Gibralter said.

Louis hesitated, knowing he was about to get his head chopped off. Shit, at least it would stop the headache. "Someone got the call," he said. "It was four minutes long."

Gibralter's eyes didn't waver. "I have a wife, Kincaid. Maybe they chatted for a few minutes."

Louis lowered his eyes. Stupid, stupid.

"So, if we are done discussing Lacey," Gibralter said, "I have something I want to take up with you, Kincaid."

Louis tightened. Now what?

Gibralter went to the credenza and took one of the swords off the wall. "This is a samurai sword," he said. "Do you know why I have it here, Kincaid?"

Louis felt Jesse shift nervously at his side. "No, sir," Louis said.

"I keep it to remind myself of what honor is. We spoke of honor once, didn't we?"

"Yes, sir," Louis said slowly.

Gibralter's hand traveled over the ornate hilt. "The samurai code was a simple one," he said. "The business of a samurai consisted of reflecting on his station in life, in discharging loyal service to his master and in deepening the trust and fidelity of his fellow warriors."

Gibralter looked at Louis. "You think maybe a samurai might have something to teach a cop?"

"I'm sure he would," Louis said. Where the hell was this going?

Gibralter carefully set the sword back in its holder. "I spoke to a man named Bob Roberts today. Name ring a bell?"

The hairs on Louis's arms came alive and he was suddenly aware of his heartbeat. It was moving up, mixing with the pounding in his head. "Can we discuss this in private?" he said.

"No. I think this is something Officer Harrison should hear."

"Sir, this—"

"We are under siege, Kincaid," Gibralter said. "Any man on this force can take a bullet for you at any time. I think they should know how you plan to repay them."

Suddenly, Louis knew what was coming, and there was no way he was going to be able to explain it.

"Officer Kincaid spent a couple of interesting days in Mississippi federal court last year, didn't you?" Gibralter said.

"Yes," Louis said tightly.

"Officer Kincaid testified against another police officer by the name of Lawrence Cutter. What were the charges, Officer Kincaid?"

"Civil rights violations," Louis said.

"What'd he do, Officer Kincaid? Call you a jigaboo?" Gibralter asked.

Louis went rigid. "Larry Cutter—"

"Shut the fuck up when I'm talking to you!" Gibralter shouted.

Louis felt a tremor rush through his body, a signal of the rage building inside. He didn't want Jesse to hear this without knowing the truth. He turned to him.

"Jess, the man tried to kill me. He tried to hang—"

"I don't care what he did!" Gibralter interrupted. "You turned on your own, and cops don't turn on their own!"

"Sir, I think—" Jesse said quietly.

"No, you don't!" Gibralter snapped.

Louis glared at Gibralter. "Are you firing me?"

Gibralter shook his head. "I have no intention of making it easy for you. If you leave here, it will be because you quit or because your stupidity gets you killed."

"Jesus, Chief," Jesse whispered hoarsely.

"That's enough."

For a long moment, it was quiet in the office. From outside came the murmur of the other morning-shift men, punctuated by the ring of the telephone. Finally, Gibralter turned away from them.

"Dismissed," he said.

Twenty-four

They rode in silence. Louis drove, his hands locked on the wheel, his eyes never wavering from the road. The snow had given way to sleet and Louis flicked on the wipers to keep the windshield from icing over. For a half hour, the silence between them built, like ice on glass. It was Jesse who finally broke it.

"Tell me about this cop."

Louis shook his head. "Forget it. It was a thousand miles away, a thousand years ago."

"Louis, for chrissake, tell me."

"I said forget it. I have."

"Right. That's why the veins are popping out of your temples. Tell me, damn it, why'd this guy try to hang you?"

"You heard enough."

Louis stared straight ahead. They were heading southwest, passing through farmlands, flat acres of white nothingness that blended with the slate-gray sky.

"What? You think because I'm white, I can't understand? Is that it?" Jesse asked.

Louis glanced at him, then looked back at the road.

Jesse let out a snort. "Man, you're fucked up, you know it? You're emotionally constipated and it's fucked up your head and now you're transferring your anger."

"Spare me your psycho-crap," Louis said.

"You're angry at the chief and you're transferring it to me."

"Bullshit."

Louis turned the wipers up a notch. They rode in silence for another ten miles until Jesse gave him directions to turn.

"Chief has ordered us all to double up," Jesse said.

"On patrol?" Louis asked.

"Yeah. Did it while you were away. Says he doesn't want anyone riding alone right now."

Louis nodded. At least Gibralter was finally taking precautions to protect his men. He glanced at Jesse, wondering if he should try to explain about Larry Cutter. What was the use? Even if Jesse understood, the other men wouldn't. And Gibralter would make sure every last man on the force found out. Shit, what the hell was the matter with the man? Was this part of some plan to break him just because he had let Lacey go? Or was it just because he had challenged him on the Lacey kids, the call from Lovejoy and about getting outside help?

"You found letters from Cole?" Jesse asked, interrupting his thoughts.

"Yeah, in Lacey's room," Louis said.

"What did they say?" Jesse asked.

"Not much. He's proud of his dad for, quote, 'killing that nigger,' unquote."

Jesse shook his head. "Guess the kid hasn't gotten any smarter."

"What you mean?"

"I busted him once, when he was about eleven, for shoplifting. He had a smart mouth then too."

Louis tried to conjure up an image of Cole at eleven. The only thing that came to him was the five-year-old Cole with the cigarette burns on his back.

"He was abused. Did you know that?" Louis asked.

"So what? Plenty of abused kids turn out okay," Jesse said tersely.

"Well, it kind of puts a different spin on—"

"It's no excuse for being an asshole," Jesse snapped. He shook his head. "I hate that kind of talk. It's crap, like the chief said about the vets, blaming everything on post-traumatic stress. It's like nobody wants to take responsibility for their actions anymore."

Louis bit back his thought, that Jesse could be talking about his own temper.

They survived the rest of the drive on a diet of small talk about the case. It was eleven-thirty by the time Louis turned the Bronco down a freshly plowed road and under an iron arch that said RED OAK CORRECTIONS FACILITY FOR BOYS. The road cut a wet black ribbon through the high drifts, leading to an ugly Kleenex-box building in the middle of a treeless field of snow. The compound was surrounded by a high chain-link fence topped with barbed wire. In the distance were some basketball hoops. Jesse looked back at the gate as it closed behind them.

At the entrance, Louis pushed the button. The guard peered at them through the glass door and he buzzed them in. After signing them in, the guard directed them down a gloomy corridor to a door marked WARDEN LITTLE.

"Officers Kincaid and Harrison to see Warden Little," Louis told the secretary. "He's expecting us."

She buzzed, and a moment later, a small bald man in a gray suit came out of his office.

"Officers," Warden Little said, greeting them with a weak smile and weaker handshake. "Can I offer you some coffee?"

"No, thanks," Louis said. "We'd like to see Cole Lacey."

"No problem. I've secured Cole in our visitor lounge. We find it's more conducive to getting the boys to relax. It's comforting to them to have some homey surroundings."

"Cole Lacey's comfort level is no concern of ours, Warden," Jesse said, following Little down the hall.

Warden Little glanced at him as he pressed the elevator button. "Well, we won't argue the sociological fine points of juvenile crime, officer. But let me assure you, many of my boys here are victims, just like those you seek justice for."

"Tell that to Stephanie Pryce," Jesse muttered as they entered the elevator.

"Pardon?" Little said.

"We have reason to believe that Cole Lacey's father killed two police officers," Louis said.

"I see. That reminds me." Little reached in his breast pocket. "Here's the visitors log you asked for."

Louis took the paper, straining to read it without his glasses. Finally he handed it to Jesse.

"Here it is," Jesse said. "Lacey was here on November 11. One day after getting out of Marquette. He was here again on Christmas Eve."

The elevator deposited them on the second floor. A muscular guard in a khaki uniform stood by a door, his arms crossed, a baton and cuffs hanging from a gunless belt. His nameplate said HAYNES. He unlocked the door and advised them to knock when they wanted out. Louis waited until Little had left before turning to Jesse.

"My way, right?" Louis asked quietly.

"Scout's honor."

They went inside, the heavy door locking behind them. The pale blue room was small and it reeked of pine air freshener. The small single window was hung with flowered curtains, frost visible between the bars. At the table in the center of the room sat a slender teenager. He wore the regulation blue pants and a denim shirt, which ballooned around his thin chest. He sat, dark head bowed, bony hands clasped together on the table, legs wrapped around the metal folding chair.

Louis cleared his throat.

Cole Lacey's keen brown eyes moved from Louis's shoes up, over his uniform, up to his face. As they skipped over to Jesse, Cole's posture changed slowly from the languidness of an arrogant teenager to a stiffness that Louis read as fear.

Cole stood up and slowly moved around the back of the chair, like an alley cat trying to sidle away from predators. "What do you guys want?" he asked.

"Sit down," Louis said.

"No."

Louis reached over and grabbed Cole's shoulder. The boy tensed, but allowed himself to be set back down in the chair. Louis pulled a metal chair from the wall and sat down across the table from Cole.

"We want to ask you about your father," Louis said.

"Haven't seen him," Cole mumbled.

"Don't lie to us."

"Fuck you."

Louis leaned across the table. "Look, Cole, your father is wanted for the murder of two police officers. We tend to take things like that rather personal, you understand me?"

Cole lowered his head. His nape was red from the fresh scrape of a razored haircut. "I don't know nothing about that."

Louis slapped one of Cole's letters on the table. "Look at me," Louis said, raising his voice.

Cole eyed the letter, then lifted his gaze. "That's private stuff. You got no right to it."

"You want to tell us what you and your dad talked about during his visits?"

Cole's eyes drifted away.

Louis sat back, drawing in a breath. "I'm going to explain something to you, Cole, and I want you to listen very carefully. This thing with your father is going to end one of two ways. One, you tell us where your old man is, we arrest him and when you get out of here, you can go visit him because he'll still be alive."

Cole's eyes flicked up to Jesse, who was standing behind Louis, and then down to the table.

Louis tapped Cole's face, just light enough to get his attention. Cole's jaw twitched as he stared at Louis.

"Or two, we can hunt your father down like a dog," Louis went on, "and when you get out of here five years from now, you can plant flowers on his grave."

"I don't know nothing."

"Okay, then let me tell you what *we* know," Louis said. "We know your dad told you what he was going to do. We know he didn't live around here and that you did. We know *you* know where he is now."

Cole glared at him. "I'm not telling you guys shit."

"This is no time to go brain-dead, Cole," Louis said slowly, unable to hide his growing anger. "We *will* find your father. If we have to hunt day and night, ass deep in snow, we will bust open every damn cabin door, look behind every fucking tree and under every fucking rock. Because he killed two cops, Cole. You have any idea what that does to another cop's mind?"

"Ask me if I care," Cole muttered.

"You care about your father's life?"

Cole gave a laugh of derision. "Yeah, sure. I *care,* man. I care so much my heart is fucking breaking."

Louis glanced back at Jesse, who was standing motionless, arms folded over his chest, staring at Cole with undisguised contempt.

"Okay, well, maybe you care about saving your own skin then," Louis said, looking back to Cole.

"You can't do anything to me," Cole said.

"Wanna bet? The law says you get out of here when you're twenty-one," Louis said. "If we find out you know something about these murders, we're going to charge you with everything we can. That means next time you'll be tried as an adult and do you know where you go then?"

"You can't connect me to this shit," Cole spat out.

"You ever been to Jackson State Penitentiary?"

Cole laughed. "Sure, right. Now you're gonna take me on one of those 'scared-straight' tours? Huh? Are ya?"

Louis rose slowly. Cole watched him, the smirk slowly sliding off his face. He pressed himself back into the folding chair, so far his body seemed to meld with the metal.

Louis came around the table and stood in front of Cole. "You want a tour, asshole?" Louis asked.

Cole tried to muster another smirk, but it came out as a

grimace. "Yeah, give me a tour, nigger," he said, the last word dying to a whisper.

"What did you say?"

Cole wouldn't look up. He stuck his thin legs out, extending them toward Louis's feet. Louis kicked them. The chair scraped the floor, nearly folding. Cole grabbed the table for support, but ran smack into Louis's face.

"Listen to me, you little piece of shit," Louis whispered between clenched teeth. "We're pissed. And when cops get pissed, they don't care if assholes like you die."

Louis could feel Cole's breath on his face and could see something in the kid's eyes. The kid knew where Lacey was. He knew, goddamn it.

"You gonna hit me?" Cole said, trying to smile.

Louis grabbed Cole's chin. "Look, you little prick! You like it here? You like this place? Five years is a long time. How'd you like to make it two?"

"What?" Cole croaked.

"You tell us where your old man is and you walk out of here on your eighteenth birthday."

Cole's eyes flicked from Louis to Jesse and back to Louis. Louis could almost see the wheels turning in the kid's brain. Cole pulled his face away, rubbing his chin.

Louis took a step back, folding his arms over his chest. "Offer expires in ten seconds," he said. He had no authority to make such a deal, but Cole didn't know that.

"Why should I tell you anything?" Cole spat out.

"Five seconds."

"I ain't giving you my old man."

"You're stupid, Cole," Louis said.

A slow grin came over Cole's face. "Yeah? Who's stupid, man? You had him and let him go."

Louis lunged, grabbing Cole's shirt. He jerked him from the chair, shoved him backward and slammed him against the wall.

Cole threw up his hands, a mixture of fear and anger glazing his eyes. "You fucking pig!" he squealed. "Get your hands off me!"

Louis's hand tightened around Cole's throat. "Talk to me!"

Cole glared, his nostrils flaring. "Fuck you!"

Louis drew back a fist. His eyes flicked back to Jesse, who had moved forward, his face tight with shock. Louis looked back at Cole, then at his hand, inches from Cole's face.

A tear had squeezed out of Cole's eye. "Go ahead," he whimpered. "I don't care. I don't fucking care."

Louis's hand began to tremble. For a moment, no one moved. Then, with a violent shove, Louis sent Cole reeling back into the chair. It folded with a loud clang, sending Cole sprawling to the floor. Cole's legs pedaled against the linoleum until he had pushed himself back against the wall. He had bitten his lip and a trickle of blood appeared at the corner of his mouth. He ignored it, wiping angrily at the tear on his cheek.

Louis stared at the boy. Then slowly his eyes dropped to his hand, still curled into a fist. His heart was pounding and he suddenly felt very hot. He walked woodenly to the wall. He leaned heavily against it, wiping a hand over his brow.

Jesus, what am I doing?

Louis glanced at Jesse, as if suddenly aware he was in the room. Jesse was rooted by the door, his face clouded with confusion and something else, something that Louis recognized, with a sick feeling, as approval.

Louis moved to the door and banged on it. Haynes appeared, his eyes moving from Louis to Cole and back. "He give you trouble, officer?" he asked, his hand moving to his baton.

Cole stood up slowly, his eyes flashing new confidence in the presence of Haynes. "Always my fucking fault, isn't it, Haynes?" he said.

"Watch your mouth, Lacey."

Haynes reached out and grabbed Cole by the neck of his shirt. "Let's go," he said, shoving him toward the door.

At the door, Cole twisted to look back at Louis.

"You are dead, man," Cole said softly. His hard eyes took in Jesse. "You're both dead motherfuckers."

They stepped out into the cold sleet, pausing to zip their jackets.

"Give me the keys," Jesse said.

"No," Louis said.

"Give me the fucking keys."

Louis dug them out and almost threw them at Jesse. He walked briskly to the cruiser, jerked open the passenger door and got in. Jesse got in, but made no move to start the car. Louis was staring out the windshield, his jaw muscles moving. Finally he looked over at Jesse.

"You going to start this thing?"

"Not 'til you tell me what that was all about."

"Just start the damn car."

Jesse rubbed the orange rabbit's foot. "Look, Louis, I need to know. What the hell happened back there?"

"Nothing."

"Don't tell me 'nothing.' The man I saw in there is not the same man I know."

"What do you mean?"

Jesse shrugged. "It's just not you. I mean, it's not bad, but it's just not you."

"Start the car, Jess."

Jesse sighed. "Gonna be a long ride home."

They pulled out of the lot and headed back to the interstate. Louis dropped his head back against the seat. He was glad Jesse had let it go. If he hadn't, he would have probably been forced to admit that he didn't know what had happened in that room with Cole Lacey.

He closed his eyes. Jesse was right. That wasn't him back there. Or was it? He had felt something back there, something foreign and dark, something that had crawled up from deep inside him. Standing there over that stupid kid, giving him shit, making him shake, it had felt . . . *good*.

"What we going to tell the chief about this?" Jesse asked, breaking into his thoughts.

"Tell him whatever you want," Louis muttered.

He closed his eyes again, letting the hum of the tires take him back down into his thoughts. He could, he knew, rationalize his behavior. Cole knew where Lacey was, and they had every right to get that information out of him. Christ, he could have made it really hard on the kid. But coerced testimony was illegal and wouldn't hold up in court. And it was wrong.

Jesse suggested they stop at the White Castle to pick up lunch, but Louis said he wanted to go right back to the station. He wanted to get the damn report done on Cole. Jesse dropped him off, and Louis went right to his desk, pulling a blank report from his drawer.

He paused, pen over paper. What the hell did he write? Subject uncooperative and belligerent? Interrogation failed due to officer's lack of control?

"You get anything out of Cole?" Dale asked.

"No. The kid's cold as the damn lake," Louis answered without looking up.

After thirty minutes, he sat back and read what he had written. His usually straight handwriting had an unmistakable angry slant to it. He was always careful not to let his emotions color a report, but this thing with Cole had pushed him into a different state of mind.

Louis crumpled the report and tossed it in the trash. No way would Gibralter accept this. He liked his reports ice cold, just like his own damn blood.

The door opened and Jesse came in. He walked to Louis and dropped a greasy White Castle bag on the desk.

"I brought you some anyway. No pickles, no onions."

Louis mumbled a thank-you. A second later, a door banged against the wall and Louis looked up to see Gibralter emerge from his office, wearing his parka. Louis's eyes followed Gibralter as he went to Dale and held out a paper.

"New assignments. Post it. I'm going home," Gibralter said.

Louis bent back over the report. The smell of the hamburgers in the bag at his elbow was making him feel sick and he pushed it away.

He felt someone standing behind him and looked up. Jesse was holding a piece of paper, a pained look on his face.

"Now what?" Louis asked.

"He's splitting us up," Jesse said.

Louis took the paper from Jesse and stared at the new schedule in disbelief. Shit, he was going on swing shift with Ollie.

Twenty-five

One drink before he went in. The bottle was cold in his hand, but the Jack Daniel's was hot on his tongue. Jesse twisted the cap back on, set the bottle on the seat of the Bronco and stared at the front door to the chief's house.

A light went on in the living room. Jesse drew in a deep breath and popped open the door, knowing that his courage was fading faster than the dying daylight. He had to do it. He had to talk to the man, find out what was going on. Why had the chief split him and Louis up?

His shoes scrunched on the hardened snow as he moved up the walk. He rang the bell and heard the chimes echo through the house. The door opened, silhouetting the chief's wife, Jean, in a golden light. She frowned slightly, then seemed to recognize him and switched on the porch light.

"Jess. What are you doing here?"

"I need to talk to the chief. He here?"

"Of course. Come in."

She stood aside, holding the storm door. Jesse stepped inside, stomping his boots on the throw rug near the door. He glanced at the white carpet and stomped again.

"You haven't been over in a long time, Jess," Jean said, taking his coat and hanging it on the hall coat tree.

"I know. I'm not interrupting anything, am I?"

"Of course not," she said with a smile.

She walked away, and Jesse let out a small breath of relief. The woman had always made him nervous, but he didn't know why. Maybe it was just because he had never gotten the chance to get to know her. But how could he? As close as he was to the chief, they never socialized and the chief never talked about his personal life.

Jesse waited in the foyer while Jean Gibralter went to the den to get her husband. He tried to remember the last time he had seen her at any police function. She never went to anything. But then, neither did Julie anymore; she said she hated standing around while the men talked shop.

A door opened and Gibralter emerged. He came over to Jesse.

"What's wrong?" he asked.

"Nothing's wrong. I . . . ." Jesse looked at Jean, who had curled into a chair near the fireplace with a book on her lap. "I just wanted to talk to you."

"About what?"

"It's kind of personal," Jesse said quietly.

Gibralter frowned, then motioned for Jesse to follow him into the den. Gibralter closed the door, then went to the bar to turn down the scanner.

"Beer?" he asked, opening a small refrigerator.

Jesse didn't want one, but he accepted the can of Budweiser Gibralter pressed into his hand. Gibralter moved to a stool at the bar where he had spread out his reloading gear.

"What's the problem?" Gibralter asked, hoisting a hip onto a bar stool.

"I want to know why you split Louis and me up," Jesse said.

"I don't need to explain my actions to you, Jess." Gibralter picked up a shell casing and carefully poured powder into it.

"I know. But Louis is my partner."

"We don't have partners in this department, you know that."

Jesse came forward and set the beer on the bar. "I know that, too. But you doubled us up—"

"That was temporary."

"Well, maybe it shouldn't be."

Gibralter leveled his eyes at Jesse.

"I mean, I like riding with someone," Jesse said. "I've learned shit from Louis. He's—"

"Your friend?" Gibralter asked.

Jesse hesitated. "Well, yeah, I guess he is."

Gibralter turned back to his shell loading.

Jesse stared at Gibralter's broad back, then moved around near the bar so he could see Gibralter's profile. "What? Is something wrong with that?"

Gibralter didn't look up. "In this job, there must be a blind faith, an unbreakable trust, or we can't function."

"I don't understand."

"Kincaid is a lone wolf. He is a cop without loyalty, without purpose."

Jesse shook his head slowly. "I think you're wrong, Chief. Louis has purpose. His purpose is . . . Well, it's the law."

Gibralter picked up another gold shell casing. "Trust me, Jess."

Jesse fell silent, frustrated. Finally, after a moment, he added, "Chief, I need to say something here."

"Don't."

"Damn it, I'm going to." He hesitated, then spoke quickly. "It isn't all Louis's fault that Lacey was cut loose. If I had told him about the raid, then maybe he would've made a better call."

"It's more than that."

"What? That thing in Mississippi? I don't—"

"It's more than that too."

Gibralter held the newly made bullet between his thumb and forefinger, moving it so it caught the light.

"See this?" he said softly. "This can take a life or it can save a life. We decide."

Jesse waited. He knew there was no point of doing otherwise when the chief was in this kind of mood.

Gibralter finally looked over at him. "We enforce the law, right? But what is the law?"

Jesse wondered if Gibralter expected an answer this time. He was relieved when Gibralter put aside the finished bullet and picked up another empty casing.

"What is the law?" Gibralter repeated. "A bunch of statutes in a courthouse somewhere? A set of old leather books in a lawyer's office? Nine old men in black robes?" Gibralter shook his head. "People want to see the law as this beautiful, clean-running stream. But it's not like that. It can't be because there is always someone kicking up the bottom or throwing in shit."

Jesse stared at him, uncomprehending.

"That's what Kincaid does," Gibralter said.

Jesse moved to a chair and sat down.

"I don't think he can be trusted." Gibralter said. "You *can* trust me. You know that, don't you, Jess?"

"Sure . . ." Jesse bowed his head, running a hand through his hair. When he looked up, Gibralter was watching him.

"You remember that New Year's Eve you showed up at my house at three A.M. shit-faced?" Gibralter said.

Jesse nodded slowly.

Gibralter took a swig of beer. "You were seventeen. You ran away from the halfway house and you showed up on my door-step, half frozen and drunk from that Boone's Farm shit you stole from the party store."

Jesse nodded again, his gaze going to the floor.

"You sat on Jeannie's new white sofa, dripping on her new carpet. You were trying so damn hard to look tough. You said your girlfriend dumped you. What was her name?"

"Dee Dee," Jesse whispered.

"You said you had called your father." Gibralter paused. "You remember what he told you? He told you that your running away was the best thing that ever happened to your family. He told you not to call back. You remember that, Jess?"

Jesse said nothing.

Gibralter came over to stand at his side. "You asked me for a glass of water. I went into the kitchen and you picked up my service revolver off the bar."

"You saw that?"

Gibralter nodded. "I knew what you were thinking of doing."

"You would have let me do it?"

Gibralter put a hand on Jesse's shoulder, cupping the knotty muscle. "Jess, the gun was empty."

"Jesus," Jesse breathed, looking away. He rose, going to the window.

"But I knew you wouldn't do it," Gibralter said. "You didn't let me down then and you never have since. And I know you never will."

"I still don't get it," Jesse said after a moment.

"Get what?"

He turned to look at Gibralter. "Why'd you split us up?"

Gibralter's eyes softened, taking on an almost paternal warmth. "Sit down, Jess. I'll tell you," he said.

Twenty-six

The blackness stretched before them, a tunnel of trees, asphalt and night sky. The snow, caught in the glare of the cruiser's headlights, rushed toward them out of the dark void.

"Looks kinda like the *Enterprise* at warp speed," Ollie said.

Louis didn't reply. He sat back in the passenger seat, adjusting his body to get the gun butt out of his ribs. He was tired, beyond tired and moving fast toward exhaustion. All his life he had been a light sleeper, and had learned to function on five hours of fitful sleep. But the churning wake of the week's events had left him storm tossed, with the burning eyes, heavy limbs and dulled brain of a drowning man. And now, he was riding night shift.

Louis closed his eyes and leaned his temple against the cold window. He wasn't going to make it through the shift awake. New Year's Eve. The drunks would be out in force soon.

"You haven't said a word for two hours, Kincaid," Ollie said.

Reluctantly, Louis opened his eyes and looked over. Ollie Wickshaw was tall and thin, all angles, elbows and eggshell skin. He had a weird mechanical way of moving, as though he were built from Erector set parts. Louis had watched him earlier that night as he got into the cruiser, folding his body down into the seat like one of those old-fashioned wooden carpenter rulers.

Louis focused on Ollie's hands gripping the wheel. Like the rest of him, they were a road map of veins. His fingers had the pale brown tint of a chain smoker. Ollie reached up on the dash for his pack of Kools and with a few snaps of movement had the cigarette lit and in his mouth.

"They say *I'm* the man of few words around here," Ollie said.

Louis cracked the window. "It's not personal."

"I know."

They rode another mile and Louis looked at his watch. It was almost 1:00 A.M. and he hadn't eaten. They hadn't had a call in an hour.

"Is there someplace open to get something to eat?" Louis asked.

"On New Year's? Jo-Jo's about it." Ollie pushed a brown bag toward Louis on the seat. "You can share my dinner. Got some carrots and celery sticks in there and a soy burger. You ever tried soy?"

Louis sank deeper into the seat. "No."

"Tastes just like hamburger, but you gotta know how to work it, you know, seasonings. Cumin is good. And there's this Cajun spice stuff I get over in Grayling. I buy it by the case. I'm a vegetarian. Gave up meat eight years ago. The other guys think I'm a little strange, but meat's bad for the arteries. You ever seen a picture of an artery coated with plaque?"

"Nope," Louis said. "You ever seen a picture of a smoker's lungs?"

Ollie glanced at him, blinked twice, and looked back out at the road.

Louis sighed, resting his head back against the seat. Wickshaw didn't deserve this. It wasn't his fault Gibralter was such a prick. He had just decided to apologize when Ollie spoke.

"You have to know him."

"Who?" Louis asked.

"The chief. He's not what you think."

"Right."

"He's an Aries."

"What?"

"That's the chief's sun sign. Aries."

Louis rolled his eyes. Not that shit.

"Aries have an inbred desire to be in charge. To be number one. All the great leaders were Aries." Ollie reached down to snuff his cigarette out in the ashtray. "What are you?"

Don't even answer this, Kincaid.

"I bet you're a Scorpio."

"How did you know that?"

"I do charts. You ever had your chart done?"

"No. It's bullshit."

Ollie was quiet for several miles. They passed the road to the lake and Ollie made a left turn. The headlights illuminated a sign that said: U.S. 33—4 MILES.

"Where and what time were you born?" Ollie asked.

Louis stared out the window. "Five-thirty A.M. Mississippi."

"Ah."

"What does that mean?"

"It means you have Libra rising. Of course, I would have to calculate the exact hour to be sure, but it's a fair guess. Libra is the sign—"

"I don't care."

"Of beauty and fairness. Its symbol is the balanced scales. You must get very confused sometimes."

Louis didn't reply. He watched Ollie use his free hand to open his Ziploc bag and pull out a carrot.

"Scorpios are very moody and often immerse themselves in the morbid and sometimes violent aspects of life," Ollie said, between bites of the carrot. "You probably have a Mars or Mercury in Aries, which would account for your love of police work. Aries is the god of war and rules police and the military."

"So why am I confused?" Louis asked. He couldn't believe he was asking this nut anything.

"Because Libra is your secondary ruler and Libras are very peaceful by nature. Totally nonviolent. So, you see, you have this urge to subject yourself to violence, yet your gentler nature abhors it. Thus, the confusion."

Louis stared at him.

"Want a carrot?" Ollie asked.

Louis nodded and took one.

"Should I go on?" Ollie asked.

Louis nodded slowly, munching on the carrot.

"I bet you like very passionate women."

"Doesn't everyone?" Louis laughed. The laugh trailed off quickly. He didn't need to be thinking of Zoe right now.

"No, not really. But you like women who drive you crazy, physically and mentally. The woman you will marry is elusive by nature, mysterious and probably loves the water."

"The water?"

"As do you."

"I never thought about it one way or the other."

"You should," Ollie said, looking at him. The dashboard lights caught Ollie's benign eyes. "The water is where you need to settle."

"Well, I get the feeling the chief is not going to let me do that. I don't think he wants me here."

"It doesn't have to be here. There's lots of water in the world." Ollie held out the Ziploc. "Another carrot?"

Louis shook his head. They drove on without speaking for several miles while Louis stared out at the swirling snow. The radio belched a burst of static. Ollie reached over to turn down the volume.

"Hey, Ollie," Louis said finally.

"Yeah?"

"I'm sorry."

"For what?"

"For that crack I made about smoking."

Ollie's veiny temples twitched. "Forget it. I should quit anyway. Would make my wife happy. But it's my only vice left." He suddenly slowed the car and did a U-turn.

"What are you doing?" Louis asked.

"The Castle might be open. I mean, if you're desperate."

"Thanks, man."

They were heading back toward town now. After several miles, Louis spotted the neon halo of the White Castle hamburger joint arching above the dark trees. Ollie swung the cruiser up to the curb and shoved it into park. Louis moved to open the door.

"Jess is a Virgo," Ollie said. "Virgo rules your twelfth house."

"What's that?" Louis asked. "The house of partners?"

"Your house of secrets," Ollie said.

Louis stared at him for a moment, then closed the door. He went inside and ordered six burgers, fries and a coffee. He watched his burgers sizzle, then glanced back at Ollie through the sweaty glass. House of secrets. What crap.

He paid for the burgers, grabbed the greasy white bag and walked out, checking his watch. Only three hours to go. He started across the damp parking lot, thinking of Jesse. And then Zoe's face flitted across his mind, hovering there for a moment like a phantom. He paused, popped off the coffee lid and took a sip. His eyes were burning from fatigue and he looked across the parking lot, trying to focus on the black stand of pines. A ground fog had left the lower trunks shrouded, making the huge trees look as though they were floating in the night. House of secrets. His house, but whose secrets?

Louis climbed back in the warm car and opened the bag.

"Don't suppose you want one?" Louis said, offering the bag of fries.

Ollie shook his head with a smile and pulled the cruiser out of the lot. They rode on in silence as Louis downed the burgers. He found himself watching a small medallion that hung from the rearview mirror, lulled by its hypnotic sway. It took a moment before he realized it was an arrowhead.

"What's with that?" he asked, pointing.

Ollie gave him a half-smile. "You sure you want to know?"

Louis finished the last fry and stuffed the trash in a bag. "Yeah, I'll bite."

"It's a jasper quartz arrowhead," Ollie said. "The Indians believed it had special powers to keep them safe against their enemies."

"Didn't work too well against the white man, did it?"

Ollie let the remark go. Keeping a tight grip on the wheel, he headed the car through the center of town. Louis stifled a yawn and leaned back in the seat, watching the arrowhead sway back and forth. The dispatcher's voice ignited the silent radio to life. Ollie turned up the volume.

"Loon-8 and Loon-11, we have a report of a trash fire at mile marker 7, County Road 329, two miles off Highway 33. Do you copy?"

"Great," Louis said under his breath. He keyed the mike. "Ten-four, Central. We're en route."

County Road 329 was a dark, two-lane road that stretched east toward Lake Huron. It was bordered by acres of open, snow-covered meadows that loomed out to the ridges of the Huron National Forest. It was a stark, almost alien-looking landscape, white open patches of emptiness set down in the deep, dark canyon walls of the ancient pine trees.

The brush fire was clearly visible as the cruiser rounded a final curve. Ollie pulled over to the shoulder, leaving the rear of the cruiser on the asphalt.

Louis got out first, standing near the door of the unit. There wasn't a house or an electric light of any kind. Just the rotating red and blue lights of the cruiser and, far off in the meadow near the trees, the eerie orange glow of the fire.

He reached for his flashlight and shined it into the open field. The fire was burning high in an old oil drum. He trained the light on the distant pines, casting feeble arcs into the shadows there. Nothing.

Kids, probably just kids. He drew in a deep breath of cold air. But why were the hairs on his neck standing up?

Everything he knew about Lacey told him that the man

wouldn't strike in a place like this. He had shot both his victims when they were in places where they felt safe, places and situations where a cop was least likely to be acting like a cop. This was too . . . set. It wasn't Lacey's style.

The trunk of the cruiser popped open and Louis jumped.

"What are you doing?" Louis hissed.

"Getting your vest," Ollie said.

Louis set the flashlight on the hood of the car and stripped off his jacket. Ollie held the heavy vest out to Louis, who pulled it on. The wind whipped against his back as he fumbled with the Velcro tabs. Shivering, he hustled back into his jacket.

"Where's yours?" Louis asked.

"I'm wearing it."

Louis picked up the flashlight and swept it again over the meadow, looking for some sign of a vehicle. There was nothing, not even a track in the pristine snow.

"Could be kids," Ollie said.

Louis shook his head. "Only reason to set a fire way out here is to burn something you don't want anyone to find." He didn't add what he was thinking, that maybe they had stumbled upon evidence Lacey was trying to hide, that maybe there was another dead cop out there somewhere.

"Well, whatever it is, we've got to check it out," Ollie said.

"I'll go," Louis said, looking at the fire.

"I think I should."

"Why? Did your horoscope tell you that?"

"Actually, it said I should avoid confrontations on the job today."

Louis put on his gloves. "Well, that settles it. I'm going."

Ollie nodded and reached in the car to get the radio. "Central, I'm staying with the unit. L-11 is on foot."

Louis climbed the snowbank and started out into the field. Away from the cruiser, the darkness engulfed him and he felt his heart begin to beat faster. He stepped carefully, the powdery snow growing deeper with each move. The fire was an orange blur against the black wall of trees.

He squinted, knowing his lack of sleep had affected his eye-sight and probably his thinking. He felt as if every nerve in his body was trembling with adrenaline.

Suddenly, he sank to his knees in the snow and he fell for-ward, catching himself on his hands. Shit, shit. He got up, yanked off his gloves and shook out the snow. He wiped down the flashlight and turned to look back at the cruiser. It looked small and far away. Ollie, standing by the driver door, looked even smaller.

As he neared the drum, he could smell gasoline and hear the faint crackle of the fire. He aimed the flashlight at the drum. The snow at its base was packed down, but he still could see no prints leading anywhere.

The voice pierced the quiet and he jumped. Edna . . . Christ, it was just Edna, her voice coming from the portable radio on his belt. She was asking Ollie for a code-4 to make sure they were all right. He heard Ollie respond.

Louis stopped a few feet short of the drum and scanned the snow. Now he could see prints, sloppy and distorted in the snow, as if someone had moved around the drum at length. The prints led off toward the pines.

He picked up a stick and stepped forward, poking the stick into the drum. It hit something solid, sending a blizzard of orange embers up into the sky and the fire blazing to new life. He lifted a burning rag out of the fire and tossed it into the snow. Damn it. He couldn't tell what was in there. It could be a body for all he knew. He had to put it out.

"L-8," he said, calling Ollie from his portable, "I'm going to throw some snow on it and see if I can determine what's burning."

"Ten-four."

Louis threw the stick aside and stuck the radio back on his belt. He bent down to scoop up some snow.

Something snapped in the distance. What was it? A branch? An animal?

Louis looked back toward the cruiser. A chill prickled his spine and his hand jerked to his radio.

A loud crack fractured the silence and at the same time, something hit him hard from behind, slamming him to the ground. He couldn't breathe. Frantically, he tried to raise his face from the snow and immediately felt a sharp pain somewhere near his spine. He coughed, fighting for breath, trying to wipe the snow away.

God, God . . . he was hit.

Another crack pierced the quiet. Struggling up on his elbows, he wrenched his radio from his belt and keyed it with trembling fingers.

"Central! Central! Shots fired! Shots fired! I'm hit!"

Edna immediately hailed Ollie. There was no response from him. Louis lay still, trying to think. Head back to the cruiser? Wait for backup? The radio trembled in his hand.

"L-11, where are you hit?" Edna demanded.

"In the back!" he gasped. He keyed his radio again. "L-8! L-8! Do you copy me?"

There was no answer and he lowered his head, his fingers tightening around the radio. He had to get back.

He forced himself to his knees, and ripped his gun from his holster. *Move! Move!* his mind screamed.

He pulled himself behind the oil drum, facing the pines. He peered into the dark wall, trying to slow his racing heart. Slowly, he realized the pain in his back was not getting worse. Christ, the vest! The bullet had hit the vest. But Ollie had a vest, too. Why hadn't he answered?

Edna's voice crackled over the radio, still trying to raise Ollie. Another rifle shot zinged overhead and snapped branches far to his right.

"Central," he said breathlessly. "Sniper fire. Repeat, sniper fire, no visual, no visual."

"L-11, what is your location?"

"Road 329 . . . in a field. We're separated!" His voice

sounded hollow, almost feeble. The sound of it sent a spasm of terror through him. He was scared. Jesus, he was so scared.

Edna called to Ollie. "Advise code-4, Loon-8."

Louis stared at the radio. "C'mon, man, answer," he whispered.

Edna came back to Louis. "Loon-11, what is your condition?"

"I'm okay! I'm okay!"

"What is your proximity to Loon-8?"

"I . . . about eighty feet."

Louis took a deep breath, his heart pounding. He wiped his face, keeping his eyes trained on the trees.

"Loon-11, advise. How many shots fired?"

"Three . . . no, four!"

"Do you have a direction of fire?"

Louis looked at the trees to his left. "Shots fired from the east, Central. It's quiet now."

"Can you determine shooter's location?"

Louis wet his lips. "Negative. Negative."

Edna came back, her voice steady, but underscored with fear. "Loon-11, be advised Loon-5 and 6 are 10-8. ETA seven minutes."

Visions of the shooter ambushing the units raged in his head. He wanted to scream into the radio, but he forced his words out slowly. "Central, repeat, no location on shooter. Advise all units to proceed with caution."

The oil drum at his back was hot, but he shivered as the wind swirled the snow around him. He rubbed his hands on his thighs, his fingers tingling. Somehow, he had to get back to the cruiser.

The fire in the oil drum was slowly dying out, but he needed the cover of darkness. He scooped up two handfuls of snow and tossed it in the drum. The fire sizzled and died.

He began to creep on his knees, his eyes probing the darkness, his ears pricked for anything that moved. His bare hands grew numb as he inched through the snow toward the cruiser.

He kept waiting for more shots. He knew that even in the darkness he had to be visible, his uniform dark against the snow.

A rustle of brittle branches drifted to him from his left. He froze. The sound came again, farther away this time. Then he saw him, just a flash of movement near the road. He was coming from the eastern trees, visible only for a second as the red and blue lights of the cruiser swept over him. Then he was gone.

Louis struggled to his feet and started running.

The lights caught the figure again as he emerged from the brush and crossed the road. He was only twenty yards away, angling away from Louis. He carried a long, dark object. A rifle.

The man moved quickly, expertly, through the white beams of the cruiser's headlights, then disappeared behind it.

Louis froze, thrusting his arms rigid in front of him, his gun aimed. "Stop! Stop!" he shouted. "Stop, you mother-fucker!"

Two shots, that was all he was going to get. He held his breath and squeezed the trigger. A flash exploded in front of him and he had to blink the runner back into focus. He fired again.

He couldn't see where he was shooting. Then he saw him again. He was almost to the trees on the opposite side of the road.

"Loon-11. Loon-11. Are you code-4?" Edna called.

Damn it! Damn it! Louis ran, stumbling into deep drifts. He fell and struggled to his feet, raised his gun and fired again as the man leapt into the trees. Branches splintered as the darkness swallowed him up.

"Son of a bitch!" Louis yelled.

"Eleven! Advise code-4!"

His chest was tight, his heart thundering. Fucking bastard! Not again. Not again! He wasn't getting away again!

He gripped his weapon and emptied it at the trees, the gun bucking in his hands, the explosions reverberating in the night.

Click, click, click. Hammer against empty chamber.

Louis lowered the gun, panting. With trembling hands, he jammed the speed-loader into the cylinder and slapped it shut. "You fucking bastard!" he shouted to the darkness. "Motherfucking bastard!"

"Loon-11, advise your status!"

He started to run toward the cruiser, but his legs bogged down in the heavy drifts. In the distance, he heard an engine roar to life and ran toward it. He stumbled up onto the asphalt in time to see two red taillights disappear into the night, heading east on County Road 329.

"Loon-11! Advise your status!" Edna called.

Louis ran back to the cruiser and froze.

Ollie was slumped in the seat, his leg dangling out the door. His eyes were open, his gun still in his hand. He was shot in the throat. Blood was gushing from the wound, covering the dark blue fur of the nylon parka.

"Loon-11. Please advise your status!"

Ollie's lips were moving. His eyes were locked on Louis, frightened, birdlike. He was alive. Jesus, he was alive.

Louis seized the radio off the dash. "I need an ambulance out here now!" he shouted. "Now!"

Ollie lifted his trembling hand. Louis took it, gripping Ollie's fingers in his. They felt damp and cool as clay. The blue veins pulsated under pearly skin.

"Central, where is my backup!" Louis yelled into the mike, bracing his elbow on the hood.

Ollie's fingers wiggled limply in his. "Help me," he said, his voice thick with blood.

Jesus, everything was red. Ollie's throat, his shirt, the car, the lights. Oh, Jesus . . . He had to stop it, he had to stop it.

Louis tossed the radio on the dash and leaned in the car, placing his hand on the wound. Warm blood oozed over his skin and he could feel Ollie's weak pulse under his fingertips.

"Hang on, man," Louis whispered. "Hang on."

"Loon-11, what's the situation out there?" It wasn't Edna's calm voice now. It was Gibralter's, hard and firm.

Louis reached across Ollie for the radio, but froze as he saw Ollie's eyes looking up at him. They were dull. It took a moment before he realized the pulsating under his fingers had stopped.

He slowly withdrew his hand, staring at it. For a second, the radio traffic stopped and it was absolutely silent.

A deep, slicing pain moved through him, doubling him over. He grabbed the door of the cruiser, pressing his bloody hand to his forehead.

"Loon-11!" Gibralter shouted.

Louis squeezed his eyes closed, his fist banging on the roof of the cruiser.

"Kincaid!"

Numbly, he reached back for the radio. He turned away from Ollie and clicked on the radio, but when he tried to speak, the words caught in his throat. He knew what he needed to say. He had heard it before a hundred times. But not for real. On television and in the movies. Not for real. Not for real.

"Central . . . we have . . . we have a 10–99."

He looked up quickly, up into the snowflakes.

"Officer down."

There was silence. Then, suddenly, the radio burst alive with urgent voices. Other Loon Lake officers, and on the other channel, the sheriff's department.

Edna silenced them all with a few words. "Hold all traffic. Loon-11?"

Louis wiped his face with his sleeve and looked down the empty road in the direction of the sirens. He raised the radio back to his mouth, lowering his head into his hand.

"Suspect is armed with a large-caliber . . . rifle. In a vehicle of unknown description . . . headed . . . headed east on Road 329."

"Eleven!" Gibralter shouted. "What kind of description is

that? What happened out there? Did you return fire? Where are you?"

"I don't . . . affirmative, affirmative."

The sirens were closer, the wails rising and falling on the wind. In his clouded head, they sounded almost human.

His fingers gripped the radio as his mind grappled to hold on to some sense of reality. He could smell the blood on his hands, strangely metallic. Ollie's blood. He looked down at his hand. It was covered with blood. The radio was covered with blood. His pants legs were stained with blood. He stared at it in morbid curiosity. It was black . . . not red, black.

"Loon-11!" Gibralter yelled. "What's happening out there?"

Something drifted into his dulled mind in that moment, something about the rifle. He keyed the radio. The words flooded forward on a wave of anger and he could not stop them.

"Coward!" he spat into the radio. "He's a fucking coward! Lacey used a goddamn nightscope! He didn't have a chance! Ollie didn't have a chance!" Louis's voice cracked into a sob and he gulped in a cold, icy breath.

"Kincaid!"

"We can't catch him! We need help. Damn it, can't you see that? We need help!"

"Loon-11, pull yourself together!"

Louis threw the radio down to the wet asphalt. It bounced and gave out a final burst of static. He lifted his face to the sky. He could feel the flakes settling on his face, feel each one, so terribly gentle.

Twenty-seven

His teeth were chattering and he clenched them to make them stop. He looked up into the black sky, trying to find a place to store the vivid, bloody images that swam in his mind. So many sounds. Wailing sirens. Radio static. Shouts. All these men shouting and he was doing nothing.

A door slammed and Louis spun around. Ambulance, just the ambulance. It pulled away slowly, with no sense of urgency.

Someone touched him and he turned. Jesse was a silhouette against the glare of the spotlights aimed at Ollie's cruiser. For a second, the voices and sirens seemed muted.

Jesse reached for him. Louis stiffened, pulling back. But the need for touch, for human contact, was too strong. Slowly, he surrendered to Jesse's embrace. He closed his eyes, lowering his head to the stiff nylon of Jesse's jacket.

"Harrison!"

Jesse pulled back, leaving a void of cold wind. Louis blinked to focus on Gibralter's silhouette as it came toward him.

"How did this happen?" Gibralter whispered hoarsely.

How did this happen? How did this happen? Louis's eyes drifted to the spotlit cruiser, dark forms crawling around it, over it, in it.

"Kincaid! How did this happen?"

It happened because I let Lacey go. It happened because I went into the field and Ollie stayed by the cruiser. It happened because I couldn't get back to Ollie in time. It happened be-

cause I didn't react fast enough, I didn't shoot straight enough, I didn't, I didn't, I didn't . . .

"I want your report tonight," Gibralter said, bringing him back.

Did he say "Yes, sir," or nod? He wasn't sure. All he knew was that Gibralter had turned away. In the glare of the lights, Louis was vaguely aware of Jesse hovering somewhere nearby. The sounds came to him again—the voices, the radios, the rush of noise that hurt his head.

"Damn it . . . damn it."

It took him a moment to separate the words from the noise. It was Gibralter repeating the words to himself.

"Damn it . . . why him?"

The last two words made Louis look up. *Why him?* He looked over again at the cruiser and in his mind saw Ollie lying on the front seat, felt the warmth of Ollie's blood as it pulsed against his hand. *Why him?*

He looked back to see Gibralter watching him. The words were unspoken but there in his eyes. *Why not you?*

Gibralter turned and walked away.

Louis moved woodenly back to Gibralter's Bronco. He reached in the driver's side and picked up a clipboard. He slowly unzipped his jacket and fumbled for a pen. His hand touched the rough nylon of the vest. For the first time, he became aware of its weight, became aware, too, of the dull ache above his kidney where the vest had stopped Lacey's bullet.

He threw the clipboard to the seat and yanked off his jacket. He tore at the Velcro strips, pulled the vest over his head and threw it to the floor of the Bronco. He stood for a few moments, breathing heavily. He shut his eyes tight.

Stop, stop . . . *stop!* He opened his eyes to look at the shapes moving around him. State troopers, deputies, crime-scene techs. He saw the familiar blue parkas of his own department's officers. He saw, far off in the snowy field, the play of flashlights as men searched for where Lacey had been hiding. The men were doing their jobs. He had to pull himself together to do his.

He picked up the clipboard and sat down on the edge of the passenger seat, pulling his jacket up over his shoulders. He faced away from the field and the lights.

Slowly, the words came. They came, the words that explained what had happened, pouring out onto the lined form. They were the words of his job, words like *suspect, victim* and *pursuit* and *shots fired,* words unweighted with emotion. Safe, efficient, unhuman words, and he found comfort in their blankness.

When he was done, he set the report aside and leaned back in the seat. A huge wave of fatigue rolled slowly over him, and he had to fight to keep his eyes open. He pushed himself up, put on his jacket and got out of the Bronco.

He searched the crowd for Gibralter, finally spotting him standing by the open door of Ollie's cruiser. Louis walked over to him, not looking at the blood-soaked interior.

"The report is finished. What do you want me to do now?"

"Go home," Gibralter said, not looking at him.

"Chief—"

"I said go home."

"I need to be here."

"This isn't about what you need, Kincaid. You're on administrative leave pending psychiatric evaluation."

"A shrink? I don't need a shrink."

"It's departmental policy. Make an appointment in the morning."

"I can help search—"

"We don't need you," Gibralter said. He turned away before Louis could answer. "Evans!" he called out.

The other officer looked up and trotted over.

"Evans, take Kincaid home."

"Wait a minute," Louis said, moving into Gibralter's line of vision. "I want—"

"I don't care what you want," Gibralter said sharply. "In your mental state, you're no use to us. Now go home."

Louis walked stiffly to Evans's car and got in, unable to look at Evans as he started the cruiser. They pulled slowly away and were soon engulfed by the darkness and quiet.

Louis leaned his head back on the seat. A thought penetrated the fog in his head. "Did they find it?" he asked dully.

"Find what?" Evans said.

"The card."

Evans hesitated. "Yeah."

"Where was it?"

"On the floor of the cruiser."

Louis closed his eyes. That's why the motherfucker ran near the cruiser, to throw in the damn card.

"What was it? What card?" Louis asked.

"Eight of clubs."

Eight. Eight? Just like Ollie's call number.

Something inside him stirred. Fred Lovejoy's number was ten. "Radio numbers," Louis mumbled softly. "He's using their damn call numbers."

Evans glanced at him. "What?"

Except Pryce. Pryce's number was two, not one as the ace of spades would indicate. Why hadn't Pryce been tossed a two?

Evans brought the car to a sudden stop. Louis looked up, saw he was home and jumped out of the cruiser without a word. He went inside and walked to the kitchen. He uncapped the bottle of Christian Brothers and took a long swallow. It dribbled down his chin and he coughed, setting the bottle down. Bent over the sink, he wiped his chin with his hand.

You're no use to us. . . .

His hand was trembling. He brought it up to his face, turning it over slowly. He stared at his nails, rimmed with dried blood. He turned on the faucet, grabbed a Brillo pad and thrust his hands under the water, tearing the pad across his nails. Finally, he threw it aside and turned off the water.

There was a knock, and his eyes shot to the door. His hand went to his holster. It was empty; he had turned over his gun at the scene as routine procedure.

"Louis?" a soft voice called. "Louis? It's Zoe."

He let out a breath, went slowly to the door and opened it. She stood there in the darkness of the porch, her head uncovered, her face shadowed. She waited, and finally he moved aside and she came in.

The cabin was dark, the only light filtering in from the kitchen. She looked around, her eyes coming back finally to him. He saw them move down from his face to his chest. He had forgotten he was still wearing his police parka, the front stained brown with Ollie's blood.

He turned away, going to the sofa. He switched on a small light and slipped off the jacket, throwing it in a corner. He sat down, leaning forward, hands on his knees, closing his eyes. After a moment, he felt the sofa sag with her weight as she sat down next to him.

"I heard what happened," she said.

Her voice was distant in his brain, childlike, fearful. He didn't want to answer. He was afraid his own would sound the same.

"I had to come," she said.

He shook his head slowly, not daring to look at her. He wanted to ask her why she had come back, but he didn't want to hear what he knew was the truth, that she came back out of pity.

"Go away, Zoe," he said softly.

"Louis . . ."

"I need to be alone right now."

She touched his back. "Don't push me away. I understand—"

"Please . . . please go. Now, please." He started to pull away, but her hand moved up to his neck, pulling his closer.

"Don't," she said.

He tried to push away, but her hand grew firmer. "Don't," she said.

He began to tremble and shut his eyes.

"Don't," she whispered.

Something ripped inside his chest and he fell against her. Her arms encircled his back and she pulled him to her. He began to cry. She held him, stroking his face, until he fell exhausted into sleep.

Twenty-eight

Louis stepped out onto the porch, stretching his arms up over his head. He looked left, to where the setting sun had left a smudge of orange over the western trees. Dusk had always been his favorite time to run.

He hadn't run in years, except for that one time with Zoe, and was probably risking a muscle pull, but he didn't care. He had to get out. Running had always helped him clear his head, helped him think straight, and God knew he needed help in that department right now.

Stretching his calves, he thought about his appointment earlier that afternoon over in Grayling with the psychiatrist Vincent Serbo. He was a phlegmatic old fart, used to treating depressed housewives and wigged-out military types from the base. He told Louis that in his thirty years of practice he had never seen a police officer. He seemed fascinated by the smallest detail of cop life.

Not that Louis had volunteered much. He knew that seeing a shrink was standard procedure after a shooting, especially when it involved another cop. But he didn't share his feelings with friends, let alone strangers.

Besides, it was all crap anyway. Seven stages of grief . . . shit, who needed it? Ollie's death had been a hit to the gut, but he would deal with it and get back to work.

He stepped off the porch, swinging his arms to get the blood moving, and started down toward the shoreline.

"Hey, Louis!"

Louis turned to see Jesse walking down the road toward the cabin. He was in uniform, but there was no sign of his cruiser.

Jesse came up to him. "Where you headed?"

"Going for a run," Louis answered. He hadn't spoken to Jesse since the shooting. They hadn't talked about anything since Gibralter had split them up. As glad as he was to see Jesse, Louis had trouble meeting his eyes.

"Where's your unit?" Louis asked.

"I was over at Dot's after shift and decided to take a walk, do some thinking. Been doing a lot of that lately, thinking."

Louis nodded. "How'd it go at work today?"

Jesse gave a sigh. "Everybody's pretty upset. Chief sent Florence home because she wouldn't stop crying."

Louis nodded again and looked out to the lake. He wasn't sure he wanted to talk about Ollie's death, even with Jesse. Shit, was that denial or what?

"Lou, can we go inside?" Jesse asked.

"Sure."

They went back in the cabin. Jesse pulled off his parka and sat down on a chair, wringing his hands, trying to warm them. He seemed edgy, even more than he had after finding Lovejoy. There were only two cops left now from the raid: himself and Gibralter.

"You want a drink?" Louis asked.

Jesse shook his head.

Louis picked up a half-finished can of Dr Pepper and took a drink, leaning against the counter to wait for Jesse to bring up whatever was obviously on his mind.

"So," Jesse said, "how'd the thing with the shrink go?"

"It's bullshit, a game," Louis said with a shrug. "I'll tell the guy what he wants to hear and get back to work."

Jesse just looked at him.

"What?" Louis said.

"I don't know, Louis," Jesse said. "I think you should take this a little more seriously."

Louis gave a laugh of derision. "Jess, spare me your amateur analysis."

"You shouldn't just shrug this off. I mean, Ollie died right—"

"Jess," Louis said, cutting him off. "Enough. I'm all right."

"You're not all right. I heard the tape."

Louis turned. "What tape?"

"The radio transmission. You sounded fucked up."

Louis stared at him. "Gibralter played the tape for you?"

"He played it at briefing." Jesse shifted on the chair, suddenly uncomfortable. "He used it as a kind of training thing, played it for all of us and said that with Lacey out there we had to keep cool heads and—"

Louis threw the empty soda at the sink. "Son of a bitch!"

"Louis . . ."

"Son of a bitch!" He stalked across the room, turned and went back. He picked up the small lamp off the end table. "Motherfucker . . ."

Jesse jumped up. "Louis!"

Louis set the lamp down with a thud and went to the fireplace. He braced himself against the mantel, head down.

"Nobody thought anything about it," Jesse said weakly.

"Shut up, Jess," Louis muttered. "Just shut up for a minute." After a moment, he turned. "Why is he doing this to me?"

Jesse was watching him intently. "Sit down," he said quietly.

Louis didn't move. But something in Jesse's eyes finally compelled him to sit down on the edge of the sofa.

"He knows," Jesse said.

"Who?" Louis asked.

"The chief."

"He knows what?" Louis said sharply.

"About you and Jeannie."

"Jeannie? Who the fuck is Jeannie?"

Jesse looked at him oddly. "His wife."

Louis shook his head. "Wife?"

"He knows . . ." Jesse hesitated, his face pained. "He knows you two are having an affair."

Louis stared at Jesse in shock. "He thinks I'm fucking his *wife?*"

Now Jesse looked stunned. "Aren't you?"

"No!" Louis said quickly. "I've never even met his wife!"

"Wait, wait," Jesse said, shaking his head. "Who *are* you fucking?"

"That's none of your business," Louis snapped. He paused, trying to calm down. "Zoe, her name is Zoe Devereaux."

Jesse was quiet for a moment. "I don't know any Zoe, and I know everyone here."

"She's not from here, she's from Chicago. She rents a cabin up on the north shore. She's an artist."

Jesse's expression clouded. "Artist? What does she look like?"

"She's . . . she's small, half-Asian and . . ."

Jesse waited for him to finish and when he did not, he continued for him. "Dark hair, light-colored skin, like you?" he said.

Louis stared at him.

"She likes French stuff," Jesse added. "She paints . . . pictures of snow and trees."

Louis stared at him, then walked off toward the kitchen. Jesse shook his head slowly, watching Louis's back. He stood up. "I guess I'd better let you—"

Louis turned quickly. "Why the hell didn't you tell me sooner?" he demanded.

"I just found out," Jesse said slowly.

"How?"

"He told me. The other night, before Ollie was killed. I went over to his house to talk to him about splitting us up and he told me."

Louis started to say something, then just shook his head. He turned away again, unable to face Jesse. The only sound in the cabin was the dripping of the kitchen faucet and Louis's breathing.

"I couldn't believe it," Jesse said softly, wanting to fill the silence. "I mean, I always thought she was strange, but when he told me about her cabin and all the weird shit—"

"How long?" Louis demanded.

"What?"

"How long has he known?"

Jesse looked uncomfortable. "About a week. He told me he suspected something and went to her cabin one morning to talk to her. That morning he was late for briefing? You remember . . ." Jesse's voice trailed off.

Louis was staring at him vacantly, as though he wasn't really hearing Jesse's voice.

"He said he saw a drawing of you, something she did," Jesse said quietly. "That's when he knew."

Louis hung his head.

Jesse glanced at the fireplace, then back at Louis. "It's not like it's all your fault," he said. "I mean, she lied to you, man."

Louis couldn't move. The anger was building fast and it was taking every ounce of strength he had to keep from hitting something.

"Louis, the woman is strange," Jesse went on. "From what the chief told me, it's like she's leading two lives, like she's got some multiple personality dis—"

"Shut up!"

"Sorry."

Again, silence. Finally, Louis turned to face him. "Why are you telling me this?"

Jesse didn't answer.

"I thought he was your friend, your great fucking mentor or something. Why are you telling me?"

"I wasn't going to," Jesse said. "I mean, he is my friend and he is the chief. But he's riding you because of this, not because of Lacey, and he wants you out."

"So why doesn't he fire me?"

"I asked him. He said he doesn't want her to feel sorry for you. He said if he fires you, you'll be a martyr in her eyes."

Louis shook his head.

It was quiet again. "Louis—"

"Go home, Jess," Louis said, not looking at him.

"Look—"

"Go home, please."

Jesse slowly pulled on his parka and started toward the door. As he passed the counter, he touched Louis's shoulder. Louis pulled away.

Jesse left, closing the door softly behind him. Louis stood, head bowed, hands braced against the kitchen counter. Finally, he looked up, surveying the room for his coat. He scooped it off the chair and was out the door. It was dark, but a waning moon bathed the lake in a spare gray light. He squinted, picking out a light on the far side of the lake. He got into the Mustang and started it.

It took only fifteen minutes to reach her cabin. It was dark. He hurried up the steps, flung open the screen and pounded on the door. There was no sound from within. He pounded again. He saw a curtain move and looked to the small window. The black cat stared at him with calm wide eyes.

"Zoe!" he yelled. "Zoe!"

His voice caromed through the pines, her name echoing back to him, fading into the black, silent night.

"Zoe!" he shouted.

Echo. Silence. The whisper of wind in the trees. He looked to the window. The black cat was gone.

He stumbled back off the porch, his gaze moving up over the cabin. He stood there, staring at it for several seconds, then turned and went back to the car.

Twenty-nine

Ribbons of muted color against the brilliant cobalt sky. Blue. Brown. Black.

They had all come. The state troopers in their navy blues. The Oscoda County sheriff deputies in their chocolate browns. A neighboring town force in their cadet blues. Another in their ink blacks. A fourth in their seal browns. They stood, in a mute, unmoving mass, around Ollie Wickshaw's casket.

The eight men of the Loon Lake Police Department were positioned in the front, dressed in dark blue, double-breasted overcoats and pristine white gloves. From his position as a pallbearer, Louis watched them, struck by the contrast created by the extravagant coats and the pain-etched faces of the men. He thought back to earlier that morning. He had almost been late because he couldn't bring himself to put on the uniform.

His gaze traveled to the family sitting stiffly in the chairs in the front. Ollie's wife stared at the flag-draped coffin in a dry-eyed trance. A daughter of about twenty sat on her left, weeping softly. An older son sat on his mother's right, holding her hand, staring off into the distant trees.

Louis's eyes drifted over to Gibralter, standing stiffly nearby; then he scanned the crowd, wondering if she had come. He didn't see her and closed his eyes.

The minister's voice droned on. Louis tried to listen to what the man was saying, tried to use the placating words to block all thought. He concentrated on the voice until it was a soft drone in his head, a mantra of numbness.

A gunshot pierced the quiet. He jumped.

He braced himself for the second and third rounds of the traditional salute. Quiet again. He let out a ragged breath.

He felt a nudge. Jesse was urging him to the casket. He took his place with the others and helped fold the flag into the tight triangle. He watched as Gibralter went to Ollie's wife and handed her the flag. Gibralter hesitated, then bent to kiss her cheek. He shook the son's hand and stepped back in line.

The warble of a bugle drifted on the cold breeze. Louis caught Jesse's eye. Jesse looked terrible, eyes red rimmed from sleeplessness, skin ashen with tension. Louis looked at the ground as he fought back the tightness in his throat.

When the last note died, he looked up. Ollie's son rose and went to a small wooden box positioned just outside the canopy. He opened a latch of the cote and there was a flurry of movement. Ollie's prized homing pigeons circled upward. Louis watched them, white wings against blue sky. They dipped west and disappeared.

Slowly, people began to move away. Ollie's wife and children lingered, talking to friends. Louis stood rigidly, gazing blankly at the crowd.

"She never comes," Jesse said softly.

Louis looked at him.

"Jean. She never comes to funerals. Her father—"

"I know."

"Come on," Jesse said, tugging his sleeve. "Let's go."

The Loon Lake officers were walking off to a nearby tree where Gibralter was waiting. He and Jesse joined them. For a moment, the men just stood in silence. Finally Gibralter cleared his throat.

"This is the third time we have gathered to bury one of our own, the third time we have said good-bye to a friend," he said, his voice soft but firm. "Let us now ask that we do not have to gather here again." Gibralter bowed his head and the others took their cue.

Louis closed his eyes, feeling the wind on his neck.

Gibralter's voice broke the silence. " 'The glories of our blood and state are shadows, not substantial things. There is no armor against fate. Death lays his icy hand on kings.' "

The men began drifting away, parting to allow Louis a view of the cemetery. He glanced at Jesse at his side. "You ready?"

"Yeah, let's get out of here," Jesse said softly.

"Kincaid," Gibralter said.

Louis turned.

"When can I expect you back at work?" Gibralter asked.

"I don't know," Louis said. "The shrink hasn't said."

"Let's see if we can step it up some. We need you on the street."

Louis looked hard at him. *You didn't need me New Year's Eve, you son of a bitch.* He looked away. The hell with it.

Jesse touched his sleeve and gave a nod toward the cruiser. They started toward the cluster of cars.

"Chief Gibralter!"

The voice sliced through the air. Louis turned.

"I'll be damned," Jesse whispered. "It's Mark Steele."

A tall man was walking boldly across the snow, his black overcoat flipping in the wind, two similarly dressed men following behind. The man's hair was as black as his coat, his face whipped pink from wind. A gray cashmere scarf hung around his neck, and a speck of red, a tie, was visible between the lapels of the coat.

"It's about fucking time," Louis muttered. He went to a nearby tree, positioning himself within earshot.

Jesse sidled up to him. "Louis, let's go," he urged.

"No, I want to hear this."

Gibralter had turned toward Steele and was lighting a cigarette, his hands cupped over the match. Mark Steele stopped a foot before Gibralter, the flunkies lurking in the background.

"Steele," Gibralter acknowledged curtly. He flung the match to the snow and blew a stream of smoke into the cold air. "Nice of you to show up for my officer's funeral."

"I'm sure he was a good man," Steele said.

"But that's not why you came, is it?"

"No."

Gibralter took a drag on the Camel. "I don't need you."

"It's not a matter of what you need anymore," Steele said. "I'm taking this over."

"I'm not going to let you do that," Gibralter said.

"You have no choice." Steele paused, leaning closer. "How many more are you going to bury?"

"This is *our* problem."

"Not anymore."

Gibralter stared at Steele. Then he tossed his cigarette to the snow, turned sharply on his heel and walked away. He brushed past Louis without looking at him.

"Jesse, come on," Gibralter said brusquely.

Jesse shot Louis a look and followed Gibralter up over a slope toward the cruisers. Louis looked back to see Steele heading to an unmarked black sedan. The two flunkies hurried to open the door.

The cemetery was emptying fast, the cruisers and cars pulling away in a slow line, exhaust plumes curling up into the blue sky. Louis spotted Jesse and Gibralter standing near the hood of Jesse's cruiser. They were talking heatedly, Jesse shaking his head. Finally, Jesse hung his head and Gibralter slipped an arm around his shoulders.

It was clear that Jesse was falling apart, and what was that son of a bitch going to do to help him? Probably laying another of his fucking loyalty guilt trips on him.

Louis's gaze moved back to the gravesite. Ollie's black coffin glistened in the sunlight. Two cemetery workers hovered nearby, impatiently waiting to finish their task.

Shivering, Louis stuck his hands in the pockets of his overcoat. His right hand closed over something small, hard and cold, and he pulled it out. It was the snowflake obsidian Ollie had given him on Christmas Eve. On impulse, Louis had slipped the thing in his pocket as he went out the door that morning.

Louis looked at the small black stone for a moment, turning it over between his fingers. With a last look back at the coffin, he started up the snowy slope to his car.

Thirty

The Mustang rounded the curve in the road, and Louis saw the sign: LOON LAKE—12 MILES. It had been a pain in the ass, but it was over. That quack Serbo had given him a full release to go back to work. The rational part of him knew it was too soon. He'd seen cops who came back only a few days after a traumatic incident and almost always they cracked. But he had to get back to work, if for nothing else than to get back some of his dignity.

Fragments of the sessions with Serbo floated back as he drove, and he shifted in the seat.

It had been the first time he had told a stranger about his real mother, Lila. It had been the first time in years he had said the name of the father who had deserted him, Jordan Kincaid, and peeled back the thin layer of anger that covered his heart.

It was also the first time he had told anyone he was afraid. He admitted to Serbo that his confidence was broken, his nerves shredded. And, at the end, he had talked of Gibralter.

It hadn't been easy. How could you tell a shrink you thought your boss was out to get you without sounding like a paranoid? How could you explain to a stranger you were involved with your boss's wife without looking like a complete fuckup? And how could you admit you didn't know how to fight back?

Serbo had offered only one observation. "Maybe you should deal with your chief as you do this man Lacey," he had said. "You have studied Lacey's life, looking for his weakness.

Maybe you need to do the same with your chief to level the playing field."

Louis shook his head. Shit, if Gibralter had any human frailty, he sure the hell wasn't going to let anyone see it.

Louis approached the station, slowing. The lot was filled with strange sedans, and a shiny blue chopper sat like a giant insect on the courthouse lawn next door. Mark Steele had taken over, just as he had promised.

Louis was forced to park near the supermarket and walk back to the station. Inside, it was crowded with strange men who, with their bland faces and black wingtips, looked like J.C. Penney catalog clones. One corner desk had been taken over as a command post, stocked with extra phones and heaped with files. The place even smelled different. No fire in the hearth, just the stink of cigarettes.

Louis noticed Dale's radio was not playing. There was also no sign of Dale. He went over to the dispatch desk.

"Hey, Flo."

She looked up and smiled. "Oh, Louis, I'm so glad you're back," she said, jumping up. "Let me get you a coffee—"

"No, don't get up. Listen, where's Dale?"

A frown creased her face. "Out on patrol. Chief put him with Jess."

Louis shook his head. Damn, Dale had no business out on the street.

"Things are not the same here, Louis," Florence said softly.

"I know," he said. "Is the chief in?"

"Yes, but he hasn't come out of his office in the last hour. Want me to buzz him?"

Louis nodded. Florence paged Gibralter on his intercom and his voice came back, telling her to have Louis wait. Louis's eyes drifted up to the wall and he saw that Ollie's portrait had been hung next to Pryce's and Lovejoy's, all with black bands. Four days had passed since Ollie's death. Jesse had told him that there had been no sign of Lacey.

He felt a rush of cold air at his back and turned to see

Steele come in. Steele went straight to the command desk, pulling off his black overcoat with a vampirish flourish and handing it off to an aide. Rubbing his hands, he went to the coffeepot and poured a cup, using Jesse's mug.

Florence looked at Louis and frowned. With a shake of her head, she turned back to the dispatch radio.

"Kincaid."

Louis looked at Gibralter standing at his office door. Gibralter's eyes focused briefly on Steele, then back on Louis. He waved him to the office. Louis hesitated as Zoe flashed into his head, followed by a disturbing image of her with Gibralter. Jesus, was that always going to be there now, every time he looked at the man?

Louis went in, closing the door behind him. Gibralter was sitting at his desk. His uniform shirt was crisp, but there were circles under his eyes and a shadow of whiskers on his jaw. The office had a slightly fetid smell, an odor of cigarettes and body musk. Louis spotted a Styrofoam takeout container in the trash and a bottle of Aramis on the credenza.

"You have something from the doc?" Gibralter said.

Louis held Gibralter's eyes for a moment, looking for a clue in them about Zoe. Gibralter had trusted Jesse with his secret and had no reason to suspect that Louis now knew. There was nothing new in Gibralter's eyes, Louis finally decided, just the same contempt that had been there before.

Louis pulled the papers from his shirt pocket and handed them to Gibralter.

"It says you need to continue to see him," Gibralter said. "You have other problems I need to know about, Kincaid?"

"The future visits are routine. I can come back to work."

Gibralter nodded stiffly. He fished in a drawer and pulled out a paper. "Now I have something for you," he said, holding it out.

Louis came forward and took it. The Loon Lake city seal jumped out at him. It was a letter of reprimand. *Conduct un-*

becoming a police officer, improper and inappropriate radio traffic, profanity and blatant unprofessionalism . . .

"What is this?" Louis said, looking at Gibralter.

"You know what it is."

"I don't deserve this."

Gibralter swung the chair around to the credenza and switched on a tape recorder. The tape crackled with static and then Louis's voice filled the office.

"Jesus . . . Jesus . . . Coward! He's a fucking coward!"

"Kincaid, pull yourself together!"

"Turn it off," Louis said sharply.

Gibralter turned it off and the room went silent. He held out a pen. "Sign it."

Louis didn't move.

"Sign it or I'll add insubordination."

Louis stared at the letter in his hand. *Quit, Kincaid, just quit and walk away. You don't need this, you don't need this damn job and you don't need her.*

Gibralter started to reach for the paper.

Ollie's face came back to him in that moment. Ollie's face splattered with blood and his pleading eyes. He grabbed the pen from Gibralter, scribbled his name and thrust the paper back at Gibralter, throwing the pen on the desk.

"Can I go now?" he asked tightly.

"No. I think you need a few days in the office."

"I have a release for full duty."

"I don't care what you have. I decide when a man is fit for duty." Gibralter reached down below his desk for an empty box. He tossed it across the desk and Louis caught it against his thighs.

"Take down the Christmas decorations."

Gibralter's eyes didn't waver, but Louis could see the net-

work of tiny red veins around the cold blue irises. The man
was cracking, just like the rest of them.

Suddenly, something snapped inside Louis. The room
shifted, everything shifted. As he stared into Gibralter's eyes,
the impotent rage burning inside him was mutating into a cold
anger. He realized in that instant he had made a decision. He
wouldn't quit and leave Jesse, Dale, or any other cop, at Lacey's hands.

But what could he do? Gibralter wasn't going to let him
work the case. And now Steele was in control of the search,
the arrest, of everything.

Then he knew. He would help Steele. He would do whatever
he could to help Steele catch Lacey. He didn't want to be
caught in a damn ego war, but Lacey had to be stopped. If it
meant taking sides against Gibralter, he would do it. He would
do what he could and then get the hell out.

"Am I dismissed?" Louis asked tightly.

"Get out of here."

Louis left the office and went to his desk, tossing the box
in a corner and sinking into the chair. Taking a stand against
Gibralter was a dangerous move. He had to play it carefully.
Very carefully.

Level the playing field. But how could he find something
to neutralize Gibralter?

He glanced at the phone. He grabbed the phone book and
dialed the *Argus,* asking for Doug Delp.

"Delp here."

"Delp, this is Kincaid. Can I buy you lunch?"

"Sure. Dot's?"

"No." Louis paused. "Jo-Jo's."

"That shithole out on 29?"

"Yeah. Ten minutes, okay?"

He spotted Delp in the gloom of Jo-Jo's, sitting at the end
of the bar. There was no one else in the place except for a

drunk slumped over the table in a corner booth. The bartender eyed Louis's uniform as Louis slid onto a stool next to Delp.

"Nice place," Delp said, stirring his coffee.

Louis ignored him, motioning to the bartender to bring another cup.

"Where you been?" Delp asked. "I called the station."

"Therapy."

"Oh, yeah. How's it going?"

"Fine." The bartender set a mug of coffee in front of Louis. Louis stirred in three sugars and took a sip. He grimaced and pushed it away.

"Okay, what's with the secrecy?" Delp asked. "Don't tell me you're ashamed to be seen with me."

"I need a favor," Louis said.

Delp studied him for a moment. "What?"

"Do you know anyone at a newspaper in Chicago?"

"Got a buddy at the *Tribune*. Why?"

"Somebody who's been around a while, maybe on the police beat?"

Delp leaned forward. "This is about Gibralter, isn't it?"

Louis tightened. He sure hoped he could trust this asshole. "I want to know why he left Chicago."

"Why?"

"Can you do it or not?"

"Where you going with this?"

"I can't tell you."

"Not yet, you mean."

Louis hesitated. "All right. Not yet."

Delp shook his head. "Promises, promises."

"Look, Delp, can you help me or not?"

Delp shrugged. "I'll see what I can do."

Louis started to get off the stool. "I have to get back."

"Hey, wait," Delp said. "I got something for you."

"What?"

Delp hoisted a beat-up leather briefcase onto the bar and

pulled out a manila envelope. "The photos you asked for, the leftovers from the raid. I found some extras in the morgue."

Louis slid back onto the stool. He opened the envelope and sorted through the black-and-white photographs. It was just standard newspaper stuff: shots of the cabin, the backyard, a sliding glass door, a broken window. There was a photo that showed an indentation in the snow that looked like a snow angel splashed with black that he recognized finally as the spot where Johnny Lacey fell after being shot.

"Nothing here," Louis said, setting them down.

"Try these," Delp said, holding out a second envelope.

"What's this?"

"Postmortems."

"I already saw them."

Delp slipped out a stack of photos. "Not all of them. I found some stuff that didn't get printed the first time."

"How do you know?"

"Photographers use a hole punch to notch the edge of the negatives they want to print," Delp said. "These weren't notched."

Louis sifted slowly through the photos. Many were just different angles of those he had already seen, but he paused at one. It was a closeup of a hand, life-size but still small and delicate, obviously Angela's hand. It was palm down, fingers splayed, and across the back, between the first set of knuckles and the wrist, was a half-circle bruise. He knew he had not seen this picture in the case file. Why had it been left out?

"That one's weird, isn't it?" Delp said, sipping his coffee. "What you think that bruise is?"

Louis said nothing.

"Looks like maybe someone stepped on her hand with a boot heel," Delp said. "Or maybe it's a horseshoe?"

Louis started to stack the photographs, but Delp laid a hand on them. "Something else," Delp said. "Did you notice the initials on the raid photographs?"

Louis picked up a print of the cabin's sliding glass door. He hadn't bothered to look at the initials the first time. "A.R. Who's A.R.?" he asked.

"Arnie Rogers."

"So what?"

"So don't you think it's strange that Arnie took the crime-scene photos?"

"Common in small towns."

Delp shook his head. "I checked other files. Gibralter always had his men do the pics, before the raid and after."

Louis was silent, remembering that Ollie had been the photographer at the Lovejoy scene.

"And get this," Delp said. "I found out a local doc by the name of Boggs did the autopsies. Don't you think that's strange too?"

Louis slipped the photographs into the envelope, not wanting Delp to know that he did think it was strange. Why hadn't Gibralter called in Ralph Drexler, the county medical examiner?

Picking up the envelope, Louis slid off the stool and tossed a five on the bar. "Listen, Delp," he said, "don't call me at the station."

"What's the matter? Things getting rough there?"

"Just don't call."

"What if I get something on Gibralter?"

"I'll call you. When?"

Delp shrugged. "Can't say, man. Haven't talked to my bud in Chicago in a long time. He might have forgotten all about me."

Louis resisted the urge to say something smart. He started for the door.

"Hey, Kincaid," Delp called, and nodded toward the envelope in Louis's hand. "A thank-you would be nice, you know."

"You'll get your thanks," Louis said.

"Promises, promises," Delp mumbled.

Thirty-one

Louis sifted again through the autopsy photos, then slipped them back in their manila envelope. He placed the envelope in his desk drawer, under some other papers, and locked it.

He glanced up at the clock. Four-thirty, still a half hour until shift end. Shit, his first day back and he was already going crazy from riding a damn desk. He glanced down at the cardboard box. But no matter what Gibralter threatened to do, he wasn't going to take down the damn Christmas crap.

He looked at Gibralter's door. The office was locked and dark. Gibralter had gone home early for once.

"Jim!"

Louis swung around at the sound of Steele's voice. He was standing at the wall map. An aide hurried to his side.

"How many men we have out there today?" Steele asked.

"Three dozen, sir."

"Is Chopper One up?"

"Not yet. Fuel line problem."

"Call Lansing. Get another."

Steele picked up a yellow highlighter and marked off an area on the map. Louis assumed it was an area that had already been searched. He heard a snort from Florence, who was incensed Steele had marked up the map.

Steele went back to the command desk and sifted through some papers. His face looked a little haggard, lines visible around the raven-black eyes.

"Jim, did you get that Lacey background I asked for?" Steele asked.

The aide thrust out a thin folder. Steele scanned it and dropped it on the desk. "This is just his rap sheet," Steele said, his voice edged with irritation.

Louis watched the exchange, thinking about the thick Dollar Bay file. The phone on the command desk rang. Steele picked it up and started arguing with someone about getting more tracking dogs.

Louis rose and went to the coffeepot. He poured out a cup, and leaned against the wall, sipping the coffee, his gaze wandering down over the command desk. He spotted the case files for Pryce and Lovejoy, the two playing cards, encased in plastic, stapled to each.

He wondered what kind of legal arm-twisting Steele had gone through to get Gibralter to relinquish them. But Steele had no reason to know about the Dollar Bay file, and obviously, Gibralter had not volunteered it. Well, if he was going to help Steele, this was as good a place as any to start.

Steele finished his call. He sensed Louis's presence and turned, a flash of impatience on his face.

"Yes?"

"I overheard you talking about Lacey's background."

"So?"

"There's a file on Lacey compiled by the cops in Dollar Bay. It's got everything you need."

"Where is it?"

"You'll have to ask Gibralter."

Steele studied Louis. "Why are you telling me this?"

"Lacey's ex-miliary, knows how to survive outdoors. You'll need everything you can get to find him."

Steele smirked. "I suppose you think you know him."

"I know he's gone to see his son. I think the kid knows where his father is."

Steele's eyes narrowed, then drifted down to Louis's name badge.

"I also know he's got a good motive," Louis added.

Steele paused, then fished out a folder from the pile on the desk. Louis saw the case number and knew it was the raid file.

"I read all about his motive," Steele said, waving the file. *"You* gave him motive. You should have been able to talk those kids out of that cabin."

Louis bit back his anger. For a second, he wanted to spit it right back in Steele's self-satisfied face that he *agreed* with him. But as he stared at the file in Steele's hand, he realized it was thin, too thin. The original was at least an inch thick.

Steele tossed the file on the desk and turned away.

Louis stared at the file on the command desk. He could see Gibralter not giving Steele the Dollar Bay file, just to piss Steele off. But why withhold information from the raid file?

"Excuse me," Louis said.

Steele turned slowly.

Louis nodded toward the raid file. "That isn't complete."

"I chalked it up to your department's incompetence."

Louis tightened. Asshole.

Steele was staring at him, as if trying to see inside his mind. "Officer," he said quietly, "what are you trying to tell me?"

"Just that I've seen the complete file, and that isn't it," Louis said.

"Are you saying Gibralter is withholding information?"

"I don't know."

"He's given me everything I asked for."

"He didn't give you the Dollar Bay file."

Steele picked up the file, then his eyes went to the two aides hovering nearby and then to Florence. He gave Louis a nod to follow him. Louis hesitated, then followed.

Outside, they stood by the door. It was cold, but no wind blowing. Two Loon Lake officers, just coming on night shift, eyed Louis as they passed. Louis looked quickly away.

"All right, what's going on here?" Steele asked, waving the file.

Louis felt an uneasiness come over him. Suddenly, he wasn't sure *what* exactly was going on, at least as far as his own motive. No matter what he thought about Gibralter, he was still his chief. Did he really want to put the reputations of other cops on the line because he was pissed at him?

You were not there, Kincaid, you don't know what really happened. You're letting your anger get in the way.

"Officer, you're wasting my time," Steele said.

But he was almost certain that Gibralter had left something out of the file he gave to Steele. Anyone reading Gibralter's report of the raid, and those of the other men, would say the Loon Lake cops had acted in self-defense. But it was also possible to see their actions as overly aggressive. In fact, in a larger department, the raid would have routinely gone to internal affairs for investigation. Gibralter knew that; he had worked in a big city department. But Gibralter also knew Steele had made a career out of carving up cops. Was he just trying to protect himself and his men from Steele?

Shit, be careful, Kincaid. You don't know what's going on here.

"Officer?"

Louis met Steele's eyes. "I am not sure, but I think the original file might contain something that could be misconstrued or—"

"Are you suggesting Chief Gibralter has a reason, other than his personal dislike of me, to withhold information?"

Louis was taken aback. "Look, I don't know—"

"What do you know?"

Louis shook his head. Man, this guy was a prick.

"You show your chief little respect, Officer Kincaid," Steele said.

Louis stared at him. This wasn't going right at all.

Steele started back and then turned to Louis. "You're telling me about the Dollar Bay file and Cole Lacey is appreciated," he said. "But if you have a problem with your chief, deal with it. Don't use it to bullshit yourself into my good graces."

Louis flushed with embarrassment and anger.

Steele went inside.

Louis just stood there, stunned. He stared at the streetlights for a moment. They flickered on in the quickly darkening dusk. Shit, now he had lost Steele, too. He went back in.

He glanced at the command desk. Two aides were there but Steele was gone, apparently leaving by the locker room back door. Louis looked over at Florence. She was staring at him oddly.

This was nuts. He was going nuts. He had get out of here. He hurried into the locker room to change. He emerged and was halfway out the door when he heard Florence calling his name.

"Louis! Telephone!"

He hesitated, hand on the door. "Who is it?"

"A man. Wouldn't tell me his name."

Slowly, Louis came back to his desk. He picked up the phone.

"Yeah?"

"Hey, it's Delp."

Louis sank into his chair. "Look, man, I told you—"

"I know. I didn't tell the old biddy who I was. Jesus, what's with you?"

"What do you want?"

"I got what you asked for."

Louis sat up straighter. "That was quick," he said quietly.

"Hey, I'm good. What can I say."

"What did you find?"

"You tell me first what you're looking for."

"Just tell me."

Louis waited, hearing papers being shuffled at Delp's end. He glanced at Florence, but she was busy with the dispatch mike.

"Okay, back in '68, there was a drug scandal," Delp said. "Seventeen Englewood cops were indicted for possession and conspiracy to sell drugs, extortion and bribery."

Louis let out a soft breath. "He was dirty?"

"No. My buddy knew the guy working the cop shop then. He said Gibralter was squeaky clean. But the DA figured Gibralter knew something and pressured to him to testify with a grant of immunity. Gibralter refused."

"What happened?"

"Gibralter went to jail for contempt. He got off the hook though. The DA got what he needed somewhere else."

Louis pulled out a notebook, but then decided not to write it down. Besides, it wasn't damning; it was totally in character for Gibralter.

"That it?" Louis asked.

"No, one more thing. In 1973, Gibralter was involved in an incident on the force," Delp said.

"Incident? What does that mean?"

"He was a sergeant, thirty at the time. Something happened when he was on patrol. Couldn't find out what. Whatever it was, Gibralter was riding the desk for months afterward."

Louis tapped the pencil on the desk. "Shot in the line of duty, maybe?"

"Could be. Engelwood's a tough place. But here's something interesting. Three weeks after Gibralter was taken off the street, three gang members went down on drug charges. Came out of nowhere and rumors had it the kids were railroaded by the cops."

"Did it have something to do with Gibralter?"

"Don't know."

"Shit, man, what *do* you know?"

"I know that it's been bricked over."

"What?"

"They ain't talking about it, Kincaid. Not even ten years later."

"Is that why he left Chicago?" Louis asked quietly.

"Doubt it. He made captain soon after the gang thing, but never rode patrol again. He came here about a year later."

Louis rubbed the bridge of his nose.

"You still there, Kincaid?"

"Yeah. Is that it?"

"Yup."

"Okay. Listen, thanks, Delp."

"If you want to thank me, get me an interview with Steele."

"Can't help you there. He runs his own show."

"Well, if anything breaks, don't forget me, okay?"

"I won't."

Louis hung up and sat back in his chair, his eyes going to Gibralter's locked office door. The contempt charge was understandable, given Gibralter's code of conduct. But the gang thing was less clear. It would have taken something pretty damn drastic to keep a cop like Gibralter off the street. And something told him that Delp was wrong, that whatever it was, it had driven Gibralter out of Chicago.

"Louis?"

He looked up at Florence.

"I forgot to tell you. The chief called for you."

"When?"

"When you were outside."

He stared at her but could read nothing in her bland face.

"Did he say what he wanted?" Louis asked.

"No. Just wanted to know where you were."

"What did you tell him?"

"That you stepped out." She blinked. "Was that okay?"

He nodded woodenly. He realized he was sitting there in his University of Michigan jacket. And that he was sweating.

Rising quickly, he unlocked his desk drawer and pulled out the envelope of photographs Delp had given him. For a second, he couldn't find his copy of the raid file and in his paranoia wondered if Gibralter had found it. With relief, he found it stuffed under some papers. Without a word or a look back at Florence, he left.

Thirty-two

The contents of the raid file were spread out on the bed before him. Louis rubbed his face, trying not to give in to his fatigue and disappointment.

It was here. It had to be. He just couldn't see it. Something had gone wrong that night, and there was something in this file about it that Gibralter did not want Steele to see.

What had happened? And who was involved? His gut was telling him it was Jesse. Shit, the guy had lost it just busting a harmless hippie. Had he done something at the cabin that Gibralter felt compelled to cover up?

Louis slid off the bed and went into the darkened kitchen, got another Dr Pepper and returned to the bedroom. He popped the top and took a long drink, his eyes scanning the papers and photos.

Jesse's report was on top, the last thing he had been reading. He stared at it, taking another drink, then froze, the can at his lips.

It was typed.

Louis picked it up. He hadn't noticed it before. Dale had said Jesse couldn't type, that he was always allowed to write out his reports. Louis himself had seen it, Jesse's distinctively heavy, right-slanted scrawl. He had seen it on the hippie report, on Mrs. Jaspers's reindeer report and Stephanie Pryce's statement.

Setting the soda can down, Louis read Jesse's report again. Something about it didn't ring true. The wording, the grammar, the phrasing were wrong. Jesse was an emotional man, someone who couldn't stifle his feelings, even when writing a routine report. And what had Dale said about Jesse being upset after the raid? This report wasn't written by someone emotional, with a kid's blood fresh on his uniform. This was too perfect, too . . . cool.

Louis flipped to the end of the report. It was signed, but with just "Jesse Harrison," not with Jesse's trademark triple-underlined signature and usual postscript: NO MORE THIS REPORT.

Louis pulled out Ollie's report. The wording was virtually identical to that in Gibralter's and Jesse's. Lovejoy's version was the same. Louis shook his head. Every cop had his own way of writing reports. What were the chances four cops would have the same style?

He rummaged for Pryce's report. It was typed like the others. But as Louis read, he became aware that its phrasing and grammar were different, with small idiosyncracies not obvious in the others. He set it aside and dug out the diagram showing the positions of the officers surrounding the cabin. Jesse, Ollie and Lovejoy all ended up in the backyard with Gibralter. But Pryce had been ordered to maintain his position in front. There was no way he could have seen what happened in the backyard.

All right, so Gibralter might have been the author of all the reports except Pryce's. But would Steele even notice that? There had to be something else.

Louis turned to the crime-scene photos, stopping finally with Johnny Lacey's shotgun-shattered face. It was a Xerox, but it clearly showed the hole from the shotgun blast. It was centered on Johnny's left cheekbone, maybe about the diameter of a half-dollar, spreading outward, taking out his left eye and brow. It was also obvious that the shotgun had been fired at very close range, at a slightly upward angle.

Louis stared at the Xerox. There was another mark, this one barely noticeable, on the right cheek. But was it just a shadow created by the copy machine?

He pulled out a separate manila envelope, the one Delp had given him. Sifting through the postmortem photographs, he found a closeup of Johnny Lacey's face. It showed the second mark clearly, and it wasn't a shadow. It was a rectangular bruise, about an inch-and-a-half long with two short, parallel lines.

Louis fished through the papers on the bed and found the autopsy report, looking for an explanation for the bruise. There was nothing.

He picked up the autopsy photo again, staring at the strange bruise. Its shape was too perfect, too regular, too familiar. Suddenly, he knew what had caused it. It was from the cylinder of a handgun.

His mouth went dry as he slowly realized what had happened. Jesse had beaten Johnny Lacey to death. Jesse could not have been holding a shotgun in his right hand, as the reports said, because he had been holding his handgun, the gun he used to beat Johnny to death. The shotgun blast had came later, after Johnny Lacey was dead. Someone had blasted off Johnny Lacey's face in an attempt to hide evidence of the beating.

Louis picked up the autopsy report again. The cause of death was listed only as "Accidental shotgun wound to the left orbital area." There was no mention of any other injuries. Louis stared at the name on the form. Merlin Boggs, M.D.

Suddenly, the pieces were falling into place. This had to be what Gibralter did not want Steele to see. Jesse had beat Johnny Lacey to death and they had covered it up. They got a gullible local doctor to do the postmortem and a small-town reporter to take the crime-scene photos. They kept it in the family, led by Gibralter who believed that loyalty was more important than anything, even the life of a teenage kid.

"Goddammit," Louis muttered.

He stared at the papers spread over his bed. What was he going to do now? Turn it over to Steele? If this could be proven, Jesse and Gibralter could end up facing conspiracy or even manslaughter charges. But did he really have enough evidence?

He slowly shook his head. Shit, after what happened today, he had no credibility with Steele. If he went to him with only a photograph and his suspicions, Steele would kiss him off for good. He needed hardcore proof.

He started to gather up the papers and photographs off the bed, but then stopped. Someone was knocking on the door.

Jesse? Christ, he couldn't look him in the eye, not now.

The knock came again. Louis went to the front door.

"Louis?"

It was Zoe.

"Louis? Are you there?"

He waited, hoping she would leave. He hadn't seen her since the night Ollie was murdered. He had awakened sometime before dawn, alone on the sofa, and they hadn't spoken since. Several times, he had dialed Gibralter's home, only to hang up when he heard her answer.

"Louis?"

He flipped on the porch light and opened the door. She stood, looking up at him questioningly, seeing something in his face. There were things he wanted to say, questions he needed answered. Instead, he turned away, going into the living room.

"It's freezing in here," she said softly, pulling off her jacket and red wool hat.

Louis knelt to toss two logs in the grate. It wasn't until the fire was burning that he finally turned to face her.

"Louis, what's the matter?" she asked. When he said nothing, she came to him, her hand raised to touch his face. He jerked back.

"Don't," he said brusquely. He moved away, going into the bar.

"Louis, what is the matter?" she asked again.

"You lied to me," he said.

She didn't move. When she didn't say anything, he turned and faced her. "You lied to me," he repeated.

She stared at him, then slowly, her face crumpled. She went to the sofa, sitting woodenly on its edge.

"You're married," he said coldly. "When were you going to tell me that?"

"Tonight. I . . . Louis, please—"

"Right."

She looked away, holding her arms.

"He's my chief, for chrissake!" Louis said.

She shut her eyes, as if trying not to cry, and he turned away in anger. "How could you lie to me?" he demanded.

"I didn't lie."

He came forward to stand in front of her. "You lied about him, Zoe. Shit, that isn't even your name. You lied about who you are, for God's sake."

Her eyes glistened up at him. She didn't say it, but he saw it there in her eyes. *So did you.*

"Why?" he asked.

She didn't answer.

"Why?" he repeated.

"I don't know," she said, her voice quavering.

"You know."

She met his eyes. "I can give you all the clichés, Louis. I can say my marriage was over years ago. I can say he's changed, I changed. Is that what you want to hear?"

"I don't know what I want," he said, shaking his head.

"This isn't easy," she said sharply.

Her anger was unexpected. It deflated his own somehow. He moved to the window, not wanting to look at her. "Do you love him?" he asked.

"I don't know. I did. I don't know anymore."

He gave a mirthless laugh, leaning his forehead against the cold glass.

"I'm not happy. I haven't been for a long time. Part of it

is this place, but it's more, it's . . ." Her voice trailed off, breaking slightly.

He didn't want to hear it. An affair, a neglected wife, it was a damn cliché and he didn't want to be part of it.

"All right, so the marriage failed," he said. "Lots of marriages fail. But I don't get it. The fake name, the cabin. What the hell was that? Do you take other guys there too?"

"No. You're the only one." She took a deep breath and let it out slowly. "He got me the cabin about two years ago. I wanted to have a place to go. He had work, and I wanted something of my own. I started painting there, something I hadn't done in ten years. I found two kittens living in the crawl space so I kept them there, because Brian hates cats."

Louis thought of the sensual cabin, with its draperies, music, pillows, candles and incense. He couldn't see Gibralter tolerating any of it.

"What about your name?"

"I read it in a novel once, and I always wanted to go to France. I never used it before that night by the lake when I saw you. It just . . . came out."

Her voice had trailed off to a whisper. "I always hated the name Jean. I never felt like a Jean."

Louis came back to stand near the fireplace, looking down at her. "Why didn't you tell me you were married?" he asked, his anger still simmering.

"Would it have made a difference?"

"Yes."

She stared at him. "It must be comforting to have such a reliable moral compass."

He couldn't tell if she meant it to be sarcastic. "You could have left him," he said.

"We've been together since I was nineteen. We had . . ." She paused. "He needed me."

"I can't see him needing anyone," Louis said.

"He wasn't always like this," she said. "In the beginning, back in Chicago, it was different."

Louis looked away. He didn't want to hear about the joys of Brian Gibralter's young married life. She saw Louis's reaction, but went on.

"When Brian was a rookie, he used to come home at night so excited about the job, so sure he was doing good," she said, her eyes going to the fire. "But he got transferred to Engelwood and things changed. He started talking about the bad things, the junkies, the thirteen-year-old hookers, the man who pulled a hunting knife on him after he pulled him over for a broken tail light." She paused. "One night, I found him sitting at the kitchen table in the dark, still in his jacket. I finally got him to tell me what it was. He had arrested a man who had bashed in the head of his girlfriend's baby with a baseball bat because the baby wet his pants."

Louis didn't respond.

"He stopped talking to me about work after that. He said I couldn't understand," she said.

Louis thought of the night Ollie died. Even as she had held him while he cried, he had thought the same thing.

"I didn't fit in with the other wives and I was very lonely," she said. "I started taking the el downtown for classes at the Art Institute, but Brian made me stop. He said I'd get raped or mugged."

He heard her voice break. Her face was streaked with tears.

"It got worse," she said flatly. "He yelled at me for not locking the door when I went down to the laundry room. He yelled at me for not ironing the crease sharp enough in his uniform pants."

"You should have left him," he said.

She looked at Louis. "I wanted to, but I had no way to support myself, no job. I didn't even have a high school diploma." She gave a small laugh. "I needed him."

"I thought you had a sister," Louis said.

She nodded. "She told me I could come stay with her. I even had a suitcase packed, but then something happened and I couldn't leave."

"What?"

She looked at him warily.

"What happened?"

"Brian," she said. "Something happened to him and I couldn't leave him."

He could see something in her face, pain, guilt maybe, and he knew she had to be referring to the incident that Gibralter's department had covered up, the event that Doug Delp had been unable to unearth. He waited, tense. A part of him, the man who had been deceived, didn't want to hear one more damn word about Brian Gibralter. But the other part of him, the cop part, needed to know.

He sat down next to her. "What happened?"

She pulled in a breath, wiping her eyes with the sleeve of her sweater.

Louis went to get her a Kleenex. He sat down again, waiting. "What happened?" he repeated softly.

She looked away, unable to meet his eyes. "I didn't find out until weeks later. He wouldn't tell me. He had been to a doctor, someone the department made him see. I think the doctor was the one who told him to tell me."

Louis waited. The wind picked up outside, sending a low whistle through the windowpanes.

"He was on patrol alone because his partner was out sick. It was March. I remember because it was very cold for March." Her voice dropped to a soft monotone. "He turned into an alley, thinking he had seen something suspicious. They had been watching the neighborhood—there was a lot of gang violence. He should've called for help, but he didn't."

Louis suddenly knew where this was going. What he didn't know was how bad it would be.

"They . . . kids . . . a gang . . . they jumped him. He was alone and they jumped him. They took his gun."

Louis shook his head.

"Then . . ." She squeezed her eyes shut. "They held his

gun on him and made him undress. They stripped him. It was so cold that night. But they left him there, naked."

It took her almost a full minute before she was able to speak. "They handcuffed him to a fire escape in the alley and beat him. Then they spray painted . . . things, words, things all over his body."

She took a breath, and the rest rushed out in one long sigh. "He was there for hours before another unit came by and found him."

"What happened to the kids?" Louis asked.

"Kids?" She seemed bewildered. "The gang? He didn't want them prosecuted because then he would have had to tell the whole department what had happened. The cop who picked him up and one or two others, including his captain, were the only ones who knew."

Louis remembered what Delp had told him, the drug bust for the gang members that came out of nowhere.

She had stopped crying. She was just sitting there, staring vacantly at some point over Louis's shoulder, as if she didn't even know he was there anymore. When she focused back on his face, there was a naked look in her eyes, as if what she had just told him was about her, not her husband.

For several minutes, they just sat. He listened to the wind pound the glass and the crackling of the fire. Her soft voice interrupted the silence.

"We came here about a year later. He didn't even tell me about the ad in *Police Chief* magazine. He just told me we were going, that he could start over, build his kind of department."

Louis leaned back on the sofa, closing his eyes.

"I thought things would change," she said softly, "but they didn't. I didn't fit in here either."

He knew she was talking about being black, or half-black/half-Asian. Loon Lake wasn't like some backwater boonie in the South, but it was undeniably white. White in its racial makeup and white-bread in its small-town mind-set. He had come to feel like an outsider in the short time he had been here. He could only guess how a lonely woman like Jean Gibralter could survive.

He moved to hold her, to comfort her the way she had him, but he stopped. There was no future for them. He knew that now, even if he hadn't been so sure an hour ago. His anger toward her had dissipated, but he knew he wasn't beyond judging. Even if, after this ugly mess was over, she decided to leave her husband, he was not sure he could give his heart to her again. He wasn't sure he could trust her again.

"I think I'd better go," she said, rising.

She went quickly to the door, putting on her coat. He rose and stood watching as she pulled on her gloves. She looked up.

"I'm sorry, Louis. I'm sorry I lied to you," she said.

The door opened, a flurry of snow blew in and she was gone.

Thirty-three

Louis swung the Mustang around a turn and up the hill. The bald tires spun on the snowy road but finally caught hold. The car moved slowly up through the pines.

A small sign marked the entrance to the driveway: LITTLE EDEN, and the pines parted to reveal a clearing with a large log cabin in the center.

Louis pulled up in front and cut the engine. He frowned, seeing the smoke curling from the chimney and the shiny white Ford Bronco parked at the side. He picked up the raid file from the passenger seat and searched for the owner's name. Eden, David and Glenda. Damn, they were here now? He hadn't counted on having to deal with anyone.

He had decided to come to the cabin only that morning, not telling anyone at the station. It had been an impulse, partly to get Zoe out of his head, but mainly because he was hoping to find something to back up his suspicions before he went to Steele. But as his eyes traveled over the cabin, he knew he had no idea what he was looking for.

The front door opened and a man stood behind the storm door, staring at the Mustang. Louis got out and started up the shoveled walk. The man didn't seem to relax any seeing Louis's uniform.

"Mr. Eden?" Louis asked.

He cracked open the door. "Yes?"

Louis held out a hand. "Officer Kincaid, Loon Lake police."

The man shook his hand tepidly. He was about fifty, balding, beefy, and swathed in a red sweater with reindeers prancing across his chest. He had the buffed-pink look of a successful, middle-aged man, buttressed by his wealth and unaccustomed to such sordid things as visits from cops. Louis remembered reading the Edens were from Dearborn, the man a management type with Ford. He wondered why he hadn't sold the cabin after the raid.

"I'm sorry to bother you this morning, Mr. Eden," Louis said. "I didn't know anyone would be here."

"We don't come much anymore," Eden said simply, "just over the holidays."

A woman's face appeared behind him. "What is it, David?" she asked.

"Nothing, Glenda. Go back inside."

She gave Louis a blank look and retreated. "What do you want, officer?" Eden asked.

Louis took off his sunglasses, remembering something his lieutenant back in Ann Arbor had told him, that nobody liked talking to a cop in sunglasses. He realized he disliked it when Jesse wore his.

"I would like to look around," Louis said.

"What is this about?"

"Just a routine follow-up, sir."

"It was five years ago," Eden said flatly.

"I know, sir. We're closing the case officially. I just need to take some notes."

"Is this really necessary? I don't want my family upset."

"I don't need to come inside, Mr. Eden, or talk to anyone. This will only take a minute, I promise."

David Eden hesitated, then gave a curt nod.

"Thank you, sir."

Louis could feel the man's eyes on him as he went back to the Mustang. Finally he heard the door close.

Louis gathered up the raid file and stood back to look at "Little Eden." The property was large, enough so that no other cabins were visible. The woods in front had been cleared to provide an impressive view of Loon Lake below. The cabin itself was a new prefab structure, the kind built from blueprints bought from the back of a home-decorating magazine, and it had the contrived rustic charm of a Disney World exhibit. It was secluded and private, a perfect place for a gang to hole up, even if it didn't look like the kind of place where two kids would die.

Louis dug through the file, finding the diagram that detailed the positions of the bodies and the officers. It gave no sense of what the place really looked like. But it was always like this. The dry starkness of reports and diagrams never prepared you for the physical reality of a crime scene. That's why he had always liked to see the places where things happened, like Pryce's house. Maybe it was just vibrations, intuition, like Jesse had said. Whatever it was, it always helped clear his thinking.

He reached back into the car and picked up a second folder, which held the extra crime scene and autopsy photographs. Tucking both under his arm, he set off around the north side of the cabin and into the backyard.

The back was cleared about sixty feet from the cabin to where the heavy woods began. There was an aluminum Sears shed off in a far corner and a large woodpile, but nothing else on the lot. Louis turned to face the cabin. He was facing due east and had to bring up his hand to shield his eyes from the sun.

The back of the cabin was plain compared to the front, with two windows on the first floor and a sliding glass door that opened onto a snow-heaped deck. There were three windows on the second floor and a large satellite dish on the roof.

Louis fished Gibralter's report from the file. He needed to refresh his memory on the sequence of events.

Pryce had been the first on the scene, calling for backup after the kids refused his order to come out. Gibralter, Jesse, Ollie and Lovejoy had arrived soon after. Even after tear gas was fired into the cabin, the kids refused to come out. At this point, Gibralter was in front with Pryce, Jesse in the back, with Lovejoy and Ollie positioned on either side of the cabin.

According to the report, Johnny Lacey ran out the back door, took off toward the woods and was tackled by Jesse about twenty yards from the cabin. *"Officer Harrison's shotgun discharged, hitting suspect in the left front facial area. Suspect died at the scene."*

Louis turned and looked at the woods. He could almost picture the way it went down. He could see Johnny Lacey bolting out the back. He could see Jesse chasing him, the way he had chased Duane Lacey in the snowy field outside Jo-Jo's. He could see Jesse losing it, the way he had with the hippie. He could see Jesse going into a rage and bludgeoning Johnny's head.

What had happened after that? Was it Ollie or Lovejoy who had pulled Jesse off Johnny Lacey? And who had been the one to pick up the shotgun and blast off Johnny's face to cover up the beating?

Louis let out a deep breath. Jesse, Gibralter, Lovejoy, Ollie . . . He tried to picture them standing over the body. He tried to imagine one of them pulling the trigger of the shotgun. He could almost hear the echo of the shot in the trees and smell the powder burn in the clean air. But he couldn't see who had done it.

He lowered his head. He didn't want to see any of this.

When he looked up, his eyes picked up a flash in an upstairs window. He brought his hand up to shield his eyes. Someone was standing there. He pulled out his sunglasses and slipped them on.

It was a teenage girl, about fourteen. She was wearing a red sweatshirt and a bunch of silver bangle bracelets that she twisted nervously as she watched him. He guessed she was the Edens' kid and wondered briefly if she knew about the deaths at her vacation home.

Louis stared at her. Angela and Cole. Had they seen what happened in the backyard?

He went back to Gibralter's report. Cole had been found hiding in an upstairs closet, armed with a shotgun. He could have seen something and then hid. But Angela had appeared at the back door *after* Johnny was killed.

> *At this time, suspect #3 exited the premises through the rear door, armed with a small-caliber handgun. She positioned herself on the deck and announced she intended to shoot the officers unless they allowed her to leave the scene. Officers Wickshaw and Lovejoy ordered the suspect to drop her weapon. Suspect refused. Suspect then raised her weapon and fired at officers. Officer Wickshaw discharged his weapon, fatally wounding suspect in chest.*

Louis shook his head. It didn't make sense. Angela Lacey had no prior record involving guns; none of the kids was on drugs, according to toxicology reports. Why did she overreact? Why didn't she just surrender?

He knew there was no point in reading the other reports; they were duplicates of Gibralter's. But maybe there was something different in Pryce's. He fished it out, scanning it:

> *I heard Officer Harrison request assistance in a foot pursuit. I heard a female screaming and a shotgun discharged. I offered assistance, but was directed to remain in my position. At exactly 16:35, I heard a handgun discharged. Exactly five seconds later, I heard a second shot.*

Because Pryce had been ordered to stay out front, his perspective was limited, but he had heard Angela scream. Louis looked back at the Eden girl in the window upstairs. He couldn't prove it, but he was certain now that Gibralter had lied about Angela in his report. She had been standing at the door when her brother was killed and she had fired that gun because she was afraid they would kill her too.

Why had they let her get out of the cabin in the first place?

And why hadn't they shot to wound, not kill? He stared at the sliding glass door, trying to imagine Angela standing there, pointing the gun. He tried to imagine what was running through her head.

Nothing. No feelings, no vibrations. It had been five years, and the trail was cold. It wasn't like the Pryce house. No one spoke to him here. No one was alive.

Reluctantly, he opened the raid file again, looking for something, anything, that would trigger his brain. He stopped on the photograph of Angela's body. He held it up, comparing it to the cabin itself. The photo showed Angela slumped near the right side of the sliding glass door. He could tell her exact position because part of an electrical box was visible in the upper corner of the photograph. Nothing . . .

He pulled out a second photograph, this one the closeup of Angela's hand. He stared at the odd, scythe-shaped bruise across the back of her hand. What the hell had caused it?

Something made him look up.

It was the girl at the window. She was still standing there, watching him, twisting her silver bracelets.

Bracelets . . .

His hand crept back under his parka to the small of his back. He pulled out his handcuffs.

He stared at them for a moment; then his eyes went back to the cabin, scanning the back, finally finding what he was looking for. The conduit snaked up, out of the electrical box, just a few feet from the sliding glass door.

They had handcuffed her. She could not have fired the gun. They had handcuffed her to the conduit.

Something in his memory stirred and he quickly pulled out Pryce's report. It hadn't registered a moment ago, but he knew the way Pryce's mercurial mind worked, knew the kind of details it recorded. He drew in a breath. There it was.

At exactly 16:35, I heard a handgun discharged. Exactly five seconds later, I heard a second shot.

Pryce heard two shots in five seconds. Not one shot and what should have been the instantaneous return fire of an officer acting in self-defense. But five full seconds. That was the way Pryce's mind worked, not in "approximately" or "about" but "exactly." If Thomas Pryce said five seconds, it was the truth.

Five seconds . . .

Nothing in the normal duration of everyday life. But it was everything in the split-second time span of a crime.

Five seconds . . .

Just long enough for someone to react, to plan, to create a new reality.

Louis stared at the electrical conduit, seeing Angela Lacey, seeing everything, with a horrible clarity. Closing the folder, he went up onto the deck. His eyes scanned the conduit. Six feet above the deck, there was a gap between the cabin and the conduit, large enough to slip a cuff through.

Angela was about five feet tall, which meant they had to raise her arm over her head to cuff her. The bruise on her wrist, he knew now, would not have been made from the cuff alone. It was caused by an extreme restriction of blood flow.

Louis stared at the conduit. He could see her now. He could see her, hanging there by one arm, the weight of her body pulling her down, constricting her wrist against the metal cuff. Weight . . . dead weight.

Angela Lacey had appeared at the back door, just as the reports said. She saw Jesse beat her brother and saw them blow off his face. They used the cuffs to control her while they dealt with Jesse's mess. She never had a gun.

Someone, one of the four, shot her. It was Ollie, if the report was to be believed. She fell, still chained to the conduit. Five seconds later, a second gun was fired. It was the Hammersmith Beretta, a "throw-down," one of the oldest tricks in the book. They had fired it into the air to simulate returned fire, then they planted it in Angela's hand to make it look as though she shot first.

They had erased her, just as they had erased the evidence of her brother's bludgeoned face.

Louis pulled in a deep breath. There was no way to prove any of it. It was still just a theory, and he could be wrong, his imagination running wild. Ollie and Lovejoy couldn't talk; they were dead. Gibralter would never admit to anything. And Jesse . . .

Louis felt his stomach turn. Ollie and Lovejoy were conspirators, each guilty in his own way. But Jesse was the catalyst, the reason it happened. He had let his rage take over, and then had let Gibralter cover it up.

Clutching the folders, Louis stepped off the deck. He looked up at the window. The girl was gone.

As he stared at the cabin, a wave of sadness came over him, surprising him as it flowed in to mix with the other emotions. He was angry at them; he felt betrayed by them. They were cops and they were monsters.

But now what? What could he do about it? Go to Steele and tell what he knew? No—what he *suspected?* All he really had were pieces and gut instinct. He couldn't go to Steele with that.

He went quickly back to the Mustang, got in and started the car. He needed some hard evidence. He needed to get the throw-down.

Thirty-four

Louis scanned the shelves beyond the grating. Somewhere in the evidence room was the throw-down, but there was no way he was going to get to it without Dale's key.

He turned to face the chaos of the station. Ringing phones, anxious radio voices, the muted bark of dogs outside. Cords snaking over the floors, maps hanging on the walls. Suits, lots of suits. The smell of sweat, cigarettes and burnt coffee.

It was worse outside, the lot filled with state sedans and television vans, two from Detroit and one from Chicago. That morning, Louis had to fight his way through the knot of shivering reporters and cameramen. No one bothered to stick a mike in his face; they knew every Loon Lake cop was under a gag order. And they were waiting for Steele anyway.

Louis surveyed the room. No sign of him.

"Louis," Edna called out.

He looked over to see her holding out the phone. "It's the *Lansing State Journal*. She wants a quote."

As Louis pointed to one of Steele's aides, he saw Dale hurry in the front door. He was wearing his police parka, his face red from the cold. He spotted Louis as he pushed through the crowd to the locker room, and quickly looked away. But not before Louis saw the distress in his eyes. Shit, the kid never even frowned; something was up. Louis followed him.

Dale was sitting on a bench, still in his coat, head in his hands.

"Dale?"

His head jerked up. He looked like he was going to be sick. "What's wrong?" Louis asked.

Dale ran a shaky hand over his face. "I didn't know what to do. I didn't know how to stop him."

"Who?"

When Dale didn't answer, Louis sat down next to him. "Who?" he pressed.

"Jess," Dale said. "Jess . . . he . . . I didn't know how to stop him."

Louis felt his stomach knot. "What happened? Where's Jesse?"

"I don't know where he is," Dale said. "We went to Red Oak. The chief sent us, told us to do whatever we had to do to make Cole talk." Dale drew in a breath. "I knew Jess would get rough, but I didn't think—"

"What did he do?"

"I don't know. It happened so fast!"

"Dale, calm down, tell me."

"Jesse slammed him around a little, you know, knocked him out of the chair. Cole just got madder and madder and started yelling at Jess, telling him he was next, that he was going to 'die special' . . . That's what he said, Louis, said Jess was going to 'die special.' "

"What else? What else happened?"

"Jesse kept shouting at him to tell us where his old man was, and Cole started calling him stupid and . . . and . . ."

Louis heard a door open. Voices bounced off the tile. He leaned closer.

"Jess lost it, Louis," Dale whispered. "He took his baton and swung it at Cole's head like it was a baseball. Caught him in the mouth, I think." Dale wiped his sweating face with his sleeve. "I saw blood, Cole spit out blood, and he fell over. Jess hit him in the ribs and his balls." Dale took a breath. "I couldn't watch after that."

"What happened then?" Louis asked.

Dale looked at him. "He stopped. He just stopped and

looked at me, like, with this look on his face, like, why the hell didn't I stop him? Jesus, what was I supposed to do? I couldn't stop him!"

Louis pulled back. "Where is he?" he asked tightly.

Dale shook his head. "I don't know. We got out of there quick. Cole was laying there, holding his balls. We got out of there quick."

Dale's voice caught and he looked as though he was going to cry. Louis went to the sink, wet some paper towels and brought them back.

Dale covered his face with the towels, then looked up at Louis. "I should've done something," he said.

"Jesse's sick, Dale."

"It's my fault, I—"

Louis cut him off. "It's not your fault, damn it. It's Gibralter's fault."

"The chief didn't say to—"

"He sent you and Jesse out there knowing exactly what would happen," Louis said. "He knew what Jesse would do and he knew you couldn't stop him."

Dale was staring at him. Louis began to pace, shaking his head. "Chess," he said. "It's a fucking chess game to him and he used you and Jesse."

The locker room door banged open again, letting in the voices and telephones. Two cops eyed Louis and Dale, then moved to a different part of the locker room.

"I'm sweating like a pig," Dale said softly, peeling off his parka. His uniform was pitted with stains and he rose, taking off his shirt.

"You going to be all right?" Louis asked.

Dale nodded, pulling a knit shirt from his locker and putting it on.

"Louis?"

"Yeah?"

"Thanks." Dale changed into jeans and picked up his coat. "Well, I better get home."

"Dale, hold on a minute."

Louis waited until the voices at the other bank of lockers died and the door slammed shut again.

"I need a favor," Louis said. "I need to get in the evidence room."

"What for?" Dale asked.

"Can you just trust me on this one?"

Dale reached into his pocket and handed Louis the keys. "It's the small silver one with the red mark."

"Thanks," Louis said. "Dale, there will probably be some fallout from this Cole thing. You know that, don't you?"

Dale nodded.

"Just tell the truth. You'll be okay." Louis put a hand on Dale's shoulder. "And stay away from Jesse."

Dale nodded again.

Louis went back out to the office, making his way through the crowd to his desk. He drew up short. There were two German shepherds sitting obediently by the desk. They eyed Louis as he carefully reached between them to open a drawer and pull out a folder. Stepping back, he headed to the evidence room.

Unlocking the padlock, he slipped inside. He yanked on the light and turned to look at Edna. She was deep into her book and Milanos.

He scanned the shelves, looking for the evidence from the raid, finally spotting the box marked LACEY, JOHNNY/AN-GELA. He hoisted it down to the floor and using a pair of nail clippers, cut the sealing tape.

The evidence log was on top. Putting on his glasses, he scanned it for the gun. It was listed, a 9-mm Beretta, but there was no serial number. Setting the log aside, he turned to the box's contents. There was a sweatshirt, a brown-stained bullet hole visible through the plastic bag. He came across a small baggie holding a shotgun shell and a misshapen bullet that he guessed was the one taken from Angela's chest. Finally, his hand touched something hard and he pulled out the Beretta.

He held the plastic tight, down against the barrel. Damn, the serial number had been filed off. Without it, there was no way to prove it was a throw-down. A lab might be able to raise the number, but he knew that only Steele could make that happen now.

Louis poked his head outside the grating and scanned the room. It had thinned out some, the search called off because of darkness.

"Hey," Louis called out to one of Steele's aides. "Steele around?"

The man looked over. "Nope."

"Where is he?"

The man glanced at his watch. "Probably at about 35,000 feet right now."

"What?"

"He's the keynote speaker at some banquet in Detroit. Starts at nine. He said not to interrupt him unless Lacey is either in custody or dead."

Louis rubbed his forehead. His eyes drifted to the sweatshirt. He pulled it from the plastic bag, laying it across the open box, revealing the hole and brown stain just below the MACKI-NAW ISLAND lettering.

From the folder he had brought in, he pulled out the autopsy photo of Angela's chest. The bullet hole was dead center in her chest, but the one on the sweatshirt was lower. He moved the sleeve up, as if her arm had been raised over her head, and the hole in the sweatshirt fell into place, center of the chest.

He stared at the sweatshirt, his anger rising. How the hell had they expected to get away with this? And where had they gotten the throw-down in the first place? They wouldn't use one of their own weapons and there was no easy black market in a location like this. The most logical answer was that the gun had come from another evidence bag that no one had reason to ever open again.

He started moving bags and boxes, searching randomly, trying to remember anything from the case files he and Jesse had gone through. His eyes scanned every name and number, but nothing registered. Then he stopped, his eyes locked on a brown bag tucked far back on a top shelf.

HAMMERSMITH #75-88961. The dead motorcycle guy who had been arrested in Loon Lake eight years ago for drawing a weapon.

He pulled down the bag, slipped his finger under the dried, cracked tape and reached in. His fingers hit something sharp and he withdrew them. Cursing, he pulled out a broken beer bottle, set it aside and carefully patted down the bag. Nothing. No gun. It should have been there and it wasn't.

He pulled the evidence log out of the bag. Hammersmith's gun was listed, a 9-mm Beretta, serial number SYL61829.

SYL61829 . . . the number in Pryce's notebook, the number he had written on the back of the legal pad.

Louis felt his skin grow cold. Pryce knew. He knew that Hammersmith's Beretta had been used in the raid.

Pryce knew about what happened at the cabin, and it explained a lot of things. It explained Pryce's secrecy and his sudden desire to get out of Loon Lake. But why hadn't he done anything with the information?

"Louis?"

He spun around.

It was Edna. She was standing just outside the grating. "The chief just called for you."

"What did he want?" he asked.

"I don't know. He just asked if you were still here."

"Did he say anything else?"

"Just wanted to know if Mr. Steele was here too."

Edna gazed at him over the top of her cat's-eye glasses. For several seconds, she just looked at him as she munched on a cookie. "Want one?" she asked suddenly, holding out the bag.

Louis shook his head. She withdrew the bag, her eyes drifting down to the sweatshirt draped across the evidence box and then back up to Louis. She trudged back to the dispatch desk, shooting Louis a final look over her shoulder.

Louis let out a long breath. Jesus, had she told Gibralter he was in the evidence room? Had someone else seen him? No, no, he was getting paranoid. No one in the department could possibly know what he was doing. But why the hell was Gibralter checking up on him? Christ, maybe he was just trying to find out if he was with Zoe.

He was clammy with sweat, and the small, warm room seemed to close in around him. It hit him in that instant, the gravity of what he was doing. He wasn't just breaking the rules; he was breaking the code among cops. He was turning against his own.

Gens una sumus. "We are one family."

Had Pryce had the same doubts? Had he come to the same choice? Is that why he hadn't acted on what he knew? Had he simply decided to turn his back and get out? But there was no way to know what Pryce's plan had been because it was cut short by Lacey.

Louis put the beer bottle shard back in the Hammersmith evidence bag. He hesitated, then folded the log and slipped it in his pocket. Refolding Angela's sweatshirt, he put it back in its evidence box, but stuck that log in his pocket too.

He picked up the plastic-wrapped Beretta, turning it over in his hands. With a look back at Edna, he turned his back and slipped the gun in his belt, under his shirt. After putting the raid box back in its place on the shelf, he left the evidence room, locking it behind him.

Edna didn't look up at him. No one in the office did, as he went back to his desk. He stopped short.

The two German shepherds were staring at him. A trickle of sweat made its way down his back. Holding his breath, he reached between the two dogs for his jacket. Slowly, very slowly, he backed up, moving toward the door.

Thirty-five

The damn Mustang wouldn't start again. Louis looked at his watch, deciding against calling Dale for a jump. The kid had his own problems after yesterday's mess with Cole.

Grabbing the black garbage bag off the seat, Louis climbed out, slamming the door. It was snowing, a wet snow that coated everything like heavy cake icing. Gray clouds hung low in the morning sky and a mist hovered over the lake. Hefting the bag under his arm, Louis turned up his collar and started to walk.

A church bell clanged somewhere in the distance. A few cars puttered down the street. Everything seemed to be running in slow motion this morning, even his mind. He hadn't slept. Partly, it was because he was afraid that Gibralter would discover the Beretta missing from evidence.

But mainly, it was because he was uneasy about what he was going to do this morning. He had decided to go to Steele with the evidence he had against Jesse and Gibralter. It had to be done, he knew that. But that didn't make things any easier. It didn't make his thoughts less chaotic.

As he walked, he had a vision of Jesse and Gibralter being hauled off in handcuffs, the damn TV cameras capturing it all for national feed.

He could see Steele standing there, spewing out his self-righteous crap about corrupt cops. As much as he hated what Gibralter and Jesse had done, he couldn't stand the idea that Steele would come out of this with another notch in his belt. What did Steele know about cops? The man had never worn a uniform, had never known what it felt like to be pushed to the limit.

He himself knew. He had felt it that day at Red Oak when he knocked Cole Lacey back in the chair. He knew what it felt like to teeter on the edge.

Louis rounded the corner onto Main Street. The garbage bag under his arm held only the Hammersmith gun, the evidence logs and a copy of the raid file, but it felt heavy.

Another image flashed into Louis's mind. Jesse's face caught in the glare of headlights that night they rode with Lovejoy's body in the flatbed truck. *I wanted to be a cop. . . . I had to be a cop.* He could see Jesse standing in Lovejoy's cabin, staring at that stinking dog cage. Shit, Jesse would eat his gun before he'd go to prison.

Louis gripped the garbage bag tighter to his chest. But there was no turning back, no room in his head for second thoughts. Kids were dead. Soon, cops' careers would be dead.

Maybe even his own. Until last night, he hadn't really considered his own position in this mess. But now he could see it clearly. His own career was about to go on life support. Some cops might agree with his decision to turn in his chief, but he would still be ostracized, branded a traitor.

Gibralter's words came back to him in that moment, that day he told Jesse about Louis's testifying against Larry Cutter. *Is this how you plan to repay your fellow officers?*

He stopped a block from the station. There was a large crowd of reporters and a new van, with NBC NEWS on its side. Louis saw Delp in the middle and turned left to duck in the back way.

Delp spotted him and hurried over. "Hey, Kincaid!"

Louis ignored him. Delp fell into step with him.

"Give me a quote, man."

"About what?"

"Cole Lacey."

"Don't know what you're talking about."

Delp pulled a folded newspaper from his coat and thrust it in Louis's face. The headline said: COPS BEAT JUVENILE.

Louis stopped and took the copy of the *Lansing State Journal*. He looked back at the crowd. "Steele show up yet?" he asked.

Delp shook his head. "That's what we're all waiting for."

"Can I keep this?"

"Sure. Were you there?"

Louis shook his head, heading to the alley.

"Does the kid know where his old man is?" Delp asked, keeping pace.

"I don't know."

"Was anybody else there besides Harrison and McGuire?"

"I don't know."

"What'd the kid say?"

"Look, Delp, give me a break here."

Delp stopped. "Give you a break? I've busted my ass for you and you won't give me shit. I had to read this in the fucking *Journal!*"

Louis faced him. "Look, when we get Lacey, you'll be in on it first."

Delp's lips drew into a thin line. "You can't make good on that promise anymore. It's Steele's show now. You guys are as out of the loop as me."

Louis shifted the bag with the Beretta in it, staring at Delp. For a moment, he considered telling Delp what he knew. Right now, right here, he could hand him the garbage bag and the biggest story of his life. Why not? Eventually the press was going to find out anyway. The glare of publicity was too bright; it would have to reflect into the shadows of the raid. Why not just leak it all right now to Delp and get out of the way?

Louis's eyes went from Delp to the NBC truck. No, it wasn't right. He had made his decision and he would see it through.

"You're right, Delp, I can't help you," Louis said. He turned and started to the back door of the station.

"Fucking cops," Delp muttered.

Louis made his way through the locker room and out into the office. The place was nuts-to-butts with state flunkies, troopers and K-9 cops. A television in the corner was tuned to a newscast. Louis pushed his way through the uniforms watching it.

A talking head from the Lansing station was giving a report on Cole Lacey, the kid's juvie mug superimposed in one corner of the screen. The news guy was saying that the "young inmate was in fair condition" at Red Oak. They cut to Warren Little standing outside the center, giving a statement.

Louis looked around for Dale but there was no sign of him. He pushed his way to his desk, setting down the garbage bag. He was pulling off his parka when Steele came in through the front door. Steele had obviously just run the gauntlet of reporters outside and his eyes snapped with anger.

"Where's Gibralter?" he demanded of the room at large.

Heads swiveled, troopers gazed at him through the steam of their coffees, but no one answered.

"Where is he?" Steele said, raising his voice.

Gibralter's door opened and Steele spun around.

"You got something to say to me, Steele?" Gibralter said.

"Where are they?" Steele said sharply. "Where's Harrison and McGuire?"

Before Gibralter could reply, Jesse came forward. "We're here," he said. Dale was trailing behind, his eyes sweeping the crowd nervously.

"In the office, now," Steele demanded, nodding to Gibralter's door.

Jesse and Dale moved past Steele, neither looking at Louis. Gibralter and Steele followed them in and the door closed. The murmur of the office resumed.

Louis sat down at his desk, his eyes going to the garbage bag. There was no way he could bring this up right now; it would have to wait. He opened his drawer, dropped the bag in and locked it. Pulling the *Lansing State Journal* from his parka, he put on his glasses to read the story.

It was sketchy, with Warren Little as the only source and the reporter covering her attempt to get quotes from Gibralter with the old crutch, "Loon Lake police did not return *Journal* calls." Louis tossed the paper aside.

Gibralter's door opened and all heads snapped up.

Jesse came out first, head down, walking fast toward the locker room. A few seconds later, Dale emerged, heading more slowly in the same direction as Jesse. Louis was debating whether to follow him when Steele's voice drew his attention back to Gibralter's door.

"Your men interfered with an on-going criminal investigation that I have made clear is out of their jurisdiction," Steele was saying to Gibralter.

Louis tightened. The asshole was grandstanding.

Gibralter said nothing, his eyes never leaving Steele.

"They are facing criminal charges," Steele went on, "and you, sir, will be lucky not to go down with them."

Steele went back to the command desk, his aides quickly circling him. Louis watched Gibralter, but the man had not moved a muscle.

"We have a sighting."

All eyes swiveled to one of Steele's men, holding a phone. Louis felt his pulse quicken.

"Where?" Steele asked.

"Highway 33, twelve miles north of town."

The office eddied with noise and action. Steele moved to the center of the room, lifting his hands. "Listen up!" he shouted.

The crowd quieted.

"In the wake of the Red Oak incident, I must remind you of an additional obligation," Steele said. "We must conduct ourselves with the utmost professionalism. We are under the microscope now, gentlemen, and every move we make will be scrutinized. I do not want any witnesses touched, harassed or antagonized. I do not want one citizen angered. Do I make myself clear?"

It was quiet, but a current ran through the room, the charge of adrenaline.

"I know how you feel about this suspect," Steele went on, "but if we get a track on Lacey, there will be no quick triggers, no hot heads. I want it by the book."

Louis looked at Gibralter. As he gazed at Steele, Gibralter lifted his cigarette to his lips and took a long, slow drag. His face was like granite, but there was something new in it. Louis stared at Gibralter, trying to read it. Jesus, it was fear. It barely registered, just a flicker in the eyes, but it was there. Gibralter didn't want Lacey caught alive; he wanted him dead. He needed him dead, so he couldn't talk about what Cole had told him about the raid.

Steele left, going out to face the reporters. Louis looked back at Gibralter. He was gone, his door closed.

Louis rose and went to the locker room. Jesse was gone, but Dale was there, pulling on a sweatshirt. He looked at Louis as he approached.

"It didn't work, Louis," he said.

"What didn't?"

"Telling the truth. Steele says I could be arrested for . . . hell, I was so nervous I forget. Assault and coercion and something else."

Dale hung up his uniform shirt, running a hand down the front.

"What happened in there?" Louis asked.

"Steele was ripping Jesse apart, saying he was out of control, a renegade. He called him stupid." Dale looked at Louis. "I had to say something, so I said to Steele what you said to me."

"What?" Louis asked.

"That Gibralter sent us, and he did it knowing what Jesse would do."

Jesus, the kid had guts. "What did Gibralter say?" Louis asked.

Dale's face clouded. "He denied it, just out and out denied

it. I couldn't believe what happened next. Steele was telling Gibralter that Jesse and me should be fired. Next thing I know, the chief turned to Jesse and said, 'You're through.' Just like that."

Louis shook his head. "What about you?"

Dale pulled on his parka. "Jesse tried to tell him I didn't do anything and I tried to tell Steele I wasn't a real cop and I didn't even have a gun, but he wouldn't listen. He was yelling, saying we weren't fit to *wash* a uniform let alone wear one. And the chief was just watching, not saying a word."

"So he fired you, too?"

"I quit."

Louis stared at him in disbelief.

"I can't work here anymore," Dale said. "I just can't."

"Dale . . ."

Dale zipped up his parka. "I gotta go," he said briskly. Dale brushed by him, heading back out to the office. He stopped, then slowly came back.

"Guess I better go out the back," he murmured.

Louis reached out to put a hand on his shoulder, but Dale moved quickly away. Louis heard the door close and let out a slow breath.

This stunk, every damn part of it. Jesse was beyond his sympathy now, even if Gibralter had sacrificed him to Steele. But damn it, Dale didn't deserve this.

Louis went back out to the office. The men had dispersed and only two of Steele's aides lingered. Steele was still there, on the telephone. With a glance at Gibralter's closed door, Louis unlocked his desk drawer and pulled out the garbage bag. He went over to the command desk and stood, waiting.

Steele hung up the phone and swiveled around to face Louis, his eyes dark with anger. "What do you want?" he snapped.

"I need to talk to you," Louis said.

"I don't have time."

"I have something—"

The phone shrilled impatiently. "Do something about these phones!" Steele yelled.

Louis held out the bag. "You need to see this. It's—"

Steele stood up. "Listen you little ass kisser. There are real cops here working damn hard to save your incompetent asses. Steele grabbed his overcoat off the chair. "Now get out of my way, I have a chopper to catch."

Louis stepped around the desk, blocking Steele's way. "Look, I need to talk to you. Now!" he said.

"Make a damn appointment!"

He brushed by Louis, knocking him aside.

Louis glared at Steele's back, debating whether to follow him and shove the damn garbage bag down his throat right in front of the cameras. He saw one of the aides looking at him.

"What are you staring at?" Louis demanded.

The suit gave a shrug.

"When's your boss coming back?"

"In the morning." The aide smiled. "You want to make an appointment?"

Louis felt his hand curl into a fist. The hell with Steele. He would see this through himself, take the damn evidence wherever he needed to take it, give it to NBC or the fucking FBI, if he had to. They liked to bust cops, too.

He went back to his desk, tossed down the bag and dropped into the chair. Make a damn appointment. Fuck him.

Make an appointment.

He was staring vacantly at Pryce's doodles on the blotter, the curlicues and numbers fading in and out.

Make an appointment . . .

Slowly, a phone number came into focus in his head. He looked down at the blotter, at the number. He grabbed the phone and dialed it.

"Michigan State Police. How may I direct your call?"

Louis swiveled to look out the front window. He could see the chopper lifting off. "Mark Steele's office, please."

"That line is busy. For future reference, the extension is thirty-one."

Louis hung up. He unlocked his desk drawer and pulled out Pryce's small notebook. He flipped through it, stopping when he found the right page.

C.L. J.L. CIS @ 5661 X 31.

C.L. was Cole Lacey.

J.L. was Johnny Lacey.

CIS was Chief Investigator Steele.

And 5661 X 31 was his phone number.

Make an appointment . . .

Shit, that was exactly what Pryce had done. Pryce had found the proof about the raid that he needed to bury Gibralter and the others and he planned to take it all to Steele.

Louis redialed the state police, asking for extension thirty-one this time.

"Chief Steele's office," a woman answered.

Louis introduced himself, explaining he was investigating the death of a police officer and needed to track the officer's last movements.

"How can we be of help?" she asked politely.

"I need to know if Thomas Pryce made an appointment with Chief Steele around the end of November," Louis said.

He heard pages turning. "No, no . . . I don't see one."

Louis started to thank her when she interrupted. "I do have one for December third, but Officer Pryce didn't keep it."

Louis thanked her and hung up. His thoughts began to coalesce, coming together with cold certainty. Pryce had found out that something about the raid was dirty and started his campaign to get out of Loon Lake. But something happened to make him change his mind and he decided to go after Jesse and Gibralter.

Pryce was going to Steele. He had been within days, maybe hours, of taking down four respected police officers for the murders of two kids. But then Lacey surfaced and began his rampage, blowing Pryce away.

What a stroke of luck for the Loon Lake police.

Louis felt a chill creep up his back and he turned to see if someone had opened the door. No one was there. The cold spread slowly through him and with it came a horrible new thought. Luck . . . Was it really luck?

Gibralter's words came back to him, and the coolness with which he had spoken them.

Gambit, you know what a gambit is, don't you?
No, sir, I never learned chess strategy.
A gambit is when you sacrifice one of your pieces to throw an opponent off. . . . The permanent sacrifice . . . a move that elevates the game to artistry.

Had Gibralter somehow found out what Pryce was going to do? Had Gibralter killed Pryce to silence him?

Louis ran a hand over his forehead. No, no, his mind was outracing all logic now. Gibralter had been involved in the deaths of the Lacey kids, but no matter how threatened he felt, he would never kill one of his own men.

Gens una sumus. But Pryce wasn't one of his men, one of the family. Pryce was an outsider.

A shadow moved behind the glass of Gibralter's door. Louis held his breath as his eyes followed it. He felt suddenly nauseous, lightheaded. He rose quickly, picked up the garbage bag and threw Pryce's notebook inside. Grabbing the bag and his jacket, he bolted for the door.

Thirty-six

Louis set down the pen and leaned his head back on the sofa, closing his eyes. For the last three hours, the same looped tape had been running through his head, and everything on it was leading him to the same conclusion: Gibralter had murdered Pryce.

It didn't matter how Gibralter had found out Pryce was on to them. Gibralter had decided that "a permanent sacrifice" had to be made, and with Jesse, had formulated a plan to kill Pryce.

But Lacey . . . That was the ingenious part. However they had found out about Lacey, they had used him. Lacey was, after all, the perfect suspect, a wacko vet with a hard-on toward authority. A suspect who would not be able to defend himself because Gibralter had always intended Lacey to be conveniently shot and killed during his capture. That was why Gibralter had not wanted any outside help.

Louis opened his eyes and looked down at the legal pad in his lap, at the notes he had made in the last couple of hours. He stared at the names at the top of the page: PRYCE . . . and next to them, OLLIE, LOVEJOY.

It all fit. Except for one thing. There were three dead cops, not one. Three.

The theory had come to him only in the last hour, a second theory about the three deaths, a theory so grotesque he had immediately dismissed it. But it wouldn't go away and he was finally forced to confront it.

Had Gibralter also killed Ollie and Lovejoy? Had they some-how also become threats? If Gibralter was desperate enough to kill two kids and a cop, why not two others?

The idea was outrageous, that Lacey didn't kill anyone, that Gibralter had somehow engineered the murders to make them look like Lacey's work before Lacey had a chance to make his own move. But it explained why Lacey had gone home to Dollar Bay and complained to Millie that "everything was fucked up."

Louis read again the notes he had written under Lovejoy's and Ollie's names. What could have happened to make Gibral-ter turn against them? Did they know Pryce was going to ex-pose them and try to come clean? Or, after five years of keeping the secret, did they just crack?

Ollie . . . He could see how guilt could have consumed him, especially if he had, in fact, been the one to shoot Angela, as the reports said. Ollie was a docile man, just trying to slide into retirement. And Ollie knew Pryce was troubled and had given him the serenity crystal. Had Pryce confided in Ollie, trying to turn him to his cause? Had Ollie cracked under the pressure?

Lovejoy . . . He was different. He was an old drunk living off a medical settlement, but he was friendly with Gibralter. Had Gibralter tried to enlist his help in the plan to eliminate Pryce? Had that been the subject of the ten-thirty phone call the night before Lovejoy's death? And had Lovejoy balked, thereby sealing his own death?

Louis took off his glasses, rubbing his eyes. *If you're going to move on this, be right, Kincaid.*

Motive . . . It was there.

Means . . . Both Gibralter and Jesse carried twelve-gauge shotguns in their cruisers.

Opportunity . . . He could see that, too.

Pryce's death was clear, the details born from the echoes, scents and ghosts in Pryce's empty house. Gibralter had been the one to plan everything out, right down to duplicating Lacey's fatigue jacket and boots. But Louis was sure Jesse had done it, maybe out of some perverse need to impress Gibralter.

He could see Jesse driving into the darkness of the park, taking the shotgun down from the rack and calmly walking to Pryce's house. He could see him pulling the trigger and running to the backyard, crisscrossing the yards to avoid the dogs. Only Jesse didn't jump fences well and he snagged the jacket on the last fence, leaving the scrap.

Lovejoy's death was also easy to imagine. He could see Gibralter going to the fishing shanty at dawn, renewing the argument they had begun the night before on the phone. He could see Gibralter raising the shotgun, holding it low so the trajectory would match Lacey's height.

He could almost see the look of confusion on Lovejoy's face as he realized what was happening. Was the generator on, covering the sound of the shotgun blast? Had Gibralter returned later to put Lovejoy in the ice, thinking that by spacing the deaths over weeks they would appear more like the pattern of a serial killer?

But Ollie's death . . . He couldn't see it as clearly as the others. Ollie had died from a sniper's bullet. But who had fired it? How much time had elapsed between the shooting and Gibralter's first radio transmission? Enough for Gibralter to make it from the field back to his cruiser hidden nearby? Or had Jesse been the shadow he had seen running across the field?

Louis shook his head. He couldn't remember; the details of that night were too blurred. Except for one: the bullet in his own back, stopped by the vest. Who had fired it and why? Did they intend to kill him along with Ollie, or had they fired at him just to make it look convincing?

He closed his eyes. He wasn't sure. Damn it, he just wasn't sure about any of it. And he couldn't accuse Gibralter of murder until he was.

Gibralter . . .

No matter what route his thoughts took, they always came back to Gibralter and what kind of man he was. Louis thought about the two events in Chicago. An investigation that had tested Gibralter's definition of loyalty, and a gang attack so humiliating it had driven him from the job.

What kind of man was he? A cop who put loyalty above anything else? A paranoid who would do anything to avoid crucifixion by Mark Steele? A genius capable of planning the perfect murder?

And where was Louis's own place in the plan? Why had Gibralter given him the Pryce case in the first place? There was only one answer. Gibralter needed someone to lead the investigation away from himself and Jesse and right to Lacey.

He needed a pawn and I was perfect.

A sudden pounding at the door made Louis turn, his heart jumping against his sternum. He lunged for his belt lying on the counter and pulled out his gun.

"Louis!"

Shit, it was Jesse.

Louis put the gun back in its holster and moved to the door. Jesse hollered for him again and Louis swung open the door.

"What do you want?" Louis hissed.

Jesse's face was red from the cold, his hair flecked with snow. "I wanna talk. . . . Can I come in?"

Louis's hand balled into a fist at his side as the stink of whiskey floated up to him. Shit, Jesse was drunk. Louis started to close the door in his face, but Jesse stuck his arm in the door.

"Hey! Louis! I wanna talk, man!" Jesse said.

Louis stared at him. Okay, he wanted to talk, and he was drunk. Maybe drunk enough to talk about things he didn't want to talk about. Louis stepped back and Jesse stumbled in, dropping his keys as he fumbled with the zipper on his parka.

"I guess I'm a little tipsy," he said, looking at Louis.

Louis reached down, picked up the rabbit's foot and stuffed it roughly in Jesse's jacket.

Jesse fell backward. "Hey, man, what's with you?"

Louis turned away, going into the living room. He stood,

his back to Jesse for several moments, trying to quell his anger. But he couldn't hold it in.

"You son of a bitch," he said, turning.

"Huh?"

"I know what you did."

Jesse frowned. "What you talking about?"

"Angela and Johnny Lacey. I know how they really died."

For a moment, nothing registered on Jesse's face. Then slowly, comprehension penetrated the alcohol fog. He closed his eyes and bent forward slightly, as if he were going to vomit.

"Fuck," he muttered.

"Is that all you've got to say?"

Jesse staggered to the sofa and sank down onto it. "How did you find out?" he mumbled.

"That's not important."

Jesse covered his face with his hands. "It was an accident," he said.

"It was murder."

"You don't understand."

"Then tell me."

Louis waited, fearing Jesse was going to clam up, but then Jesse let out a slow shudder. "We were outside the cabin," he said. "It was really cold and I was antsy, you know?"

Jesse looked away. "I mean, I had just busted these kids and here they were out again, messing up somebody's property and life. I was mad going in."

When Jesse didn't go on, Louis resisted the urge to prod him.

"We were standing out there in the snow, listening to them yelling at us to go fuck ourselves," Jesse said. "I guess I made up my mind before that back door ever opened that someone was going to get hurt." He fell silent again, staring at the fireplace.

"What happened?" Louis said.

"The back door opened and he took off running, so I went

after him," Jesse said. "I jumped him and we fell in the snow. He was a big kid, but I got on him and started swinging . . ."

"With your gun?" Louis pressed.

Jesse looked up at him with unfocused eyes. "Gun . . . my gun."

"You don't remember?"

"Bits and pieces, that's what I remember," Jesse said, the words slurred. "I had my gun out, we all did, because they had guns, too. But I don't remember using it."

"You beat him to death with it," Louis said tightly.

Jesse squeezed his eyes shut. "I see his face. . . . I see it and it's changing, getting redder and redder. . . ."

The room was silent again, except for the crackle of the fire. "What happened next?" Louis demanded.

"Someone pulled me off him," Jesse said softly. "I had . . . blood . . . I had blood all over me."

"He was dead?"

"I don't know. The chief said he was."

"Then you shot his face off?"

Jesse shook his head. "I remember the chief ordering Ollie to do it and Ollie yelling back that he wouldn't. It happened so quick. I didn't see who did, just heard the shot."

"Where was Angela?" Louis asked.

Jesse's voice dropped to a whisper. "I looked up and I saw her standing up on the deck. Then they were cuffing her and she was screaming."

"Who shot her?"

Jesse turned his head. "The chief."

Louis walked slowly to the dark kitchen, unable to look at Jesse another second. He heard Jesse sniffling.

"Why did you let him do it?" he asked without turning.

There was no response. Louis turned. "Why, goddamn it?" he demanded.

Jesse was crying. "I don't know, I don't know."

Louis came back to stand in front of him. "You know!" he yelled in his face.

"I was scared!" Jesse said. "I was scared, all right? He said I'd go to prison. He said my life would be over!" He shook his head slowly. "And he was the chief! All my life, all my fucking life, no one treated me like he did. He fixed it and I let him."

Louis glared at him. Jesse shielded his eyes with a trembling hand.

"I'm sorry," Jesse said hoarsely. "Christ, I'm so sorry that girl had to die."

"Her name was Angela."

"Okay! Angela!" Jesse shouted. "I know she had a name, I always knew her name. It was Angela Lynn. I *know* who she was!"

Louis backed off and Jesse slumped into the cushions.

"Gibralter wrote your report, didn't he?" Louis said.

Jesse nodded.

"And the others, too?"

Jesse nodded again.

"Who investigated this?" Louis asked.

"We did and then the city council had a hearing. It was a joke. We told them what happened and they believed us. They always did."

"What about the kids' mother?"

"Mother?"

"She didn't try to do anything about it?"

Jesse shook his head. "I saw her at the hearing, but she never said anything the whole time, just sat there listening, with this weird look on her face. She left town a while later, after Cole went to Red Oak."

"What about Cole? Did he see what happened?"

Jesse shook his head again. "I don't know. Ollie and Fred found him hiding upstairs."

"What about Pryce? Did he see anything?"

Jesse looked up. "Pryce?"

"Did he see what you did?"

Jesse shook his head.

"You're sure?"

Jesse looked up at him. "He was out front. . . . He . . . I don't know, I don't know."

Louis stared at Jesse, trying to read his reddened eyes. They were filled with confusion—or was it fear? Jesse looked away. Louis pressed closer to the sofa. He had to find out how far they had gone to cover up the mess.

"You knew Pryce suspected you, right?" he said.

Jesse wouldn't look up at him.

"Pryce suspected something was dirty, and you all knew it," Louis said.

"Pryce was—" Jesse stopped himself.

"Pryce was what?"

Jesse stared into the fire, his face streaked with sweat and tears.

"Pryce was going to expose you," Louis said. "He knew about Johnny and Angela and he was going to turn you all in."

Jesse frowned, his eyes locked on the fire.

"Pryce was going to take everything to Steele and Gibralter knew it and told you," Louis said. "So you killed him."

Jesse's eyes shot to Louis.

"You found Lacey—"

"Lacey?" Jesse interrupted.

"You planned it all out so he'd take the rap."

Jesse was shaking his head, his mouth agape.

"You killed Pryce, you and Gibralter," Louis said, leaning down on the arm of the sofa. "How'd you do it? How'd you find Lacey?"

A glimmer of comprehension registered in Jesse's eyes. "Lacey? Wait, wait," he said, holding up a shaking hand.

Louis knew he should just shut up and let Jesse talk, but his anger was pushing him forward now.

"How'd it feel?" Louis said, leaning down into Jesse's face. "How'd it feel when you pulled the trigger and saw Pryce fall? How'd it feel when you heard Stephanie scream?"

"No, no . . ."

"You were this close," Louis whispered, holding two fingers in front of Jesse's face. "This close to being behind bars, your worst fear."

"No, I didn't—"

Louis's hand balled into a fist and Jesse tried to squirm away. "How'd it feel?" Louis hissed.

Jesse swatted Louis's hand and jumped to his feet. "No!" he yelled. "I didn't kill Pryce! Lacey killed Pryce!"

Louis grabbed his arm. "You *used* Lacey! You killed Pryce and used Lacey to cover it up!"

Jesse jerked away, stumbling back. "You're nuts! Lacey killed—"

"Yeah, stick to your story! You were stupid enough to let Gibralter suck you into one murder, why not more? Why not Ollie and Lovejoy? Tell me this, you bastard, who shot me in the back? You or him?"

Jesse stared at him, his face twisted.

Louis drew in a deep breath. Now that he had said it, put his thoughts into words, it didn't seem so outrageous. For a second, he felt a small pang of sympathy for Jesse, but it dissipated fast, replaced by rage. He couldn't see Jesse as any kind of victim in this.

"Give it up," Louis said.

Jesse was shaking his head, raking a hand through his hair.

"Maybe you can strike a deal for Gibralter," Louis said.

"No," Jesse said quickly. "No, no."

Louis reached out to grab Jesse's arm, but Jesse spun away, stumbling against the counter and knocking over a stool. He pulled himself upright and started to the door.

"Where are you going?" Louis said.

Jesse didn't answer.

"Stop, Jess, now," Louis said, moving toward the door.

Jesse glared at him. "Either you arrest me or let me get the fuck out of here."

Louis started to the counter to get his cuffs from his belt, but Jesse moved more quickly, pulling out his gun and pointing it at Louis.

Louis stared at the gun, not moving. "Jess, this isn't the answer."

"Let me go, Louis. I've got something to take care of."

Jesse moved slowly toward the door.

"Don't do this, don't make it worse," Louis said.

Jesse flung open the door and ran out, the door banging against the wall and slamming closed behind him.

"Jess!"

Louis grabbed his gun, ran to the door and jerked it open. He ran outside and stood for a moment, scanning the darkness. He went quickly around the side of the cabin. Jesse's cruiser was parked where he had left it. Louis circled the cruiser, peering inside. An empty Jack Daniel's bottle lay on the seat.

"Jesse!" he shouted.

He ran up the driveway toward the main road. He stopped, looking off into the night. Fresh boot prints led off down the road in the direction of town.

"Fuck," he murmured.

He had blown it. He had tipped his hand and let Jesse get away. And now he was probably on his way to alert Gibralter.

Louis looked down the road and scanned the dark trees. He shivered. He had been walking in Pryce's shadow for weeks and now, like Pryce, he was a threat.

He went quickly back into the cabin. He locked the door and pulled all the curtains closed. He paused to survey the room, then dragged around a chair from the corner to face the door. He turned off the lights.

The walls of the cabin pulsated with the light of the dying fire. Picking up his gun and portable radio, he sat down in the chair. He pulled the afghan up around his chest and over the gun resting in his lap.

Thirty-seven

The cabin was dark and cold. He had let the fire burn out, not wanting to have any light detectable from outside.

The phone rang, but he ignored it. It was the fourth time it had rung in the two hours since Jesse had left, and each time, he had let it ring. This time, though, it wouldn't stop, and finally he jumped out of the chair and grabbed it.

"Yeah?"

"Louis?" It was a woman, a voice he didn't recognize.

"Who is this?"

"Julie Harrison, Jesse's wife. Is Jesse there?"

"No, Julie. He was, but he left hours ago."

"Oh, God . . ."

He could hear the fear in her voice and wished he had lied.

"Do you know where he went?"

"No, I don't. Julie . . . Julie?"

She was crying.

"Listen, Julie—"

She had hung up. Louis set the phone back in the cradle and returned to his chair. He pulled the afghan over his shoulders and laid the gun in his lap. He massaged his right hand; it was stiff from gripping the gun.

He glanced at his watch. Just past eleven. His whole body was stiff with tension, but sleep was out of the question. He had decided on his plan—just get through the night until the morning, when Steele was due back from Detroit.

A crackle of static drew his attention to the portable radio on the table at his side. "All units in area, stand by for a BOLO."

Louis picked up the radio, turning up the volume on Edna's voice. "L-1 advises to be on the lookout for L-13. Subject has not been in contact with his residence and is reported missing."

Louis listened as Edna gave a brief description of Jesse. Damn him. His wife was going crazy worrying about him and the asshole was probably passed out in a snowdrift somewhere.

He tensed. A light appeared against the curtain, the wash of headlights on the trees. He heard a car and then silence as the motor died. He shrugged off the afghan and gripped the gun.

Footsteps on the porch, heavy, a man. A knock.

"Kincaid! You in there?"

It took a second for the voice to register. Gibralter.

Louis rose slowly, holding the gun at his side as he slid along the wall toward the kitchen.

"Kincaid! It's the chief. I need to talk to you."

He looked out the kitchen window and saw the Bronco. His chest tightened and he flexed his fingers around the grip of the gun. What was Gibralter doing here? He didn't come to kill him, not in the Bronco, right here at the cabin. He was too smart for that.

Louis went to the door. "What do you want?" he called out.

"I'm looking for Jesse," Gibralter called back.

There was something strange in Gibralter's voice, a quiver of concern.

"Kincaid? His cruiser's here. Is he there with you?"

"He left."

"When?"

"Two hours ago."

There was silence on the other side of the door and then Louis heard the retreat of footsteps from the porch. He went quickly to the kitchen window. Through the falling snow, he could see Gibralter shining a flashlight into Jesse's cruiser. He headed back to the porch and pounded again on the door.

"Kincaid? Let me in. I need your help."

Louis hesitated, debating what to do. He slipped the gun in his belt at the small of his back and unlocked the door.

Gibralter's silhouette filled the door frame. "Why do you have the lights out?" he asked.

"I was asleep," Louis said.

Gibralter took a step inside. Louis switched on a lamp, blinking in the light. Gibralter glanced around the cabin, his eyes coming back quickly to Louis. "Jesse's missing," he said.

"How do you know?"

"Julie's called the station twice. He didn't make it home."

"Maybe he stopped for a drink," Louis said. He was careful to stand a good ten feet away.

"On foot? There are no bars between here and his place."

Louis watched Gibralter carefully, trying to reconcile what he knew about the man with what he was seeing in his eyes, a strange look of dread.

"What was he doing here?" Gibralter asked.

"He wanted to talk."

"About what?"

"About you firing him today."

"Was he drunk, Kincaid?"

"Wasted."

"Why'd you let him leave on foot?"

"We argued. He ran out."

Gibralter paused, his eyes steady on Louis. "I fired Jess to protect him."

"He doesn't see it that way."

Gibralter let out a sigh. "I know. I didn't handle it well."

Louis stared at him. *Bullshit.*

"Kincaid, I need your help. I've got a bad feeling about this and we've got to find him."

"What about Steele?"

"I tried. He's gone until tomorrow." Gibralter's face hardened. "The moron he left in charge told me to go fuck myself."

"What about your own men?"

"They're already searching. Edna called here twice trying to get you. Didn't you hear the phone?"

"I told you, I was asleep."

"That's why I came out here, thought maybe something happened to you."

"Why'd you think that?"

"Lacey shot at you once," Gibralter said. "He'll do it again."

Louis just stared at him.

"Come on, get your coat," Gibralter said.

"I'm not going with you," Louis said.

"Why the hell not?"

For a second, Louis thought of confronting Gibralter with what he knew about Angela and Johnny, and with what he suspected about Pryce and the others. But if it was true that Jesse was missing, then Gibralter was still in the dark. And it was foolish, even dangerous, to alert him to what he knew. It would all come out tomorrow anyway when Steele got back.

Gibralter was waiting for an answer. When he realized Louis was not going to go, he nodded grimly and started down off the porch. He stopped and turned back to face Louis.

"I've got blood on my hands," he said softly.

Louis stared at him.

"Three of my men are dead, two of them because I was too proud to get help," Gibralter said. "Jesse and I are the only ones left. I have to find him."

Louis tried to read the emotion in Gibralter's eyes, but all he could see in the red rims and dull stare was fatigue and stress. The man looked pulled too tight, as if he knew everything was coming to an end.

Gibralter squinted at him through the falling snow. "I don't like you, Kincaid. You know that, it's no secret. But I don't want to lose any more men, Jesse or you. Now will you come with me or not?"

When Louis didn't answer, Gibralter shook his head and walked away. As Louis watched him, his heart quickened. Jesus, what if he was wrong? What if Lacey had killed all three cops? What if Jesse was lying out in the snow, easy prey for Lacey's scope? No matter what Jesse had done, he deserved a trial, not a sniper's bullet in his back. And no matter what he himself thought of Gibralter, he couldn't sit here like a coward while the others were out searching.

"Wait!"

Gibralter turned.

"Give me a minute to get ready."

"Dress warm," Gibralter said. "We might end up on foot."

The wipers kept up their monotonous rhythm as they drove slowly up toward the main road. From the radio came Edna's steady murmur, directing the other men on their search. Gibralter reached down and keyed the mike.

"Central, this is L-1. I'm 10-8 with L-11, joining the search." He clicked off. "You sure he went in this direction?" Gibralter asked Louis.

"It's the only road up away from the lake," Louis said.

"Maybe he went down to the lake."

"No, I saw his prints." Louis was training the outside spotlight on the snowy shoulder. "He was too drunk to drive. Maybe he tried to walk home."

"That's three miles from here."

It was quiet except for the groan of the wipers and an occasional spurt of radio voices. Louis moved his elbow so he could feel his gun against his ribs under his parka. He hadn't bothered with the bulky uniform belt, just stuck the gun and his cuffs in the belt of his jeans.

"Can you see any prints?" Gibralter asked.

"No, but they're probably covered by now."

"Shit, maybe he headed in the other direction."

"There's nothing out that way."

They crept on, Gibralter slowing the Bronco to five miles an hour.

"Hold it!"

Gibralter braked. Louis swung the light low on the shoulder. "What is it?"

"Boot prints." Louis got out, training his flashlight down in the snow. Gibralter was quickly at his side, shining his own light into the snow. The prints formed a faint but staggering pattern into the darkness of the road ahead. They followed them for several yards, walking in the headlight beams of the Bronco idling behind.

The prints ended abruptly in a flattened area of the snow. "Looks like he fell here," Gibralter said.

Louis swung the flashlight out into the field beyond and then across the road, finally picking up the prints again. They walked on, following them for another ten yards, then the prints stopped again in another flattened area. But this patch was larger, messier, the snow shoved away in spots down to bare ground. There were several dark spots, almost covered with a light dusting of new snow. Louis knelt to brush it away. It was blood.

Gibralter's breath, stale with cigarettes, was at his ear. "Christ, what happened?"

"A struggle of some kind," Louis said.

Gibralter swung his flashlight ahead down the road, but there were no more prints. He straightened. "He killed him," he said.

Louis looked up. Gibralter's face, caught in the reflection of their flashlights on the snow, was drawn with pain. To his amazement, Louis saw tears in the man's eyes.

Gibralter met his eyes and looked away. He turned and started back to the Bronco.

Louis looked again at the blood in the snow. A gnawing started in his gut, a gnawing that came from his guilt for letting Jesse walk out of the cabin.

"Jesse!"

Louis swung around. Gibralter was standing in the beams

of the Bronco, staring out into the field, hands cupped to his mouth.

"Jesse!" he shouted into the darkness, his voice echoing back to him.

"Chief," Louis called out.

"Jesse!"

"Chief!" Louis called out sharply.

Gibralter's head snapped toward Louis.

"He's not here," Louis said.

Gibralter turned away and went back to the Bronco.

Louis scanned the field again, in desperation, trying to find something, anything. But there was nothing. No Lacey, nobody. No . . . body.

Lacey had left the others dead, out in the open to be found. Where was Jesse's body? Louis trained the flashlight down again at the blood spots. There was so little, too little for a gun wound. Had Lacey subdued Jesse and taken him somewhere else?

Something drifted back to him in that instant, words, a threat. Who had said it? Dale, it was Dale, telling him what Cole had said to Jesse after Jesse attacked him. *You're going to die special.*

Louis hurried back to the Bronco and got in. "Chief, I think there's a chance Jesse might still be alive," he said.

Gibralter was staring vacantly out the windshield.

"Chief, listen to me. If Lacey wanted Jesse dead, he'd have shot him and left him, like the others," Louis said. "Something is different this time."

Gibralter looked over at him. "What are you talking about?"

Louis hesitated, then told him what Cole had said. "I think he's taken Jesse somewhere."

"Why?"

Louis hesitated. "He wants you and he knows you'll come after Jesse. But I also think he wants to torture him for what he did to Johnny."

Gibralter stared at him.

"I know what Jesse did at the cabin," Louis said. "And I know what you did to cover it up."

Gibralter's eyes went back to the windshield. Louis could see his jaw moving as his mind chewed on this revelation. He wasn't about to tell him what he knew about Angela.

"You can't protect him anymore," Louis said slowly. "Not if you want to save him."

Gibralter shut his eyes. It was quiet for a moment.

Gibralter's voice was strained when he finally spoke. "We did what we had to, Kincaid."

"That's for the courts to decide," Louis said.

"There are many versions of the truth. Everyone sees the one they need to see."

"That's not important right now."

Gibralter gave a tired nod. "I suppose not."

The Bronco fell quiet except for the low murmur of the radio.

"We're going to have to get ahold of Steele," Louis said.

"I told you what his man said to me," Gibralter said, his voice rising in anger.

"But with his men, we can search—"

"Search where?" Gibralter interrupted him. "We can't find Lacey. No one can. It's useless."

Gibralter was right. With all of Steele's resources, no one had come close to finding Lacey's hideout. No one even knew where to start looking.

"Cole," Louis said. "Cole knows."

"He won't talk," Gibralter said.

"We have to try."

"How? We can't get near Red Oak now."

"Then we bring him here."

"They won't release him to me."

"They would on a court order," Louis said.

Gibralter looked over at him. Louis could not read what was in his eyes.

"Why are you here?" Gibralter asked quietly.

"I want to find Jesse," Louis answered.

"But you don't trust me," Gibralter said.

"No. But if there's a chance Jesse is alive, I want to find him."

"Even if he's guilty? Even if I am guilty?"

"I told you, that's for the courts to decide."

Gibralter held his eyes for a moment, then put the Bronco in gear. "Let's go," he said.

"Where?"

"Judge Frazier's place. He'll do the order. He owes me."

"What about Steele?"

Gibralter glanced at him. "He'd block it. You know that."

He was right. There was no way Steele would sanction Cole's release for questioning, even if it meant helping Jesse. If they were going to do this, they would be on their own.

Gibralter was waiting, watching him, his face drawn in the orange glow of the dashboard lights. Louis looked out the windshield to where the beams faded into the darkness.

"All right," he said. "Let's go."

Thirty-eight

The guard looked down at the paper in his hand, then back up at Gibralter. "Maybe I better call Warren Little," he said.

"That paper tells you everything you need to know," Gibralter said.

Louis hung back, watching. The guard glanced nervously at the phone on his desk.

"Look," Gibralter said, leaning forward. "Go get Cole Lacey or in the morning you're going to find your fat ass covered in brass-plated shit from here to Lansing."

The guard handed the paper back and disappeared down the hall. A metal door clanged, echoing in the hallway. Louis glanced at his watch. It was past midnight. He felt a bead of sweat make its way slowly down his back, but he didn't know if it was from dread over Jesse's fate or his own. He knew when he agreed to this scheme that they would not be taking Cole back to Loon Lake. He knew there would be no by-the-book questioning under the watchful eye of Steele's men. He knew Gibralter would do whatever was necessary to make Cole talk. What he didn't know was if he had the stomach to go along with it.

The door clanged again. The guard was shoving Cole ahead of him. Cole wore only a denim shirt, pants and work boots. There was a large gauze patch on his forehead. When he saw the blue parkas, he froze. The guard tried to prod him forward, but Cole wouldn't move.

Gibralter went to him and held out a police parka. "Put this on," he said.

"Fuck you, man."

"Then freeze your balls off, I don't care," Gibralter said. He grabbed his arm and yanked him toward the door.

"Hey! Where they taking me?" Cole yelled back over his shoulder. The guard turned away, going back to his desk.

Outside, Louis followed closely behind as Gibralter led Cole to the Bronco. Cole was squirming and spitting out obscenities, his lank hair whipping around his face. Louis opened the back door and Gibralter pushed Cole in, then slammed the door.

Louis got in on the passenger side and flipped on the heater. Gibralter immediately turned it off, nodding toward Cole. Louis glanced back at him through the metal grating. The kid was huddled into the seat, shivering, his eyes wide with fear. Louis zipped up his jacket and stared straight ahead. The doubts began to crawl back.

Weeks ago, he never would have thought he could do something like this, break the rules, even his own. But all bets were off now, he was in new territory, and he had no idea what else he was capable of doing.

"Where you taking me?" Cole asked.

Gibralter eyed him in the mirror. "To hell, you little prick."

"What's going on?"

"We're tired of dicking around, Cole. We want your old man. Tell us where he is and we'll take you back."

"Fuck you."

Gibralter slammed on the brakes, sending Cole bouncing forward to the metal grate. Gibralter spun around, gun drawn. Louis's eyes locked on the barrel.

Cole dove behind the seat. Gibralter pulled the trigger, the blast echoing in the truck. Louis jumped, afraid to look back. He turned to see a hole in the backseat.

"Get up," Gibralter said.

Cole's pale face appeared above the seat.

"Put on the fucking jacket. Now."

Cole drew the parka over his thin arms, fighting tears. Louis detected the faint smell of urine.

Gibralter steered the Bronco off the highway and drove deep into the trees, plunging them into a cavern of darkness. They drove on, through the trees for several miles. Then, suddenly, Gibralter braked and killed the engine. For several seconds, it was silent. Louis watched as the windshield quickly sheeted over with a blanket of snow. The sound of Cole's ragged breathing drifted from the back.

"Get him out," Gibralter said to Louis.

Louis opened his door and stepped down into ankle-high snow. Opening the back door, he motioned Cole to get out. When Cole shrank back against the seat, Louis reached in and grabbed the police parka, dragging Cole out.

He dumped him into the snow. Cole leapt to his feet, his eyes darting to the trees, but Louis caught his parka, jerking him back. Cole's fist shot out and Louis threw up an arm, blocking the kid's weak punch. He wrapped one arm around Cole's neck and reached back for his cuffs. Cole twisted, going for the gun in Louis's belt.

"You stupid shit!" Louis said.

He shoved the kid away, his grip still tight on the parka. He set the gun on the front seat and dragged Cole a few feet away from it. He had no idea where Gibralter was going with this, so he set Cole against a tree, directly in the headlights' beams. Cole squinted, bringing a hand up to his eyes.

"Here," Gibralter said, coming up behind him and holding out Louis's gun.

Louis slipped it back in his waistband. He watched Gibralter break off a tree branch and walk toward Cole.

"Where is he?" Gibralter said.

Cole was looking at the branch in Gibralter's hand. "I don't know!"

Gibralter brought the branch down across Cole's face. Cole let out a squeal and stumbled back, covering his face. When he lowered his hands, Louis saw a thin line of blood across his cheek.

"Cole," Louis said quickly. "Just tell us."

Cole glared at him. "Fuck you, and fuck Harrison!"

Louis glanced at Gibralter. The kid knew.

Gibralter started toward Cole, who backed against the tree. Gibralter pulled him forward by the parka.

"Drop your pants," Gibralter said.

Cole's eyes shot to Louis.

With one swift move, Gibralter reached out and ripped Cole's pants open, popping the plastic button. Cole tried to stop him, but Gibralter smacked the branch against his arms.

"Stop! Stop!" Cole yelled.

Gibralter yanked at Cole's pants, working them down his thin hips. Louis watched, his heart hammering. What was going on? Then, suddenly, he knew. The child abuse report in the Dollar Bay file. Cole had been sodomized as a child and Gibralter knew it. He was going to use it to break the kid.

Cole started to scream.

Jesus, Jesus! Do something, Kincaid. Stop this now!

But before he could move, Gibralter shoved Cole face-first into the snow. Cole's bare skin glistened in the headlights. He was sobbing.

Louis grabbed the branch. Gibralter spun to face him.

"Enough," Louis said through clenched teeth.

Gibralter glared at Louis, then wretched the branch free. He tossed it down and took a step back. For a moment, Louis thought Gibralter was going to hit him and he braced himself to fight.

"You sorry son of a bitch!" Gibralter shouted. "How dare you stop me!"

"You're over the edge!" Louis shouted back.

Gibralter's fist came up, but Louis was ready and deflected it. But the blow was powerful and he stumbled back, falling in the snow. Gibralter towered over him.

"Jesse's dead and you're defending this piece of shit! What kind of cop are you?" Gibralter yelled.

Louis grabbed a tree to pull himself up from the snow. Gibralter walked a few feet away, turning his back. He was looking off into the darkness.

Louis looked around. Cole was gone. Then, incredibly, he heard laughter. Gibralter was laughing.

Louis trudged through the snow and grabbed Gibralter's sleeve. "He's gone! What the hell's the matter with you?"

Gibralter pulled his arm away. He reached into his parka pocket and pulled out matches and a cigarette. Cupping his hands around the match, he lit it. Louis watched his face in the match's glow.

"You're crazy," Louis said. "You're fucking crazy."

"There is no genius without some touch of madness," Gibralter said softly, tossing the match to the snow.

Gibralter headed back to the Bronco. Louis followed, furious. But before he could say anything, Gibralter produced a black box, about the size of the cigarette pack. It was flashing a red light and giving out a faint *ping*. Gibralter held it out, moving his arm in a wide arc toward the distant trees. It was a tracking device that responded to a sensor, a sensor that Gibralter had imbedded in the police parka Cole was wearing.

"You wanted him to run," Louis said.

"Of course. Stupid little prick."

"But what if he hadn't? What if I hadn't stopped you?"

"I knew you would."

For a moment, Louis was paralyzed with anger and a feeling of impotency. "You son of a bitch," he said.

"No time for insults, Kincaid," Gibralter said, placing two speed-loaders in the holder on his belt. "We've got a job to do."

"Forget it. This is nuts. I'm not going along."

"Why not? It was your idea, remember?"

Gibralter laughed and tossed a flashlight at Louis. Louis

caught it against his chest, "Get ready," Gibralter said, his smile fading.

Louis moved to the open passenger door and for a moment just stood there, watching as Gibralter pulled on his gloves. The man was crazy, stone-cold crazy. His eyes drifted to Cole's prints. They were fading fast in the falling snow, but with the bug, he was easily tracked, and there was no need to hunt him by themselves.

Louis reached in the Bronco and keyed the radio. The static pierced the quiet, and Gibralter's face appeared over the roof.

"What are you doing?" he demanded.

"We need help. We need to call this in, admit we blew it and get some help." He keyed the mike again. "Central, this is L-11, do you—"

A sharp bang, an explosion of sparks. Louis jumped back, holding his hand. Smoke poured out of the dashboard, clearing to reveal the shattered radio. Louis looked up to see Gibralter holding his gun.

"Let's go," Gibralter said. He stuck the gun in his holster, slammed the Bronco door and started away.

Louis pulled out his gun and flipped open the cylinder. It was empty. Gibralter had removed the bullets while he had been distracted struggling with Cole.

Louis began to tremble, the wind creeping up under the parka and seeping through his wet jeans. He glanced around, at the black pines and rolling drifts. About ten yards ahead, he could see the beam of Gibralter's flashlight.

Jesus, what was he going to do? He didn't know where in the hell he was. He couldn't stay here and freeze to death. And he couldn't let Gibralter go on after Cole alone. If Cole did lead him to Lacey, Gibralter would kill them both.

Louis pulled on his gloves and picked up his flashlight. It was nearly two-feet long and heavy in his hand. He weighed its potential as a possible weapon, knowing Gibralter would not let him get close enough to use it. He stuck his empty gun back in his belt.

"Kincaid!" Gibralter's voice echoed back to him through the trees.

Louis closed the passenger door and reached back to shut the back door. His eye picked up a spot of color on the floorboard and he froze.

It was an orange rabbit's foot, its chain broken.

Louis picked it up, his heart beating faster. He had seen it, back at his cabin just hours ago. Jesse had dropped it and he had stuffed it back in his parka. What was it doing here?

Louis's eyes went to the metal grate that separated the front from the backseat. A cold knot formed in his gut. Jesse had dropped the rabbit's foot in the Bronco. But he would never get in the backseat behind the cage. Not unless he was forced to.

Gibralter had Jesse. But why? And where was he now? Was he alive?

"Kincaid!"

Louis looked up. Gibralter's flashlight ahead cut a faint path in the blackness. Louis put the rabbit's foot in his pocket and started toward the light.

Thirty-nine

Darkness and cold. They were closing in on him, tightening their grip on his mind, on his body. He trudged on, through the drifts, his eyes never leaving the beam from his flashlight. It was all he had, that light. It was his only defense against the fear that was growing inside him. The light . . . and his brain. They were the only weapons left to him now.

"Stop."

Louis did not turn at the sound of Gibralter's voice behind him. He heard the faint *ping* of the tracking device.

"Left, ten o'clock," Gibralter said.

They moved on slowly, as they had been doing for the last hour. Or was it longer? Louis was losing sense of time, just as he was losing sense of place and himself. He was shivering, unable to stop it, and his fingers gripping the flashlight were numb. His toes were numb. His mind was growing numb.

Is this how it ends, this numbness? Is this how I die?

He bit down hard on his lower lip, almost drawing blood. Anything to stay alert. He stuck his free hand in his parka pocket. It found the rabbit's foot. He gripped it, his mind finding a focus again . . . Jesse.

He stopped suddenly and turned around. It was going to end soon. However it did, whatever was going to happen to him, he needed to know the truth.

"Where's Jesse?" he asked.

All he could see was the light Gibralter was shining in his face. "What did you do with him?" Louis asked.

When Gibralter said nothing, Louis held up the rabbit's foot. He couldn't see Gibralter's face.

"It doesn't matter. You don't have to worry about Jesse anymore," Gibralter said.

"You killed him," Louis said flatly.

Gibralter said nothing.

"You killed him. Why?"

"He made the wrong choice."

"Choice? What choice?"

Louis heard the click of a gun hammer.

"Move," Gibralter said.

He trudged on, trying to think. What choice had Jesse made? Had he finally turned against Gibralter? Had Jesse been going to turn himself in when he left the cabin?

Louis stopped again and turned. "You killed Pryce, too, didn't you?"

"You're wasting time, Kincaid."

"Jesse's dead. They're all dead! It doesn't matter anymore, that's what you said!"

It was quiet except for the ping of the tracking device in Gibralter's hand.

"Did you? Did you kill Pryce?" Louis demanded.

"I made a permanent sacrifice," Gibralter said.

There. He had his truth. Louis shut his eyes, turning his face upward. The snow was cold and wet on his face. It was a moment before he could bring himself to speak again.

"You coward," he whispered. "You were afraid and you killed him. You fucking coward."

"Pryce was the coward," Gibralter said. "He didn't have the guts to do what had to be done. He didn't understand that our strength comes from our unity."

"*Gens una sumus,*" Louis said, shaking his head.

Gibralter's chuckle drifted to him. "You're learning, Kincaid." He tipped the gun barrel, motioning him to move on.

Louis didn't move. There were still too many questions. "How did you find out he was on to you?"

Gibralter didn't answer.

"How?" Louis shouted.

"I was lucky. I got a call I never should have got."

"From who? Who told you what Pryce was doing?"

"Steele's secretary," Gibralter said with a small smile. "She called the station one day. Dale transferred the call to me. She said she was calling to say she had to change the time of Pryce's appointment for December third."

Louis stared, stunned.

"I told her I'd pass the message along."

"You killed Pryce on the basis of that?"

Gibralter shook his head. "I suspected he was turning before then."

Louis waited. Gibralter seemed to be trying to decide how much to explain.

"He was looking for a job. I got calls for references," Gibralter said. "I didn't think much of it at first. Pryce never seemed to really fit in here."

"It had to be more than that. What else tipped you off?"

"Dale."

Louis shook his head.

"It's not what you think," Gibralter said. "Dale didn't know what Pryce was up to—he was just pissed that Pryce was messing up his files. Dale came to me, it was around Halloween, asking if he could put locks on the file cabinets to keep everybody out. He was mad at Pryce, said he never put things back. He showed me a file Pryce had left a mess."

"The raid file," Louis said. "Pryce made a copy."

Gibralter nodded. "I started watching him after that. I followed him one day when he went back to the Eden place. I checked evidence and knew he'd been in there. I saw that the seal on the Hammersmith bag was broken."

"You knew he found the throw-down," Louis said.

"Yes, but he didn't take the gun. He wasn't as smart as you."

Louis was shivering hard and clenched his teeth together to keep them from chattering.

"Walk," Gibralter demanded.

"What about Ollie and Lovejoy?" he said.

"What about them?"

"Did you kill them, too?"

Gibralter stared at him, his breath visible in the beam of the flashlight. "Do you believe in fate, Kincaid?"

Louis didn't answer.

" 'There is no armor against fate. Death lays its icy hand on kings.' "

Louis recognized it as part of the quote Gibralter had delivered at Ollie's funeral. It hadn't meant anything to him then because he didn't believe in fate and the words had sounded like simply part of an epitaph. But now, here, the words sounded cowardly, like an excuse.

"Fate?" Louis said angrily. "It was their fate to die?"

"For every action, there is an equal and opposite reaction," Gibralter said. "Things were set in motion that day at the Eden cabin, things that no one could stop. Is that fate? I don't know. All I know is things must come to their inevitable conclusions."

Louis turned and walked on, the cold inside him growing as his thoughts turned to his own fate. Gibralter planned to kill him tonight. He knew too much, just like the others. He felt the cold steel of his empty gun against his skin.

Think, think! Find a way to beat him. Find a weapon.

He stopped again.

"Kincaid, you're getting on my nerves," Gibralter said.

"You're going to kill me, aren't you," Louis said.

"Get moving."

"What are you waiting for?" Louis yelled. "Why don't you just shoot me right now!"

"What, and make you a fucking martyr in her eyes?"

Louis swung his flashlight to Gibralter's face. Gibralter

moved, but not before Louis saw the tightness in his expression.

"Who? Zoe? Is that—" Louis demanded.

"Her name is Jeannie!" Gibralter interrupted, pointing the gun at Louis's chest.

Louis held his breath. Gibralter slowly lowered the gun.

"You're going to take a bullet in the back tonight, Kincaid, but it won't be mine," Gibralter said. "Now move!"

Louis walked on through the drifts, his mind churning as he realized what was going to happen. Gibralter knew he would have to face an investigation when this was over. Any bullet found in Louis's back would come from Lacey's gun. Gibralter would make sure of that. He had thought of everything. Every maneuver was designed, every move thought out three steps ahead. How could he get the advantage?

Zoe.

He had seen something in Gibralter's eyes when he had said her name. It was small, almost undetectable, but it was there. A weakness, a fissure, a way in.

"Zoe," he said.

From behind came only the crunch of boots on snow.

"Zoe," he repeated, more loudly.

Silence.

Louis gave a small laugh as he walked on. "She likes to be called Zoe. You didn't know that, did you?"

"Shut up."

Louis's heart was hammering, but he knew he had to get Gibralter off balance. "Zoe," he said loudly. "That's what she wants me to call her when we make love."

Silence. Louis drew in a harsh breath of cold air.

"You know what Zoe told me? Zoe told me you haven't been able to satisfy her in years."

"Stop!"

Louis stopped, but didn't turn.

"Turn around."

He faced the light, squinting.

"You want to play games?" Gibralter asked.

Louis could not see if the gun was pointed at him. *Ping-ping-ping.* The faint sound of the tracker matched the pounding of his pulse in his ears.

"You know what an endgame is, Kincaid?"

Louis remained silent, his hand going up to shield his eyes against the light.

"The endgame is the final strategy in chess," Gibralter said. "It's when most of the pieces are lost and the king is forced into action. Amateurs think the king can be taken at this point. But in the hands of a master, the endgame can have any number of outcomes."

Gibralter moved his flashlight away from Louis's face. Louis could see him smiling, shaking his head.

"Zoe, Jeannie, it doesn't matter to me," he said. "Weak move, Kincaid. A weak move from a weak man."

He motioned with the gun toward the trees. Louis turned and trudged on. He was shivering violently now, the cold overtaking him. There had been no response about Zoe. A normal man would have retaliated. But there had been nothing.

Think! Think!

Gibralter was a man, and every man had a weakness. Where was Gibralter's? But this wasn't a normal man. This wasn't even a man. This was nothing but a gun, a badge and a fucking uniform.

A cop. Not a man, just a cop.

A cop . . . Attack the cop, not the man.

Louis forced himself to let out another laugh. It echoed in the darkness. "A weak man! I'm a weak man!" he yelled. "That's the ultimate insult to you, right, *Chief?*"

He charged the final word with sarcasm, knowing Gibralter would pick up on it. He forced out a chuckle. "Nothing worse than a weak cop, right, Chief?"

Gibralter said nothing.

"What makes a weak cop? Why don't you define it for me,

Chief?" Louis said. "Why don't you tell me so I can get my badge to shine as pretty as yours?"

Louis kept his eyes on the dim path created by the flashlight in his shaking hand.

"A weak cop doesn't break the rules, right, Chief?" Louis yelled back over his shoulder.

The crunch of boots on snow.

"A weak cop doesn't let his macho ego lead him into a dark alley alone without calling for backup, right, Chief?"

Silence.

"A weak cop doesn't let a bunch of punks take away his gun, right, Chief?"

Louis listened for the click of a gun hammer.

"A weak cop doesn't end up naked, spray painted, and hand-cuffed to a fire escape, right, Chief?"

Jesus, what am I doing?

He drew in a shuddering breath and forced out one last laugh. "And a weak cop doesn't end up riding a fucking desk because he's too scared to go back out on the street and do his job, right, Chief?"

"Stop!"

Louis froze. He shut his eyes, waiting. For a bullet, a blow to the back. Whatever it was, he wanted it go come fast. *Just let him come close. Just close enough, just one swing of the flashlight, one chance . . .*

"Did she tell you that?"

The voice came from the same distance behind him, but for the first time, it sounded different, colored with a whisper of effort.

"She told me everything," Louis said.

There was a long silence. It was so quiet Louis could hear the snow's kiss as it touched the ground. Quiet, so very quiet.

Too quiet.

The *ping* had stopped.

Louis turned slowly. Gibralter was looking down at the

tracking device in his gloved hand. It was now giving off a soft steady tone.

"He's stopped," Gibralter said. He looked off into the dark pines and then pointed his gun at Louis.

"Let's go."

Forty

Louis could smell the burning wood before he saw the cabin's lights. The scent drifted to him, faint but definite, and he stopped.

"Smoke," Gibralter said softly behind him.

They moved on slowly, quietly. Finally, Louis saw a glimmer of light in the distant trees. The snow had stopped and a silver moon was out, bathing the forest in a sickly glow. Off in the distance was a small boxy shape—a cabin.

Louis stared at it in disbelief. They had found it. The whole scheme with Cole, the tracking device, it had actually worked. For a moment, he felt a rush of adrenaline. It was replaced quickly with dread. Now what?

"Son of a bitch, there it is," Gibralter said, his voice closer now. "Switch off your light."

As they crept nearer, they saw it was not a cabin, but a small, rough-hewn hut. It listed slightly under the weight of the snow, a tendril of smoke curling from a pipe in the dilapidated roof. The place was probably a deserted storage hut left over from the long-dead logging trade. No wonder they had not been able to find Lacey.

As they came up to the small clearing, Louis's eyes went to the red pickup parked in front. His pulse quickened. Lacey was here.

They had approached the hut from the front, but the two front windows were boarded shut, the door closed. The light they had seen through the trees had come from a small window on the side.

Gibralter moved around to Louis's left, standing about five feet away. He was surveying the hut and the truck.

"Let's go. Stay in front of me," he said softly.

They crept up to the truck. From his position near the front wheel, Louis could make out the outline of a shotgun in the rack. Gibralter peered inside the open bed and carefully lifted a tarp.

"He's got an arsenal here," he whispered, nodding toward the boxes. "Probably more inside."

"Give me back my bullets," Louis said.

"Forget it."

"You're going to need my help. Lacey's dangerous and the kid knows guns," Louis said, his voice low but urgent. "You go alone, you're going to lose."

"This way," Gibralter whispered, swinging his gun back over his shoulder toward the trees.

Louis had no choice but to obey. Gibralter followed him back to the cover of the trees. He seemed to be looking for something in them.

"Stop here," he said. "Toss me your gun."

Louis didn't move. What was this? What was he doing now?

"Gun," Gibralter hissed.

Louis pulled the empty gun from his belt and flung it at Gibralter. He caught it and stuck it in his parka.

"Get out your cuffs," Gibralter ordered.

Louis stuck his flashlight into his waistband and retrieved his cuffs. Despite the cold, he felt a hot flush of terror spread over him as he realized what Gibralter was going to do.

"Do it," Gibralter said, pointing the gun at him.

Louis didn't move.

"Do it! Now!"

With trembling hands, Louis slapped one cuff on his right wrist.

"Other one, over that limb," Gibralter ordered, pointing with his gun.

Louis looked up at the bare limb. It was about three inches in diameter, sturdy but just big enough for the cuff. With a look at Gibralter, he snapped it on.

"Key."

With his free left hand, Louis dug in his pocket for the key and threw it at Gibralter. It bounced off his chest and Gibralter knelt to pick it up from the snow.

Gibralter slipped it into his pocket, then smiled at Louis. "Scared?"

Angela Lacey flashed into Louis's mind. "Fuck you," he whispered.

For a second, Louis thought Gibralter was going to laugh. Then, incredibly, Gibralter brought a finger to his lips, like a child signaling another to be quiet. He turned and headed back to the pickup truck.

Louis watched him as he crept around the back of the truck and toward the hut. He was moving toward the open window on the side and Louis knew he was going to try and take Duane Lacey and Cole by surprise, gun them down in cold blood.

Do something! Yell! Warn them! No! They'll panic and end up dead.

He twisted the cuff against the limb, pulling it, but it wouldn't move. He glanced back at Gibralter. He was nearly to the window.

With his left hand, he pulled the flashlight from his jeans. Reaching up, he placed it over the limb and grabbed each end. Using himself as dead weight, he swung his legs back and forth, trying to break the limb. It swayed but held. He edged the cuff out on the branch and tried again, his breath coming hard and fast as he bounced.

A loud snap split the quiet. He fell to the snow.

He scrambled quickly for the cover of the trees. From his

position near the hut, Gibralter looked back, scanning the darkness.

Louis's eyes darted to the pickup. The shotgun, he needed to get the shotgun. He started toward the truck, but a sudden light made him duck back.

The door of the hut opened. A figure came out onto the porch. It was Lacey. He was holding a shotgun ready at his side, surveying the trees. He waited for a moment, then stepped off the porch and started toward the pickup.

Suddenly, out of the corner of his eye, Louis saw movement. Gibralter, moving into firing position, raising his gun.

Move! Now!

Louis darted from the tree to the truck. Lacey had opened the truck's door and started to turn, his ears picking up a rush of sound. Louis tackled Lacey, slamming him against the open door. Lacey let out a grunt, but kept a tight grip on the shotgun.

Louis threw his full weight against Lacey, grappling for the shotgun as Lacey tried desperately to swing it down into position to fire.

"Get off me!" Lacey yelled.

"Shut up, goddammit, shut up!" Louis said.

A shot rang out. Louis wrenched Lacey into a neck hold and scuttled back for the cover of the open truck door. Louis slammed Lacey against the door, and Lacey's grip on the shotgun loosened just long enough for Louis to grab the barrel and twist it out of Lacey's grasp. Louis tightened his arm around Lacey's neck, pulling his back against his own chest. Frantically, he scanned the trees, but there was no sign of Gibralter.

Lacey's fingers tore at Louis's arm around his neck. "You're gonna die, motherfucker!" he yelled.

"Shut up! I'm trying to save you!" Louis hissed in his ear.

But that only drove Lacey into a greater fury. Louis swung the butt of the shotgun into Lacey's face. Lacey stopped struggling, momentarily stunned.

A flash of silver caught Louis's eye and he squinted into

the darkness, trying to make out Gibralter's outline in the faint illumination given off by the truck's dome light. Gibralter's badge glinted a second time as he emerged from the shadows in front of the truck.

His gun was drawn, pointed at Lacey's head. Louis tightened his grip on Lacey's neck, his heart jumping to his throat. He knew he couldn't rotate the shotgun up quickly enough to use it against Gibralter.

Lacey was coming alive again. Then suddenly he froze, and Louis knew he had seen Gibralter, too, standing just four feet away.

"Say good-bye, asshole," Gibralter said.

Louis tried to spin but was caught between the door and truck. He braced for the bullet he knew would rip through Lacey and into his own chest.

Gibralter's gun exploded, and Louis was pushed into the door. He felt a dampness trickle down his face as Lacey went limp in his arm. Louis forced his eyes open.

Lacey was deadweight. Louis let him slip to the ground. He reached up to his face and his fingers came away wet with Lacey's blood and brains.

Louis glared at Gibralter. "You bastard!" he yelled, lunging at him, shotgun raised over his head.

He slammed the shotgun down, catching Gibralter on the right shoulder. Louis drew it back again, this time with both hands and aiming for Gibralter's head. Gibralter threw up his arm and ducked away.

Another blast exploded, shattering the truck's window and showering them with glass.

Louis dropped to the ground and crawled around the back of the truck, away from the porch. He crouched by the front wheel and drew in several quick breaths, his fingers iced to the shotgun barrel. His eyes frantically searched the darkness for the source of the shot and for Gibralter.

"Kincaid."

Louis spun to his left. Gibralter was crouched by the back

wheel, holding his shoulder with his left hand, his right hand still gripping his revolver.

Louis swung to aim the shotgun at him.

Gibralter looked at it, then laughed softly. His eyes drifted up to the porch.

Louis followed his gaze. The front door was open a crack, letting out a trickle of light from inside. Louis could make out the outline of a woodpile on the porch. But he couldn't see Cole. He had fired on them. Had he gone back inside?

"Cole!" Louis called.

"Stay back or I'll shoot again."

He was still out on the porch, probably crouched down behind the woodpile.

"Cole! Put the gun down!"

"Fuck you! I'm not crazy." The voice sounded small.

"Cole! This isn't the way to end this!"

Louis glanced at Gibralter, but he was watching the porch.

"Cole, you don't have to die!" Louis called out. "You can give up right now. Nothing will happen to you."

Cole's laugh came out as a cry. "Tell that to Johnny and Angela!"

Louis shook his head. The kid had seen what had happened at the raid. "Cole, listen to me," Louis said. "I know what happened to your brother and sister. I can help you make things right."

Cole didn't answer.

"I have proof, Cole! I have evidence you can use to prove what you saw!"

"Fuck you!"

Louis heard a low chuckle and looked over to see Gibralter shaking his head.

"Cole! Listen to me! The men who killed your brother and sister, they'll pay, I swear! But you have to stay alive to tell the truth!"

The sound of shuffling feet came from the porch, followed by the thud of a log falling.

"Cole? Are you listening? You have to trust me!"

"You're one of them, man!"

"No! No, I'm not!" Louis glanced at Gibralter. He could see the contempt in his eyes. "Cole, think about Johnny! He wouldn't want you to die like he did! I can protect you!"

Louis heard Gibralter laugh again. "Right, Kincaid, you keep feeding him that bullshit. Go ahead, draw him out. Give me a clear shot."

A second gunshot split the quiet, peppering the front of the truck and making Louis duck back.

Louis swung the shotgun at Gibralter. "Shut up! He can hear you!"

Gibralter shook his head and looked back at the porch. Louis lifted his head again, straining to hear something on the porch. Nothing, except the crack of a shotgun opening. Cole was reloading. There was a small thump, then the sound of something rolling across the wood porch.

"Cole?"

"Fuck . . . fuck," Cole whispered.

"Cole, that was a shotgun shell. You dropped it."

"I have more!"

"I don't hear them going into that gun."

Cole was silent, but then came more shuffling and another log falling. He heard Cole curse softly.

"Cole, you're out of shells," Louis said. "And if you try for the door, you know I'll have to shoot you. I don't want to do that."

Louis waited. He saw Gibralter rise slowly, one hand on the bed of the truck, the other holding the revolver.

"Cole, throw the gun out," Louis yelled. "I'll come up there and get you."

"No! Stay back! He'll kill me!"

"I can protect you."

"Like you protected my dad? You held him while he killed him!"

"I was trying to save him. You've got to believe me."

"Fuck you, fuck both of you," Cole said hoarsely, his voice dying to a whisper. "Fuck everyone."

Louis stood up. "Cole, I'm coming up."

With a look at Gibralter, he started slowly around the front of the truck. He knew Gibralter wouldn't shoot him in the back with his own gun, but he prayed he was right about Cole being out of shells.

"Don't, don't . . ." Cole's words were more plea than threat.

"Cole, I'm in front of the truck," Louis said calmly, glancing back at Gibralter. Gibralter had rounded the back of the truck. Louis leveled the shotgun at him.

"Stay there," he said. "You're not touching this kid."

Gibralter stared at him. Louis braced the shotgun against his side, his finger on the trigger. With his left hand, he pulled the flashlight out of his belt and shined it up on the porch.

The beam fell across logs. Louis swung it back to Gibralter. He hadn't moved.

Slowly, Louis sidestepped up to the hut, his eyes darting between Gibralter and the porch. He reached the step.

"Cole, I'm coming up."

A whimper from behind the logs.

Gibralter took a step forward. Louis swung the flashlight to shine in his face.

"You lift that gun, you're dead," Louis said.

"There is no dishonor in death, Kincaid," Gibralter said softly. *"Seppuku . . ."*

Louis shined the light back to the porch and it picked up a spot of blue, Cole's denim shirt. He was crouched behind the woodpile.

"Cole?"

Easy, easy . . .

Louis heard a sound and swung his light back to Gibralter. His gun was moving.

Louis spun to the porch and his flashlight caught Cole's face only for an instant, just long enough to give Gibralter a target. Louis swung the beam away.

He saw the flash of Gibralter's gun go off. His own hand jerked back on the trigger of the shotgun and it bucked violently against his ribs.

An explosion of noise, followed by echoes that seemed to pound in his head. Then it was quiet.

Gibralter was lying on the ground, his body dark against the snow. His palm was up, the revolver inches away in the snow.

Louis stared at him, his chest heaving.

Cole moaned.

Louis swung the flashlight beam around, picking up Cole lying on the porch.

No, check Gibralter first. Eliminate the threat.

He fell to his knees next to Gibralter and pressed a finger to his throat. Nothing. He tried the wrist. Nothing. There was a large black hole in the blue nylon of the parka.

Gibralter was dead.

Forty-one

Louis gathered both revolvers and the radio from Gibralter's body and hurried up to the porch. He knelt next to Cole, propping the kid's head on his knee.

"Where are you hit?"

"In the belly . . . God, it hurts. Fuck . . ."

Louis caught Cole under the arms and dragged him inside the hut. He spotted a cot in the corner and carefully lifted him up on it as Cole screamed in pain. In the spare light of the room's single kerosene lantern, Louis looked down into Cole's pale, sweaty face.

He pulled up Cole's shirt. Blood was pouring out of the small, black hole below Cole's rib cage.

"What are you doing?" Cole asked, his eyes frantic.

"Put this on it. Keep pressure on it," Louis said, grabbing the army blanket from the foot of the cot and handing it to Cole.

"I'm going to die," Cole said.

"No, you're not."

"I'm going to die. I'm going to die." Cole was crying.

"Cole, stop. Listen to me. We've got to get some help. Tell me where we are."

"I'm bleeding! I'm going to die!"

"Cole! You're not going to die! Now help me. Tell me where we are, damn it!"

Cole wiped his face and pointed across the room. Louis saw a scarred footlocker.

"Maps," Cole said.

Louis went to the locker and jerked it open. He rummaged through the dirty clothes and debris, finally pulling out two maps. The first was nothing but a series of undulating circles, a topography map that he couldn't read. He tossed it aside. The second one he unfolded was a county map that detailed every highway, road and landmark, even the old logging roads. He brought it back to Cole.

"Where are we?" he demanded, holding it up to Cole's face.

Cole's eyes were closed. Louis shook his shoulder. "Cole! Show me where we are!"

Cole's eyes fluttered open and he struggled to focus. With a shaky finger, he pointed to the map, leaving a bloody smudge. He fell back with a grimace.

Louis grabbed the radio and called Loon Lake. A voice came back to him, Edna's voice, the sweet sound of Edna's nasally voice.

"L-11? Where are you?"

"Edna, listen carefully. I need a flight-for-life chopper. And contact Chief Steele—"

"Chief Steele? But he isn't—"

"Find him! Tell him . . ." Louis hesitated. Christ, he hated to say all this over the radio. "Tell him I have one injured suspect and a 10-99, officer down. Tell Steele I need him now. Repeat, I need him—"

"Louis, Chief Steele isn't going to—"

"Tell him I have Lacey. Tell him he's dead."

Louis read off the longitude and latitude of the hut's location, along with the nearest roads. He signed off, knowing it would still be hard for anyone to find them. There was nothing to do now but wait.

Louis touched Cole's face. It was cold, and his breathing shallow. Louis glanced around the hut for another blanket, finally spotting the blue police parka crumbled in a corner. He got it and spread it over Cole's chest.

"Cole," he said. He had to keep him conscious somehow.

Cole didn't open his eyes, but Louis could see the slight rise and fall of his chest beneath the parka.

"I'm sorry you had to see your father die like that."

Cole opened his eyes. "He knew you'd get him," he whispered. "He knew he was going to die and he didn't care. He just wanted to finish it."

Louis shook his head. "I don't think your father killed anyone. I think that's just what you want to believe."

"He did!" Cole said with a grimace. "He killed those cops. I know he did."

Louis pressed Cole's shoulder gently back into the cot. "Cole . . ."

"He showed me, he showed me the cards."

Louis tensed. "What cards?"

Cole brought a hand out from under the parka and pointed again to the footlocker.

Louis went the locker and dug down through the debris again. A pack of Bee cards was on the bottom. He slid the pack open. There were only three cards, bound with a rubber band. Louis pulled it off and fanned the cards. All had the drawing of the skull and crossbones on the back. Louis turned the cards over.

There was an ace of hearts, a king of diamonds and a two of clubs.

The ace symbolized one, Gibralter's call number. The king was number thirteen, for Jesse. But the last card . . . a two? Pryce's call number had been Loon-2. But Pryce had been thrown an ace of spades. This card had never been delivered.

He stared at the cards in his hand and suddenly he understood. *Two* killers . . . There had been two.

All along, he had wanted to tie all three murders to one killer, and he had gone back and forth between Lacey and Gibralter. But now he saw clearly that there had been two.

First there was Lacey. Driven by his demons and need for revenge, he had killed Lovejoy. Gibralter had discovered Lovejoy's body in the shanty and realized it was Lacey's work.

Gibralter had then killed Pryce to silence him, duplicating Lacey's methods and motive as his cover.

That was why Lacey had retreated to Dollar Bay, telling Millie that "everything was fucked up." That's also why he waited so long to continue his rampage before finally killing Ollie.

Louis let out a tired breath. Gibralter had cold-bloodedly thought out every detail. From finding out Lacey's boot size to putting his friend's body in the ice hole so Pryce would be mistaken as Lacey's first victim, not a copycat killing.

Gibralter had thought of everything, even down to duplicating Lacey's signature of the death card. But Gibralter had missed one small thing. He didn't realize Lacey was using the cops' call numbers. He had thrown the ace of spades down on Pryce, assuming it would look like a racial insult.

"Hey . . ."

Louis turned. Cole's face was white and tear-streaked in the lantern's glow. Louis went to him, lifted the parka and saw that the blanket under Cole's hand was soaked with blood.

"Don't let me die," Cole whispered.

"I won't."

Cole closed his eyes.

A heaviness came over Louis. He had no right to make any more promises to Cole Lacey.

Forty-two

Louis could hear the faint *whirr* of the chopper as it sat waiting in the clearing beyond the trees. He watched as Cole was brought out on a stretcher. A minute later, the chopper rose above the trees and moved off into the darkness. It was only then Louis turned back to face Steele and the question he had asked.

"Answer me," Steele demanded. "You expect me to believe this shit?"

"Cole will back it up," Louis said.

"That stupid kid?" Steele said. "Hardly a credible witness."

Louis's eyes swept over the chaos of men surrounding the hut. Fatigue had numbed him to the cold, but the ache inside lingered. He hurt, every part of him hurt.

"I told you the truth," Louis said.

"Your chief is dead," Steele said through clenched teeth. "The goddamn suspect is dead and the kid will probably die. You expect me to believe Chief Gibralter orchestrated this insane operation and then shot down the suspects in cold blood?"

Louis stared at him. "It's the truth. All of it."

"You better hope Cole Lacey lives long enough to back up your story, Kincaid. If he doesn't, you can add murder to the long list of criminal charges I'm going to hit you with."

Steele turned, took several steps, then came back. "I've seen a lot of stupidity in my time, but this takes it all," he said. "What the *hell* were you thinking?"

"Jesse. I was thinking about Jesse."

"Who?"

"Jesse Harrison," Louis snapped. "My partner."

"Who is also dead."

"I'm not so sure."

Steele stared at him, shaking his head. "You know something, Kincaid, Gibralter is not the only lunatic in this fucked-up department. Lacey abducted your partner and left him dead somewhere. Not Gibralter, not your *chief*."

Louis held up the rabbit's foot. "This belongs to Jesse. He had it with him earlier tonight at my cabin. I found it in Gibralter's Bronco."

Steele stared at him. "So where is he then?"

"I don't know, but I'm going to look for him."

Steele shook his head. "You're not going anywhere tonight. You're on suspension."

"You don't have the authority," Louis said. "I'm going to look for Jesse."

"I could arrest you and detain you for hours."

Louis closed his fist around the rabbit's foot. "Look, I know Gibralter. I know how he thinks. Now let me go so I can join the search."

Steele's eyes hardened as the wind blew snow across his face. Louis shook his head in disgust and turned to walk away.

Steele's voice sounded behind him. "Lockhart!" he called, waving to a trooper just exiting his car.

Louis turned. Steele met his gaze briefly, then looked at the trooper. "Take Kincaid back to town."

Lockhart nodded and opened the back door to his cruiser. Louis slid in the back. He pulled his parka up around him. The stiff nylon was raw against his face.

"Turn up the heat, will you, guys?"

Lockhart's partner nodded and after a few minutes, the back began to warm up. Louis stared at the backs of their heads through the mesh screen as the cruiser bounced down the snowy hill. After a while, it hit a logging road and Lockhart sped up as he threaded through the trees toward the highway.

Where would Gibralter have taken Jesse? To his own home? To Zoe's cabin? Neither of those choices made sense. Shit, he wasn't sure Jesse was even alive. If Jesse had decided to turn against Gibralter, he might be dead out in the woods somewhere.

Think. Think. Think about the man. Think like he thinks.

Even if Jesse had turned, he couldn't see Gibralter killing him. It was more logical that he do something to intimidate Jesse until he could win back his loyalty. But what? Gibralter had always used people's weaknesses to control them: Cole's fear of abuse, Louis's need for justice, Zoe's fear of being alone. Gibralter controlled Jesse all his life. How would he do it now?

The cruiser rumbled over one last set of rocks and hit pavement. The black road stretched out into the night.

Louis closed his eyes. Gibralter would take Jesse to a place that instilled fear, a feeling that if he didn't come around, he would die. It would also be a place where Gibralter could return to, once again playing the role of savior.

Louis stared out the fogged window as the lake came into view. He wiped away the condensation with his sleeve. There was a faint pink glow in the eastern sky, dawn. Out on the dark expanse of the lake, he saw a soft glow. A lantern, someone firing up a fishing shanty.

His eyes swung to the mesh screen that separated him from the two troopers.

Louis put a hand on the screen.

Lockhart glanced back. "What are you doing?" he asked.

Louis looked back at the lake. He knew. God, he knew.

"Turn here. Turn left up here," Louis said.

"What?"

"I said turn left. Here!" Louis shouted.

Lockhart cruised on past the snowy side road. "Where?"

Louis hit the screen with his palm. "Stop! Jesus Christ, turn around. Turn around now!"

Lockhart backed up, swung the cruiser around and started down the narrow road.

"There," Louis said, "at the end, by the shore. That green house. Pull in there."

The cruiser edged closer, bogged down by the deep drifts.

"We're going to get stuck," Lockhart warned.

"Fuck it," Louis said. He moved to open the door, but realized he couldn't. It only opened from the outside. "Let me out. Come on, let me out!"

Lockhart stopped the car and jerked open the back door. Louis jumped from the cruiser and ran through the snow. He fell, scrambled up and rushed on.

When he hit the porch of Lovejoy's cabin, he tore off the yellow crime-scene seal on the door and pushed. It was locked.

"Goddamn it!" he shouted. He kicked at the door, then kicked again. Using his full weight, he shoved at the door with his shoulder and it sprang open.

He stumbled through the dark living room, grappling for lights. The walls were like ice, the air so cold it burned his lungs. He tripped on a small table, kicked it aside and ran on. He hurried through the darkness, shoving open the bedroom door at the end of the dark hall.

His hand shot to the switch and he slapped at it, flooding the room in light. His heart stopped.

Jesse was in the dog cage, both wrists handcuffed to the wire, his head resting against the cage, the dog blanket across his legs. His face was covered with a light frost, his lips were purple and there was a thin line of dried blood on his cheek.

Louis dropped to his knees, stuck his hand through the wire and pressed two fingers against Jesse's neck. A pulse. He could feel a pulse.

"Jesus Christ," Lockhart whispered from behind him.

Louis threw out his hand. "Give me your cuff key."

Forty-three

A rush of warm air greeted Louis as he pushed through the double glass doors of the hospital. Seeing his police parka, the woman at the reception desk nodded at him, and he hurried to the elevator.

Only nine hours had passed since he had pulled the trigger on the shotgun, and only a little more than that since he had carried Jesse's half-frozen body out of Lovejoy's cabin. But it felt like a lifetime had passed, as if the world had been tilted onto a new off-balance axis.

Early that morning, he had checked Jesse into the hospital, then gone to the station to write his report for Steele. The report had stretched to seven pages. He had left it in a sealed envelope, not wanting the mob of reporters to get wind of it before it was necessary.

At home, he had tried to sleep. But finally, he had given up, showered and put on a fresh uniform. He thought of going to Zoe. Someone, another man in a uniform, had already been to see her that morning, to tell her about her husband. He wondered if they told her how he died. He wondered if they told her who had killed him. He knew he would have to face her soon. He just didn't know how.

Finally, not knowing where else to go, he had come to the hospital. He wanted to be at Jesse's side when he woke up.

Louis punched the elevator button and waited.

"Kincaid."

Louis didn't turn at the sound of Delp's voice coming from behind him.

"I knew you'd show up here," Delp said. "I've been waiting."

"What do you want, Delp?" He punched the button again.

"A quote I can print."

"I can't talk about anything yet. It's still under investigation."

"But you shot Gibralter, right?"

The door opened and Louis got in. Delp followed.

"Did you shoot Lacey, too?"

Louis wouldn't look at him.

"Come on, man," Delp pressed. "You promised me the story."

The door opened and Louis stepped out. Down the hall, he saw a trooper standing outside Cole Lacey's room, talking to a tall man in black. It was Steele. Steele looked up at the sound of the elevator, staring down the hall at Louis.

Louis hesitated, then walked slowly toward him. Steele saw Delp trailing behind and shot him a contemptuous look.

"Leave us alone, please," he said to Delp.

"I've got a right to—"

"Get lost," Steele hissed.

With a frown, Delp moved away. Steele waited until Delp retreated behind the window of a waiting room.

"I read your report," he said. "I also spoke to Cole Lacey. Your stories don't jibe."

"What?"

"Cole says you both took him from Red Oak, that you held him down while Gibralter threatened to sodomize him with a branch, and that you held his father while Gibralter shot him."

Louis shook his head slowly.

"He also says you talked him into throwing down his weapon, then shot him."

"He's lying."

"Ballistics showed your gun fired both the bullets we dug out of Cole and his father."

"I told you, Gibralter had my gun."

"Cole says that after you shot him, you fired on Gibralter for no reason at all."

"Jesus Christ, Steele, does that make any sense to you?"

Steele just stared at him.

Louis ran a hand over his eyes. "Look, I went along with Gibralter's plan, but when I knew it was getting out of hand, I tried to stop it. When Gibralter told me he killed Pryce, I knew he was going to kill Cole, too. I went along to stop him. I tried—"

He stopped, seeing the disdain on Steele's face. He leaned back against the wall. "It's all in the damn report."

Steele was silent, studying his face. "Kincaid, your fellow officers tell me you and Gibralter didn't like each other. I saw your personnel file, the reports Gibralter wrote up on you. You yourself tried to tell me he was dirty. I think this was more personal than what's in that report."

Louis stared at him. Had he found out about Zoe? If that came out, no one would believe him. Everyone would think he killed Gibralter because of her.

"Steele, listen," Louis said slowly. "I am a cop, a good cop, whether you want to believe it or not. Gibralter was crazy. I shot him to save a sixteen-year-old punk who didn't deserve to die. I'm not sorry."

Louis pushed himself off the wall. "I'm going to see Harrison."

Steele caught his arm. "Out of professional courtesy, I will give you a few minutes with your partner, then one of my men will arrest you."

"On what charges?"

"Obstruction of justice, attempted sexual assault on a prisoner, conspiracy, excessive force and anything else I can think of. And unless that kid changes his story, I'll add homicide."

Louis jerked away and started down the hall to Jesse's room.

He paused, watching Steele disappear into the elevator. Damn it, he wasn't going to let this happen without a fight. He back-tracked to Cole's room.

Cole's eyes snapped up as the door opened. When he saw Louis, he looked back at the television.

"I want to talk to you," Louis said.

"No way, man."

Louis moved into Cole's line of vision. "I saved your life. Why didn't you tell Steele that?"

"Why should I?"

"Because it's the truth. And it's about time someone started telling the truth."

"Yeah, like you guys know something about telling the truth. They're dead, they're all dead because of you." He paused. "Even my fucking old man."

"There was nothing I could do about your father, Cole."

"What about the rest of it, huh? You didn't have to take me out of Red Oak! You didn't have to stand there while he hit me with that tree! You didn't have to . . . fuck. Just forget it."

Louis grabbed the remote from Cole's hand and clicked it off. "I didn't have to kill a cop to save you either."

Louis tossed the remote onto the bed. Cole's eyes went to it, staying there.

Louis moved closer to the bed. "Look, my life is in your hands, Cole. I'm asking you for help. I'm asking you to tell Steele what happened out there last night."

"Fuck you," Cole murmured.

"All I'm asking you to do is tell the truth!"

"Someone has to pay!" Cole shot back.

"For what? For Johnny, for Angela? Christ, Cole, I wasn't even there! Why are you trying to bury me?"

" 'Cause you're a cop. Someone has to pay."

Louis shook his head in disgust. "Justice, huh? Is that what you want? Is that what this is all about? Let me tell you about justice. If you don't tell what happened, the man who shot Angela will be buried with honors. The man who beat your brother to death will go on being a cop. And me, the man who saved your ass, will go to prison. And you . . . You will go back to Red Oak for five more years."

Cole was staring at him.

"Your anger will eat you up, you'll end up in jail," Louis went on, "and ten years from now, someone will kill you with a shiv in the shower at Marquette and you'll be buried in a prison cemetery."

Louis shook his head. "That isn't justice, Cole, that's stupidity."

Cole's eyes glistened with tears, but before they could fall, he looked away.

"Cole, tell the truth," Louis said. "Forget about me. You owe it to your brother and sister. If you don't tell the truth, no one will ever know what really happened. Tell the truth about five years ago and about last night."

"Who am I supposed to tell?" Cole spat out. "That asshole in the suit? He's a cop. I ain't talking to no more cops."

"Okay. How about a reporter."

Cole frowned. "What? Like on TV?"

"Newspapers," Louis said.

"He'll write down what I tell him?"

"If it's the truth."

"Will Harrison go to jail?"

"I don't know. That will be up to a judge."

Cole wiped at his eyes, looking up at Louis. "But people will know, right? They'll know about Johnny, they'll know he wasn't really bad? They'll know Angela didn't do anything wrong? They'll know, right?"

"Yes."

"And they'll know I was too scared to do anything that night?"

Louis imagined the frightened eleven-year-old, huddled in the closet of the Eden cabin. "Yes, they'll know," he said.

Cole's eyes fell. He picked at the edge of the blanket. "All right. I'll tell him."

Louis stepped out into the hall. The trooper had found a chair nearby and was deep into his magazine. Louis saw Delp sitting in the waiting room. He waved, catching his attention and motioning him down. Delp hurried down the hall.

"Get out your notebook," Louis said. "You're going to get the biggest story of your life."

"You're awake."

Jesse looked up to see Louis standing at the door.

"Yeah, on and off."

With a grimace, Jesse tried to sit up straighter in the bed. Louis came forward and slipped an arm behind his back, helping him.

"Thanks." Jesse held up his bandaged hands. "Doc says I might lose a finger, maybe a toe."

"I'm sorry," Louis said quietly.

Jesse shrugged, his gaze dropping to the bed. Louis let out a breath, not knowing where to start.

"I know what happened," Jesse said. "Dale was here earlier and told me what he knew."

"He told you I shot Gibralter?"

Jesse nodded.

Louis hesitated. "I'm sorry for what I said, when you came to my cabin to talk. I was wrong."

Jesse shook his head slowly. "You weren't wrong about Johnny Lacey."

"But the other stuff, you—"

"Forget it," Jesse said quickly. "If you hadn't accused me of those other things, I would have never figured things out, that the chief . . ." His voice trailed off.

When Jesse spoke again, it was in a whisper. "I was on my way to see him, you know," he said. "He picked me up on the road and I told him it was over, that we couldn't keep the raid quiet anymore."

Jesse paused, not looking at Louis. "That's when he told

me everything. He told me we had to see it through together. But I couldn't anymore, not after he told me he killed Pryce."

"You told him you were turning yourself in?" Louis asked.

Jesse nodded. "That's when . . ."

"He put you in the back of the Bronco," Louis finished.

Jesse picked at the gauze on his left hand. It was quiet except for the hum of a monitor above the bed.

"I was laying in that cage," Jesse said softly. "I was laying there and after a while, it was like the cold affected my brain or something and I could see things real clear. I saw what he did, what he was. And I saw what I did, really saw it."

He looked at Louis. "I knew I was going to die, but I saw it was, like okay, suddenly." He shook his head slowly. *"Seppuku."*

Louis looked up. "What?" he asked softly.

Jesse looked at him vacantly.

"That last word you said."

"Seppuku?"

Louis nodded. "Gibralter said that, in the woods."

Jesse held his gaze for a moment, then leaned back in the pillows with a tired sigh. "It's Japanese."

"What does it mean?"

"It's how a samurai commits suicide, you know, when they ram their sword up into their guts? They do it as punishment, when they've dishonored themselves."

The room was silent again. Louis rose and went to the window, staring out at the gray day.

"Jess, I have to tell you something."

"What?"

Louis turned to face him. "Cole's going public. He's telling what he saw during the raid."

Jesse kept his eyes locked on Louis for several seconds, then lowered them.

"You're going to lose your job, maybe worse," Louis said quietly.

Jesse was staring at his bandaged hands. Louis turned to the window again.

"Louis?"

He turned.

"Would you do me a favor?"

"Anything."

"Call Julie for me. Ask her to come over here."

Louis nodded and moved woodenly toward the door.

"Louis?"

He turned again.

Jesse's eyes were bright with tears. "You did the right thing."

Forty-four

He had to leave the Mustang at the bottom of the hill and walk the rest of the way up. When he reached the cabin, he paused.

What was he afraid of? That she would look different now? What was a woman supposed to look like after her husband was shot to death? Was he afraid of what she would say? What did a woman say to the man who had killed her husband?

He knocked. For a long time, there was no answer, but then the door opened and she stood before him. Her eyes narrowed against the bright sunlight as she looked at him.

"Can I come in?" he asked.

Zoe nodded and moved away. He came in and she closed the door. The drapes were closed, the lights low. As his eyes adjusted, he made out the cardboard boxes stacked near the door. The paisley sofa was gone, and most of the other furniture. He looked to the fireplace. The Manet print had been taken down.

"What's going on?" he asked, turning to her.

"I'm closing the cabin," she said.

"Why?"

She rubbed the sleeves of her baggy red sweater, looking around, at anything but him. "I don't know. I don't feel right here anymore."

"Zoe . . ."

"Don't call me that, please," she said softly.

She moved away, going to a table to pick up some books.

He watched her as she stacked them in a box. She moved slowly, as if something hurt deep in her bones. He heard a sound, a soft mewing, and turned. Two animal carriers sat by the door. He could see the white cat behind the grating.

"You're going away?" he asked. Where?"

"Chicago."

"When?"

Her eyes met his. "Tomorrow, after the funeral."

"Zoe, we have to talk."

Her eyes brimmed. "About what, Louis? What can we say to each other now?"

"I'm sorry," he whispered.

She spun away, covering her face with her hands.

He was rooted to the floor by the sound of her crying. He wanted to hold her, but he was afraid she would push him away.

"I don't blame you," she said softly.

He closed his eyes.

"Brian died a long time ago," she said. "If anyone's to blame, it's me."

"Zoe—"

Louis took a quick step toward her, touching her arm, but she pulled back. She wiped her face with her sleeve and brushed a strand of hair back from her face. She looked around the room, her eyes dark with fatigue and confusion.

"She's gone," she said softly.

Louis felt something cut into his chest. "Zoe . . ."

"I have to find her."

She knelt to look under a chair, then rose and pulled back the curtains. Louis watched her, suddenly afraid she was breaking down.

She looked up at him suddenly. "I can't leave her here," she said, her eyes bright with tears. "Help me find her, please."

Suddenly, he understood. The other cat. She was looking for the other cat, the black one.

She went into the studio, calling her name. Louis drew in a slow breath and scanned the room, looking for the animal.

Zoe came back into the living room. "Isolde, I can't find her," she said, her eyes frantic.

"She's here somewhere," Louis said.

"I have to find her now. I'm leaving tomorrow, there's no time. I have to go, I have to—"

Louis grabbed her shoulders. "Zoe, stop. Come on, stop. Calm down."

She stared up at him, then started crying again. He held her, stroking her hair, letting it all pour out of her, even as he struggled to hold his own emotions in. He held her until the crying dwindled and stopped.

Finally, she pushed gently away from him, wiping her face, unable to meet his eyes.

"I have to go, Louis," she whispered.

She moved away and he closed his eyes. When he opened them, she was standing by the door, wearing her coat. She was holding one of the carriers, waiting.

He went to the door and she opened it. They stepped out into the bright sunlight. She didn't look back as she went down the snowy walk, the carrier bumping awkwardly against her leg. She didn't look back at him as she opened the door of her Jeep and put the carrier in the back. He waited, standing with his hands in his pockets. Finally, she faced him.

"I loved you," she said softly. "Was it wrong?"

He felt his heart tear. "No," he said.

She hesitated, then nodded slightly. Her dark hair glistened in the sun, her eyes locked on his.

"When will you be back?" he asked.

"I don't know," she said.

The question was there, in his head, but he knew there was no need to ask it. Nothing was possible for them. He had known that when he walked up the hill.

He focused on her eyes, on her lips, her face, her hair, focused on every detail so he would remember. He would remember the taste of brandy on her mouth, the curve of her hip, the smell of patchouli.

She got in the Jeep. She looked back at the cabin, then at Louis.

"She might have gotten outside," she said absently.

"I'll look. I'll find her for you."

She nodded woodenly and started the engine.

"Good-bye, Zoe," he said.

She smiled slightly. Then swiftly, she turned, put the Jeep in gear and pulled away.

He watched the Jeep disappear down the hill. He turned and looked back at the cabin. He let out a breath, so long and raspy that it hurt his lungs. He was so tired, a sudden hollow feeling overtaking him, as if the last of his emotions had drained out of him with Zoe's departure. He started down the hill.

He didn't know what made him stop and look back at the cabin. But when he did, he saw something at the window. A small black form. A cat.

It sat there calmly, staring back, its green eyes luminous slits in the sun.

He stared at it, transfixed. Its tiny pink mouth moved, a silent meow behind the glass.

Damn . . .

Shaking his head, he went back into the cabin. The black cat came right to him, rubbing against his legs.

"Damn," he murmured.

Picking it up, he put it in the empty carrier sitting by the door. Moving quickly, without looking back at the dim room, he left with the carrier, stepping back out into the sun.

Forty-five

He rubbed his arms, watching the coffee dribble into the pot. It was the last of the can and he knew he was only going to get one or two cups out of it. Damn. It was too cold to go out and get more and the Mustang hadn't started in days anyway.

Something touched his leg and he looked down to see the black cat rubbing against his calf.

He pushed it away gently with his foot, thinking about Zoe. He had called several times about the cat, but she had never responded. He assumed she had left for Chicago and finally had left a note in her mailbox, telling her he had the cat.

He glanced down at the animal. It sat staring up at him, its tail swishing slowly back and forth on the linoleum.

With a sigh, he looked back at the slow drip of the coffee-maker. Finally, he pulled out the pot and stuck the mug under the drip, staring out the window as he waited for it to fill. Frost obscured the windowpane. He reached up and used the sleeve of his sweatshirt to wipe it clear.

Sunny . . . first time in a week.

The pine trees stood tall and unmoving in their crisp green uniforms with their white epaulettes of snow. He shivered, glancing down at his feet in their old tube sox. His big toe was poking through a hole in the end. He used his other foot to turn the hole under as he pulled the cup from the machine. He stuck the pot back and walked to the table, sliding into the chair. Taking a sip of coffee, he picked up the stack of mail he had neglected for the last three days.

A large manila envelope caught his eye, and he stared at the Detroit return address with no name. He opened it.

It was a copy of the *Detroit Free Press,* the most recent Sunday edition. As he snapped it open, a note floated to the table. He picked it up and read the unfamiliar scrawl.

> *Thanks. I owe you one. Delp.*
> *P.S. How's the weather up there?*

"Jerk," Louis muttered.

He looked at the front page. He couldn't miss the big headline on Delp's freelanced feature story: THE KILLING SEASON. And the small blurb below that: "On a cold winter day, two teenagers were murdered. Five years later, the cops who did it are brought to their final justice."

It was a long article, but he read all of it, and when he put it down, he was left with a begrudging respect for Delp. He had done a good job on the article. It was painstakingly researched and written with the sensitivity of a good novel, and between the lines anyone could read the unspoken theme: that the Lacey teenagers were not the only victims.

Louis dumped sugar into the mug and stirred the coffee, thinking about Jesse. He was facing felony murder charges for beating Johnny and conspiracy to cover up Angela's death. Gibralter was dead, his reputation shattered. Zoe was gone, her life shattered. And he . . .

Louis sipped the coffee, thinking now of his own fate. Steele had dropped felony charges against him after Cole told the truth and recanted his statement about the Red Oak abduction. But Steele had still made an example of him, telling the TV reporters that "the actions of Louis Kincaid, while technically legal, were still unethical. I intend to pursue a charge of obstruction of justice, if only to ensure Kincaid does not remain a police officer in the state of Michigan."

Louis poured more sugar into the coffee. It didn't matter anymore. He had already quit. He would survive. He would survive, he told himself, if his bitterness didn't eat him alive. He had warned Cole against it, but he could see it happening to himself these last couple of days. He had changed somehow, on some very basic level, and it arose from something more than just what had happened with Zoe or even the fear he might never work as a cop again. He felt adrift, his faith in the power of his badge destroyed, the idea of what he *was* shaken. Nothing was black and white, as he had believed, especially truth. Truth was nothing but different perspectives, refracted through the prisms of people's pain. It was ever-changing, unreliable, not to be trusted.

He turned back to the rest of his mail, sifting through the junk flyers and bills. His eyes locked on a small envelope with a Flint return address. It was from Stephanie Pryce. He ripped it open.

The note was short, poignant, an acknowledgment for unraveling the truth about her husband's death. She had added a postscript, the Churchill quote from Pryce's funeral plaque. Louis read it, a hand rubbing his brow.

The only guide to a man is his conscience . . . with this shield, however fates may play, we march always in the ranks of honor.

He put the letter back in its envelope. Rising stiffly, he went to the living room. He stood for a moment, his lassitude threatening to overtake him. He felt something rub his leg and looked down. It was the black cat again.

"Don't you have someplace to go?" he asked, irritated.

It was getting cold. The fire was burning down; he needed to go outside and get more logs. Slipping on an old pair of loafers and a University of Michigan jacket, he stepped out onto the porch.

The bright sunlight made his eyes water, the cold air made

his chest ache. He started toward the log pile, then paused, his eyes going out to the lake.

It glistened in the sun, its white blanket broken only by the ripple of a lone snowmobile. The sound of its motor drifted in to him, fading as it headed away, toward the north shore. He walked down to the shoreline, and stood looking out over the flat white expanse, his hands thrust in his pockets.

His fingers closed around something small and hard in his pocket. He pulled it out. It was a black stone, the snowflake obsidian Ollie had given him. He held it up to the sun. *It is the stone of purity, that balances the mind, body and spirit.*

More of Ollie's words trickled into his mind, something he had said about finding his place, where he needed to be, something about water. What had he said?

But then, Frances Lawrence was in his head, too, whispering. *People have places on earth where their souls feel comfortable, Louis, places where they feel at home.*

His fingers closed around Ollie's snowflake stone, and he remembered: *The water is where you need to settle, Kincaid. It doesn't have to be here. There's lots of water in the world.*

He stared out at the frozen lake. This was not the place. He had thought it would be, but it wasn't. Right now, he wasn't sure where he did belong.

The only thing he knew for sure was that he had to go on trying to find it. Gripping the hard black stone, he turned and started back.

ABOUT THE AUTHOR

P.J. Parrish has worked as a newspaper reporter and editor, arts reviewer, blackjack dealer and personnel director in a Mississippi casino. The author currently resides in Southaven, Miss. and Fort Lauderdale, Fla., and is married with three children, three grandchildren and seven cats. P.J. Parrish is currently at work on the next Louis Kincaid thriller. Please visit the author's Web site at www.pjparrish.com.